THE SONS OF
SORA

W9-AJQ-236

THE SONS OF SORA

THE EARTHBORN TRILOGY BOOK 3

PAUL TASSI

Talos Press

Talos books may be purchased in bulk at special discounts for sales promotion,
corporate gifts, fund-raising, or educational purposes. Special editions can also
be created to specifications. For details, contact the Special Sales Department,
Skyhorse Publishing, 307 West 36th Street, 11th Floor, New York, NY 10018 or
info@skyhorsepublishing.com.

Talos® and Talos Press® are registered trademarks of Skyhorse Publishing, Inc.®, a
Delaware corporation.

Visit our website at www.talospress.com.

10 9 8 7 6 5 4 3 2 1

Library of Congress Cataloging-in-Publication Data

Names: Tassi, Paul.
Title: The sons of Sora / Paul Tassi.
Description: New York : Talos Press, [2016] | Series: The Earthborn trilogy; book 3
Identifiers: LCCN 2015036382 (print) | LCCN 2015039147 (ebook) |
ISBN 9781940456393 (softcover) | ISBN 9781940456492 (ebook) |
ISBN 9781940456492 (epub)
Subjects: LCSH: Imaginary wars and battles—Fiction. | Extraterrestrial
beings—Fiction. | Space warfare—Fiction. | BISAC: FICTION / Science
Fiction / Adventure. | FICTION / Science Fiction / Space Opera. | GSAFD:
Science fiction. | Fantasy fiction. | War stories. | Adventure fiction.
Classification: LCC PS3620.A86 S67 2016 (print) | LCC PS3620.A86 (ebook) |
DDC 813/.6—dc23
LC record available at http://lccn.loc.gov/2015036382

Cover design by Paul Tassi, Victoria Maderna, and Federico Piatti

Printed in the United States of America

1

The war raged on.

Noah was surrounded. He couldn't see them in the mist, but he heard their footsteps on the ancient stone. They were sprinting around his position to flank him. The rest of his team was gone; he'd heard their screams on his radio before the feed went silent.

He was the last one standing, and there was no way he was getting out alive.

Checking his magazine, he knew he should have listened more closely to the Watchman's lessons about conserving ammunition. He only had enough charge for another handful of shots. Too much had been wasted on a sniper far out of his range, an enemy whom he'd ultimately had to flee from anyway, lest he lose his head in the exchange.

His armor was hot and his helmet felt like it was suffocating him. But he didn't dare remove it; its HUD data was proving too invaluable. The display showed him the approximate positions of the shapes in the woods, tracking their footsteps on the forest floor and their heat signatures. They were using the same sort of tech to see him. His team should have been better prepared. There was no way they should have been wiped out like this.

The downed stone pillar he hid behind was starting to feel like a grave marker. Noah needed to retreat into the temple if he was going to have any shot of taking at least a few down with him before he joined his fallen squadmates. Breathing heavily, he gradually inflated himself with enough confidence to make the run.

It's fifty feet. Their view is obstructed. They'll miss.

But would they? Noah was a larger target than most. He was nineteen in Earth years, but towered over everyone in his unit. The strength that came with his size was often a blessing in combat, but it wasn't advantageous when dodging enemy fire.

They'll miss.

He finally convinced himself it was true and lobbed his last pulse grenade over the top of the fallen pillar. The moment he heard it detonate, he took off toward the crumbling stone archway behind him. Even if it hadn't fried anyone directly, the afterglow would wreak havoc with their sensors and targeting systems. At least he hoped it would.

He heard the blasts of the first two shots coming from somewhere behind him to the left. Neither hit him, and he didn't slow his pace. The door was close, twenty feet, ten. One final shot whizzed by the side of his head so close he felt his hair stand on end, but he dove through the entrance and found himself in a much more secure place. From outside he heard the dismayed cries of his enemies as they berated each other for failing to take him down as he fled. Noah breathed a sigh of relief. But he wasn't comforted for long; he knew there were many other ways into the temple. He had to move quickly.

There wasn't time to admire the workmanship that had gone into the murals etched into the stone corridors around them. Gods, monsters, warriors, the usual. The only thing he was interested in were the secret passageways the ancient architects had built.

Noah hurdled a stone altar, long absent of anything resembling a sacrifice, but almost tripped over the body that lay sprawled on the other side. He quickly crouched over it and pulled back the helmet. It was Kadoma, one of his squadmates. Her dark features were serene and calm, her eyes closed. Noah quickly remasked her, then scoured her body for anything useful, his face devoid of emotion for his fallen ally.

Even with his size, it wasn't practical to dual-wield her rifle, though he did take its mostly full clip. She'd barely had a chance to fire at anyone before being hit. He pulled another pair of pulse grenades from her hip and the sidearm pistol from her ribs. He'd lost his own in a bout of hand-to-hand combat outside, an encounter he'd walked away from unscathed. The same could not be said for his opponent.

More footsteps made him fumble one of the grenades, which rolled under the altar. He was forced to leave it there as he sprinted into an adjacent chamber. Voices whispered and two armored figures crept into the room he'd just left. They spoke English.

"He was here," the first one said.

"Are you sure you know how to read those sensors?" the second said. "You weren't just tracking the corpse?"

Noah peered around the corner and saw the second figure lightly kick the downed Kadoma.

"I know the difference between—"

Noah had heard enough. He spun out from the wall and planted his feet. With their backs to him, the shots from the pistol were precise.

A blue flash of light exploded off the back of the helmet of the first figure. The second only had time to curse and pivot around before another pair of blasts dropped him. Now there were three bodies at the foot of the altar. The old gods would have been pleased.

Noah took two steps forward before he heard a click and felt a barrel press into the back of his neck plating.

"Drop it," came the voice.

Noah shook his head, furious he'd let this happen. He reluctantly chucked his pistol toward the pile of bodies and felt his rifle ripped from his back by a gloved hand. The width of the barrel pressed against him indicated a scattershot housing. The weapon was a close-range killer, perfect for a maze like the temple.

"Nice work," Noah said.

"Haven't had a live capture in a while. Much more valuable, they tell me," said the voice from behind him. Noah started to peer around his shoulder cautiously.

"But you know what?" the voice continued. "I'm not quite sure I care."

Noah knew enough about who was in that armor to understand what was about to happen next. The scattershot's trigger was pulled at the exact moment Noah whipped around to knock it sideways with his elbow. The noise was deafening, but he regained his balance and threw a punch into the armored figure's forearm, causing the gun to clatter to the ground. Immediately, the soldier whipped out a pistol from his belt with his other hand, but Noah blocked his arm and the shot went wide.

Using all of his famed strength, Noah grabbed the soldier's wrist and neck and shoved him into the opposite wall. Noah wrenched upward, raking the figure along the stone. The soldier's feet now dangled above the ground. The pistol fell from his grasp, but the moment the metal clinked on the floor, the soldier brought both his knees up and they connected directly with Noah's chin. Noah staggered backward, eyes full of stars, and the figure dropped to the ground, rubbing his neck where the armor had been bent inward to a painful degree by Noah's grip.

When he regained his senses, Noah tried to land a haymaker, but only succeeded in splintering the stone behind his target. Pain shot through his two largest knuckles. The soldier was incredibly quick, and caught Noah with a nanosuit-amplified one-two punch to the ribcage, which cracked his armor plating. As he doubled over, the soldier righted him with an uppercut that caused Noah's helmet display to short out. A second punch detached the helmet from its housing entirely and it bounced haphazardly across the stone floor.

Noah finally managed to block, deflecting a pair of lightning-fast kicks from the smaller figure. On the third attempt, he brought an elbow down on the soldier's thigh, which caused him to cry out in pain and limp backward. Noah seized on the opportunity and charged. Unfortunately, the nimble, wiry soldier deftly moved sideways and caught Noah by the elbow as he did so. He flung Noah directly into the wall, headfirst, and Noah felt pain explode through his now unarmored skull. He flipped around, barely able to keep his balance. His vision was spotted with red-and-black blotches, but he could see the soldier removing his helmet with one hand, as he pointed the retrieved scattergun at him with the other. The familiar, sneering face slowly came into focus.

"Alright, Erik," Noah said, panting. "Take me in. You got me."

Erik's dark hair was plastered to his forehead with sweat. His bright green eyes stood out against his tanned skin, and burned with a mix of rage and delight.

"As I said, I don't really do live captures."

Noah slowly shook his head and extended his hand outward.

"You don't have to—"

"You lose again, brother," Erik said as he pulled the trigger. There was a flash of blinding light. Noah saw nothing but darkness.

2

Dubai.

The word was on his lips, as it was nearly every time he woke. But as soon as it appeared, it drifted away again, forgotten.

Light crept into his eyes as he opened them, and a blurry face began to take shape. When he recognized it, he couldn't help but grin, despite the throbbing agony inside his head.

Sakai returned the smile, brushing her long brown hair over the top of her ear. Her facial features took more from her father, a man from the once great Earth-nation of Japan, but her body was her Brazilian mother's, with light caramel skin and graceful curves at her hips.

"I can't believe you're awake already," she said as her narrow eyes widened in surprise. "The silvercoats said a close-range stun round to an exposed head would have you out for a day at least."

Noah slowly pulled himself upward and rested on his elbows. His armor had been stripped away and he was clad in his fiber undersuit. He looked around the med bay and saw both teams of his unit being treated for various minor injuries. All had risen from the unconsciousness caused by the stun rounds. The exercise was over. His team had lost again.

He rubbed his eyes and felt a light kiss on his forehead. He smiled at Sakai, who somehow managed to look radiant despite being drenched in sweat and splattered with mud.

"You went out early this time," he said, swinging his legs off the side of the gurney where he rested. Machines nearby beeped indicators of his vitals.

"Tehran was being an idiot," she said, exasperated. "I told him they were nested by the log pit, but he wanted to go in anyway. I tried to save his ass, but Quezon fried both of us."

Quezon was helping his half-sister Kadoma to her feet. He was the only one in the unit who was even close to Noah's size. He stood only an inch or two shorter than Noah, despite being three years younger, like nearly everyone else was. He met Noah's eyes and nodded.

"Where's my brother?" Noah asked.

"Getting ripped by the Watchman," she replied, failing to mask a smile. "He wanted to see you also when you were awake, but I don't think he knew you'd be up this soon."

Noah lumbered to his feet and found his nerves tingling. The stun rounds of combat training weren't burning plasma, but they packed a hell of a punch that would linger for hours or even days.

"Might as well see what he wants," Noah said, and bent way down to give the diminutive Sakai a kiss. Everyone was small compared to him, but she was especially so. He knew at least a few of the others had unflattering nicknames for the pair of them, probably concocted by Erik. The rest of Sora knew him by a more grandiose title of honor: the Last Son of Earth. He'd be forever identified by a planet he didn't even remember.

But the Sorans were determined not to let him forget. That was one of the many purposes of Colony One, living and training quarters established on the continent of Losara for the thirty-eight humans still known collectively as the "Earthborn." Though Noah was the only one that identifier described accurately. The rest had been birthed in tanks on Sora, assembled from the twelve comatose humans Alpha had brought with him from Earth. In addition to his parents, of course.

And then there was Erik, the First Son of Sora. He was Lucas and Asha's trueborn son, while Noah had been a stray they'd picked up during their harrowing escape from Earth. Erik was seventeen in the still-used metric of Earth years, with the other Earthborn all sixteen, bred together in a litter.

Noah stepped outside and took in the fresh air, which was a relief from the off-putting antiseptic scent of the med bay. Rolling hills filled with lush pine greenery spread out around him, and the compound itself rose out of the ground ahead.

Colony One was a university, military training ground, and secure dormitory all wrapped up into one. It was built over the ruins of a long-dead holy city destroyed, during one of Sora's countless wars, nearly thirty thousand years ago. Most of the old architecture had been swallowed by the surrounding foliage, but they still utilized some of the more intact sections for training, like the temple where Noah had just met his fictional end. But most of the buildings around him were shiny and new. The government had spared no expense assembling Colony One for the Earthborn. The thirty-eight of them were far too valuable to simply be allowed to melt into the general public. They'd be targets for fanatics, or at best simply become extinct within a generation. It had been revealed that, despite their nearly identical physical similarities, Soran and human biology were incompatible with one another, and an attempt to reproduce between the races would result in the death of both the child and the mother, of either race.

That was why Colony One was formed. It was supposed to be the foundation for a human-only society that would allow their sub-species to someday grow back to its former glory, many thousands of years from now. In the Colony they were taught about both their current home, Sora, but also their former planet, Earth. Everyone, Noah included, spoke fluent English and Soran. Though English hadn't been the most commonly spoken language on Earth, it was the tongue of the original Earthborn, Lucas and Asha, so it became adopted as the old planet's official language. As such, it was taught to everyone in the Colony, student or employee.

They learned the histories of both worlds, though Earth's past was full of more than a few holes. Everything the Sorans knew about the planet had come from Alpha's pre-invasion research, and as smart as he was, he hadn't managed to preserve the complete annals of human history. Still, Noah was fascinated by stories of the major wars of the Romans, Greeks, Huns, Chinese, Germans, and Americans. There was much to learn from them, even if the technology had changed over time.

Unfortunately, the real war, the one with Xala, was still a more pressing concern. It was why they were diligently trained at arms, despite no actual intention to ever send such valuable citizens into battle. But homeworld strikes were still possible, and with humanity on the brink of extinction, they needed to know how to defend themselves, perhaps more than any other civilians on the planet.

Noah walked past the angular, multi-peaked pyramid of the technology nexus and toward the Watchman's quarters, where he expected to find his brother. He approached a pair of Earthborn, already discharged from med bay, it seemed, and out for a walk on the grounds. Lyon had brown eyes with chestnut curled hair and was spawned from a French father and Australian mother. Veria was Greek-Filipino, her features dark and rich. Each of the tank-borns usually did extensive research into their countries of origin, but it was hard to really feel a sense of national pride given their current circumstances. It was more for curiosity than anything else, and despite different points of origin on the globe, all that mattered was that they were all from Earth. The thirty-eight of them had grown up together here, the last of their kind.

Lyon and Veria had been a pair for as long as he could remember. Both smiled as he reached them.

"Heard your brother really went all out this time," Lyon said. Lyon had been on the rival squad, and Noah was pretty sure he'd killed him in the opening moments of the conflict, but he didn't say anything to rub it in.

"Sure did," Noah said, putting his palm to his still throbbing head.

"He's a maniac," Veria bristled as they passed by each other. "He's going to go too far one of these days and someone's going to really get hurt."

In truth, this had already happened many times. Erik's careless disregard for the rules of engagement had resulted in the hospitalization of a few of the Earthborn. But even major injuries were treatable with the colony's state-of-the-art med tech and full-time staff of silvercoats. The Watchman kept devising new and more terrible punishments for Erik after each new offense, but he always ended up laughing it off and continued to treat the rules as mere suggestions.

There were plenty of rules in Colony One, namely that everyone be where they were supposed to be, when they were supposed to be there. Meal and rack time was strictly regimented, and everyone was up at 0500 every day. The most important rule, however—one that Erik frequently broke—was that they were not to leave the compound. Colony One wasn't a prison. There were plenty of field trips for the group, and you could request a special escort to many destinations on the planet. A year or so ago, Sakai learned that there was an ancient library in Ghurain that had a few eighty-thousand-year-old tomes in it. She'd put in a request to visit, and a heavily armed escort had taken her and Noah there for a few days. Their security detail when they were out on such excursions, or even safe inside the colony, was enormous, though there had been only a few attempts of outsiders attempting to invade. Some remnant Fourth Order lunatics had attempted to "cleanse Sora of the plague of humanity." The most successful among them got about three miles outside the colony before they were shredded by auto-turrets.

Erik was something else though. He was always illegally leaving the compound, either by digitally hacking his way through security or just good old-fashioned sneaking. If he put half as much effort into his coursework as he did his escape attempts, he'd be the top student in the colony. Rather, he was content slipping past security and being scooped up by one of his many rich Soran socialite friends who whisked him away to party until colony guards tracked him down and hauled him back.

For as much as Noah and Erik sparred, they were still brothers in each other's eyes, despite not sharing genes. Erik would often invite Noah to tag along for his escapes and subsequent debaucherous evenings, but Noah would always refuse. While Erik was brash and bold, Noah was reserved and contemplative and had little interest in such things. He was content to exercise, study, ascend the stairs to the White Spire, or simply spend time with Sakai.

Oddly, of all the rules in place at the colony, fraternization between the genders wasn't restricted at all. It was practically encouraged. There were no rules about sleeping arrangements, so long as everyone was awake and dressed by the appropriate hour. As such, couples were gradually formed as the Earthborn hit puberty and nature and hormones took over. Sex was commonplace, though all were informed that they had been temporarily sterilized so as not to rapidly explode the human population. Having children at the ages of fourteen, fifteen, sixteen, or even nineteen in Noah's case, would interfere with their education. There was plenty of time for that later, they were told. This lack of restriction was so they'd learn how to function as a normal society would, once it was time to gradually start rebuilding the human race.

Noah's stature and rugged appearance had made him a frequent target of the girls in the colony. Not to mention he held something of a place of honor as the famed "Last Son." But despite their nearly universal affection for him, Noah had been enraptured by only one of them, the enigmatic Sakai. He had been with her and her alone for well over a year now. Despite a lack of official rules regarding relationships, two were universal among the Earthborn themselves. You never pursued someone else who was officially paired (though that had been known to occur), and the tank-borns would obviously never pair with anyone with whom they shared a father or mother. To ask any of them, the idea was simply nauseating. Whether that was a natural reaction or the avoidance had been genetically engineered into them, it was hard to say.

As Noah approached the Watchman's head office he saw Wuhan, Sakai's half-brother, leaning against the side of the entryway eating a purple piece of fruit. He still had most of his plating on. Wuhan was Japanese-Chinese, named after a city in one of his parents' home countries. It was how all of the tank-bred were given their names at birth.

"What are you in for?" Noah asked.

Wuhan shook his head.

"Nothing this time, surprisingly. I'm just here to file a travel request for Rhylos."

Noah scoffed.

"Good luck. Didn't he reject you the last three times?"

Wuhan nodded.

"Yeah, but I've been kill leader the last few exercises. I'm hoping that wins me some points."

"It's won you a target on your back from everyone else," Noah said.

Wuhan shrugged and flicked the pit of the fruit into the brush.

"Well, the only ones I'm scared of are you, and you're on my squad, and your brother. But lucky for all of us, he doesn't seem to take the exercises seriously. God help us if he ever does."

"He did today," Noah said.

Wuhan winced.

"Yeah, I heard. Scattergun to a naked cranium? How are you conscious right now?"

"Kyneth's blessing," Noah replied with a smile.

Wuhan rolled his eyes.

"Sure. Anyway, I'm pretty sure your thing takes priority over mine. I can hear the yelling from here."

Wuhan stepped aside and Noah entered the Watchman's quarters. The walls were sterile, devoid of anything resembling decoration. Noah followed the sound echoing off the metal walls until he found what he was looking for.

Erik stood stiffly with his arms behind his back as Watchman Tannon Vale was berating him. Despite the older man's intensity, Erik's gaze was fixed past Vale and out the window, which overlooked the eastern mountains. He looked bored. Tannon didn't stop when he saw Noah enter, and continued his tirade.

"—and where in our combat scrolls does it say anything about executing prisoners at point-blank range? And with a scattergun? You could have given your brother brain damage!"

"He's a tough guy, Watchman," Erik said diplomatically. He always regarded Tannon very formally, but his tone usually carried a sharp tinge of sarcasm.

"As miraculous as it is that he's standing here now, that's not the point. You're a danger to yourself and everyone in this colony when you refuse to respect the laws that have been put in place for your protection. You'll run the circuit a dozen times tonight before lights out and think about that."

"Requesting permission to be expelled from the colony, Watchman," Erik said, still standing at attention in his full armor plating.

"If only I could," said Tannon. "But you know better than that. Just don't let this fixation you have with provoking your brother go any further. One of these days he'll have had enough and make you wish you hadn't."

"He tried today, Watchman," Erik said, a faint smile crossing his lips.

"Noah," Tannon said, addressing him for the first time, "Try harder next time. Maybe you can teach him a lesson that I can't."

"Yes, Watchman," Noah replied, also now standing at attention.

"At ease," Tannon said. "I didn't call you here about this."

Erik glanced at Noah. Standing side by side, the two couldn't be more opposite. Noah was tall and thick with muscle. He had buzzed sandy-blond hair and oceanic blue eyes. His cropped undersuit revealed the large burn that spread across his shoulder and arm, a remnant from a homeworld he couldn't remember.

Erik was a combination of the two greatest heroes of the era. He had Lucas's hard jawline, nose, and mouth, but the rest of him was all Asha, with her wild black hair and piercing green eyes. Two years younger than Noah, he was almost a foot shorter. But he was lean and hard and spry. When he wanted to be, he was the best fighter in the colony and was smart as a whip to boot. Too smart for his own good, his instructors often said.

"What is it, Watchman Vale?" Noah asked.

Tannon sat down behind a sprawling desk alive with holographic displays. He looked tired, and his age was finally starting to show, which was rare in Soran culture. His short reign as High Chancellor had taken a lot out of him. He'd devoted nearly his entire few years in office to first distancing himself from the crimes of his sister, who was discovered to have committed genocide and treason on a shocking scale before her death at the hands of the rebel Hex Tulwar. Tannon knew nothing about her crimes at the time, and had barely gotten the trust of the public back. But the Vale name was forever tarnished after Talis's sins. The new High Chancellor, Madric Stoller, had granted him the position of first watchman at Colony One, supervising and training the young Earthborn. Some saw it as less of an honor and more of a form of exile. It was often a difficult job, but Tannon said it still felt like retirement compared to serving as an admiral or ruling as High Chancellor.

His last act before abdicating office was to clear the names of Lucas and Asha as supposed conspirators working with Hex Tulwar and the Fourth Order to assassinate his sister and destabilize the planet. He tasked the smartest living being he knew with the job of unraveling Tulwar's attempt to frame them. Alpha relished the opportunity to clear his friends' names and spent months of painstaking work piecing together video and audio tracks that the now-dead Tulwar believed he'd completely wiped from the palace security feeds. What he had manipulated to make the Earthborn look guilty, Alpha unwound to show the truth. Tulwar alone was the traitor, and Lucas and Asha were exactly who they claimed to be. It was a relief for a world desperately in need of heroes. Though some still reviled the Earthborn, and probably always would, most continued to see them as a symbol of hope in the endless war with Xala. When it was revealed what they'd done on Xala during the Battle of Altoria, the public at large went back to worshipping them.

"They want you for the anniversary this year," Tannon said. "Stoller himself made the request."

Erik cursed under his breath.

"Again?"

The anniversary of Altoria was coming up in a few days time. The battle was named after the green gas planet in the Soran solar system where the two massive fleets had clashed all those years ago. It was when Lucas, Asha, Alpha, Zeta, and Mars Maston traveled to Xala itself to spark the Xalan uprising and disrupt the enemy's communications. Only through their work had the Soran fleet been able to break the Xalans in the black of space, barely three billion miles away from Sora itself. The shattered enemy force limped out of the system only to find all their colony planets in open revolt when they returned. Their citizens had learned the truth Alpha's father had uncovered before his death. The premise of the entire interstellar war was built on a lie that Xalans were a sovereign race with a homeworld destroyed by Sora, when in fact they had been slaves genetically engineered from Sorans themselves, mercifully banished to the barren world after a violent uprising.

"I thought the point of living here is that we can be zoo animals with no visitors," Erik continued, losing his formal tone.

"The people need reassurance the next generation of Earthborn are still our committed allies. It's a symbolic gesture that unites our two planets." Tannon didn't sound particularly convinced himself.

"We don't have a planet, Watchman," Erik shot back. Tannon glowered at him.

"From what I can tell, you like the spotlight," Tannon said. He pulled up a feed of the Stream that was playing a video of a drunken Erik at a nightclub in downtown Elyria with his friends a few weeks earlier. A scantily clad Soran girl was tucked under each of his arms. He stumbled and fell, pulling both down with him.

"I didn't know you were a frequenter of the gossip feeds, Watchman," Erik said with a sly smile.

"Only when it involves one of my charges illegally going off-site where any madman could murder or abduct him," Tannon said, annoyed.

"They can try," Erik said coldly.

"When do we leave, Watchman?" Noah asked, eager to get out of the colony, no matter the reason. It had been too long.

"Tomorrow. And no, you can't bring Sakai, so don't even ask."

Noah figured as much, but knew she'd be disappointed. Sakai loved Elyria. A holographic photo of the two of them at a state dinner in the Grand Palace's throne room had a permanent place next to her bed.

"I'm heading off-world for some sort of damned summit, so I won't be here when you get back," Tannon continued. "But I've told security to keep extra eyes on you," he said, glaring at Erik.

"Is that all, Watchman?" Erik said, assuredly eager to return to whichever Earthborn girl he was currently sleeping with. Was it Penza or Tula now?

"Dismissed," said Tannon.

There were three full moons as Noah ran the thousand-stair climb toward the White Spire that night. In truth, it was actually 1,653 stairs—Noah had counted—but that didn't roll off the tongue as easily, he supposed.

Sakai was sleeping when he stole away for one of his many midnight runs to the spire. She'd come with him a few times, but after a hard day's training, climbing that high to pray at a temple to gods she didn't even believe in was usually the last thing she wanted.

The White Spire was the oldest building in the entire compound and was placed high up on the backside of a mountain. It was still under the protection of Colony One's security, but far removed from everything else. The temple was perfectly intact, unlike other similar structures that lay in ruins on the colony grounds below. The faithful always believed it was because the gods had blessed it, keeping it safe from harm for untold millennia. But chances were it was simply too far from any possible conflict, and it had been prevented from falling into natural decay by Zurana's Anointed, who had lived there for as long as the structure had existed. They weren't immortal, but their order was devoted, and when one sister died they'd send another in her place. As they all wore white woven veils at all times, it was impossible to tell who was a new recruit or a two-hundred-year-old crone, other than perhaps by judging their gait as they moved through the stone corridors.

Noah reached the 1,653rd step and gazed up at the glorious structure before him. The White Spire was actually many spires, all carved from stone, that thrust hundreds of feet upward into the night sky. From a distance, they looked like a single unit. All the building's stone was white marble, and it was hard to believe how long the temple had stood intact. Before Colony One had been established, many faithful would make pilgrimages to the spire, and they were dismayed now that they no longer could. It was one of the oldest sites of worship on the planet.

Two colony guards nodded curtly at Noah as he entered the temple. Both were heavily armored and armed, as the spire was in a rather exposed location. There were even more guards inside.

Noah couldn't really explain how he'd come to appreciate the faith of the people who had once tried to kill his parents and frame them for murder and treason. He'd studied all the religions of both Earth and Sora, but was inexplicably drawn to the Tomes of the Forest and the knowledge they contained. When he first reached the White Spire years ago, he felt a peace he couldn't explain, and he had been coming to pray ever since. No, he didn't know if the First Man and Woman, Kyneth and Zurana, were actually sitting on oak thrones listening to him, but it made him feel better all the same.

There were no other patrons that night. He'd spotted Quezon up here a few times in recent weeks, but the chapel floor was currently vacant. Round, flat stones rose out of the ground, all curved around a central towering statue of Zurana, the First Woman herself.

Noah took up a kneeling position on one of the stones. Many of the white-robed and veiled sisters were doing the same, but others were attending to unlit candles or sweeping the floor with wiry brooms. Coming here was like stepping back in time thirty thousand years. Almost nothing had changed in that span, right down to the sisters' holy garments and the carefully arranged pattern of the prayer stones.

Sitting back on his heels, Noah placed his hands on his thighs and lifted his head toward the vaulted ceiling. He spoke in a whisper.

"Zurana, hear my prayer. Protect our colony from those who would do us harm. Guard Erik and me on our journey tomorrow. Bless our soldiers in the field, and their families still at home."

He paused.

"Keep Asha safe, wherever she may be. May she find whatever she's looking for."

Noah knew where Asha was supposed to be. The official word was that she was back on Makari, helping the Oni there shake off the last remnants of Xalan occupation. The colony there had given birth to the quickest and most volatile uprising, with a large Xalan resistance force already in place and a native human population to agitate things further.

But whether Asha was there or not was anyone's guess.

Things had been good for a few years, which Noah could still remember. Asha had returned home from Xala injured, but alive.

With Lucas gone, she did her best to be a mother to him and Erik. They lived in exile, as Tannon and Alpha were still trying to clear the Earthborn for their supposed crimes, but they had each other, and that was enough. Noah's memories from that time were faint, but warm.

Eventually, when Noah was seven and the Earthborn were absolved, Asha was called back into service as the war escalated. Noah and Erik were brought to the newly built Colony One and assigned caretakers and tutors during their formative years. Asha was out on assignment frequently, stopping by the colony to see the boys when she could. But over time, her missions became longer, her visits more spread out. When they saw her a few years back, she was distraught and wouldn't speak about where she'd been. Later, it was Alpha who told them that she'd been caught trying to commandeer a long-range null core in order to travel to Xala to look for Lucas.

Noah confronted her about it, and she confessed that she never believed Lucas was dead. If only they would just let her have a ship, she swore she could find him.

It was heartbreaking to hear her say those things with such conviction. But it was also worrisome, an indicator she might literally be losing her mind. Whether she was actually on Makari right now or cruising toward Xala in a stolen spaceship, Noah had no idea. But either way, she wouldn't be at the anniversary ceremony tomorrow, as she hadn't for the last ten years or so.

When Noah prayed for her to find what she was looking for, he didn't mean the long-dead Lucas. He meant peace of mind, something that seemed to forever elude her.

Noah fell into a deep, meditative state after finishing his verbal prayers, as was traditional for the faithful. The world fell away around him, and his mind was full of light and color and nothing else. Then someone whispered in his ear.

Dubai.

Noah jumped, turning around from side to side to see who had spoken. But there was no one. Even the praying sisters were gone now. Continuing to scan the room, he caught a glimpse of one veiled sister staring at him through a half-open doorway across the chapel. As soon as he noticed her, she scurried out of sight. But she was too far away to have been next to him a half second ago.

He didn't understand why the word had kept coming to him in dreams the past few weeks, and this was the first time he'd heard it during prayer. It sounded familiar for some reason, but he couldn't place where he'd heard it before.

The ice moon passed over the middle skylight of the cathedral. The hour was late. Noah's sore legs were thankful that the trip down the stairs was much easier than the way up. As he left, he still felt like he was being watched, a familiar feeling during his time spent at the spire.

Noah gazed up into the trillions of stars as he stepped outside.

May the gods save you, Asha. Wherever you are.

3

Noah woke at 0430 and found Sakai crippled with abdominal pain. It wasn't a cause for concern; these issues cropped up every so often around the colony. The silvercoats deemed it a forest parasite they couldn't vaccinate against. They'd give her some meds, tell her to rest, and she'd be back to 100 percent soon after. In this instance, however, it did serve to reassure her that she couldn't have gone with Noah to Elyria even if it was allowed, which was some small comfort to her.

"Be safe," she said as she flattened his high-collared formal jacket against his chest. He could see her trying to hide the pain she felt in each movement, but still, she smiled. Noah had mercifully avoided the parasite so far.

Noah let her crawl back into bed, grabbed his travel case, and set out toward the colony docking bay.

The shuttle was already waiting for him, as were the two heavily armed escort ships that would accompany them to Elyria. A guard took his case from him and the hatch of the shuttle opened upward with a hiss. Noah was surprised at who he found inside.

"Hi Theta, I didn't realize you were coming."

Alpha's daughter was sitting across from him with her claws perched delicately on her knees. She had the coveted white coloring of her mother, Zeta, but the gold pupil rings of her father. She was how old now? Thirteen? Her translator collar had been tuned to a higher-pitched tone to match her youth, though there were still traces of a metallic echo.

"Hello Noah, I hope my presence isn't an inconvenience for you or your brother," she said meekly.

"Of course not. We're glad to have you," Noah replied, though Erik was still nowhere to be found inside the shuttle. "Are you coming to see Alpha?"

Theta nodded.

"Yes, and I believe he requested a visit from the pair of you as well."

Noah took a seat across from the Xalan. Even though she was far younger than he was, she was only a few inches shorter. Once she was fully grown, he knew he would be looking up to her.

Theta was wise beyond her years as well, and was unquestionably the smartest being employed at the colony. Even at her young age she ran the technology nexus almost single-handedly, teaching the Earthborn both Soran and Xalan schools of science and working on government projects in her free time. Many assignments had her partnering with her parents, as they could easily collaborate from afar. Her presence in the colony was meant to keep her safe. She couldn't stay on any of the Xalan worlds, which were all too unstable and far away from her parents. At the colony, she was meant to socialize with the Earthborn, who were somewhat close to her age, even if they were of a completely different species. She was shy, but well-liked by the group as an instructor. Noah in particular had made an effort to reach out to her over the last few years since she'd arrived, but to this day she still seemed afraid to think of him as a friend.

"Alright, let's get a move on," said Erik as he spilled into the seat next to Theta, not even glancing in her direction. He was in similar formalwear to Noah, but his pants and coat were horribly wrinkled and smelled unwashed. Noah supposed he'd worn them out during one of his many mini-vacations away from the colony.

"Hello, Erik," Theta said at a volume that registered just above a whisper.

Erik turned to look at her, just now seeming to notice she was there. Only he could overlook a six-foot-tall Xalan sitting next to him.

"Oh, hey," he replied, but it was enough to make Theta's white cheeks turn the slightest shade of pink. It was obvious to most that Theta had some sort of affection for Erik, though she never admitted as much. Erik likely had some idea, which was why he was always asking her for favors. Sometimes it was coursework extensions or equipment upgrades, but Noah had a feeling that when the colony's security grid magically went dark in one quadrant while Erik snuck out, it was her untraceable handiwork.

The hovercraft began to rise and Noah watched the colony fall away behind a six-inch-thick indestructible viewscreen. The two military escort craft could be seen on either side of them, and their own pilot had the dividing screen up. The guards weren't supposed to get friendly with the Earthborn, lest they be emotionally compromised when it came to their protection. They often came off as cold as a result, but any one of them would trade their life for one of the Earthborn in a heartbeat if need be.

They ascended up the side of the dark mountain that housed the White Spire, and Noah watched it as they passed. Small, pale figures milled around in the gardens and soon turned into mere specks.

From this distance, the colony did look a little like a prison, only the walls were a thick canopy of trees and the closest city was three hundred miles away. Yes, they could leave, but only under heavily armed guard, the way captives would. However, life at the colony had plenty of freedoms to go with its restrictions, and at times it was almost *too* comfortable. Men younger than Noah were fighting and dying out there in deep space and on foreign worlds, yet he was waking up each day with a beautiful girl under his arm and a full staff of Sorans dedicated to his education and fitness. Lucas and Asha had been allowed to contribute to the war effort. Why couldn't he? He'd broached the subject many times with Tannon, but was met with increasing hostility each time he brought it up. Noah came to realize that Tannon felt somewhat responsible for Lucas's death, and he had no plans to let either of his sons meet the same fate. Noah could understand his position, but it didn't make the situation any less frustrating.

If Erik felt the same way about their removal from the war, he didn't let on. Truth was, Noah and Erik rarely had anything approaching a serious conversation. Erik never wanted to talk about their parents and seemed to resent them, both living and dead. Lucas had died so that they, and the rest of Sora, would survive. It was hard to hate him for that, but he was gone all the same, and they'd grown up with half a parent at best. Asha had tried, but thought the colony would raise them better than she could. Now she was off on her fool's quest chasing after a ghost, and the brothers simply had to deal with her absence. It wasn't just Erik who resented them. Sometimes, Noah had to admit that to himself.

A few hours later, Noah found himself staring up at his father. Lucas's monument was a hundred feet tall and carved entirely out of one mammoth piece of stone, as were all the other statues that lined the promenade of the Grand Palace. The first two, all the way down by the entrance, were of Kyneth and Zurana themselves. Then, in pairs, the rest watched over the long, ancient path to Elyria. There was Ruul the Conqueror, Ayl the Lord of Starlight, Ulissa Cliffbreaker, Merenes the Martyr, Sha'len the Holy, and dozens more, all known as the greatest warriors of their era and the heroes of tales told to Soran children worldwide.

Now, two new pedestals had been erected. To Noah's right stood Lucas, clad in Guardian armor, clutching his famed rifle, Natalie. To Noah's left was the towering form of Mars Maston, the famous commander and his father's friend, who was also killed on the mission to Xala. Maston met Lucas's gaze, his arms folded and a pistol dangling from his hip.

Noah could remember seeing Lucas's face in person only through deep concentration. He'd been so young when Lucas had left for Xala; there were just mere glimpses of him lodged in his mind, and he wasn't even sure if those were real. For all he knew, he could have subconsciously absorbed them through the endless number of times Lucas's face was cycled through the Stream.

He remembered being very cold in a wooden house with a fireplace. Sitting on Lucas's lap, his father was telling him something, but he could never hear his voice. Rather, Noah had to be content with the farewell Lucas had recorded on his Final before he'd landed on Xala. Noah used to watch it every day when he was little. Then it was once a week. Then once a month. Now, he couldn't remember the last time he'd played it, or even where the file was saved in his datacluster. But by this point he'd memorized most of it.

"Lead them," his father had said in the video, assuming Sora would revere the young Noah someday.

"And look out for your mother and brother."

It made Noah sad to think he'd failed to do either. Asha was racing through the stars with an apparent death wish. Erik pursued every possible chance to rebel, and hardly looked up to his quiet big brother in any way other than literal. Sora adored Noah from afar, but the only thing he'd managed to lead so far had been the tiny cluster of Earthborn at the colony. Even then he still answered to a slew of instructors, guards, and Watchman Vale.

Noah hadn't been paying attention to whatever Madric Stoller was saying, nor to the massive crowd that was assembled before them. Mercifully, they weren't making him speak this year. He was just supposed to be scenery, a reminder that the offspring of the Earthborn were still alive and well and contributing members of society. Though that last bit was certainly a farce.

Stoller winning the High Chancellorship had made him twenty years younger, somehow. He'd easily shed fifty pounds, but was still built like a tree trunk. Even at well over a hundred years old he hadn't allowed his mustache and hair to turn white, and likely never would. The man had simply stopped aging thanks to the best treatments and genes money could buy, as well as quite a few new replacement organs along the way, if the rumors were true.

Since his rise to power, Stoller had brought something of an iron fist down on Sora. His first priority after taking office had been to make sure any and all government opposition groups were smashed and dismantled. He claimed it was to avoid another Fourth Order nightmare scenario, where they had collaborated with the Xalans to subvert the Soran government. But if the Stream was accurate, there were reports that even peaceful antigovernment organizations were being harassed and their leaders were mysteriously disappearing. These days the Stream didn't say much to that effect, but Noah suspected it was because Stoller had taken a more personal investment in what did or didn't air on the Stream regarding his administration. A few overly critical newsmen had ended up missing as well. Still, the people celebrated Stoller's rule as a return to order for a planet thrown into chaos by Talis Vale's treachery. With internal strife quelled by force, Sora's full attention could be devoted to the more urgent war with Xala.

Noah hadn't had much personal interaction with Stoller himself other than at state affairs where he was pressed about colony life or recent sakala highlights as small talk. Rather, Noah was more familiar with Stoller's son, Finn, who had taken a shine to Erik and was one of his more frequent partying pals whenever his brother made his escapes. Finn was present on the promenade and was whispering to Erik as his father spoke. Mercifully, he looked nothing like the elder Stoller, and instead had rather angular features with light auburn hair and blue eyes. He was thin as a rail, but was handsome enough thanks to a combination of good genes from his now-deceased actress mother and better genes that Stoller had paid a fortune to inject into his embryo, as the rich so often did with their progenies. Noah didn't particularly care for Finn. He credited him as a bad influence on Erik, but he had to concede that maybe it was the other way around.

Noah looked up at the statue of his father once more. High Chancellor Stoller had claimed that he and Lucas were good friends, and he used that to his benefit whenever possible, always invoking the fallen war hero's name when it was required to make a political point. "And I know if Lucas, Savior of Sora, were here today, he would be proud of the way our military has secured his adopted homeworld, and how we've driven the monstrous Xalan hordes back to their dying planet."

Funny, Noah had never heard Stoller refer to Alpha or Zeta as the "Saviors of Sora," despite the fact that it was their work that sparked the Xalan colony uprisings. But he supposed they were part of "monstrous horde," and couldn't be given such credit. He was glad Theta wasn't there to hear this.

Noah wondered what Lucas would actually make of all this if he were standing next to him, not as a statue, but in the flesh. It was hard to know the mind of a man he could barely remember meeting. All he had were stories and all those seemed to say that Lucas probably wouldn't like Stoller's chancellorship very much at all.

Stoller said something else, then motioned toward Noah and Erik. The crowd gathered before them went wild, letting out cheers and raising fists in the air. The brothers shared a knowing look, but each forced a smile for the swirling camerabots. They might as well just make the next pair of statues the two of them, so they wouldn't have to keep coming to these things.

Thankfully, Noah and Erik were allowed to skip the stuffy dinner at the Grand Palace following the ceremony. Though Noah remembered snippets of his time spent living at the palace in his youth, he wasn't particularly fond of visiting after Tannon Vale had left office and Madric Stoller sat in the metaphorical throne. Instead, Erik convinced their escort to swing by downtown Elyria for a rack of roasted Yutta ribs, which they ate on the ride to their final destination.

A few miles outside Elyria, the Merenes Military Base was very old but was constantly being upgraded to maintain its distinction as the most advanced weapons research facility on the planet. Though Alpha worked at many installations both on- and off-world, this was his most frequent haunt.

A pair of Soran Defense Initiative dreadnoughts were docked at the base when they arrived, each getting fitted for their pair of white null cores. It had taken just over a decade to synthesize the proper element that allowed Sora's SDI troops to travel further and faster in space than ever before. It was perhaps Alpha's most valuable contribution to the Soran war effort. It allowed Sora's ships not only to respond to Xalan threats faster but also to reach their enemy's five conquered colony worlds—all once inhabited by human civilizations in millennia past—to assist in the uprisings that were taking place there.

The Xalans had possessed the advanced technology of the white null core for ages, and it allowed them to expand without consequence and gain the upper hand in the war, even against such a resource-rich planet as Sora. The white core was also what allowed them to invade Noah's homeworld of Earth in the first place. The fact that Alpha had gifted the knowledge to the Sorans should have gotten him his own statue, but the Xalan didn't care about such things. The SDI had spent the last five years fitting every possible ship with a white core. Winning the war on the back of that advancement would be reward enough for Alpha, he always said. Still, neither he nor the SDI were satisfied with just faster ships, and he'd been designing weapons and defense systems for them in the interim while the null element synthesized.

Their hovercraft landed and Theta was there to meet them at the gate.

"I trust your event was suitably exciting?" she asked, her gold eyes darting between them.

"Oh, it was a joy," replied Erik as he carelessly tossed a Yutta bone to the ground.

"I am delighted to hear it," answered Theta, who still hadn't managed to grasp the concept of sarcasm. Noah knew that Theta would have loved to have been in attendance on the palace promenade—a place she'd more than once remarked was breathtaking—but of course Stoller would never allow that.

"My father will be pleased to see you," she said, motioning them to come inside. "He is always renewed by your visits."

Alpha's section of the base was blocked by endless security checkpoints, all of which they were waved through after careful molecular screening. Their Earth DNA was something of an all-access pass in and of itself most places, though the rest of the Earthborn wouldn't be privileged to see this base if they were visiting. It was one of the most secure installations on the planet.

They passed rows and rows of rooms where Alpha's assigned Soran technicians were bringing his many projects to life. Noah saw prototype energy weapons test fired and hulking mech suits stumbling around, but most doors were locked tight, embedded in thick walls with no windows.

The final door at the end of the hall led to a massive circular chamber. It was a far cry from the sort of cramped quarters Alpha was normally known to work in, but he'd done his best to make it crowded by filling the room with mountains of machinery. Noah didn't know what more than one or two devices around him actually did, even with Theta's technological tutoring.

Alpha stood up from behind his massive curved desk when he saw them.

"Greetings!" he said heartily and walked around to welcome each of them with a claw clasp to the shoulder. Noah heard the seams in Eric's jacket rip and saw him wince. Alpha had probably inadvertently broken skin with the six-fingered metal appendage that had replaced his lost left hand.

Alpha released his grip and played with a few controls, which powered down some of the noisier machines in the room.

"How goes the war?" Noah asked. Alpha wasn't technically supposed to tell them, nor was he technically supposed to know certain sensitive information, but the Sorans simply had no way of restricting his access to their databases with how plugged in he was to their systems. They simply had to trust him. And in turn, he trusted them.

"The Xalan Council is proving surprisingly resilient, considering I watched them all perish years ago at the hands of the Desecrator. Though the resistance has made many colonies catch fire, there is still an order to the military I do not comprehend. Logic dictates a new council now rules in the old one's stead, yet the communications Zeta has intercepted say nothing to that effect. It is as if the Xalan forces are being guided by ghosts. Each commander and general operates independently, yet they retain a huge amount of coordination and control with their forces. It defies reason."

"What about Makari?"

Alpha nodded and pulled up a video feed. Contained within was footage of the human-equivalent Oni living in ruined Xalan bases and cities. They were the only colony planet with a surviving human population, however small. Periodically in the video, a Xalan or two would wander through the streets who had to be resistance or civilian.

"The chieftain Toruk managed to unite the last of the Oni clans and has come to the aid of the resistance. The native population coupled with the uprising has been enough to purge the whole of the planet of Xalan forces. The fleeing troops have been picked off by Soran blockades, and now transports are bringing food and relief to the surface. Zeta is onboard one of them."

Noah glanced at Theta who looked a touch forlorn. Perhaps she thought she'd be able to see her mother during this visit. Granted they saw each other often, but video feed communication came with a certain degree of sterility, especially when Xalans were concerned.

"Where's Asha?" Erik interjected. "I thought she was on Makari."

Alpha flipped through some more footage.

"She was present for the battle at Moonwater Bay."

The video footage showed the blurry, small shape of a woman on a beach cutting through Xalan armor, surrounded by legions of dark-skinned Oni.

"But she has since been reassigned."

"Reassigned where?" Erik asked.

Alpha brought up another screen and scrolled through a flurry of symbols.

"Ah, she has been tasked with tracking and eliminating the Black Corsair."

Erik and Noah looked at each other. Noah shrugged. Alpha read their minds.

"The general public is not being told about the Corsair, though whispers are spreading."

"Who is he?"

Alpha tapped a file marked "classified."

"Unknown. Data points to a Chosen Shadow, but one with a taste for extreme brutality."

"Is there any other kind?" Erik asked disdainfully.

"It would seem to be a unique case. The Corsair has wreaked havoc on supply lines over the past few months. He completely cut off food relief to the Soran asteroid colony in the Eroch System. The entire base starved to death, and the supply ships meant to reach them were found drifting in the asteroid field full of psionically dismembered corpses. The Corsair's ship was nowhere to be found, and all data drives onboard the Soran vessels were erased completely, leaving no record of his raid."

Noah was incredulous.

"This is one ship, and one Xalan?"

"It is not known if he has a crew with him, though yes, he does have a single ship. Cloaked and incredibly fast. He has been spotted in systems that should be months apart mere days after his previous strike."

"A new type of core?" Noah asked.

"I see no other explanation, though I cannot comprehend the physics behind it. Nor who on Xala would be capable of creating such a thing."

"And they're sending Asha after him?" Erik asked with concern.

"She volunteered. The Corsair butchered one of the first Soran relief fleets heading to Makari, which is when the SDI began to deem him a pressing threat. The last I heard, Asha was attempting to track him through the Kettler Quadrant."

"She's got a goddamn death wish," said Erik under his breath, visibly annoyed. Noah was similarly unsettled.

"Tell them about Earth, father," Theta chimed in from behind them, attempting to change the subject.

Alpha's eyes widened.

"Ah yes. I am surprised you did not ask sooner. This way."

He led them around a corner to a holotable projecting a large globe of their former planet, but it looked very different than any version of it they'd seen before. There were wisps of white clouds across the brown landscape. But more pressingly, there were splashes of blue underneath them. The datestamp was current.

"Is that . . . water?" Noah asked, his eyes widening.

A few years earlier, Alpha had informed them that temperatures on Earth were beginning to normalize. After reaching incredible levels of heat after the Xalan invasion and resulting nuclear war, which seared the last life off the planet, temperatures gradually began to drop years later. Alpha mused that Earth was somehow beginning to heal itself after the shock of the human-Xalan war that had devastated its surface. The ozone was reforming, the air clearing. Alpha couldn't rule out that the Xalans had managed to artificially create this new state in an attempt to salvage a planet that would have been a great prize of war had they not completely destroyed it during their assault.

"Rain has begun to fall in certain areas of Earth over the past few months," Alpha said. "Nourishing rain, not the corrosive variety that plagued the planet in its final days. The oceans remain mostly dry, but certain lakes are retaining water in areas with particularly severe downpours."

Noah was amazed. *First habitable temperatures, now actual water?*

"The Xalans have minimal forces on the ground and in orbit, but the SDI followed them. There have been a few skirmishes outside the planet's atmosphere and on the surface, but both Sora and Xala seem to be devoting few resources to investigate. Even with small amounts of pure water that could be used as fuel, Earth has almost no tactical significance in the larger war. I do not understand why Xalans are there at all, in fact. It would seem to be an inefficient use of resources. I am also picking up a few energy signatures on and around the planet I cannot identify."

Alpha looked up at the map, which pulsed with colorful dots.

"In any case, when the war concludes, I thought you would enjoy knowing that perhaps one day you may visit your homeworld again. It truly was a beautiful place before its annihilation. Perhaps someday it may be again."

Noah stared at the unfamiliar rock. In a few places where the barren oceans were starting to fill in with water, it created odd continental shapes that weren't at all what the planet used to look like, if the history scrolls were accurate. It was turning into a new world. But new or old, it would never feel like home to him. He seldom spoke of it, but Noah only truly had one memory of Earth.

Fire.

4

Noah winced as Wuhan's staff cracked across his forehead. The hammer was heavy to wield, and not the most effective weapon for blocking. For every strike he deflected from the lightning-fast wooden staff, another three would land. He was fortunate Wuhan's weapon lacked the usual blades that would accompany its tips, otherwise he might have already lost a few facial features.

The other Earthborn were gathered in a wide circle around them, and instructors were shouting advice as they fought. *Parry! Thrust! Low! High!* It was simply too much to process, and Noah took a dashing strike to the chest that sent him stumbling backwards. Wuhan grinned before attacking with a wheelhouse kick that Noah managed to negate with his forearm.

The hammer was slow, but Noah had adopted it as his melee weapon of choice nonetheless. He read about how the ancient Yalos warriors would tear through villages and strongholds using their mighty warhammers, crushing armor and bone and stone alike with their colossal strength. They conquered a third of the world in their time, before Haleo the Wise decimated their empire once he invented gunpowder. Still, for someone possessing as much raw strength as Noah, the hammer kept its allure. His training maul was made of graftstone and tulwood, not anything nearly as formidable as allium or darksteel, but it was still solid enough to leave an impression.

Wuhan whipped his staff around, and it took every bit of Noah's minimal speed to avoid more strikes to the head. Wuhan had seemingly limitless energy in combat, but Noah did see him starting to sweat. The blows Wuhan had landed on him would have felled any other combatant, but Noah still stood, patiently waiting for his moment.

Noah wiped a trickle of blood from his forehead as he circled Wuhan, who was now being more reserved with his strikes to avoid fatigue. Behind him, Noah could see Erik sitting on the amphitheater's carved stone sidelines, talking to Theta of all people. The two were whispering back and forth while Erik's latest Earthborn devotee, Penza, sat on the other side of him. She was a tall, leggy blond from Russian and Danish stock, with ghostly pale skin and sky-blue eyes that looked rather bored at present. She didn't seem terribly amused at being ignored for a Xalan. What were Erik and Theta talking about? Most days Erik barely acknowledged her existence.

Half the crowd roared when Wuhan caught Noah in the gut with a half moon strike. The other half cheered when Noah retaliated with an uppercut with the butt of the hammer. Poor Sakai remained silent when either of them was struck, not wanting to cheer for injury inflicted on either her pair or her half-brother. Erik, meanwhile, took a break from talking to Theta when either took a savage blow to cheer because he just seemed to like watching people get hurt. He was still nursing a rapidly swelling black eye from his earlier bout with Heraklion, but his foe had fared worse and was currently unconscious in the med bay.

Noah had fought Wuhan more than a few times, and certain patterns began to make themselves known in his fighting style. Noah deftly dodged a downward strike to his right, then countered with a hard cross swing that hit Wuhan in the shoulder and sent him staggering to the side. Wuhan countered with a sweep to Noah's knee, but the move was anticipated. Noah raised his foot and slammed down on the staff with all his might when it arrived, snapping the wood with a crack. Wuhan had just enough time to look surprised when the graftstone head of the maul slammed into his chest, imploding the fiberslate plating and sending him flying backward into the dust. When Noah reached him, he was writhing around coughing, attempting to reclaim some of the air that had been pulverized out of his lungs. When Noah's swings did land, the results of his strength combined with the brute force of the hammer were devastating. He offered Wuhan his hand as the instructors waved their arms to call the fight in his favor.

"Kyneth's blessing?" Wuhan asked as he got to his feet, clutching his chest.

"Must be," Noah said with a smile. He glanced over at Erik who, still deep in conversation with Theta, hadn't even seen his winning blow. Penza was now tugging on his arm in an effort to pry him away from her, and was starting to look more than a little annoyed.

Noah was still breathing heavily after the fight and let the hammer slip from his grasp and land upright on the ground with a thud. The weapon was three feet long. He didn't know how much the rectangular stone head weighed, but nearly no one other than him could effectively wield it in combat. His size might not have been great for dodging plasma, but it proved useful on days like today. Wuhan crumpled down next to Sakai, and both simply shook their heads at Noah. Thankfully, both were masking smiles. He felt a clap on his burned shoulder.

"Good fight, brother," Erik said with a grin. "Swing that thing enough and you'll hit someone eventually, I guess."

Noah just rolled his eyes and continued walking toward the med bay, where he could acquire a few liquid stitches for his forehead. Erik kept pace with him and began to speak in a hushed tone.

"So I'm out of here tonight," he whispered. "Finn's picking me up near the south gate in his Shatterstar at 0200."

It was clear now why Erik had been talking to Theta.

"You're going to get her in trouble one of these days," Noah said, annoyed.

"Who?" Erik asked with a puzzled look. "Anyway, you should come."

"You know that—"

"Yeah, yeah, I know you're a black hole of fun, but this is different. We're going to Mark's Mission."

Noah stared blankly at him.

"Oh, come on," Erik continued. "Mark's Mission? The casino supersatellite orbiting the Talosi Colony in the Deca Quadrant?"

That made Noah stop walking.

"You're going to an entirely different *quadrant*? Are you insane? The Watchman will crucify you."

Erik stopped as well and stared out into the forest past Noah.

"He won't find me. None of them will."

His tone was more somber than the destination suggested, but changed in an instant.

"Come on, it'll be a blast. When's the last time you were out of the quadrant? When we were kids? You can even bring Sakai!"

Noah threw up his hands.

"Alright, I'll think about it."

Anything to get Erik off his back. He'd never go, of course. A casino satellite? That was hardly anything that remotely interested him. It's not like the two of them even had use for marks living in the colony. But the real reason to go to the Mission was likely more about the flowing drinks and promiscuous Soran girls who would be there, which likely interested Erik more than gambling. Noah was sure Sakai would love that.

"He's going out of the quadrant to go to a floating *casino*?" Sakai said incredulously. She did not, in fact, love it.

"Mhmm," Noah muttered as he picked at the new gel stitches across his face. They were still warm, but had dulled the stinging quite a bit. By morning there wouldn't even be evidence of a cut.

"Your mother isn't the only one with a death wish," Sakai continued. "I'm shocked he hasn't been kidnapped or assassinated already. I almost wish you would go with him just so he won't be."

"Really?" Noah raised his eyebrows.

"No," she said. "But you know what I mean."

"Erik can take care of himself. He's done nothing but tell me that for the last decade or so."

Sakai shook her head.

"Poor Theta. You really think she's helping him?"

Noah nodded.

"That could cost her the teaching position she has here, especially if anything happened to him," Sakai said. "I'd hate to see that."

Noah loved how empathetic Sakai was. Many of the Earthborn were far too wrapped up in themselves. Each was their own sort of mini-celebrity on the planet, but she was always concerned with everyone else, Noah included. She once failed a final because she was busy taking care of two girls afflicted with the forest parasite when the silvercoats hadn't been able to make it to the colony because of severe storms. That was just the kind of person she was.

Too often Noah forgot that Sakai, like all the other Earthborn, was effectively an orphan. It wasn't really fair to complain about his parents being alive or dead war heroes when Sakai's father and mother were brain-dead and simmering in a bio-tank somewhere. The tank-borns had even less of a sense of self than he or Erik, and it was remarkable to see them come together to form something resembling a functioning society despite their complete lack of a past. The fact that Sakai had turned out kindhearted and selfless was impressive considering the absence of role models other than caretakers, teachers, or governmental supervisors. Noah smiled to himself, but Sakai caught him.

"What's so funny? You want to go to Mark's Mission?"

"Oh gods no," Noah said, violently shaking his head. "I'm heading to the spire."

"Not yet you're not," Sakai said playfully. She pulled him in by the edge of his undersuit and kissed him. Once. Twice. A dozen times. Soon the suit was a neat heap on the floor, and her robes had fallen away to reveal a sight to make the pain of training melt away completely. The light of three moons danced across her skin and there was nowhere else Noah wanted to be.

The climb to the spire that night was a tough one. Fall was starting to give way to winter on the continent and Noah could see his breath. Once the steps turned to ice, the time it took to ascend would triple, and the climb could quite possibly kill him. He thought the gods would appreciate the effort at the very least and show him some mercy when he showed up for judgment at the Oak Thrones.

His foe wasn't only the cold; there was the heavy stone warhammer on his back to contend with as well. The trainers always said he needed to get used to carting it around if he ever wanted to wield it in battle. While the hammer was his friend in a fight, now it was an enemy, straining his chilled muscles with each new step. He thought of the ancient Yalos, who had scaled mountains with their own hammers, and they didn't have the luxury of steps.

The winds whipped across Noah's skin as he reached the final stair. He dropped to his knee, unslung the hammer from his back, and laid it on the dusty path. His back ached, but he'd made it. Usually during hammer ascents he'd have to stop once or twice to rest, but he'd climbed straight through this time. He was getting stronger.

The moons and stars were hidden by cloud cover, and there was no one in the gardens outside. It was a bit late to be tending to plants, but he'd seen Anointed out here at all hours. Approaching the arched doorway to the spire, he prepared to surrender his weapon at the entryway as was customary when entering the sanctuary. Curiously, there were no guards there to greet him.

"Hello?" Noah called into the dark hallway after cracking the ornate doors open. He took one last look around the courtyard. Still empty, still silent.

And then he heard the scream.

Noah's head jerked back toward the doors. He flung them open and dashed inside. Torchlight flickered, casting shadows on the walls, and Noah sprinted down the corridor.

"Who's th—" he called out, but was stopped short when he tripped over an obstacle in the hallway. Picking himself up, he bent down to find the body of a colony guard, blood pooled in a wide circle around him, his weapons nowhere to be found. Noah quickly checked his pulse, but it was nonexistent, and when he pulled off the man's helmet he found vacant brown eyes staring up at the rafters.

Noah quickly tapped his communicator to call for help from the colony. His readouts were glitching and showed him no available frequencies. His comm was being blocked.

Another scream.

Noah left the dead guard and sprinted onward, his warhammer in his hands. Though he'd trained for this, the moment felt surreal, like some sort of disjointed nightmare.

The feeling was amplified a thousandfold when he turned the corner.

The white stone sanctuary was drenched in blood. The corpses of a half dozen Anointed were strewn all over the room, some draped across the prayer stones, their snow-colored robes soaked in crimson blood. All the women had their veils torn off, and many of their faces were frozen in displays of grotesque horror. Most had plasma burns across them while some had their throats haphazardly slit. There were two more dead colony guards among the bodies of the women. Neither of their radios worked and their weapons were missing.

Noah looked up at the statue of Zurana surrounded by a half-lit collection of candles.

This is how you protect your followers? Noah thought angrily. Zurana said nothing, only looked impassively over the carnage in the room.

What the hell is going on?

Noah tried his comm one more time to no avail. When he looked up, he found himself standing opposite a lone figure in solid black armor. It was pointing an energy pistol at him.

A blank-faced helmet hid the assailant's features and there were no markings on his armor plating.

"I know you," came a crackling male voice through the armor.

"The gods will curse you for this," Noah growled. "You disgrace your own order with your actions here."

"Guess again," came the icy reply.

Noah was in no mood to guess. His right hand left his hammer and he scooped up a stone bowl full of holy water next to the altar. The first shot from the man's pistol grazed Noah's neck. He didn't get to fire twice as the bowl crashed into his arm and the gun flew out of his grasp. By the time he'd recovered, Noah had already closed the gap between them.

The warhammer smashed into the armored gut of the intruder, propelling him backward over a prayer stone. He reached for another gun strapped to his hip, one taken from a dead guard, but another swing from Noah caused the weapon to instantly crumble, along with at least three of the man's fingers. His cry echoed around the chamber until it was silenced by one final crushing blow to his helmeted head. The metal caved deeply and blood, brain, and bone sprayed across the stone.

Noah blinked, stunned and silent. His face was sticky from the spatter. He'd just killed someone. It wasn't like the simulations. His blood had gone sub-zero in his veins, and he felt nauseous. He couldn't look away from his handiwork; the man's head crushed to pulp on the stone. The slain Anointed women lay all around him in silence, and Zurana still surveyed the entire scene from her perch at the opposite end of the room.

"What was that?"

Noah heard the voice echo from an adjacent hallway. He quickly dove to the wall and flattened himself against the stone.

"Let's go, they'll keep searching," came another voice.

Noah held his breath as two pairs of metal footsteps grew louder down the hallway. As they entered the room, they spotted their dead compatriot.

"Oh gods—" was all the first man could exclaim before Noah demolished the back of his head with a swing from his hammer. Unfortunately, weakened from his other strikes against metal armor plating, the warhammer's graftstone head exploded on impact. The armored man stumbled forward and hit the ground unconscious or dead, Noah couldn't be sure. Rather, his focus was on the second man, who was scrambling to turn his rifle toward him. Noah dropped the useless piece of wood that used to be his hammer and shoved the barrel of the gun upward, slamming the man into the wall.

The two struggled for control of the weapon, Noah's natural strength slowly being overpowered by the augmentation of the power armor. The man's finger slipped into the trigger and let loose a spray of rounds that caused stone debris to rain down on them from the ceiling. Noah mustered all his strength and threw the armored figure into the opposite wall. Wrenching away the rifle, Noah slammed it across the man's visor, leaving a deep gash across the metal. The man countered with a blow of his own, his metal fist meeting Noah's exposed temple, sending him sprawling on the ground inside the sanctuary. The rifle went clattering away, and the man drew a sidearm. Noah came up with a pistol of his own, pulled from the second downed intruder, now lying in a pool of his own blood. Noah was faster by a millisecond, and the man crumpled to the ground with a smoking hole in his helmet.

Noah was sprawled on his back and attempted to catch his breath, but another female scream made him leap to his feet. He didn't have time to think about what he'd just done. He left the three corpses and sprinted down the corridor clutching an energy rifle with a pistol hastily shoved into his belt.

He'd never been this deep inside the spire before. It was a maze of corridors, and he realized he was in the personal quarters wing of the Anointed. The doors to the adjacent rooms were all splintered and destroyed, and inside each one was a new body, veil ripped off and covered in blood. Noah heard whispers coming from up ahead. He peeked around the corner and saw two figures converging on another door.

"What happened to them?" the first one asked. "They're not responding."

"Probably just our jammer killing the wrong signals," the second one said. He moved into the light and Noah was stunned by what he saw. Though the first man was clad in the same black armor as the others, the second wore the olive plating of the colony guards.

A traitor.

"How can she be this hard to find? You work here!" the first man asked.

"They keep changing the room assignments," the colony guard replied. "It's this one though, I'm sure of it."

Noah started walking toward them, cloaked by the darkness of the hallway. The colony guard kicked the door in with an iron boot and Noah raised his rifle to fire.

The man died before he could.

A blast from the doorway propelled the guard into the opposite wall, the boom echoing down the hall. The first man shielded himself and cried out only to have his legs swept out from under him by another thunderous shot. A scattergun.

Noah crept toward the downed assailants. Neither stirred. Slumped against the wall, the colony guard was missing half his face. The other man lay prone with both his legs detached and pointing in odd directions on the floor.

"Hey!" Noah called out. "Don't shoot, I'm from the colony. I'm one of the Earthborn. I'll get you out of here."

Noah crept toward the lit doorway. The heavy wooden door had been knocked completely off its hinges and into the room.

"What's your name? Which one are you?" called the voice from inside. A woman, another Anointed. She sounded young.

"Noah," he replied.

There was a long pause. Blood droplets tumbled down the wall opposite from the doorway. Noah looked around nervously for more enemies in the dark, but there were none, and he could hear no more cries.

"Show me your arm," the voice said nervously,

Noah was confused, but stuck out his right arm so that it was visible in the entrance. He gave a small wave.

"Your other arm."

Noah understood now. He tore away his already ripped undersuit and thrust his left arm through the door. The burns creeping down his bicep should be visible now, a mark well known around the world.

"Alright," came the voice, still shaking.

Noah stepped into the light and prayed he wasn't going to be torn apart by a scattergun blast. He held the rifle by the barrel, off to his side just in case she saw it as a threat.

The woman in the room was still veiled, seated against the back wall pointing the scattergun toward him, her grip shaking. Flecks of blood dotted her white robes and woven mask.

"Gods, you've changed," she said, lowering her gun and pulling off her veil with one hand.

Noah stared into a pair of wide, deep blue eyes. The girl was seemed to be about his age with pale skin and short, jet-black hair. He had no idea who she was.

5

"We have to get out of here," Noah said, his eyes darting around the room and back out into the hall. He secured his grip on his rifle, content that the girl wasn't going to kill him.

"Are they all dead?" she asked, peering at the two bodies behind Noah. He offered his hand and pulled her to her feet. The girl's head barely came up to his chest.

"I don't know," he said. "That's why we have to move. I can't reach anyone on my comm. I thought these men were here for me, but they're here for you. Why?"

"I-I don't know," she said.

"Then why do you have a scattergun in your room?"

"For protection."

"Expecting a day like this one?" Noah asked, rubbing his temple with two bloodied fingers. This situation was too unreal to comprehend.

"I was told—"

"Later," Noah said, pulling her by the hand into the hallway.

"We should go out the back to the courtyard," the girl said, tugging him the other direction. He followed, assuming she knew the labyrinth better than he did. She stepped gingerly over the body of another fallen woman. Torchlight showed that the girl was on the verge of tears.

Noah kept trying his comm to no avail. A thought occurred to him. Should he even be trying to contact colony security? One or more of their own was responsible for this massacre. He thought about trying Tannon, but remembered the Watchman was attending to business off-world, far outside the range of local communication.

The pair of them emerged from a small door at the rear of the spire and entered an old graveyard filled with white tombstones in the shape of small trees. No one was there to greet them.

Almost as soon as they were out in the open, Noah's comm squealed.

"Hey, brother," came Erik's voice.

"Erik!" Noah shouted, quickly realizing he should still be keeping his voice down.

"I've been trying you for twenty minutes, where are you?" his brother responded.

"Listen, Erik, I'm—"

"Anyway, Finn and I are about to leave for the Mission, and I figured I'd give you one last chance to not be lame. I *really* think you should come."

Mark's Mission. Noah had forgotten all about it. He had to get out of here, go anywhere. His mind raced. Sure, he could take this girl to some casino for a few days while he sorted out whatever the hell had just happened. As of now, he wasn't even sure which authorities he could trust. But he could trust Erik, for all his faults.

"Erik, I'm at the spire. It's been attacked. Dozens of Anointed and all the colony guards are dead. I need you to pick us up at the rear of the mountain in the graveyard."

There was a pause.

"Shit, are you serious?" came Erik's startled reply.

"Yes. Get here. Now. Don't contact anyone."

Noah heard Erik talking to someone, presumably Finn.

"On it. See you in four."

The comm went dead. Noah immediately tried Sakai, then Wuhan, then Quezon. All were silent, switched off or worse.

Noah made his way to the edge of the cliff, which overlooked the colony. The lights of the buildings below were dimmed. There was no one stirring down there other than the usual patrols.

This wasn't an attack on the colony, he thought. *Just on the spire. Just for this girl.*

He was relieved that at least Sakai was safe. He tried her one more time with no luck.

"What's your name?" Noah asked the girl. She was standing next to a tree, shaking as the wind pierced her thin white robes. Noah had nothing to offer her for warmth. She was crying.

"You wouldn't remember. It's been so long."

Noah's eyes narrowed to suspicious slits.

"What are you talking about?"

"My name is Kyra," she said. "Kyra Auran."

A jolt ran through Noah.

"Kyra?" he said. "How the . . ."

Kyra had been Noah's best friend through his early childhood years. The granddaughter of the Palace Keeper, Malorious Auran, she had been introduced to him back when Noah's father was still alive. The two became fast friends and were inseparable for years. Even when he, Asha, and Erik were forced to live in exile, Keeper Auran had brought Kyra for visits until they were seven. After Noah and Erik had been transplanted into the colony, he never saw her again, even with Auran in charge of the installation for a spell. Noah had been told she remained in Elyria with her parents. Gradually, she had faded from his memory.

It was almost impossible to recognize her. He could barely picture her as a child anymore, though her bright blue eyes did ring some distant bell in his mind. But as long as he'd known her, she'd been blond, and her black hair now was a drastic change. Also, she'd aged twelve years, and had become a strikingly beautiful young woman rather than a bubbly child. But there was some small piece of him that could see that she was his old friend.

"Why are you here?" he finally got out. "What's going on?"

Kyra leaned against the tree. Noah looked cautiously at the exit to the spire; he'd managed to barricade it with a log, but that wouldn't stop a plasma burst. They just had to pray the invading force was all dead and no one was coming to reinforce them. Noah scanned the sky for ships. The clouds had parted to give way to an almost blinding field of stars.

"A few years after you left for the colony," Kyra said, "someone broke into my house in Elyria. My parents were killed, I was shot."

Noah started to say something, but it got lost in his throat.

"The city lawmen killed the intruders. They said one had my picture on a chip. They thought they were trying to kidnap me for ransom, because my grandfather was Keeper."

She looked out toward the colony down the cliff.

"Grandfather Auran was devastated. He treated my wound and told me I wasn't safe. I needed to go far away from him, from Elyria. Somewhere hidden. He'd been retired from running the colony for a few years by then, so he brought me here."

Kyra stared up at the towering white spires behind them.

"I've been at the spire ever since. He said the colony guards that kept the Earthborn safe would keep me safe too. He said I could even see you from time to time, but I couldn't say anything."

Noah remembered the small Anointed he'd caught staring at him from time to time. And the guards at the spire. They'd been there for her as much as they'd been there for him. For all the good it did either of them.

"I was so thrilled to see you start to come here a few years ago. I was never allowed down into the colony itself," Kyra continued. "I took my vows, I served Zurana. But I never revealed myself to you or anyone else. The Anointed ask no questions."

"I have a few," Noah said, interrupting. "No one was trying to kidnap you tonight. This was an assassination attempt, through and through. Why would someone be trying to kill you?"

Kyra burst into a fresh set of tears.

"I have no idea. My sisters. My friends. They're all—" she couldn't even finish the thought. Noah realized that perhaps he was being a bit too harsh given what she'd just endured. He was still trying to process the fact that he'd just killed three men, but he would have to deal with it another day.

"I was careful!" Kyra cried. "I wore my veil. I changed my hair like he said just in case. I kept the gun, but I never thought I'd use it! I never knew this would happen!"

"I know you didn't," Noah said, and he moved to put his arm around the shivering girl. He could feel goosebumps prickle through her robes. He winced as her head brushed across the black plasma burn on his neck.

"We're going to get you out of here," Noah continued. "Off-world, where whoever these people are won't think to look."

Kyra's chin was buried in his chest and she was still sobbing.

"You should try and reach your grandfather," Noah said. "Maybe he can help us. But for now, we need to get far away."

As if on cue, a huge ship decloaked not thirty feet away from them, hovering over the edge of the cliff. Noah jumped, pointing his rifle at the vessel, but when the rear ramp descended, it was his brother standing there clutching an energy pistol.

Where did he get that?

Erik was noticeably stunned when he saw the pair of them covered in blood, their tattered clothes whipping around from the thrust of the luxury liner's engines.

"What the hell happened? Who is this?" he called to them.

"We need to go," Noah replied, hoisting Kyra up onto the hovering ramp like she weighed nothing. He climbed in after her. The three of them dashed inside and the craft ascended into the night sky.

Inside the cruiser, a Shatterstar-class luxury vessel with apparent after-market cloaking abilities, Noah and Kyra found themselves staring at Erik, Finn, and Theta.

Noah quickly filled the shocked trio in on the events at the White Spire. Theta took Kyra to one of the guest suites and found her some non-bloodstained clothes to change into. Finn found some for Noah, but they were naturally far too tight. The group was sitting in a plush lounge area that looked like it should be one of the rooms of the Grand Palace itself. Finn nervously eyed the cushions of the sprawling white couches, which were now smeared with drying blood.

"You're *Kyra?*" Erik said incredulously as the story concluded. He had been old enough to faintly remember her presence during her visits in their youth. They didn't have many guests at their various safehouses scattered around the world while Lucas and Asha's names were being cleared in the killing of Talis Vale.

Kyra nodded. "It's nice to see you again," she said, smiling weakly. She looked visibly ill, but she was now clad in a gray mesh exercise suit and at least no longer spattered with blood.

"I'll call my father," Finn Stoller said emphatically. "He'll know what to do."

"He could help," Noah said, considering the idea. The man he'd spoken to indicated he wasn't Fourth Order, but someone attempting to assassinate the Palace Keeper's granddaughter was assuredly part of some antigovernment group. Perhaps Chancellor Stoller could be actually be of assistance; he hated such organizations with a passion.

"Just . . . hold on," Erik said. "We can't make any outgoing transmissions yet. They could have someone tracing them in the area."

Kyra looked around nervously. "I already tried to reach my grandfather."

"Did it connect?" Erik asked sharply. Kyra shook her head. "Then it should be fine, but hold off until we're in the wormhole. Comms can't be tracked there."

Erik apparently had learned much through evading colony security to go on his little excursions.

Theta had barely said a word since Noah and Kyra showed up. Noah put a hand to his throbbing head as the Xalan shot sealing gel onto the plasma wound on his neck.

"Theta, what are you doing here? You're going to Mark's Mission?"

Noah had been surprised to see her onboard. Though she helped Erik arrange these escapes, she never went with him. Noah had half expected to see Erik's newest fling Penza instead, but no one else was there except Finn and the young snow-white Xalan.

"Yes, I . . . very much enjoy . . . the gambling," Theta said unconvincingly. She threw a worried look toward Erik who was talking with Kyra. Noah knew the obvious reason she'd want to spend time with his brother, but why would he agree to bring her along? He normally wouldn't give her the time of day.

"Don't worry," said Finn, puffing his scrawny chest out from beneath his dress shirt. "You couldn't be in a safer ship. This Shatterstar has military cloaking capabilities and the purest core in existence. Nearly 50 percent faster than anything the SDI has. Father made sure we had the first one in the world."

A great use of the planet's resources, Noah thought, though Stoller's ego would actually serve them well in this case.

Finn left the room to take over for the autopilot, and Theta was attempting to console Kyra with her own brand of awkward bedside manner. Erik and Noah sat across a table from each other, with Noah downing a full pitcher of water. He still felt sick and hadn't stopped shaking since he'd arrived.

"What do you make of this?" Erik asked him. "A colony guard? Those guys are supposed to be eternally, unflinchingly loyal. This is some serious shit."

"I know," Noah said, holding the glass pitcher against his burning forehead. "I don't know who we can go to with this. I trust Tannon. Not sure about Stoller. We need to get ahold of Keeper Auran too."

Erik shook his head.

"I don't know. Guards are under Tannon's command. And isn't it convenient he's off-world for this?"

Now it was Noah who was shaking his head.

"No way, the Watchman's a hardass, but he'd never do something like this."

Erik leaned back in his chair.

"Yeah, they said that about his sister too."

Both of their gazes drifted toward Kyra. She'd finally stopped crying and Theta was showing her something on her wrist display.

"Why the hell is she so special?" Erik asked. "Who would go to this much trouble for a Keeper's granddaughter?"

Noah simply stared at the pitcher on the table.

"I don't know, but it's not the first time, according to her," he said. "The assassins . . . I'd never seen armor like that. Didn't have time to search them for ID chips, though something tells me I wouldn't have found any."

Erik turned back toward Noah.

"How many did you kill?"

Noah paused, feeling sick again.

"Three. She killed two."

"Was it . . . hard?"

Noah thought about that. The answer was no, which was perhaps the most frightening part of the whole night.

"Yes," he lied.

"I wish I was there. To help."

"Be glad you weren't."

Erik was silent for a minute. He kept fidgeting in his chair and checking the ship's readouts.

"You look like hell," he finally said. "The two of you should just hit cryo until we get to Deca Quadrant. The Mission is a good place to disappear for a while, and we can figure all this out."

Noah wasn't sure if he'd ever be able to sleep again, but he nodded. He'd call Sakai in the morning and let her know what was going on.

"I'm glad you came," Erik said. "This trip wouldn't be the same without you. It'll be one to remember."

Noah could hardly believe Erik was still thinking about girls and gambling right now. But that was Erik. Still, though, he was acting rather strangely.

Noah led Kyra down to the lower decks where a row of exceptionally spacious cryogenic pods was spread out. She looked like she was about to collapse, which was how he felt. The door opened to her pod. She brushed the dark hair out of her eyes.

"Thank you," she said to Noah. "I would have died if you hadn't come."

"Thank Kyneth," Noah said. "He must have sent me."

In truth, Noah was rather irritated with the gods at present, but he supposed they *had* spared the pair of them.

"I'm not going to be able to sleep," she said, echoing his earlier thoughts.

"You will," he said. "The intravenous compound will see to that. It's what we need right now. And we'll be safe here. We'll figure all this out."

Kyra lay down in her pod, and tubing began to sprout from the walls and snake its way into her veins. Liquid slid quickly up the piping into her arms, legs, and torso.

"I'm sorry to have dragged you into this," she said.

"We'll figure it out together," Noah said, as he began to close the pod door. "I'll see you tomorrow."

But she was already asleep as the door hissed shut. He lay down in his own chamber next to hers, and soon liquid peace was flowing through his veins. The world drifted away, as did the images of ravaged corpses and crushed skulls. Everything faded to white until only one word remained.

Dubai.

There were no flames in his dreams. Only oceans.

6

Noah woke from the chamber groggily, his head swimming from the cocktail of drugs that had kept him under for the night. The lights blinked on inside the pod and he glanced around the cavernous interior, briefly imagining the events of the previous night had been a bad dream. But no such luck.

Electrodes attached to his muscles had given him a workout while he slept, and reaching up to feel his face, he found the luxury pod had even given him a fresh shave for the morning.

Rich people, he thought as he tapped the controls of the pod and the door slid open. He stumbled a bit as he rose, but regained his footing and glanced down at Kyra's pod next to him. It was still closed. He'd let her sleep a little more. Gods knew she needed it.

Noah stretched and wandered toward the bridge where he figured he'd find at least one of the three other passengers.

Instead, he found an empty room, lights dimmed and the viewscreen shuttered by metal blinds. A pang of fear started to twitch within him.

"Hello?" he called out. Already thinking of the worst-case scenario, he wondered where Erik had put the weapons.

His stomach unknotted itself when Erik strode into the room and raised the lights.

"Christ," Noah said, conditioned to use an old English profanity when surprised. He breathed out a huge sigh. "I thought something had happened."

Erik walked past him toward the central captain's chair and sat down. Finn and Theta also entered through the doorway. All of them looked eerily solemn, even the normally hyperactive Stoller.

"There's something I need to tell you," Erik said slowly, turning slightly in the chair.

Oh gods, Noah thought. Was something wrong with Kyra? Her pod readouts had looked fine. What was—

"Or rather, show you," Erik continued, interrupting Noah's panicked thoughts.

Erik swirled his hand around inside a control cluster. The shades of the viewscreen began to open. When they had disappeared completely, Noah's jaw hung open, his heart racing.

After being frozen in place for a solid minute, he lunged at Erik, grabbed his brother by the collar, and threw him out of the chair onto the ground. For once, Erik didn't fight back. He knew he had no right to.

"Tell me that isn't what I think it is!" Noah shouted. "Tell me you're not this stupid!"

Finn cringed as Noah slammed Erik down again on the metal floor. Theta put her claw to her mouth, but neither intervened. Noah got up and shoved Erik backward; he stumbled into a holotable and steadied himself.

Noah turned to look at the planet in the viewscreen.

Earth.

Alpha's Earth, the one he'd shown them with budding oceans and lakes and bizarrely shaped continents that looked nothing like the old archive images.

"How long have I been out?"

Erik was smoothing the wrinkles in his clothes. His hair was longer, Noah now noticed.

"Three months. The Shatterstar's new core got us here incredibly f—"

Noah didn't wait for him to finish, he ran over and grabbed Erik by the throat, bending him backward over the holotable. His blood was molten. Three months? He was supposed to be in cryo for twelve hours at the most.

"Noah, stop, *please*," Theta had finally found her voice. Noah looked up at her.

"And you, you knew about this?"

It dawned on him.

"This is why you came . . ."

"I-I navigated us here. I ensured the ship could not be traced by its owner, High Chancellor Stoller, or the SDI."

"My father wouldn't exactly approve of this little excursion," said Finn in an irksome tone.

Noah wrenched Erik up and let him go. Erik coughed violently as his throat unconstricted.

"*Why are we here?*" bellowed Noah, far from the usual soft-spoken individual who was everyone's friend at the colony. His mind raced to try and comprehend the insanity he was seeing and hearing.

"Don't worry," Erik said, regaining the ability to speak. "Kyra will be safe. There are no assassins out here, I'll tell you that much."

Noah looked at the ravaged planet slowly rotating in the viewscreen.

"No assassins? What about the Xalans? Or have you forgotten who we're currently fighting a war against?"

"The ship is cloaked, we don't need to—" Finn began.

"I was *not* talking to you!" Noah snapped, and Finn closed his mouth and took a few steps back.

"Now, I'll ask you again," Noah said slowly, his hand again attached to Erik's collar. "Why are we here?"

Erik remained silent and glanced toward the viewscreen. On the planet, one red dot was pulsing, somewhere a few thousand miles north of the planet's equator.

Noah let Erik go and walked toward the display. He swept his hands out in an arc, zooming in on the point. His heart stopped when he read the identifier.

Dubai.

After catching his breath, Noah turned back around.

"We need to talk," he said, jamming a finger into Erik's chest. "Now."

The pair of them retreated to a small storage bay filled with a collection of oddly shaped boxes and janitorial supplies. Erik rubbed his neck where a distinct red handprint had formed.

"Don't blame them," Erik said. "I needed Stoller's ship and Finn's just trying to prove to his father he's a man, which he probably never will. I brought Theta to make us untraceable, and she wanted to come to impress her parents by investigating the planet's climate shift."

"I *don't* blame them," Noah said coldly, resisting the urge to choke his brother again. "I blame *you*."

"Look," Erik said, rolling his eyes, "don't you ever get tired of being cooped up in the colony cage? This was supposed to be an adventure for both of us. That's why I wanted you to come."

Noah gritted his teeth.

"You didn't say you were going to *Earth*."

"Well, if I had, you would have ratted me out the first chance you got, 'for my own safety,'" Erik replied. Noah knew that was true, but didn't acknowledge it.

"I know that isn't why you came," Noah said. "I know about Dubai."

The look of surprise on Erik's face was obvious, and it took him a second to respond.

"How?"

"I hear it," Noah said. "In my sleep, during prayer. I didn't know what it was until now. Some old Earth city. You've obviously heard it too. What does it mean?"

Erik shook his head.

"Hell if I know. Once I learned what it was, I can't explain it—it's like I was pulled here. I had to come. I didn't have a choice."

"You had a choice," Noah said. "And you've endangered the lives of three innocent people in the process."

Erik waved him off. "Theta and Finn agreed to come, they know the risks."

"They know the risks?" Noah asked. "Theta is practically a *child*, Finn is a spoiled prat who doesn't belong anywhere *near* a warzone. And Kyra didn't sign up for *any* of this."

"Well, I didn't sign up for Kyra," Erik said, crossing his arms. "This plan was in motion months ago, and what was I going to do, drop the girl being hunted off at the nearest space station? Whatever is chasing her won't find her here."

"Gods Erik, have you even thought about what you've done?" Noah said. "Sora will be losing their minds over this. We're two of the most recognizable people on the planet, not to mention the fact that you've essentially kidnapped the High Chancellor's son. And the colony, Sakai . . ."

"I left word for Sakai that you were safe, but would be gone for quite a while. I also got in touch with Keeper Auran to tell him about Kyra's attack so he can investigate while we're away."

"Give me access to the comm relay, now."

Erik shook his head.

"Can't. Theta's got us in permanent lockdown now that we're here. No communications in or out so no one can come haul us back."

"*I'm* going to be the one hauling us back," Noah said emphatically. "We're turning this ship around."

"We're not," Erik said, "and you know it."

Dubai.

The voice was clear now, and he was fully awake. Noah jumped like a specter had just whispered in his ear. He knew they should leave. But he wanted to land. He wanted nothing else but to land in that damn city. The pull. He could feel it now. He tried to speak, but saw Erik had the same look on his face. He'd clearly just heard the same thing.

"We're going. I'll leave it to you to explain things to Sleeping Beauty," Erik said as he stood up from the crate where he'd been sitting. Noah was still at a loss for words.

"It's not like she has anywhere to be."

Noah's head was reeling as he sat alone in the storage bay, leaning back against the cold metal wall. He didn't feel like facing Kyra with this news. How did the old Earth adage go? *Out of the frying plate, into the fire.*

His brother had always been reckless, but this was a new level for him. A voyage to *Earth*? Only a few Soran and Xalan elite had even dared to return to the recently healing planet, and there was no telling what they'd find in Dubai. What was so significant about that place? It hadn't come up in any Earth history they'd covered. But what *had* been discussed in class were the telepathic abilities of Chosen Shadows. The kind that could whisper in your mind. This felt like a trap.

But still, for some reason, Noah couldn't shake the feeling that he was *supposed* to be there. That despite the insanity of the situation, coming to Earth felt *right*. He couldn't explain it any more than Erik could. He knew they should leave, but he had to stay.

Besides, wasn't this what Noah had always wanted? He was sick of being trained to fight but not allowed to do so. The events at the White Spire had been horrifying, but strangely . . . liberating. Like he was finally doing what he was meant to do. Not the killing necessarily, but the fact that he'd rescued Kyra filled him with a sense of pride he hadn't felt, well . . . ever.

Alpha had told them the Xalans and Sorans had come to Earth in recent years. Why had either gone there at all, if there wasn't something of significance on the ruined planet? Had the call of Dubai somehow affected them as well? Could others hear it?

Noah sighed. He missed Sakai and wished she were there with him. She had to be beside herself with worry, and would never forgive Erik when they made it back. *If* they made it back. In truth, Noah realized, she was really the only thing he missed about Sora. Colony life had long grown dull, and he was too old and too healthy to be cooped up, unable to fight in a war that threatened to decide the fate of the entire galaxy. Perhaps on Earth he could make a difference. At the very least, he could now live up to what Lucas had asked of him all those years ago.

"Lead them."

And finally, he would be looking out for his brother.

"Let's see it, then," Noah said to Finn, who was standing in front of a large, conspicuously blank metal wall. Outside the porthole across the room, they could see the cruiser was still orbiting Earth in a low-powered stealth mode. They were drifting through a debris field of what had once been a Xalan Sentinel, a remote observation station with the capability to deploy assault drones. This one had apparently been destroyed by a Soran infiltration fleet, and their scanners picked up three other similar debris clouds nearby, along with a few other unidentified objects deemed non-hostile. Few active or intact Sentinels were still in orbit, it seemed.

"Some of this stuff was harder to get than the ship itself," Finn said proudly. He pressed a panel and the entire wall split in half, revealing an impressive display of military hardware. Before them were five sets of slim power armor, each some shade of gray or brown. Surprisingly, every body type present seemed to be represented in the line-up.

"During our voyage, I modified the two spare armor sets to fit you and Miss Auran," Theta said, motioning to two suits of dramatically different sizes.

"And check this out," Finn said, taking down a long gun from above a set of polished armor that was assuredly his. "Prototype S-class rifle. Micro-blue core. A dozen rounds a second."

Noah eyed the rifle worriedly; it looked too big for Finn's bony frame to carry, but the power armor's strength amplification was supposed to help with that.

"Are you, uh, sure you can use that?" Noah asked.

"I've had generals train me at arms since I could walk," Finn replied curtly, brushing his hair back. "They brought me in to test this personally."

Noah doubted the last part of that was true, but the first bit seemed like something Madric Stoller would demand of his son. In the press, Finn was often overshadowed by his war hero older sister, Maeren, who was currently commanding a liberation fleet laying siege to a Xalan colony planet.

Noah glanced over at Kyra, who was eyeing the dust-colored plating designated for her petite frame. In the months she'd spent in the pod, her blond hair had grown out from the black dye she wore when they first met. It was easier to see his old friend in her, though he often caught himself staring at her for a different reason. She was shockingly gorgeous—distractingly so—and Erik and Finn appeared to be hypnotized by her every move as well.

Kyra had taken the fact that they had arrived at Earth instead of a casino in the Deca Quadrant rather well. Noah suspected she was still fractured by the carnage at the White Spire, and her world was shattered regardless of whether she was hiding out on some lost planet or the galaxy's largest casino.

"I modified Miss Auran's scattergun into something more portable," Theta said, referring to the shortened shotgun-like weapon that hung next to her armor. "You will find it much lighter, I hope."

"Thank you, Theta," Kyra said, flashing a dazzling smile that made even the young Xalan blush. "But please, no more 'Miss Auran.' Call me Kyra." Theta gave a hint of a nod.

Erik twirled a pair of elongated energy pistols, which glowed an electric blue. Finn said they once belonged to an overseer in the Sorvo Republic until he lost them to Madric Stoller in a bet on a sakala match. The pistols didn't fire plasma but concentrated, flat lasers that could supposedly shear through nearly any surface as if it were paper.

Noah took his own weapon down from the hooks next to his armor. It was a sleek-looking assault rifle with less gadgetry than Finn's, but it was exceptionally lightweight and supposedly another rare item in Stoller's private arsenal that Finn had raided for their foolhardy mission to Earth. Noah waved Finn off when he began to launch into a story about the weapon's history. It was his now; that was all that mattered.

While the others were suiting up in their armor, Theta ushered Noah into an adjacent room.

"I just finished this for you," she said, pulling a long crate out from under a large, plush bed. "It would not fit in the armory."

"How much free time did you have on this trip?" Noah asked, wondering what new creation she'd concocted in addition to the other work she'd done.

"Xalans do not attain much rest in Soran cryogenic pods," she said, tapping through the virtual keys on the crate's lock. "I found an abundance of materials onboard this vessel and . . . I have witnessed many of your bouts in the colony training yard. I thought you might appreciate this item."

Theta opened the crate to reveal a long, dark warhammer made entirely out of matte black metal. The head had a wide, flat striking surface laid to the right in the crate's housing with two long spikes sprouting from the left and top of the head. It was far more elegant and deadly than the graftstone practice maul he'd been using that he'd recently employed to shatter the skulls of invaders at the White Spire. On the side of the head were two circular metal objects laced with circuitry that Noah couldn't identify.

"It is crafted almost entirely from darksteel," Theta said as Noah took the hammer into his hands. It had to be almost four feet long, but it felt like it weighed half of what it should.

"It is the same material as your mother's sword," Theta continued. Asha's black blade was legendary on the battlefield, and only a few darksteel weapons existed in the world, as it was exceptionally hard to forge the metal without incredibly complex equipment. Equipment that Theta had built from scratch in her spare time aboard the Shatterstar on their way to Earth. Noah could only shake his head slowly in amazement.

"It appears High Chancellor Stoller commissioned a darksteel statue to be made of himself for display in the dining area," Theta said. "I thought this a better use of the material."

Madric's ego to the rescue again. Noah rubbed his thumb across the grip of the maul and the metal spheres lit up at the head.

"Careful," Theta cautioned.

"What is it?" Noah asked, eyeing the blue circles of light.

"I fitted the head of the warhammer with a pair of sonic resonators. When activated, the kinetic force of the weapon is dramatically increased. But I would advise against overuse."

Noah spun the weapon around in his hands. It thrummed with energy.

"Thank you, Theta. This means more than you know."

"I only wish to continue the established bond between our families," Theta said.

"We'd call this a gift from a friend," Noah replied.

"I will agree to that classification."

Dubai.

"Did you hear that?" Noah said, looking around.

Theta cocked her head, confused. Clearly she'd hadn't.

The pull. It was getting stronger.

"Time to visit the homeworld."

7

"Sensor readouts are proving unreliable," said Theta as she scrunched up her face at a series of displays on the bridge of the Shatterstar. Finn had taken the ship as close to the atmosphere as he could manage, and thrusters were keeping them in place several hundred miles above the desert where they were supposed to land.

"What about optics?" Noah asked. Erik was flipping through some projections of the city of Dubai itself, before the fall. One of Earth's most lavish supercities, it was full of shining buildings and crystal-clear artificial pools.

"Some structures are intact, but most are destroyed, as to be expected. There is a great deal of sand," Theta said, unaware that she was stating the obvious. "There is no movement on the ground, though without adequate sensor data I cannot say for certain if life-forms are present."

"What's wrong with the sensors?" Noah pressed. Theta shook her head.

"Atmospheric disturbance, technological disruption, I cannot say for certain."

"Those are two very different things," Noah said worriedly. The pull of the city was constantly battling his gut instinct, which told him this was some sort of Xalan ambush.

"There are no other Soran troops nearby?" asked Kyra, staring out the viewscreen at the strange looking planet below.

Theta shook her head.

"The last Soran mission authorized here returned four months ago. Nothing remains aside from a few scattered Xalan signatures plan-etwide. But again, the sensors—"

Erik cut her off.

"The sensors will work as we get closer. If there's a Xalan fortress down there, we'll call it a day and head home. If there isn't, we'll land and go exploring."

Noah suspected that even if there was a Xalan fortress down there Erik would try to talk them into landing, but if that did happen, Noah would force the ship back to Sora even if he had to lock up Finn and Erik and "Dubai" started being chanted in his head all day long.

"I'm dropping in," Finn said. The viewscreen started to glow red as their hull met the atmosphere. "Better suit up."

Noah broke away from the readouts and helped Kyra finish putting on her armor. This was undoubtedly her first time wearing such a suit.

"Just remember," he said, as he fitted her shoulderplates on top of her form-fitting mesh undersuit. Her chestplate snapped up automatically and encased her torso. "Always keep two of us in your vision, and make sure one of them is me."

Kyra nodded as she put her hand into an armored glove. Noah snapped more plating around her upper arms. She looked scared. Noah hoped that his own fear wasn't showing on his face.

"Lead them."

"It'll be fine," he reassured her. "We're just going to take a look around, and we'll be on our way back to Sora in no time."

She shivered.

"Sora doesn't seem safer than here right now, to be honest," she said.

"Well, then think of this like a vacation," Noah said with a smile, which she reluctantly returned.

"Fifty out!" called Finn from the captain's chair. Noah retreated to finish donning his own armor. He clasped his new warhammer into the housing Theta had built for it on his back. The Xalan was already fully suited up and Erik was checking the readouts on his pair of pistols.

"Sensors clearing," Theta said. "No signatures in our radius."

The city was empty? Noah wasn't hoping to stumble upon a Xalan military base, but he secretly wondered if there was perhaps some surviving colony of humans that had weathered the apocalypse and somehow summoned them to return to their planet. But three-hundred-degree peak temperatures on the surface had made sure that was impossible. Sora's Colony One truly did hold the last remnants of humankind.

The revelation seemed to noticeably puzzle Erik as well. What were they looking for in Dubai if not something alive?

"Thirty," called Finn.

"Atmospheric readouts indicate normal levels of oxygen and carbon dioxide," Theta excitedly relayed. "The air is breathable! And look!"

She pointed out the window. Hovering at the edge of space was a long, colossal-looking metal shape, though it was hard to gauge its scale. A ship? Noah froze.

"A terraforming orbiter!" Theta clarified. "It must be responsible for the temperature decrease."

"Wait, that's Xalan?" Noah asked. He'd never seen anything like it. A hazy blue gas was pooling off the sides of the machine and drifting lazily toward the Earth below. Theta was recording video of the object via a tiny lens attached to her armor and scanning it with a device on her outstretched hand.

"The project was commissioned by my grandfather, but never progressed past the prototype stage. They must be testing it on Earth to gauge its effects. There have to be dozens in orbit to create the sort of worldwide fluctuations seen in the data."

The landscape of the surface was starting to come into focus. The area that was once vaguely named the "Middle East" was more of a desert than it ever was. Dubai had once been a coastal city. It sat on the bank of a vast gulf that had long run dry. Though rains had started filling in sporadic lakes and oceans elsewhere on the planet, nothing of the sort had happened here yet.

"Still nothing on the biological sensors," Theta said, indicating that if this was a trap, they hadn't sprung it yet.

Ten miles up, the city was now visible beneath them. Noah pulled up the images of the glimmering metropolis as it once was. The contrast was stark.

Once, manmade islands had been crafted off the coast. But with the water gone, all that remained were oddly shaped lumps of earth, littered with dull specks that were likely wrecked sea yachts and cruising ships. Of the few skyscrapers that still stood, all were covered in dust, and the Earth's former tallest structure, the Burj Khalifa, had apparently collapsed into nothingness.

It was odd to Noah that so much of Dubai still stood, given the tactics of the Xalan invading fleet. He initially wondered why the entire place wasn't one massive glass crater. But the reason he'd never heard of the city until now was that it had had almost no impact on the war during the sacking of Earth. The entire region's contribution to fighting the Xalans was largely negligible. As much of a threat as the other countries of Earth had thought the Middle East posed before the invasion, the actual capabilities of their armies had been weak compared to the giants of China, America, and Europe. Only the neighboring country of Pakistan was chronicled as being involved in a major battle of the war; the country had unleashed its nuclear arsenal to cripple a reinforcing wave of Xalan ships trying to ravage its neighbor, the once-populous India.

Rather, Dubai had escaped the worst of the conflict, and had apparently fallen to man and the sun rather than the Xalans. Noah wondered how many had still lived within the city for a time after the war, before the heat had burnt them all away.

"Setting down," Finn said. The ruined skyline loomed ahead of them. Rampaging fires had turned many of the buildings into mere husks, and there were few windows left unshattered. It wasn't a crater, but it certainly wasn't a city anymore either, merely a loose collection of metal and glass that looked like it might crumble completely if a strong enough wind blew through.

No one spoke as the ship touched down. They'd just landed on Earth. Noah felt like this could be some elaborate dream.

The ship wouldn't stay cloaked in an unpowered state, so they left it to the mercy of the sands and trudged up the coast toward the dead buildings. The Shatterstar had crushed the last remnants of an old marina boathouse when it landed and was surrounded by a sea of giant decaying ships lodged in the sand. The heat hadn't quite been enough to melt the fiberglass of their hulls, but many had started to sag before dropping temperatures had frozen them back in place.

The streets were littered with the primitive carriages humanity once called "cars," their paint long stripped by the harsh sands, their archaic rubber tires liquefied and caked onto the cracked roads. Many had old Earth animal emblems planted on their noses: horses, bulls, and the like. The wheeled machines were now as extinct as the creatures they were named after.

Noah heard Kyra gasp when she saw the first human remnants strewn on the road. A blackened skeleton lay prone in the street. Then another, and another. Theta scanned the bones and found that they were indeed human, not Soran, and they'd been dead for years, dating back to when the war still raged.

Theta was fascinated by everything around her, particularly the readouts that scrolled across her vision, projected from her suit. She informed them the temperature was far lower than anticipated, and oddly, the air did feel almost chilly.

Erik and Finn were mercifully silent as they walked, too awed by the magnificent decay around them to ruin the scope of their arrival with their usual quips or jokes. About a mile into their trek, it occurred to Noah that he and Erik were the first humans to walk on Earth in years. Most had predicted such a thing would never be possible again. Earth had been considered a dead planet, and though that was certainly how it looked, Theta's data said it was coming alive again, slowly.

Finally, Kyra asked the obvious.

"Where are we going?"

The group stopped. Erik and Noah looked at each other.

"Do you hear it anymore?" Erik whispered.

"No," Noah said, realizing the voice had left him now that they were in the city. It was a massive place, and they could explore it for years without uncovering whatever secrets it contained.

"I don't—" began Noah, but Theta cut him off. Surprising; she was never one to interrupt.

"I am picking up a reading," she blurted out.

"Life?" Noah asked, suddenly clutching his rifle more tightly.

"No," Theta said. "A power source."

"Coming from where?" asked Finn, holding his gun cocked against his hip like an action hero, eager to prove his worth.

Theta shifted her scanning equipment. She panned away from the looming skyscrapers ahead and up the coast. She came to rest on a strange shape a fair distance away.

"There," she said, extending a white claw toward it.

Back when there was still water in the area, the building must have floated on its own little island in the gulf. It was triangular, with one curved edge that made it look like an ancient watercraft with a tall sail. Noah remembered that such wind-powered ships had still been used on Earth before it was destroyed.

"What is it?" he asked.

"Let's find out," Erik said as he trudged forward.

The aqua-blue sky had given way to a dusky gray by the time they reached the structure. The small sun had set and hazy, dim stars hung above them. But other lights were now flickering, which made all of them uneasy.

The mammoth structure was emitting artificial light from a select few of its windows.

They arrived at a building that read "Welcome Center" in English, with some other sort of looping Earth language written above it. The others looked around nervously as Erik picked up one of a few hundred disintegrating brochures that littered the ground.

"The Burj Al Arab," he said, as he held up the picture on the front of the faded document, comparing it the damaged building ahead of them. "It used to be some sort of high-end resort."

What the place used to be did not concern Noah. He turned to Theta.

"Still nothing on the readouts?" he asked. She shook her head, tapping her display with a claw.

"But the energy source within is Xalan in origin," she cautioned.

They moved around the welcome center through a sea of marooned cars and more mummified remains. When they reached the other side, they saw that the pier that had connected the man-made island to land was badly damaged. Chunks of the road had fallen down to the sands below, along with the cars that had once sat abandoned on the bridge.

"Careful," Noah said as he slowly moved across the cracked pavement. It was a short distance to the base of the hotel, but a treacherous one.

The tower grew ever closer, and Noah eyed the lit rooms, all of which had shattered windows and tattered curtains blowing in the breeze. He took one more step forward and felt the pavement give beneath his foot.

Noah cried out and quickly leapt back. Erik hopped to safety a few feet ahead. The pavement split and a dark crack forked left, causing Kyra to lose her balance and stumble onto the collapsing section. Noah dove forward, grabbing her by the arm. She screamed as a huge swath of road dropped out from underneath her and landed with a soft thump on the sand below. Erik quickly scrambled to join Noah, and the pair of them pulled the dangling Kyra up to solid ground. Noah could see on his readouts that her heart was racing.

"Still safer than Sora?" Noah said to her, but she was too out of breath to either glare at him or express her gratitude. Still, better she were here with them than sitting on an exposed ship with no weapons. Though that was only true if the building in front of them was as empty as Theta claimed.

They soon found it was. Empty of life, at least.

Everyone gasped involuntarily as they made their way into the central lobby of the hotel. There were corpses strewn all over the place, draped over couches and on top of defunct fountains and abandoned luggage carts. Xalan corpses. Fresh Xalan corpses.

There was black blood everywhere. Some was dry, but much was still wet. The smell was unbearable.

"What in the hell . . ." Erik began, but couldn't complete the thought.

These were far from the dusty skeletons they'd seen on the way. Theta tried to regain her composure and scanned the bodies.

"T-The Xalans have been dead for less than a day," she said before succumbing to a fit of coughing that sounded dangerously like dry heaving.

Some of the dead wore armor, but most wore nothing, as was customary for Xalans who weren't in the military. Nearly everyone was next to some sort of a weapon, however, either a blade or a gun.

"What happened here?" Noah asked no one in particular.

"Soran raid?" Finn offered. The young Stoller had gone pale as milk.

Kyra held her breath and gingerly stepped around the corpses.

"Not one Soran body, or body part," she said, more unfazed than Noah thought she'd be. "Not a drop of red blood."

Theta was studying the bodies after resisting her apparent urge to vomit.

"It appears these wounds were all made by . . . Xalan weapons," she said, startled.

"Or they killed *each other*," Noah breathed.

"There's Resistance all the way out here? Why would they bother with Earth when there are uprisings all over the colony planets?"

No one had an answer for that. Noah looked down and saw one Xalan corpse clutching a thin blade that was buried in the neck of another creature next to him. The stabbed Xalan held a pistol that had ruptured the abdomen of his attacker.

The lights were dim, and the grisly scene had everyone visibly on edge. They pressed forward toward a large central staircase where the bodies started to thin out. There was Xalan electronic equipment placed throughout the room, and Theta scanned each device she passed that wasn't obviously destroyed.

"What is this place?" Noah asked her. She sifted through code on her display.

"Decrypting," she responded absentmindedly and kept walking forward, stepping over bodies. "The power source is concentrated above us."

The five of them ascended level after level up wide spiral staircases. More dead Xalans were sprawled out on the stairs. Black blood soaked into the plush red carpet. Most of the stairways weren't lit, and they had to illuminate them from lights on their armor alone. The wind whistled through the empty windows in the guest suites all around them and created unnerving screams that Noah often swore had to be coming from a living being. His readout told him that everyone's heart rates were through the roof, his own included. His only consolation was that there were no beating hearts around but theirs.

"Here," Theta whispered as they finally reached the twenty-seventh floor. A sign said "Skyview Bar" in both English and the other looped language. A dull glow was coming from down the hall. They crept around the corner and made their way through an arched entrance. Everyone was holding their breath.

Bits of tables and chairs lay in splinters all around them. The room had been stripped of its furniture. Replacing it were clusters of Xalan machinery. Holographic monitors showed various data readouts, and there were enormous empty spherical vats rooted in the floor, most of which had their glass shattered. Theta quickly ran to the closest console cluster and began wirelessly extracting data from it.

There were more bodies here, all with similar injuries to those they'd found below. The walls were marred by black plasma burns, and what little was left of the bar's stock had been reduced to a large pile of glass on the bloodstained floor.

"A laboratory," Theta said finally. Noah looked at the large, shattered glass tanks. "Operated by . . ." Theta continued, but trailed off.

"By who?" Erik asked.

"By the Genetic Science Enclave," Theta said in a panicked tone. Noah had heard that name before. Alpha had mentioned it many times. The Shadowmakers.

"Stay alert," Noah said as he made his way around the room. Massive windows gave way to a view of the city's skyline. The wind howled through fractured glass.

This was a mistake, he thought. *We should have never come here.*

Noah remembered his mother's tales of the Desecrator, the Xalan monster that had gone down the wrong evolutionary path and murdered his creators.

This is wrong.

His head started to hurt. A piercing migraine split his skull until his eyes teared up. He pressed forward next to Erik, motioning to Kyra to get behind them.

Noah stepped around the curved wall of the central bar and found one more cylindrical tank ahead. But this one was intact. And lit. And there was a figure inside.

Noah moved closer. The shape was smaller. Far smaller than any Xalan should be.

The shape was human.

Wrapped in pressurized bandages, his arms were locked into metal clamps above his head. His feet were firmly secured to the floor, encased in the base of the unit. Through the bandaging, Noah could see dark black veins snaking their way all throughout the man's body. His bald head hung down, his chin pressed to his chest.

Noah walked forward in amazement and put his armored glove on the glass. The noise sent a jolt through the man, whose head rolled up to face them.

Erik froze. Noah's heart stopped. He knew the face immediately. All of Sora would have.

Lucas opened his eyes. Not steel gray, but ice blue.

8

Lucas blinked, his vision swimming. He could see shapes moving outside the glass.

Not again, he thought. *No more.*

He dreaded these brief periods of consciousness. They only came rarely, but they were excruciatingly painful with whatever the Xalans were pumping into him that seemed to light his nerves on fire. It was already rotting his veins from the looks of it. Why didn't they just kill him already and be done with it? Why had they kept him alive at all?

There was muffled shouting coming from outside his container. Was that . . . Soran? Lucas's eyes widened. The faces were swimming in front of him, but they did look decidedly human-shaped, that much he could see as things started to come into focus. His heart leapt in his chest.

They found me.

More movement and suddenly the glass of the enclosure began to sink into the ground. Once it did, Lucas saw the four human shapes in front of him, with one lanky form that had to be a Xalan. He couldn't get his lips and tongue to move.

The Xalan pressed a button on the unit and the clamps around his arms and legs were released. Lucas collapsed to the ground, tubes popping out from various attachment points on his body and hissing as they swung wildly through the air. Three pairs of hands found him and dragged him out of the unit.

He could finally understand what they were saying.

"Lucas," one said. "Lucas, can you hear me?"

His head was fogged, and he cringed as the wind whistled loudly through the room. The sound was almost deafening. He looked up and saw a sign he'd read many times before in his rare waking moments.

"Enjoy your stay in fabulous *Dubai!*" the etching over the bar said, with the same phrase written in Arabic above it.

He blinked, and attempted to speak again, this time with more success.

"You . . . you the rescue team?" he slurred. He couldn't remember the last time he'd spoken aloud. "Is Asha here?"

He tried to rise, unsteadily, and a pair of strong arms grabbed him. Lucas tottered backward a step and came to rest leaning against the bar.

"Lucas, do you know where you are?" the voice said again. His face came into focus. He was a tall, good-looking young man with blue eyes and short blond hair. Beside him was a lanky kid, shorter with green eyes, and a girl who—

Lucas's eyes widened. It couldn't be her. He was hallucinating. But as he shifted and stepped on a piece of broken glass, the pain convinced him that he was not. He remembered the young man's question. The others looked like mere children. What sort of rescue was this?

"In Dubai," he spat out. "Earth."

During his brief lapses of consciousness, he'd managed to deduce that much, but little else about his imprisonment. He couldn't remember. The feeling was starting to flood back into his limbs. His sickly looking veins remained black, however. He wondered if he was dying. Or dead.

The young man put an armored hand on his shoulder.

"You're going to be okay now."

Lucas saw a canteen extended out in front of him. He took it, and saw it was being held by a white Xalan.

"Zeta?" he asked.

"No, I—" the creature began. She was too short to be Zeta. Lucas interrupted, his voice still strained.

"How did you find me?"

"You called us here," came a second voice. A boy stepped forward. His green eyes were familiar.

"What?" Lucas said. "How?"

Where was Asha? Why would she not be with his rescue team?

"Lucas, you won't know me, but you have to understand what I'm about to tell you," said the blond in power armor in front of him. He was tall and broad shouldered, but looked quite young as well now that Lucas could see him clearly. He looked warily at the blue-eyed girl again.

"What are you talking about?" Lucas asked.

"My name is Noah," the young man said. "And this is Erik."

Lucas blinked.

He saw the burn creeping up the young man's neck. He looked into the other boy's eyes. His world was flipped inside out in an instant.

"No," he said, backing away. "You're not—"

It was another nightmare. He had them every night. Why had he not learned by now? He stumbled forward toward his chamber. Maybe if he got back in he could get away from all this. He was tired of being taunted. This was what, the twentieth time he'd been rescued in a dream? But this one felt so real. More shards of glass dug into his bare feet.

Noah caught him.

"Lucas," he said, spinning him around toward the group, away from the chamber. "You were supposed to have died on Xala. You've been gone for sixteen years."

This can't be real, can it? Lucas didn't want to let himself believe it.

"Where's Asha?" he asked.

"Alive," the one who claimed to be Erik said. "She's been looking for you this entire time. She never believed you were dead. She was the only one."

"I can't—" Lucas's knees buckled. The blond girl caught him, her eyes darting back and forth nervously. Lucas stared at her, transfixed. *Blue eyes.*

Would-be Noah slid a broken metal console underneath him so he could sit.

"What's the last thing you can remember?" Noah asked. "What happened on Xala?"

Lucas rested his hands on his knees. The white Xalan was scanning him with some sort of device, which he waved away like a buzzing gnat.

"I-I," he stammered. Xala seemed like yesterday. Sixteen years?

"I detonated Natalie in the comm relay," he finally said. "Woke up on fire. Arms, feet, hair, burning. I was being crushed by the corpse of the Desecrator. The blast flung him into me, his plating must have shielded me from the worst of it. He smelled like he'd been cooked all the way through."

Lucas thought back to the moment. The lifeless orange eyes of the monster inches away from his own, the skin melting off Lucas's arms and legs as he struggled, screaming beneath the crushing weight of the creature's shell of a body.

Lucas looked down at his hands now. They were smooth, unblemished, as were his legs and head.

"Something pulled me out. A face. Eyes full of galaxies. They took me here."

The group looked at each other and whispered.

"And since then?" Noah pressed.

"Only awake every so often. They pumped me full of . . . something. Incredible pain. Indescribable."

The white Xalan whispered something to Noah.

"What are you saying?" Lucas called out to her. The creature looked startled.

"I-I said that the records here say you have been kept in cryostasis for nearly the entirety of your stay here. It is why you have lost all sense of time."

Lucas looked down at the ground. Pieces of a broken mirror that had once been on the ceiling were strewn on the tattered carpet. One flashed with a glimpse of his own face. He lurched backward when he saw his electric blue eyes.

"What . . . what did they do to me?" he asked. The white Xalan looked nervously at the others.

"We need to go," Noah said. "We'll explain everything on the ship." He and Erik helped Lucas to his feet.

"Is it . . . is it really you? Are you my . . . sons?" Lucas asked, his voice cracking. It was real. This was real. No more nightmares. It was over. And all it cost him was sixteen years he couldn't even remember.

"Yes," Noah said, and Erik gave him a tight-lipped nod. He saw so much of her in him. She was alive. And she'd never lost hope.

Lucas was finally able to walk on his own, though Noah kept steadying him whenever he faltered. The white Xalan had hacked together a rough bit of armor plating he could wear instead of the bandages he was wrapped in. She'd pulled the materials from the many, many corpses that littered the rooms and hallways.

"Did you do this?" Lucas said, looking at the bodies, wondering how children could have decimated such overwhelming forces. Even if some of them were *his* children.

"Did you?" Erik asked from behind him.

Lucas was confused.

"I haven't left that tank in a decade and a half, according to, uh, what's your name?"

"Theta."

"Friend of Alpha's?"

"I am his daughter."

That made Lucas stop abruptly.

"Well, how about that."

Suddenly, Lucas clutched his head, which exploded with pain. His eyes felt like they were going to erupt from their sockets. The screams were loud. So loud.

And then they were gone.

"What was that?" said the thin one they called Finn. The name sounded familiar.

"I don't . . ." Lucas said, shaking his head and squinting. He looked up at the sign on the stairwell.

OVERLOOK POOL.

"This way," Lucas said, pointing down the dark hallway. The others looked at each other nervously.

"We have to get back to the—"

Lucas ignored Noah and lurched down the hallway, pulled forward by a force he couldn't explain. Something painful. But not his pain. The pain of others.

He stumbled through a pair of shattered glass doors, his burning muscles failing to work properly with the electronic assists of the Xalan power armor attached to his legs, even if they'd been kept from atrophying during his imprisonment. Lounge chairs lay shredded around the pool, which now overlooked barren desert that assuredly used to be a gorgeous view of the gulf.

The pool was filled up with human bodies. Dozens. No, hundreds. Lucas heard the gasps of the others as they caught up with him.

The bodies were in various stages of decay, and in different states. Some had white or gray rotting skin, others were completely black, like they'd been burned to a crisp. Most had faces twisted into looks of agony. Lucas could feel their fear, their pain, somewhere deep in his mind.

What happened to them? What's happening to me?

He caught another glimpse of himself in a streaked mirror that made up part of a nearby wall. His eyes frightened him. He'd seen those eyes before. *But it couldn't be . . .*

"I need answers," he said, turning to Theta. "What is this place?"

He paused, then shouted.

"What have they done to me?"

The question echoed off the tiled floor. Theta glanced into the pool. Behind her, only a sliver of the moon cast any light on the mass grave before them. The hologram on her translator collar flickered in the darkness as she spoke.

"I am still deciphering the vast amount of data from the cores here, but as I understand it from what I have decrypted, this is a new phase of the Genetic Science Enclave's Shadow project. It was conceived just over a decade ago with the goal of transforming Sorans into Shadows, rather than Xalans."

"Am I . . ." Lucas said, as he looked in the mirror. The black veins were creeping up from his neck onto the sides of his jaw. His blue irises flashed in the darkness, catching the moonlight. His pupils were still black, at least.

"You are in the midst of the conversion process," Theta finished for him. "Results so far indicate that the process, if possible to complete, would take years for Sorans, rather than days for Xalans."

"What do you mean, 'if possible to complete'?"

Theta walked over toward the pool of dead bodies and hunched down near the edge. She pricked one with a long thin needle that extended out of her suit, then another, and another. Finally, she spoke again.

"The logs say there have been no successful conversions to date."

She looked down at a readout on her arm.

"Sorans. All of them, it would seem. No humans of Earth."

"Prisoners of war," Erik said, surveying the grisly landscape.

"Perhaps being human, not Soran, has allowed you to survive the conversion process for this long. There are slight genetic differences between the two species, after all," Theta mused.

A hundred voices called out to Lucas from the pit. Mournful wails. He shook them out of his head.

"Can you hear that?" he asked the group. Noah and Erik exchanged a worried glance.

"We need to keep moving," Noah said. "There's no telling when more Xalans might show up to investigate what happened here."

The pool howled at him as he left. Or perhaps it had been the wind the whole time.

A storm had descended upon the ruins of Dubai by the time they exited the hotel. Lightning crackled from cloud to cloud and violent thunder pierced their eardrums. The rain was falling in sheets, and Lucas wondered what was possibly happening with Earth's climate to drown a desert region like this. But he was just thankful the clouds were not red anymore, and the rain no longer burned. The planet had been mortally wounded. But it had clung to life, just as he had.

Sixteen years.

He could hardly believe it. He knew that his periods of consciousness had been brief inside the chamber, but he'd thought only weeks had gone by. A month, maybe. But they'd made him sleep for sixteen years. Made him dream.

It was astonishing to see Noah and Erik grown. Noah had sprouted into the spitting image of his father, the cannibal chief

Lucas had executed at Kvaløya. He wasn't quite as tall, but it seemed he would be someday. Lucas never planned to tell Noah about his true parentage, content simply to say that he was a stray child with a dead mother they found on their travels. That much was true, of course.

And Erik. He saw a bit of himself in his younger son, the one that actually shared his blood. Well, his old self. Before he'd lost his hair, sprouted ink-like veins and frosted blue eyes. He was built the way Lucas had been at that age, lean but athletic, and carried himself with a sense of purpose and obvious pride. But clearly there was more of Asha in him. The dark curls, the wide green eyes. And already, he saw a bit of her temper there as well.

He'd missed almost their entire lives. In between thunderclaps, Noah told him about the colony, about his girlfriend, or "pair," named Sakai, one of the tank-bred humans Malorious Auran had spawned to perpetuate the race. He was introduced to Finn Stoller, the son of the new High Chancellor whom Lucas had known and rather disliked in his past life. And Noah told him the story of how he'd become recently reunited with his childhood friend, Auran's granddaughter Kyra, after an attack at their local cathedral. There was something about Kyra that was disquieting to Lucas, but he couldn't understand why. She appeared to be a perfectly lovely girl, and Lucas shook off the feeling.

They trudged forward through the rain, his muscles relearning how to walk. He wondered how Asha would react when she saw him, the twisted Xalan experiment. But *god*, he couldn't wait to lay eyes on her again.

Lucas stumbled over a downed wooden traffic barrier, but caught himself before falling into the mess of fractured cement and broken glass that was the Dubai coastal highway. He looked up just as a flash of lightning illuminated the sky. He saw . . . a shape.

"Hey," he called out to the group in the rain. "Did you see that?"

Erik gave Noah a hesitant look. They thought he was crazy.

Another flash. The shape grew bigger in the clouds. A void that rain was simply swallowed into. Lucas stopped walking abruptly.

"Lucas, we really have to keep moving," Noah said diplomatically, but with a hint of frustration.

Another flash. Then they all saw it. It wasn't in his mind. Floating above them was a ship, the likes of which he'd never seen.

9

Noah's eyes widened as the disc-like craft descended toward them. This wasn't Lucas hallucinating again. The rain was being absorbed into the shape, and suddenly a string of lights erupted around the edge of the void. It was round and flat and had no external engine as far as Noah could see.

"Theta . . ." Noah called out, gripping his rifle tightly. The ship was getting lower. Too low. Theta was checking readouts that were completely blank.

"There is nothing," she said. "The sensors relay that nothing is here. It is impossible, but . . ." she trailed off.

Another flash of lightning revealed black shapes with singular blue lights falling from the underside of the dark ship. Heartbeats began to pop up on Theta's display. Four, eight, a dozen.

"I have seen this ship," she said breathlessly. "My father was attempting to study it for the SDI. There was only three seconds of footage of it, taken in the Makari solar system."

Noah understood. So did Erik.

"The Black Corsair," he said, raising his twin pistols toward the dark stretch of deserted highway in front of him. Of course someone had come to investigate the slaughter at the hotel lab. But him? Was it really him? Noah felt his throat constrict in panic.

The sound of claws on metal could be heard through the rain up ahead. Dark shapes leapt through the air, bounding over decayed cars toward them. Tiny lights from their power armor twinkled in the rain.

Noah looked around frantically. He saw a large overturned car that had once pulled a long metal container two lanes to his right. Grabbing Theta and Kyra by the arms, he hauled them over toward it.

"Stay in here," he said firmly. "No matter what you hear, don't come out."

"No!" said Kyra angrily, twisting away from his grasp. Noah was stunned. "You need help!" she continued. "We're armed."

Theta put up no such protest and was huddled against the side of the compartment.

"Please," Noah pleaded with Kyra. "I—"

Ignoring him, Kyra began to make a beeline back toward the others, checking the power pack on her scattergun.

Noah swore and turned to Theta.

"Send out a distress beacon to any SDI signature remotely near here," he said. Theta barely had time to nod before he slammed the container's sliding door shut.

Noah bounded after Kyra, who was disappearing into the rain. Surviving the spire had changed her, it seemed. Hardened her. Bravery was one thing, but recklessness was another. He didn't need another Erik on his hands. Noah looked up at the ship and heard yelling ahead. He sprinted faster.

He never reached the voices.

The Xalan slammed into him, propelled by the jetpack attached to the rear of his armor. It shot out a blue flame that was vaporizing raindrops in the downpour. Noah immediately lost his grip on his rifle, which clattered to the ground, and the pair of them rocketed into a nearby automobile that cratered with the impact of Noah's power armor. His head cracked against the metal and his vision went white.

He regained focus just in time to deflect the Xalan's extended pistol hand. The shot blew a hole through the passenger door of the car, and Noah countered with a power fist to the creature's midsection. He heard the Xalan's armor crunch painfully. He threw another punch at the creature's throat. It was a glancing blow, but it was enough to stagger his attacker and allow Noah to launch himself back to his feet. Gunfire could be heard coming from up ahead. He had to reach his friends.

Noah eyed the creature who was now clutching his side. The only Xalans Noah had ever seen in person were Alpha and his family. This one was taller and fully armored and had a strange symbol on his chest. If this was one of the famed Shadows, Noah knew he would already be dead.

His hammer.

He whipped out the long darksteel warhammer, which he'd almost forgotten was strapped to his back because of how little it weighed. The recovered Xalan raised his pistol again, but Noah shattered it into debris with one lightning quick swing. He found he could strike infinitely faster with the darksteel than with the colony's clunky practice mauls.

The Xalan ducked under the second swing and reached for the rifle on his back. Noah thrust the hammer forward, and its top spike speared the gun's barrel. The weapon misfired, and a small internal explosion sent shrapnel into the Xalan's hand, resulting in a howl of pain.

Noah didn't wait for the creature to pull out any more weapons. One more thunderous swing shattered the Xalan's entire chest plate and sent him flying through the already broken windshield of another car. Noah leapt into the air, his power armor lofting him eight feet up, and he came crashing down on the hood, his hammer caving in the Xalan's chest completely.

There was no time to stop and breathe. Ahead, another armored trooper was firing his gun at someone, possibly Erik. Noah sprinted over the rest of the demolished car and slid across the gravel, driving the spike on top of his hammer through the back of the creature's neck. The Xalan seized up and collapsed onto the cracked road, but whoever he'd been shooting at was now lost in the torrential rain.

Noah heard a thunderclap shockingly close by, and as he turned around found it wasn't the weather at all. Kyra stood a dozen feet behind him, holding her smoking scattergun. On the ground in front of her was a downed Xalan with a constellation of smoking holes in his back. He was reaching for his discarded rifle, but another boom from Kyra's gun removed the Xalan's head this time. He hadn't heard either of them behind him, and it very well could have been him lying there headless if Kyra hadn't been there.

Noah was just about to shout his gratitude over the howling wind when he saw a shape materialize behind her. His eyes widened and he bolted forward. Noah shoved her out of the way and she crashed headfirst into a nearby concrete barrier, just as the figure fired his weapon.

The blast caught Noah below his ribcage and sent him spinning wildly to his right. But he kept his footing and when he came around, he brought the warhammer with him. It shattered both the helmet and skull of the Xalan attacker before he could fire another shot.

Noah dropped to his knees, clutching his side. A black hole was scorched into his armor and the flesh underneath was charred. The armor had deflected most of the blow, but the plasma still burned like hellfire. He looked over at Kyra, crumpled in a heap up against the barrier. A quick scan revealed she was alive, but unconscious. Muddy water pooled around her face, and Noah looked behind him where the air was being lit up by gunfire.

Recognizing this could probably be the safest place for her in the present situation, Noah used all the natural might the gods had given him, along with the artificial strength from the power armor, and dragged the carcass of a rusted car a few feet backward so that it would shield her from view. Once that was done, he sprinted toward the rest of the gunfire.

Xalan corpses lay scattered on the cracked cement, and he couldn't remember if they were the ones he'd killed or not; the storm reduced vision to a minimum and he was disoriented. He kept running until he saw one body that looked decidedly human and froze in his tracks, his stomach dropping. Noah bent down and rolled the body over.

Finn Stoller. But he was breathing.

There was a smoking hole at his breastbone, but he was alive. His precious prototype assault rifle lay a few feet away, and had taken even more abuse than he had. A few plasma rounds had reduced it to scrap metal, and it would never fire another shot. Noah quickly dug into his pocket for some healing gel, which he hastily dumped on Finn's wound, ignoring the proper procedure he'd learned in his lessons at the colony. Even with his suit's stabilizers, his hands were shaking. All the training on Sora hadn't prepared him for this.

"Come on!" shouted a voice from the darkness.

It was Erik, and as Noah stood up, he realized his brother wasn't talking to him.

"Come on!" Erik shouted again toward a pair of Xalan solders trying to flank him from cover. He held out one of his laser pistols, but his other arm was drawn into his body. He was hurt.

Pieces of Xalans lay in a small clearing on the highway, neatly cut. Noah watched Erik fire the laser pistol at the car the two Xalans were hiding behind, and bright golden beam ripped through the metal cleanly. A howl indicated one of the Xalans had lost an appendage. The other one finally bolted upright and leveled a string of shots toward Erik. His brother dove out of the way, rolled upright again, and a new beam split the Xalan's head in half from his brow upward. The other one stumbled out from behind the automobile, missing an arm, and Erik whipped the beam across his chest, dropping him permanently. He shook out his good hand painfully as the gun was beginning to overheat.

Erik finally saw Noah walking toward him, hammer in hand. The rain was doing its best to wash his armor clean of blood, but it was still everywhere. There was more gunfire, but it was further away now.

"Where is everyone?" Erik shouted over the din of the storm.

"Theta safe, Kyra and Finn hurt, but alive," Noah yelled back, not wanting to waste words. "You?" he asked, motioning toward his brother's arm.

Erik extended his left hand. Noah grimaced as he saw that his brother had lost his two smallest fingers, with a third mangled badly.

"They'll grow me some new ones," he said, pretending like he wasn't in agony. "Where's this Corsair, anyway?"

Noah wondered if Theta was wrong. Maybe this was just a routine Xalan patrol coming to investigate the lab incident. But that ship . . .

More gunfire, and a human yell. There was only one of them left. Erik and Noah turned in the direction of the sound, but shifted their gaze upward as more blue lights descended from the dark ship. More soldiers.

They ran into the darkness and soon found what they were looking for. Lucas was surrounded by five Xalans, his hastily assembled power armor crumbling off of him, revealing the bandages and black veins underneath. He was holding the assault rifle that Noah had dropped in the opening moments of the battle. The Xalans were wielding either rifles or long electric spears. Stun weapons.

They want him alive.

Of course they did. They'd been experimenting on him for over a decade. The rest of them, however, seemed to be quite expendable.

Finally, the group circling him lunged. Two fired blue stun blasts from their weapons while three dove in with the electric polearms. Lucas unloaded the rifle into one Xalan whose face exploded immediately, but he was unconscious before could take out any more.

Noah and Erik bounded over a flattened car toward the dogpile. Erik swung the pistol up in an arc that cleaved one of the riflemen in half. After letting it cool for half a second, he whipped it to the right and decapitated another. Noah, meanwhile, had leapt onto one of the spear-wielding Xalans attempting to pick Lucas up. He jammed the butt of his hammer into the small of his back. Once, twice, until he heard the armor crack. Another Xalan trying to subdue Lucas lunged at Noah with the crackling electric spear and it made Noah's hair stand on end as he weaved out of its way. Noah swung his hammer upward. It connected with the metal pole, bent it inward, and killed its power source. Whipping the warhammer around, he planted its rear spike into the chest of the creature before turning back to the other one on the ground and crushing him with a powerful overhand blow. The street caved in around the point of impact, and Noah staggered backward from the shockwave. The entire section of the freeway shook while blue lights on the sides of the hammer glowed, then faded.

Erik stood next to him and they looked down at Lucas, out cold from the half dozen stuns he'd been hit with. Lucas the hero. Lucas the legend. Right now, he didn't really look like the god of war the stories made him out to be.

There was another flash of lightning and a figure became briefly illuminated standing on a car ahead of them. Not a Xalan, but a man.

"Finn?" Erik called out to him, but the man said nothing. More lightning. It wasn't Finn. The shape was taller, broader, and appeared to be encased in an entirely black suit of armor.

Noah's eyes widened.

Erik was sent flying over the guard railing of the overpass as if an invisible freight train had plowed into him and he tumbled down onto the flooded sands below.

Noah turned to reach for his brother, but he was gone. The air hummed with tangible energy. He turned back toward the man who had now descended from the car and was a walking toward Noah with his arm raised. He stepped over Lucas's face-down body. Noah sprinted toward him with his warhammer cocked.

And then, three feet away from the man, his hammer inches away from smashing into his skull, Noah froze. He couldn't move an inch or blink an eyelash. The man looked at him impassively.

Noah could see now that he wasn't wearing power armor. He had on a slim fiber suit, but everywhere his skin was visible it was charred black like many of the corpses in the hotel pool. His hair had been seared off, his skin was hard and cracked, but he was very much alive. The pure ice-blue eyes staring deep into Noah told him that much.

The Corsair.

A human.

No sooner had the realization dawned on Noah than he was flung backward from the horrifying face and slammed into an upright streetlight. He could barely move, and as the man walked toward him, he splayed Noah's arms out wide by separating his blackened fingers.

"W-why?" Noah managed to get out through strained vocal cords. "You're . . . one of us."

The man's voice was low and rumbled like the thunder that boomed all around them. It sounded like a multitude of voices in one.

"I serve the Archon. I hunt the Soran traitors," the Corsair growled through split lips.

Noah couldn't get anything else out as his arms were bent backward around the pole. His elbows were driven toward each other and he felt like he was about to pass out from the pain. He heard the gears crack in his armor. The Corsair's eyes burned with limitless fury, his black skin slick from the rain. The next pop Noah heard wasn't metal, but bone. His scream rebounded off every dead skyscraper in Dubai.

Out of the corner of his eye, he saw Kyra running toward them, weapon in hand, helmet secured. He wanted to yell to her.

No.

Go back.

Get out.

But his frozen throat wouldn't form the words.

The Corsair turned and saw the small shape layered in armor plating. She raised her gun. He extended his hand.

And then, an explosion.

Something ripped into the Corsair's ship above them. The man immediately turned to look, dropping Noah in the process, whose arms sprang back to a proper angle. His left arm hung loosely at his side, however, and the pain in his collar was excruciating. Kyra was knocked off her feet from the force of the blast, her scattergun falling into a deep crack in the freeway. She scrambled toward Noah.

Another explosion tore into the hull of the hovering round ship. Above it, out of the clouds came two gargantuan SDI dreadnoughts and one smaller interceptor making a beeline directly for them.

Noah couldn't find the strength to celebrate their arrival, or even move an inch. He looked on as a troop of Xalan reinforcements surrounded Lucas, dug their claws into his shoulders and hoisted him upright. The group took off with his father back toward the ship, their jetpacks blazing in the pouring rain. The Corsair launched himself from the ground to follow them, but there was no fire coming from his back as he flew into the night sky unaided. A chill cut through Noah right before he lost consciousness. The last thing he saw was Kyra's face, inverted above him.

10

Lucas woke up in the sky. He was flying.

Another dream.

He was disappointed. The last one had been so vivid. He'd really believed he had been rescued by his long-lost sons—that he was going to get to see Asha again. The good dreams were more cruel than the nightmares.

Lucas cringed as pain shot through his back. He rolled his head to the right and saw three Xalan claws firmly embedded in his shoulder. Above him, blue flames licked dangerously close to face.

Oh god.

It was no dream. Lucas watched Dubai disappear into gray mist beneath him as the dark ship grew closer. He could hear explosions. He tried to struggle, but was too weak. He couldn't lift his arms more than a few inches, and his head felt like it had been cracked open.

I hope they're alive, was his only thought. He'd completely lost track of the group when the Xalans landed. They were children, not soldiers. They never should have come. He never should have called to them, though he had no recollection of doing so.

There was something in the clouds up ahead, streaking through the rain toward him. A silver object outlined in orange flame that was getting closer and closer. Lucas heard a surprised grunt from above him.

The shape slammed into the Xalan holding Lucas. He could see in the new tangle of limbs that it was a person. The three of them tumbled through the air wildly, and Lucas could hear the Xalan screaming as black blood erupted from his body and dissolved into the rain.

And then, Lucas was falling.

Above him was the dark ship, now firing its invisible engines. In a split second, it was gone, blinking past Lucas's field of vision. In its place, Lucas saw three new ships. The cubic architecture of the SDI was obvious.

The rain was starting to let up now. Lucas rolled his head to his right and saw the Xalan's claw still embedded in his flesh. It wasn't attached to anything, having been neatly severed at the wrist. He couldn't see the ground, but knew it was approaching quickly.

Save the children, he thought.

But an orange-and-silver blur caught him.

The ground *was* close. Mere seconds later the armored figure lay Lucas down on the muddy sand. Lucas could see the freeway overpass a few hundred yards away. They were in what appeared to be an old park, with broken benches and long-dry fountains now overflowing with water from the freak storm that was starting to subside. The rain had slowed to a drizzle and the clouds were parting.

The figure rose up above him, staring at him, transfixed. The fiery jetpack was powered down. The visored helmet was removed and tossed aside.

Long black hair spilled out onto the silver shoulders of her armor. A dark sword crossed her back. Brilliant green eyes brimmed with tears. And that smile.

That smile.

"Is it really you?" Asha said, astonished. She dropped to her knees.

Lucas couldn't find the words. The pain left him. He pulled himself to his feet and Asha rose with him.

"I—" he began, but Asha threw her arms around him so tightly he might have very well rebroken a rib or two. But he didn't care. He held her as close as he could.

"I knew it," she said. "I knew you were alive. They told me—"

Lucas pulled back and stopped her with a kiss.

He never wanted this moment, this second, to end.

One dreadnought stayed behind to search for more nearby Xalan installations on Earth, while the other swallowed up both Asha's interceptor and Stoller's Shatterstar into its massive internal hangars. They were heading back to Sora, and Earth was slowly fading into a blue dot out the windows of the observation deck. The Corsair and his ship had vanished, the SDI vessels unable to destroy it before it activated its null core. It had done so just outside Earth's atmosphere, which was supposed to be gravitationally impossible, but that was an issue for another day.

The five young members of Lucas's rescue party had each been found and brought onboard. It was Theta's beacon that had drawn the SDI and Asha to their location. They had been trailing the Corsair for months, and the most recent data plotted him arriving in Earth's solar system for reasons then unknown. Only now did they understand that he'd likely been investigating the incident at the lab where Lucas had been held, and tasked with his recapture.

Noah was still unconscious in the med bay with a plasma wound, a dislocated shoulder, and a broken collarbone. The Auran girl had a concussion, but wouldn't leave his side. Erik's hand was a grisly mess, but he was awake and alert. The most dire prognosis was for Finn Stoller, who was in critical condition with a plasma round having eaten through his lung.

Lucas's own injuries had been dressed, but he'd escaped the encounter without any grievous wounds, thanks to the fact that the Corsair and his crew had been trying to take him alive. But none of that mattered now. All that mattered was her.

Asha sat across from him in the observation deck as Earth disappeared and Jupiter came into view. She no longer wore her silver armor and had on a dark green undersuit instead. She was just as beautiful as Lucas remembered, if not more so.

Lucas had been kept in stasis for the vast majority of his imprisonment, and it was as if he had instantly aged a decade and a half, with salt and pepper dotting his face and bald head. Asha, however, had the benefit of the Soran aging process, one that moved biology at a glacial pace due to their medical advances. She in no way looked her age, and Lucas still saw the fire-eyed huntress who had fought by his side for years, even if a new line or two had found its way into her face. She was still lean and hard and as insane as ever, as he'd learned when she bailed out of her ship to fly through the air and save him from abduction.

"I couldn't believe Theta's distress message," Asha said. She hadn't taken her eyes off Lucas since they got on the ship.

"*Lucas the Earthborn located, Xalans engaging, request assistance.*' I listened to it a dozen times before we arrived and still couldn't possibly think it was true."

"But you did," Lucas said with a smile. "You always have. The only one that kept looking, from what I hear."

"They almost threw me in prison for it, the assholes," she said.

Lucas continued to grin.

"Yeah, they don't much care for it when you steal their ships, I imagine."

"I could *feel* that you were alive. I can't explain it, but I just knew."

Lucas's eyes narrowed.

"Did I call you here?" he asked.

"Call me?" Asha asked, confused. "What do you mean?"

"That's how the boys got here, they heard 'Dubai' in their dreams. They say it 'pulled' them here."

Asha shook her head.

"Nothing like that," she said. "I've had my share of dreams about you, but none ever told me to look for you here. I didn't even know Earth's climate had reverted to this degree."

A Soran officer had brought them a meal, which Lucas devoured hungrily. It was barely more than a few bites of cooked meat, but Lucas had been fed gas nutrients for nearly two decades, so it felt like a five-course dining experience. After quickly clearing the minimal plate, his weakened stomach started to churn angrily. Asha had five times the amount of food in front of her, but wasn't touching it.

"I can't believe they came here," Asha said. "I knew Erik was notorious for sneaking out of the colony, but to come to Earth? He's lucky he didn't get himself killed."

"I really only just met him, but I think I know where he got that sort of instinct from," Lucas said with a sly smile.

"Do you really want to talk about death wishes?" Asha asked. "The guy who blew himself up and has been dead for sixteen years?"

"*Almost* blew himself up," Lucas corrected.

"I can't believe the Desecrator actually ended up saving you," she said, shaking her head.

"It wasn't his choice, believe me. And it cost me most of my skin." The room fell silent. Uncomfortably so. Lucas knew where the conversation had to turn to now.

"Alpha will fix this," he said, tracing the black veins on his arm with his fingers. He'd been trying to avoid direct eye contact with Asha, not wanting to unnerve her with his shockingly blue irises. She was acting like she didn't notice, but he could see a dim flicker of fear in her eyes now that he broached the subject.

"I know," she said with uncertain confidence. "Do you . . . feel any different?"

Lucas shook his head.

"No. I'm not a Shadow. I never finished the transformation, but I didn't die either. But if they hadn't found me, I would have. No one has survived the new process. They've killed hundreds of Soran prisoners trying to create new Shadows."

"Why?" Asha asked. "Why Sorans? Why you?"

Lucas stared past her.

"Theta's trying to crack their research data. What she's found so far is that, for some reason, the Xalans believe that human or Soran Shadows have the potential to be more powerful than Xalan ones. That they could be controlled and used as weapons."

"Reminds me of Alpha's Desecrator bedtime story," Asha said, "where they said that the Sorans created the monster in the Xalans' own image to hunt them down and slaughter them. Only this time it's the opposite."

"Kill me if it comes to that," Lucas said with a forced smile. But inside he was genuinely concerned. In sixteen years, who knew what the Xalans had done to his mind? He heard voices of the dead at the lab. He'd lured his own sons to their almost certain demise through some sort of intergalactic psychic projection. What else was he capable of?

Asha looked exhausted. Lucas felt the same way. He was still in pain, but also completely emotionally drained. He could hardly believe the events of the day, being reunited with his family after so many years. In certain moments it still didn't feel real, and he was having periodic pangs of panic that he'd wake up back in the tank if he shut his eyes for more than a few seconds.

Lucas pushed himself off his seat with a grimace and replanted himself across the table next to Asha. He swung his arm around her shoulder and she lay against his chest. She smelled of sweat and damp hair and blood, but it was all roses to Lucas. He had her back, and he'd never lose her again.

Xalans didn't smile. Their biology didn't allow it. They could grimace, snarl, frown, sneer, but they'd never evolved the facial muscles for anything resembling a smile.

But Lucas saw Alpha's gold-ringed eyes light up all the same on the viewscreen in the comms bay, and the tone in his metallic voice indicated he was overjoyed and overcome with emotion to see his old friend again. But Xalans couldn't cry either.

"Lucas," he said. "It cannot be."

Lucas, meanwhile, was beaming into the floating screen.

"Hello, old friend," he said, his voice wavering.

In the monitor, Alpha backed up a few steps and sat down in a tall chair in his lab.

"You were lost," he said. "I had no reason to believe you lived. I should have listen to Asha. I should have—"

Lucas cut him off.

"You did plenty, Alpha. You built the null cores that reached Earth and reunited my family. You ensured the boys were well cared for, and grew into men strong enough to save me. And now I need you to do one more thing."

Alpha nodded slowly.

"The Shadow conversion process, I have been briefed."

Alpha peered into the monitor for a closer look at Lucas's vasculature and electric eyes.

"The abominable practices of the Enclave continue, even after the death of the Council. I cannot fathom who would commission such a project, nor who would possess the knowledge to execute it. Xala has lost its brightest minds. This is the work of a madman or genius, I cannot be sure which."

Lucas sipped a drink laced with proteins that were supposed to normalize his digestion. It tasted like stale chalk.

"Can you reverse it?" he asked.

Alpha looked uncertain.

"This is a field I know little about, as my father forbid us to study it. And Shadow conversion of Sorans is something I did not know existed until moments ago. With that said, I will pore over the data my disobedient daughter extracted from the laboratory in which you were found. And I give you my word that I will not rest until you are whole again."

Lucas couldn't help but smile at his friend's boundless dedication.

"And I suppose congratulations are in order," Lucas said, "though they're about a decade late. You finally started that family you always wanted. She's quite a girl."

Alpha nodded appreciatively.

"She has her mother's looks and propensity for troublemaking," he said.

"Mhm," Lucas said with a masked smile. "I'm sure none of that is from your side at all."

"Recently resurrected and already making attempts at humor. I am glad to see they did not conquer your spirit."

"My spirit is intact," Lucas said. "It's my body and soul I'm worried about."

It wasn't a joke, and they both knew it. Alpha's tone grew more somber.

"I will help you, Lucas, as you have helped me so many times before."

11

Noah woke disoriented. Slowly remembering his injuries, he knew he should be in pain, but every bit of his body felt like it was being bathed in warm water. Opening his eyes, he saw the same sight he'd witnessed just before he'd gone under. Kyra blinked long lashes, and her lips parted into a smile.

"He's awake!" she said loudly, and Noah heard footsteps rush to his bedside. She turned back to him, words spilling out of her mouth too quickly to process. "Everyone made it out, don't worry. Asha is here, Lucas is safe. So are your brother, Theta, and Finn."

Noah let out a sigh of relief and allowed the painkillers to continue their relaxation of his body and mind. A female medical officer fiddled with some tubes attached to his immobile left arm. He felt an internal itch near his collar and instinctively scratched.

"Nanobots," Kyra said. "I remember the first time they mended one of your bones back together."

"You mean the creek?" Noah asked with a lazy smile.

"Of course I mean the creek."

Noah pulled himself a bit more upright on the bed with his remaining good arm. Kyra had a bandage wrapped around her head and some bruising near her neck, but was clearly in better shape than he was. Her hair fell down over one eye, leaving only one sphere of blue staring at him.

"I made the jump, didn't I? I said I would."

"Ah, the boasts of a seven-year-old," Kyra laughed. "And all it cost you was your tibia."

"It was worth proving you wrong," Noah shot back. He was trying not to slur, but his lips felt numb.

The attendant left them, and Kyra sat back down on her chair, picking up a scroll she'd placed there. Noah looked around the room and saw a bed a few rows down from him where Finn Stoller lay unconscious. Thankfully he'd lived through what had appeared to be a mortal wound. The kid was braver than he seemed.

Did Kyra say Asha was there? Noah's head was swimming from the drugs. He turned to less immediate matters.

"What are you reading?" he asked Kyra, motioning to the scroll. She opened it and holographic text sprung from the page. Noah couldn't recognize the language.

"A Ba'siri novel, *Shi Lor'ssa u Sho Ann'istarak*," she said in a tongue Noah didn't know. "*The Princess and the Anrok*," she translated. "Thirty thousand years old."

"You speak Ba'siri?" he asked. She nodded. "And your English is perfect. How many languages do you know?"

Kyra blushed briefly.

"Twelve," she said, which made Noah's eyes widen. "The Anointed insisted," she continued. "My grandfather made sure my education at the spire was historical, mathematical, scientific, and linguistic, not just spiritual. Though I do not know what I would do with such knowledge were I to live out my days within those stone walls. He said it wouldn't be forever, but at times it was hard to believe him."

Noah scratched his chest again. The top half of his undersuit had been stripped away completely. He found himself a bit embarrassed of the large burn covering most of his now defunct left arm, even though the entire world had been well aware of it since his arrival on Sora. He wasn't sure why he always rejected the offers for advanced skin grafts that could make him whole again. Perhaps because it felt like his last connection to his former homeworld. But now that he'd visited the place himself, maybe that thought was a bit silly. And judging from his injuries, he had a new set of souvenirs from the planet. A large bandage covered a plasma burn near his abdomen.

"What's the book about?" Noah asked, still feeling like he was floating down a river of bathwater.

Kyra brushed her hair back and the glowing words from the scroll lit up her sapphire eyes.

"Princess Elyssandria ruled over a small province called Gith, part of the larger nation of Baelrus. Several of her villages were plagued by a monstrous anrok, a now-extinct reptilian creature the size of a hovercraft. It would break fences, devour livestock, and eventually started to hunt small children who would stray from their parents."

Noah listened intently. He found himself unable to look away from her.

"Elyssandria sent men to meet the creature in battle, but its scales deflected their swords and spears, and its spiked tail inflicted grievous injuries. The beast was impenetrable, and grew larger and stronger. Soon, it was eating soldiers too."

"How did they kill it?" Noah asked. The medication was making this the most gripping story he'd ever heard.

"There was a brave warrior who loved Elyssandria dearly. He went into battle with the anrok with the intent to die."

"What? Why?" Noah asked, furrowing his brow.

"He rode into a fight he knew he could not win, and as the creature sank his fangs into him, the warrior drank a potent poison. The anrok ate him whole, but his insides melted from the slow-acting poison in the warrior's blood. The monster died, and Gith was saved."

Noah scratched again. He was getting sleepy.

"Interesting, but sounds like a children's story."

"It's actually much more complex," Kyra said defensively. "The anrok wasn't really an anrok at all."

"What do you mean?"

"The book is a political allegory for the great coup of Baelrus. Princess Elyssandra's province was being mercilessly taxed by the king, Karduke. He levied taxes on her crops and livestock, and eventually began to enlist her village's children for slave labor. When that wasn't enough, he forcibly conscripted men for his army to fight and die on his behalf."

Noah was silent.

"Gith rebelled, and threw their remaining warriors against the walls of the stone castle at the heart of Baelrus, only be to driven back. It was only when one soldier, a general named Merenes, pretended to defect that the tide was turned. He worked his way into King Karduke's inner circle, and poisoned him with a needle dagger at dinner. The king's guard killed him where he stood, but the forces of Baelrus scattered after the king's death and Elyssandra stormed the castle. On top of the ruins, she established a city named after her daughter, whom she'd conceived with Merenes before his death. Her name was Elyria."

"Elyria was a girl?" Noah asked, finally understanding the origin of Sora's capital city. Kyra nodded.

"Yes, my father used to read me the tale growing up. It wasn't until I was older I knew the historical significance. The Vales always claimed they were descendants of Elyria herself. Before there were elected High Chancellors, their family line used the connection to rule as monarchs in ages past. The claim still served them with the public even during times of democracy. Until recently, of course."

"What about your family?" Noah asked, yawning involuntarily. "With your grandfather as Keeper, I'm sure you have records dating back to the beginning of time."

"Oh, there are too many stories to number," Kyra said. "But sadly, there are no kings or queens or legendary warriors to be found in the Auran line."

"You wouldn't know it by how you were handling yourself down there," Noah said, thinking back to her bravery and stubbornness on the surface. Kyra dimmed.

"I'm tired of being a victim. Why should others die on my behalf? Why is my life worth more than yours? Or your brother's? Or his?" she said, motioning to Finn Stoller.

Noah found it hard to formulate a response, but his thoughts were cut off.

"Oh!" she exclaimed. "There's been a *very* pretty girl who has called about twenty times while you've been asleep." Kyra wore a sly smile.

Noah blinked. Sakai. Of course. Why was his first instinct not to call her after finally having access to comms for the first time in months? He blamed the painkillers.

"Right!" he said. "I just need to—"

Kyra was already standing up and punching keys on her scroll. The book faded and was replaced by a viewscreen. She handed it to Noah. A tone sounded once, twice, and then the blank screen was replaced by Sakai's face.

"Noah!" she cried when she saw him, tears in her eyes. Noah grinned.

"Finally," he said. "I am so, so sorry."

"I heard what Erik did. I'm going to kill him. Are you okay? Why are you in the med bay? No one's telling me anything."

"Ready for a long story?" he asked, and looked up past the scroll. Kyra was already gone.

Sakai listened with breathless silence to Noah's account of the past day, all of which was not to be shared with the general public. In his current state, Lucas was in no shape to be presented to the people of Sora as a resurrected hero, especially not until the full extent of what was done to him during his capture was revealed. As such, his existence would be kept a secret when they returned.

It was dark now in the med bay, and Noah was still weary from the medication.

Five, he thought to himself. *I killed five Xalans. And three men before that.*

Noah couldn't put each death out of his mind. The blood, both red and black, stained his mind's eye. Back at the colony, Noah had chatted with a few of the more relaxed guards. Most were ex-SDI, and they told him that in combat they just thought of the Xalans as bugs. Like pests needing to be exterminated. But Noah couldn't picture them like that, not when he was so close with Alpha, Zeta, and Theta. The Xalans, genetically engineered warriors that they were, had the sentient spark of life that meant it still felt like Noah had killed a person. Five of them yesterday alone. And of course the three Sorans at the spire. He wrestled with the reality of it, and prayed feverishly to the gods for forgiveness. The Tomes of the Forest allowed for killing in defense of the innocent, but Noah still felt sick about it all the same. War had always seemed so glamorous. It wasn't. While he appreciated feeling useful, he was rather horrified by it all now. The Dubai free-way. The rain. It would be in his nightmares for a long while. And that face.

Shit.

He suddenly realized he needed to tell someone about the Corsair. That he was man, not a Xalan. One that was immensely powerful. Did they know already? Had the SDI been keeping it from the public?

Noah pulled himself up and saw a dim light across the room accompanied by a hushed voice. Finn Stoller was awake and speaking into a handheld viewscreen. Noah immediately recognized the voice on the other end.

"You stole our pure-core Shatterstar and raided my armory for a fool's trip to *Earth*?" bellowed a small holograph of Madric Stoller. Noah couldn't see his face from across the room, but it was him all right.

"We rescued Lucas," Finn said. His voice was hoarse, either from fear or his injury. "We killed dozens of Xalans and fought the Corsair."

"You did not know Lucas was there, you imbecile! You followed the Earthborn brat to that planet like a whelp trailing after his master! You and the Xalan pup and that Auran girl! Do you have any idea what the press has been saying the past month? That if I can't keep track of my own son, how am I supposed to be trusted to govern a planet?"

"The mission was a success," Finn protested. "I used my training. I killed a dozen of them before—"

"You did no such thing," Stoller interrupted. "I'm reading the full incident report here and the lot of you were saved by SDI intervention."

"I just—"

"You will *never* be your sister," Stoller continued. "You never had her gift for combat. My money can buy you armor and weapons and ships, but not the will to do what must be done in war."

Noah cringed. He never liked Finn much, but it was hard not to feel bad for him with a father like Madric Stoller.

"I'm sorry, I—" Finn attempted to interject.

"Is this an open channel?" said Stoller.

"I'm just in the med bay. Noah's here, but he's asleep."

"Idiocy," Stoller muttered. "Contact me again on an encrypted line in your private quarters. I may find some use for you yet."

The corner of the room went dark. After waiting for Finn's breathing to settle, Noah pushed himself to his feet and lumbered out of the room. He needed to talk to Asha, if she really was here.

Noah stumbled around the dreadnought aimlessly for a while until an officer pointed him in the direction of the hangar bay. The ship they were in, the *Horizon,* was massive, and by far the biggest vessel he'd ever set foot in. It was amazing that so much firepower had been brought to hunt the Corsair and they still hadn't managed to end him.

The hangar held both the dust-covered Stoller Shatterstar that had been pulled from the sands of Dubai and another sleek craft that was some sort of cross between a fighter and a cruiser. Asha's ship. The arcing lines and dark hull had Alpha's fingerprints all over them, and as Noah approached the ship, he saw an English word painted on the reflective metal.

ALASKA.

An Earth province. Strange. Noah wondered about its significance. Under the letters, a long ramp descended. She knew he was coming.

When Asha heard what Noah had to say, she immediately summoned Lucas, Erik, and Theta to the bridge of her ship. Erik's decimated hand was now fully bandaged, but Theta didn't look any worse for wear, which pleased Noah. Lucas, however, looked feverish, and was clearly struggling to concentrate.

"And you saw this too?" Asha asked Erik. "It was a man?"

Erik lay sprawled out in the captain's chair, gazing out the viewscreen toward the hangar bay doors.

"I saw a shape, then it knocked me off the overpass," Erik said.

"It was dark," Noah chimed in. "Erik didn't have a chance to get a good look. But I was inches away. You have to believe me."

It turns out the SDI had been keeping no such secrets about a non-Xalan Shadow. This was the first time an eyewitness to the Corsair's destruction had survived.

"I do," Asha said. "But this should be impossible. Shouldn't it?" She turned to Theta, who looked startled she was being addressed.

"The experimental data suggests that all subjects failed the transformation process, and only Lucas was progressing as expected. The GSE theorizes that humans, not Sorans, may have some genetic component that allows the conversion to work. Though as Lucas is the only human they have had access to, it is still just a hypothesis."

"But nothing about another successful conversion?" Lucas asked. He was shivering profusely under a pair of thermal blankets and looked like he was about to pass out. Theta scrolled through readouts.

"No, but I still have yet to decrypt much of the data from the laboratory. I have forwarded it to my mother and father, which should hopefully speed up the process. Perhaps they managed to successfully convert a Soran after all. Or perhaps they located another human somehow."

"This changes nothing," Asha said. "He's still dangerous, and obviously working for the Xalans whether he's a man or not. We've never seen psionic power like that before, not even from the Council Shadows. He's devastating our aid fleets with a single ship and a skeleton crew."

Erik spun around in the captain's chair to address the group clustered around the holotable. He picked at his bandage.

"What about what he said?" he asked. "What was it again?"

"'I serve the Archon. I hunt the Soran traitors,'" Noah recited. He'd never forget the chilling multitude of voices that rose up from the man, nor what he'd said.

"'Soran traitors' is an odd phrase," Theta said. "Xala may thirst for the blood of Sora, but it was the early Xalans who betrayed their masters all those years ago. While there are many slurs and hostile phrases aimed at Sorans in our culture, I have not heard that specific one."

"And the Archon?" Noah asked. "What is that?"

There were blank stares all around.

"I have never come across the term," Theta said.

"There's no SDI intelligence on it," said Asha. "I've already run it through every database in existence."

"Is it an individual? A group?" Noah pressed.

The room was silent, but then Lucas spoke.

"It's a god," he said quietly. "The god of the Shadows."

12

Lucas blinked. He found himself in an almost pure white room, and his pupils shrank painfully as the light flooded them. His head swam, and he couldn't put together where he was, seeing only smooth walls and floors around him. It was hard to discern where the room's light source was coming from. Every surface seemed to glow.

He looked down at his body and found black veins and bandages. A voice boomed throughout the room, causing him to jump even while seated on the ground.

"Rise!"

Lucas looked around but couldn't place where the voice had come from. It bounced around the walls and floor and ceiling. Or was it echoing throughout his skull instead? He pulled himself unsteadily to his feet as the disembodied voice had commanded him.

A strange dream, he thought to himself. His eyes were bleary from the searing whiteness of the room. He nearly toppled over, but braced himself against the wall. The room was little more than a small cube.

"Where am—" he tried to form words, but his voice was so hoarse, they came out as a cracked whisper. The voice ignored his attempts at speech and hissed another command inside his head.

"Observe."

The wall opposite Lucas slid down, revealing an identical room directly across from his own. The white walls were marred by a black shape in the corner. As Lucas's eyes adjusted, he realized that it was actually . . . a person?

The figure was huddled in the furthest corner from him, hugging its knees and rocking slowly. Its face was hidden. The shape wore only tatters of fabric, and its skin was charred and black like the remnants of a long-dead fire.

Lucas walked slowly toward the figure, but mashed his arm into an invisible barrier where the wall had been. It felt like glass, but he couldn't see it and he didn't leave handprints on the surface as he pressed himself against it.

"Hey," he called out, his voice still weak. "Are you okay?" he managed to finally get out at something approaching an audible volume.

Lucas could hear weeping. The figure lifted its head, but lowered it back down quickly. It was long enough for Lucas to see that it was a woman, though her features were distorted. She had one sky blue eye while the other was a mess of inflamed red and murky brown. Only a few patches of pink skin could be seen among the black.

His bangs on the invisible barrier attracted no further reaction.

I want to wake up, he thought. Lucas had no tolerance for unsettling dreams and had endured far too many over the past few years.

The woman's wailing started to grow louder. The barrier seemed to amplify it in Lucas's own cell, rather than deflect it.

"Calm down," Lucas said. The woman ignored him. "Calm down!" he shouted, his nerves frayed. There was a small prick of pain inside his head.

Suddenly, the woman was still. The weeping stopped. She raised her blackened face and stared straight ahead, giving Lucas another look at her mismatched eyes and decaying skin. She was naked except for a few bloodied bandages strung around her, and her hair had all fallen out except for a dismal few loose strands. Many of the black patches on her body had a dusty gray tint to them, and the white floor around her was peppered with large flakes of her dead skin. It was like she was disintegrating.

"Good," purred the voice in Lucas's head. He tried to shake it out, but it hurt his neck to do so.

"Why am I here?" Lucas shouted at the ceiling, which seemed like the most logical place to direct the question for some reason.

"The creature suffers," the voice said, finally uttering more than one word at a time. The voice stung like icy wind in his mind. He'd never heard anything like it. Lucas shivered.

"You must end its pain."

The woman was still staring blankly at a point to Lucas's left, her arms still clasped around her legs. But her lips were moving. She was talking to someone. Or herself. Lucas couldn't hear what she was saying.

Suddenly, there was a loud mechanical groan, and Lucas stumbled through the now nonexistent invisible barrier, which had disappeared completely. The woman's head jolted to the right, and she looked into Lucas's eyes, now apparently seeing him for the very first time. Her blue eye was wide and wild, the brown one was permanently fixed on the floor. She tried to get to her feet.

Lucas took one step forward to help her but was immediately rocketed back by an invisible force. He hit the opposite wall with a crash that felt like it shattered half his bones, and after the burst of blinding pain subsided, he found he couldn't move. He was a solid two feet off the ground, his arms and legs pinned to the wall.

The woman reached behind her and pulled out a thin black knife that had apparently been hidden in the corner. She slammed it into wall next to her and swung herself up by the handle. She was rail thin, and it was a miracle she was even able to stand. Her single blue eye burned with rage.

"She has been promised her freedom in exchange for your life," the voice said, almost bemused.

The woman pulled the knife out of the wall and lurched toward him like the walking undead, holding the blade outward in a pair of shaking hands. Her jaw hung open loosely, and Lucas saw only a few yellow teeth poking out of her gums. Each new step left another pile of ashy skin on the ground behind her.

Wake up. Wake up.

Lucas thrashed as much as he could, but every muscle was frozen by an unseen force. He could barely move a millimeter in any direction.

"Fight," the voice commanded.

"How?" Lucas shouted. He found his mouth was the only thing he could still move. His question was met with silence.

He turned toward the woman. The black figure was in his cell now, stepping over the point where the barrier had been. She was dragging one of her feet, which was bent completely the wrong way. She was so emaciated that Lucas could count eleven rows of ribs. *Soran.*

"Stop!" he shouted. "Stop!" The woman stumbled closer.

"*Stop!*" Lucas bellowed. His brain felt like ice.

And the woman did.

She stood there, staring blankly past Lucas again, like she had after she stopped crying. She lowered her arms to her sides and kept them there.

Lucas breathed a sigh of relief. The woman had seen reason, even in her obviously shattered state.

But no. It wasn't right. The woman's face was completely vacant, like the rage that had been there moments ago was simply wiped from her entirely.

Her eye twitched. Then narrowed. Then turned toward Lucas again. The anger was coming back. She staggered three quick paces toward Lucas. She was only a few feet away now. The black edge of the knife was pointed squarely at Lucas with each new step.

Lucas kept yelling. "No, no! Stop! You don't have to—"

Three feet away.

"Drop it, please!"

Two feet.

"Stop!"

One.

Die!

Lucas hadn't said it, but he'd thought it. And that was enough.

The woman's face went blank again. Without hesitation, she turned the knife away from Lucas and plunged it directly into her own throat. She died wordlessly on the floor in a messy black heap as dark blood pooled out onto the white surface around her. Lucas's head was throbbing with cold pain.

"*You have passed the trial,*" the stinging voice said.

Lucas felt his arms and legs spring free, and he dropped to the ground in front of the dead woman. *How had . . . ? He hadn't—*

Before Lucas could process what had just happened, gas began to fill the room though unseen vents, like it was being filtered straight through the walls.

A figure strode in through the mist. Tall, dark, thin. As he drew closer, only one part of him was visible.

Eyes like galaxies.

No pupils, only a hundred thousand stars in a field of black.

"Who are you?" Lucas spat out in between coughs. His head fogged, his vision grew dark as he lay in the swirling smoke.

The voice spoke daggers in his head.

"I am the Archon. I am your destroyer. Your creator. Your god."

Lucas blinked himself awake inside the medical bay. *You know it's true,* an unseen voice said within him.

Not a nightmare, a memory.

Lucas swore he'd spent sixteen years stuck in that tank in Dubai. But now that he'd remembered, the scene was so clear to him. Like someone had just turned on a light in a dark corner of his brain. Even conscious now, he could see the twisted look of horror on the woman's blackened face, another failed experiment by the Xalans. He could hear the voice that pierced like needles in his mind. Each command, each praise.

"Good."

He'd killed the woman, but how? He'd been frozen, paralyzed completely. But he'd wanted her to die, and she had died. At her own hand.

Asha suddenly appeared in his field of view.

"Thank god," she said, visibly relieved. "It's been days."

"W-What happened?" Lucas said weakly. She gave him some water through a straw.

"You had a seizure on my ship. You've been out since."

Lucas hungrily gulped more water.

"The Archon . . ." he said.

Asha cocked her head.

"God of the Shadows? That's the last thing you said before it happened. What was that about?"

And Lucas told her, every detail still fresh and vivid in his mind.

After his seizure, even though he'd regained consciousness, Lucas's condition began to degrade. He was feverish, delirious, and barely acknowledged his visitors, and he couldn't remember who had even been in to see him. He'd forget conversations immediately after they happened, while at the same time being seared with brief flashes of memories from his time as a Xalan experiment at the hands of the ever-mysterious Archon. Lucas could remember nothing else about him, and all the new memories he found were mere fragments, not extended scenes like the ashen woman with the knife. Theta said his mind was attempting to repair the damage that had been done to it, and more and more of his time spent in captivity was starting to make its way to the surface.

Lucas wished he could forget. It had been far better when he simply woke up from a haze sixteen years later with little recollection of what had happened. But the death of the blackened woman made him question what it was that had actually been done to him.

Die.

Not a shout. Not even a whisper. Just a thought.

And she had.

Between constant treatment by Theta and the SDI silvercoats, Lucas was finally feeling better a few days later. He'd managed to squeeze into a fiber undersuit instead of a flowing med bay robe, and he was now walking laps in his own private wing, which had been given to him specifically due to his unique condition. What few other sick and injured there had been moved.

Lucas paced and watched archived Stream feeds of what he'd missed when he was away. He watched Tannon Vale plead the case for his innocence after his sister's assassination at the hands of Hex Tulwar. He watched his own statue erected on the Elyrian promenade across from Mars Maston's. He saw Madric Stoller win a landslide election and crush resistance groups to "secure the homeworld." He saw a virtual tour of Erik and Noah's home of Colony One, and the multicultural menagerie that was the new generation of Earthborn, and the last humans in existence. Often he'd get overwhelmed; it was almost too much to take in.

Lucas tossed down the scroll he'd been using for the past few hours and lay back on his bed, holding his hands to his head. The feed played audio of an old news report broadcasting word of the Black Corsair's decimation of an entire SDI dreadnought and the caravan of supply ships it was supposed to be escorting. Lucas saw the bright blue eye and the dead brown one of the burned woman in his head. Was there really another soul who had survived the process? Who had been granted all the abilities of the most powerful of the Chosen Shadows? Lucas muted the audio with a gesture and closed his eyes tightly as if it would cure his migraine.

When he opened them, the breath was sucked from his lungs. A figure stood in the doorway of the dimly lit med bay.

The man was large, too large. Larger than any man should be. He had long blond hair and a sprawling beard of a similar hue. His small blue eyes sparkled brightly underneath all the hair, and he wore scraps of metal armor mixed with cloth rags.

No. You're dead.

The cannibal chief dwarfed the room around him. Lucas scrambled out of bed and crouched as the man made his way toward him. When he spoke, his voice boomed throughout the room. Lucas couldn't understand what he was shouting.

"*Lucas!*" he bellowed. "*Er du godt?*"

What sort of ghost was this, haunting him from beyond the grave? While the last vision might have been a memory, this one was certainly a dream.

"*Er du godt?*" the chief asked again. Each step made the entire room shake.

"Get away from me!" Lucas said, scrambling backwards and tripping over a nearby chair.

What was he saying? Lucas didn't speak Norwegian, and only Alpha had been able to translate the man's dying words at Kvaløya.

"*Hva er det du ser?*" the man asked, continuing to march toward Lucas. He pointed at the scroll playing on the bed nearby. It had shifted to a new story, one that showed Noah at some state event.

Noah.

"No!" Lucas shouted. "You can't have him. You can't have Noah. He's mine!"

"Lucas, *roe ned*," the man growled.

"You were a monster," Lucas spat at him. "A murderer, a rapist, a cannibal. The worst of us."

Lucas looked down and found that he was suddenly at the opposite end of the room. The chief look surprised, and lumbered around to face him. His arms were extended and he was crouched liked a wrestler about to pounce.

"He's *my* son, not yours. You deserved to die in that desert, and he deserved to live," Lucas continued.

The cannibal chief was finally close enough to Lucas to grab his arm. Lucas felt like every bone his in forearm was snapping. He wrenched his arm upward which, much to his surprise, lifted the chief from his feet and slammed him into the ceiling, shattering the lights and sending a shower of sparks down to dance on the metal floor.

The man landed on his knees, and Lucas thrust his palm forward into his chest. The chief soared across the room and crashed into a workstation. Electrical pops gave way to blue flames, and almost immediately water began to shower the room.

The chief picked himself up, and with a loud roar, sprinted toward Lucas, his wet, wild hair matted like a drenched lion. In an instant, Lucas inexplicably found himself on the other side of the man, and drove his elbow into his back. The giant flew forward thirty feet and dented the metal fire door, which had slammed shut. He lay still as water and blood pooled around him.

I won, Lucas thought. *Time to wake up.*

But he didn't. Lucas plodded through the floor of water as more rained down from the rafters. When he reached the man, he found that the giant was smaller than he initially thought. Turning him over, his mane of hair and beard were gone. It wasn't the chief. This wasn't a dream.

Noah.

The room was suddenly illuminated by blue flashes of light. The stun rounds slammed into Lucas, and whirling around he saw the lights of a half dozen rifles in the doorway. The SDI soldiers moved in as he crumpled to the ground.

Noah wasn't moving and soon, neither was Lucas.

13

A few hours later, a bandaged Noah sat in the observation deck of the SDI *Horizon*. There was nothing to see other than the wispy streams of space and time that made up the ethereal fabric of the wormhole, but it was hypnotizing.

It was hard to shake what had happened in the med bay, for many reasons.

Noah rubbed his head, the back of which was one giant lump. The way Lucas had moved was unreal. His strength was astonishing. The crew had marveled at the security loops of the incident, watching Lucas dash in and out of frame at blinding speeds and toss the sturdy Noah around like a doll. But it had been ten times as terrifying in person. Mercifully, Noah had escaped with only a quickly healed concussion and a smattering of bruises as large as dinner plates. The SDI had taken Lucas down, and even Asha had to agree that he needed to be kept unconscious for the remainder of the voyage home, which was only another month or so.

He'd long heard tales of the combat prowess of the Shadows, but it was surreal to think his own father had become one himself. What the hell had they rescued from Dubai? It sure didn't seem like a man. Lucas was indeed a weapon, as Erik had tried to tell him, and Noah would be surprised if they ever woke him up again.

But somehow, that wasn't what affected Noah the most. Rather, it was who Lucas had *thought* he was. After he peppered Asha with endless questions she eventually unleashed the entire story on him. Noah hadn't simply been found in some ruined city and given to the pair of them by a dying mother. He was the son of a monstrous cannibal chief who had risen to power by murdering and raping anyone who opposed him. Truth was, Lucas and Asha never even met Noah's mother; she'd died in a fire they caused that consumed a slave pen housed inside a church. Lucas had killed Noah's father personally after escaping capture by his savage tribe. Asha ended the tale with the note that the chief had once been a schoolteacher before the war, as if that was supposed to help.

Despite having begged to know the truth, it was something Noah wished he could forget. He was furious at them for lying to him all these years. What else had they kept from him?

Noah didn't know what to make of being the son of one of the last tyrannical warlords of Earth. It explained his size, certainly, but what else? Would he someday grow into a monster as well?

"You won't," Kyra said after he unloaded the foremost question he had been struggling with since the revelation.

"It doesn't matter who you were born to," she continued. "It matters how you were raised. Your *real* parents are Lucas and Asha, intergalactic heroes. You were raised by the finest minds of Sora with dozens of charming Earthborn."

"But what if I go mad like him?" Noah asked.

"From what you're telling me, this man was perfectly normal before your Xalan war. An intelligent teacher. The conflict and destruction drove him to insanity, as it did so many others on your planet. It was circumstance, not genetics."

"They lied to me," Noah said through gritted teeth.

"Would you not have done the same?" Kyra asked, putting a hand on his shoulder. Her touch was electric, and jolted Noah out of his fury.

She was right, and he hated it. Still, in a few mere sentences, she'd made him feel worlds better. An impressive talent.

Noah stayed in the observation deck for another hour or so before he found his chin dropping to his chest involuntarily. To avoid passing out on the floor from exhaustion, he stumbled to the lift, which brought him to the crew quarters level that had been reserved for the intrepid Earth explorers. The other four doors were closed; Erik and the others had likely gone to sleep long ago. Noah resisted the urge to tap on Kyra's door, only a few down from his own. What did he want? To talk more? *That's not why,* whispered a voice in his head.

Noah shook off the thought. He had Sakai. Gorgeous, loving, generous, kind Sakai. And he was lucky for it. But Kyra. There was a draw to her he couldn't explain. She was magnetic, and he felt like he couldn't pull himself away from her whenever they spoke. It was more than nostalgia for times spent together as children. It went far beyond that.

Still, Noah passed by her room, and drove such thoughts from his mind.

Until a scream. And a crash.

Noah jerked his hand away from his room's door controls and turned down the hall. It was her room. Metal struck more metal. A muffled shout.

As Noah sprinted toward her door, a shirtless Erik spilled out of his room, obviously confused. He instinctively followed Noah another two doors over and mashed on the controls to her room. Angry red symbols flashed; the door was locked tight. There were sounds of a struggle inside.

Noah's first instinct after finding the door locked was to kick it as hard as he possibly could with his metal-soled boot. The door scuffed, then bent, but wouldn't budge further even after repeated strikes. It was meant to function as an airlock in an emergency, after all.

Meanwhile, Erik was sifting through the back-end system menu of the door's controls and, by Noah's fourth kick, the red light had turned green. The door rocketed upward but caught where Noah's foot had dented it inward. The two ducked under the jammed door and stumbled inside.

Kyra lay prostrate on the ground, a short syringe sticking out of her bare shoulder. Above her stood a slim figure in a stealth suit with a faceless mask who turned when he heard them enter.

Noah lunged first, but he felt his whole body convulse when the figure's forearm connected with his hand. An electrical jolt numbed his entire body and he crumpled to the ground as the figure sprinted by. The assailant ducked under a clothesline from Erik and jabbed him in the back of the leg with the electric weapon as he passed and fled out the half-open door.

Noah got to his feet and sprinted to Kyra. Erik turned and bolted out the door after the fleeing figure.

Cradling her head in his hands, Noah saw she was still conscious. A red mark on her temple indicated she'd likely struck her head. Noah looked nervously down at the vial in her arm and saw it was empty. Plucking it out, he turned it over in his hand. Whatever it had contained was already flowing through her bloodstream. *Poison.* It had to be. His heart hammered in his chest, but she wasn't convulsing, wasn't foaming at the mouth. A straight shot of something like niacyne could have killed her instantaneously, but she wasn't dead. Kyra started to speak.

"There was a noise," she said, blinking. "I woke up. I screamed. I tried to fight him. He stabbed me with something." She rubbed her arm and smeared a tiny bead of blood where the needle had been. She looked horrified when she saw the vial in Noah's hand.

"What . . . what is that?" Noah could hear her breathing constrict and quicken. "What did they do to me?"

"Can you stand?" Noah asked, having no useful answers, trying to hide the fear in his voice. He was sweating profusely and felt sick. An assassin? On the ship? In the middle of a wormhole? It was impossible.

Kyra slowly rose to her feet, and Noah saw Theta poke her head in through the doorway.

"Is everything . . . oh my," she said as she saw the destruction in the room.

Noah walked Kyra over to her and planted the empty vial in Theta's claw.

"I need you to analyze what was in this, immediately," he said as calmly as he could manage. "We have to get Kyra to the med bay as fast as possible." Noah slammed his hand on the nearby alarm control on the wall, but the unit had been deactivated. He looked down to find he wasn't wearing his communicator.

His attention was distracted by a scuffle at the end of the hall. From a distance, he could see that Erik had miraculously caught the assailant and was pummeling him on the ground through his armor with a nearby fire evaporator.

"Take her," Noah shouted to Theta. "Now!"

If anyone knew what was in the vial, it was the would-be murderer. How had Erik caught him so easily? Theta took Kyra to the lift and Noah ran toward his brother and the downed black figure.

Erik was bleeding from some sort of wound buried in his scalp and was breathing hard. He was still bare-chested, wearing only a pair of cloth pants, and Noah couldn't fathom how he'd managed to over-power a hitman in armor plating.

"Get him inside," Noah hissed, and Erik rose and grabbed the unmoving figure by the collar. Noah took one of his arms and they dragged him into the closest room, Noah's own. As soon as they were inside, Noah swirled his hand through the holographic lock, sealing them in. He pressed his own alarm panel, which began to broadcast a dull wail throughout the ship. The SDI would be there soon; there wasn't any time to waste.

They set to stripping the assailant of his armor, naturally starting with the most pressing piece, the helmet. Erik ripped off the blank visor and the fury in his face faded to disbelief.

Finn Stoller.

Noah's brain almost shut down on the spot. It didn't make any sense. *How? Why?*

Finn blinked. He was coming around. Erik and Noah shook off their shock and began stripping his plating off to ensure he wasn't concealing any more weapons. They scattered the pieces across the room behind them until Finn was left wearing nearly nothing. His face was already starting to swell where Erik had bashed him through the mask. Finn tried to sit up. Erik finally found his voice.

"Tie him up."

Noah ripped the top sheet from his bed and tore it into strips. He hauled Finn onto his desk chair and wrapped one strip tightly around his chest and the other across his thighs, pinning his arms and legs. It wasn't perfect, but it would be enough to hold Finn, who looked even scrawnier than usual when entirely stripped of clothes and armor.

"Wake. Up," Erik barked, his words punctuated by hard slaps across his friend's face. Finn's head rolled around on his chest for a few seconds, but he soon opened his eyes. His right one was red and inflamed, and the socket was already starting to bruise.

"What did you inject her with?" Noah asked, a question more pressing than how or why.

"*Tell me!*" he shouted when Finn simply scowled at him in reply.

Noah was surprised when Erik turned and stormed out of the room, but grew panicked when he came back and Noah saw what was in his hand.

"Whoa, whoa, whoa," Noah said, putting his hand to Erik's shoulder to stop him from walking toward the restrained Finn. His brother pushed past him and jammed the vertical lip of his laser pistol directly into Finn's chest.

"I am not messing around," Erik growled. "If you don't tell me what was in that vial in the next three seconds, I will carve your heart out."

Finn stared into Erik's eyes. The shock of his alleged friend being underneath the helmet had been replaced by pure rage once more. Erik's threat wasn't idle, Noah knew that, but he was frozen, wanting answers just as badly. He made no moves to stop Erik.

"One."

The alarm continued to drone outside.

"Two."

Finn's bare foot tapped nervously on the cold metal floor.

"Three."

The gun's power coils began to glow.

"No!" Noah finally shouted and lunged toward his brother.

"Alright, alright!" Finn shouted, tears streaming from his face.

Both Noah and Erik retreated a step. Erik kept the pistol trained on him.

"It's just phenexlorine," Finn said. "It was just supposed to make her . . . receptive."

Erik's eyebrows furrowed.

"Receptive to what?" Noah asked coldly.

"To . . . to me," Finn said, finally starting to catch his breath. "Have you seen that girl? I've been to a thousand parties in a hundred cities full of Sora's most beautiful women, and I've never seen anyone like her. I had to have her."

Erik remained silent, pulsing with anger.

"You were going to . . . rape her?" Noah said through gritted teeth, spitting out the last two words with disdain.

"I had to have her," Finn repeated. "No one was supposed to know. She wouldn't have remembered. Don't tell me you've never thought about it."

Every vein in Noah's body was throbbing. His hands shook as he raised them and took a step toward Finn.

"No," Erik finally said. "He's lying."

Noah stopped to look at his brother, who subsequently pulled the trigger on the laser pistol.

It didn't cut out his heart, but the gold beam exploded out of the gun and sheared off the better part of Finn Stoller's left ear. The laser tore into the opposite end of the room and sawed the door of Noah's dresser in half.

Finn screamed and thrashed violently from side to side, the left half of his face black with bits of his ear sizzling on the ground. The beam had sealed the wound instantly so there was little blood, but smoke rose from the charred patch and Finn's cries were deafening.

"*What was in the vial!*" Erik shouted, the coils on the gun heating up once more.

"It's a . . . it's a . . ." Finn stammered. He couldn't get the words out fast enough now. "It's a compound of fenephrine, sian extract, and mursotoxis," he finally got out.

"What does it really do?" Noah asked sternly, worried about the true answer after Finn had used attempted rape as a cover story.

"She'll die from a brain aneurysm in three days."

Noah grabbed his neck and Erik pressed the gun to his head.

"Wait, wait, wait!" Finn choked out. "I have the antidote. It's in my armor over there," he said, nodding toward a piece of plating that used to be attached to his forearm. "In case something went wrong or there was a change of orders."

Noah didn't understand, but he immediately yelled into the comm unit he'd grabbed off his desk.

"Theta, bring Kyra back up here now, we have the antidote."

Theta's metallic voice rang back to him.

"I have identified the compound, it is a—"

Noah cut her off.

"We know what it is, get her up here *now!*" he bellowed.

Noah turned back to Finn. "Orders? What orders? From who?"

"Isn't it obvious?" Erik said, lowering the gun from Finn's forehead. "His father."

Finn was beginning to sob now.

"I just wanted to show him I could . . . that I could . . ." but he trailed off and stared at the floor before finishing the thought.

Madric Stoller was trying to kill Kyra Auran? Why? And *he'd* sent the assassins at the spire?

"Talk," Noah said. "Now."

Finn was broken, and didn't need any more prodding from the barrel of the gun.

"It was supposed to be quiet, painless, and untraceable," he sniffed. "His agents told me where to find the stealth suit in the armory and how to mix the compounds. I was so careful. I disabled the cameras, the alarms. But the suit was too big. I tripped. She woke up, and it all went to shit."

"We don't care about your failed adventures as an assassin of teenage girls," Erik said. "Why the hell is your father trying to kill Kyra?"

"You really don't know, do you?" Finn said, smiling now through his tears.

At that moment, there was a knock on the door. Noah peered out and saw Theta and Kyra. He unlocked the controls and ushered them inside. Kyra's blond hair was drenched with sweat and her bright blue eyes were wide with fear. She put her hands to her mouth when she saw who was tied to the chair.

"Finn!" she gasped. It took her a moment, but she understood. She turned to Noah. "W-what? Why?"

Noah handed Theta a small vial of orange liquid Erik had pulled from Finn's armor. "Scan that," he said. "Make sure it's safe."

Metal boots could be heard stomping down the corridor. The SDI were coming. Noah turned back to Finn.

"Yes, why?" Noah pressed. "Why does your father want to kill her?"

Finn actually laughed now. The spot where his ear had once been was still smoking.

"How can you be so blind? How can you really not see it?" he said with an unstable smile. "She's *Corinthia Vale*, you fools!"

Noah shared a confused look with Kyra as Finn dissolved into a fit of hysterical laughter.

Kyra was slowly shaking her head, not understanding, but Noah kept staring at her. Closely. Like he was seeing her for the first time. That unmatched beauty. That magnetic pull. That laugh. That smile. He'd seen it a hundred times on archive feeds, and a hundred times more over the past few months. Standing before him was a younger, blue-eyed version of the woman once called the Soul of Sora.

Oh gods, it's true. How is it true?

14

"What is power?" the Archon purred, shielded by shadow in the darkest corner of the Dubai hotel room. "It is not the clenched fist or the ripping claw. It is not the cleaving sword or crushing hammer. It is not the burning shot or the explosive warhead. Power is control.

"These objects are *used* for control, but they are not control. True power lies not in forced action, a soul prodded toward their own demise with the whip or spear. True power is to march the soul wherever you so choose, and make them believe it was their own idea.

"This was the ruin of the old world. And it will be the ruin of your own as well. The Xalans believe they fight for sovereignty. For water. For honor. But they fight for the Archon, and always have. Their power lies in claws and guns and ships and bombs, but it is merely an illusion, gifts given to forever blind them. They march willingly toward your Sora, dying in droves for a cause that does not exist. For a future they will never see. Destruction is their sole purpose. They are an engineered plague designed for one use: your extinction. The old world must not rise again.

"This is how one destroys a civilization of billions. Not riding on a golden chariot through the streets. Not on the bridge of a shining warship. But lurking in the shadows, pulling a string here so a planet dies there. It is the only way.

"Silence is power. It allows stories and myth and legend to fill the air where previously there were none. Silence is a mystery, and can drive men mad through both its presence and absence.

"Patience is power, though few realize it. Patience is not a lack of action, but the intelligence to wait for the proper moment. It waits on the right time to act, for the right reasons, in the right way.

"But I fear time is running out. Immortality is a lie. We all perish someday, and time is relative. My days are your centuries. I must find the rest, and Sora holds the key. I required acceleration.

"The dark ones are valuable, but still weak. They are pale reflections of me, of my power. It is how they found their name, these 'Shadows' to my flame. Not for their color, but for their true nature. And if these *humans*, these *Sorans* could kill them, despite inferior biology? Perhaps I focused on the wrong race.

"Your counterpart is a useful weapon, devastating fleets on a whim on his imagined quest for vengeance, but he merely improves upon existing constructs. You. You are a new creation. Earth's human strain proves invaluable. Pity there are so few left. You will do what I have not been able to in twenty thousand years. You will bring Sora to its knees, and with it, purge the galaxy of the rest of your kind. And you will do so as if it were your own idea. I will find what drives you, and I will use it to make you laugh as you destroy everyone you love.

"I tell this to you because I am alone in this world. In all these worlds. Though you will not remember, and I merely speak with myself, as I always have."

But Lucas did remember, his brain knitting itself back together to find the words of the lost one-sided conversation as he lay in cold, forced unconsciousness on the *Horizon*. He strained to make sense of what it all meant.

15

A deal was struck.

When the SDI burst into Noah's room that night, they didn't find would-be assassin Finn Stoller tortured and bound to a chair. They found stupid rich prat Finn Stoller lying on the ground, rolling around in agony after accidentally shooting his own ear off messing with an overpriced laser pistol.

Nothing good could come of attempting to explain what had happened and handing Finn over to "authorities" that could very well be in his father's pocket. It was even less of a viable plan to kill him where he stood, though it was certainly what he deserved after his attempt on Kyra's life. The first option would let High Chancellor Stoller know they were onto him and accomplish nothing; the second would bring the full wrath of his government down on all of them, not just Kyra.

The deal they made was this. Finn Stoller would contact his father and tell him he was refusing his order to murder an innocent teenage girl on "moral grounds." Madric Stoller would curse and yell at his good-for-nothing son, but it was plausible enough to be believed. When they reached Sora, they'd release Finn to return to his father on the condition that he'd be their contact inside the Stoller administration for when it was finally time for Madric to face justice. In return, they wouldn't tell the High Chancellor that Finn had not only failed in the assassination attempt, but had been a fountain of information about the misdeeds of his father during his capture thereafter. Also, they wouldn't lop off any more of his body parts before they sent him on his way. It was a deal he was eager to take.

The only one they could trust with all this other than those who had been present was Asha, and she agreed it was not wise for the lot of them to be turned into fugitives for the second time since their arrival on Sora. In fact, most of the deal was her idea.

But there were still a few weeks to go until they reached home, and they couldn't very well lock Finn up in his room around the clock without drawing suspicion. They also couldn't let Kyra be alone at any point, given that they were on a ship full of SDI soldiers who took their paychecks from Stoller. They were Asha's unit, but even she admitted it would be foolish to say she trusted all of them wholeheartedly. She barely knew more than a few dozen of their names out of hundreds, even after being paired with the two support dreadnoughts for well over a year hunting the Corsair.

So they devised a system. Noah and Erik would alternate keeping watch over Kyra and Finn day and night. One needed protection, the other needed to be on a leash. Each night, one of the brothers would sleep on the floor in Kyra's room while the other kicked Finn out of his bed and forced him to sleep chained to his own furniture, propped up against the wood and metal. Despite the hard floor versus the comfy bed, Kyra was always the optimal assignment. Tonight, Noah was the lucky one.

The metal ground was cold, even through the blanket underneath him. The room was dark except for the ambient blue glow of the clock hologram projecting out of the opposite wall. Distant clunks of boots could be heard a floor or two below. Noah checked the readouts on the pistol he kept beneath his pillow each night. His warhammer leaned against the wall a few feet away.

Kyra was silent, but awake. Noah could sense it, even if he couldn't see her up on her bed. Finn's attempt on her life had thrown her deeper down an emotional well, that much was clear. But it wasn't because it was some great betrayal by a friend; she had barely known him. Nor was it the fact that she'd almost died; that had already happened more than a few times in her life. Rather, it was because of what he'd said.

"How can you really not see it? She's Corinthia Vale, you fools!"

Finn didn't have proof of his claim, but Kyra herself was evidence enough. She was the spitting image of the dead Vale, at least a younger version lacking Corinthia's famed prismatic eyes. The original Corinthia Vale was bred to be a leader with a genetic price tag in the trillions. Finn said that when his father discovered this new, impossible version of her living in the care of the palace Keeper's family, he saw her as a future political threat to him. This was assuming she was anything like her predecessor, one of the most eloquent, beloved, intelligent individuals on the planet. Not to mention she was beautiful enough to start wars. This was the dark side of Stoller's push to hold onto power. Yes, he'd eliminated violent antigovernment groups like the Fourth Order, but to deem a 108-pound girl like Kyra Auran an equal threat? The man was insane. But he was a problem for another day.

So who *was* Kyra? That was the ultimate question. Theta helpfully suggested she might be a secret child of Talis Vale—Corinthia's little sister no one had known existed. But there was another answer. A more likely one. It was possible Kyra was something else entirely, a word no one dared say in her presence.

Clone.

Despite genetic modification being the norm all over Sora, cloning was highly illegal and, most of the population agreed, horribly immoral.

There were all sorts of rumors about clones, and it was hard to tell fact from legend. Cloning labs had all been razed to the ground years ago by the extremely religious Chancellor Hallarian, who believed cloning the living would split the person's soul in half, and cloning the dead would mean they lacked one altogether. Medical complications with cloning were vague, and most of those records had been destroyed, Theta had told Noah privately. But there were whispers clones would go mad with age, spread deathly diseases, or produce mutated children.

Furthermore, they weren't able to contact Kyra's grandfather, Keeper Malorious Auran, for an explanation about any of this. He'd mysteriously gone missing, which only made the situation worse.

They didn't talk about clones with Kyra.

"Are you awake?" Kyra finally said in the darkness. Noah's eyes sprang open from drifting shut after hours of staring at the ceiling.

"Yeah," he replied, his voice hoarse. He rolled sideways on the ground toward the bed, but she was still hidden from view.

"Can't sleep again," she said. Noah didn't ask why. He knew.

"We'll be home soon," Noah said.

"Don't have a home," Kyra replied quietly.

"You can stay at Colony One. If you haven't noticed, we've got plenty of room."

Kyra was quiet, considering or ignoring the offer, he couldn't be sure. She changed the subject.

"Know any good stories?" she asked.

Noah considered that.

"None with warriors and beasts and brilliant political allegory," he said.

"I've heard enough of those," she said. "Tell me an Earth story."

An Earth story? That threw Noah. Though it was technically his home planet, he hadn't been raised there. What he knew of Earth he had found in the archives and through Alpha's compiled data. Most of the fictional tomes he'd come across were vast and complex.

"You know," he finally said, sitting up so he could see Kyra curled up on her bed, her eyes reflecting the dim blue light of the clock. "I did come across one a few years ago in the Earth Archives. It was a thin paper book, one that had pictures on every page."

"A children's scroll?" Kyra asked.

"I don't think so. I'm pretty sure it was some sort of illustrated Earth fable."

"How does it go?"

Noah closed his eyes and tried to picture the pages. The ink had been blurred and smeared, the pages crusty and decaying, but he'd read it through many times all the same.

"There was a child on a distant planet. His civilization was in turmoil in the midst of a civil war. The world's core had grown unstable, and was tearing the planet apart. It was dying."

Kyra lay her chin down on her arms to look at Noah as he continued.

"His parents were his planet's greatest scientists, so they put him in a ship and pointed it toward Earth. His world was destroyed shortly after, and he was the last of his kind."

Noah tried to remember what happened next.

"An Earth family found him and took him in. They found their sun gave him powers beyond those of any human. He could fly, he could fight, he could save those no one else could. He was a god among mortals.

"He defended Earth from threats both from within and without, domestic and alien. Powerful foes who would kill for profit or power or no reason at all. He had many friends, some with powers like him. He loved a girl, a reporter. He could never be hurt, could never age. He was Earth's sentinel for all of time."

Noah stopped. The silence hung there. Finally Kyra pressed him.

"So what happened to him?"

Noah shook his head.

"I don't know. I think there are more books out there chronicling his tales. More colorful pages. It's too bad he was just a myth. He might have saved Earth from the Xalans."

"Oh I don't know," Kyra said. Noah could feel her smile even in the darkness. "I think he sounds a lot like someone I know."

"How so?" Noah asked.

"The last son of a dead planet. A strong warrior trying to defend those he loves in his adopted world."

Noah fell silent, considering the parallel for the first time.

"I'd certainly be better at it if I could fly," he smirked.

Kyra laughed and rolled back into bed out of sight. It was good to hear her laugh again. It had been too long. The sound of it made him ache.

"Who was the woman? The one he loved?" she asked.

"Just a woman. A human."

"She had to be something special to win the affection of a god."

"She was pretty in the pages. And always knew just what to say to him. But a life with her was always just out of his reach."

"I hope they ended up together," Kyra said, yawning.

"I'm sure they did," Noah replied, lying back down on the floor. Sleep soon found both of them.

Noah flew in his dreams.

The next day, Noah wasn't so fortunate. He now had day duty with Finn, meaning he was attached to him at the hip for meals, which were usually the only times they'd let him out of his room. His father hadn't tried to contact him again after Finn "refused" his mission, but the boy was in better spirits after realizing he wasn't going to be thrown out an airlock.

Noah and Finn were seated near the door in the mess. They were joined by Asha, who had recently made a habit of scraping up any remaining dirt Finn could dish out about his father.

"It's funny," he said. "You all hating him so much. He actually loves you." He nodded toward Asha. "He's practically obsessed. It's like you're the second coming of Corinthia Vale or something."

Noah and Asha glared at him.

"Too soon?" he asked, stuffing half a precisely cut sandwich in his mouth. He scratched the bandage on the side of his head. They'd already been able to grow him a new ear onboard. Ears were one of the easiest body parts to synthetically reproduce, Noah had learned. Lucky for Finn. Erik's replacement fingers weren't yet ready for attachment.

"Anyway," Finn continued, "after Lucas died and he became High Chancellor, he actually had a plan to marry you."

That made Asha choke on her bite of paleplant salad.

"He . . . *what?*"

"Yeah. Said you'd be great to show off at events, not to mention the whole 'joining two worlds' thing that the public would eat up."

Noah eyed Asha's fists, which were clenched so hard her knuckles were white.

"But then you sort of went crazy, and he decided to send you off to kill some Xalans instead. I think he realized you'd make a better soldier than lady of the house."

Noah had to stifle a chuckle at the thought of his mother married to Madric Stoller. A union like that would have lasted from the time they were joined to a few hours later when Stoller tried to lay hands on her and she sliced them off.

"I don't care about your father's pathetic crush," Asha growled.

"Did you know," Finn continued, grinning mischievously, "that he had a full-res holographic sim model commissioned of you? You should see the amazing detail from every angle—"

Finn cried out as the metal tip of Asha's boot dug into his calf under the table.

"Enough," she said in a violent whisper. "Tell me something I actually want to know."

Finn's face was contorted in pain. He'd involuntarily crushed a biscuit with his hand.

"Fine," he said, grimacing. "I'll tell you that despite his affections, he's going to be excited for your boyfriend to show up on Sora again. With those powers? He's going to think he's found the answer to his little war problem."

"Lucas is in no shape to fight," Noah said. He spotted Erik and Kyra entering from the opposite end of the room and watched as they sat down at a table far from them. Kyra glanced nervously at Finn from a distance. Even if they were keeping up appearances, there was no way they were letting him within a hundred feet of her again.

"Maybe not, but my father will want that science for his own. He's been trying to run his own experiments with Soran Shadow mutation. Or something like it."

That caught their attention.

"What?" Asha exclaimed.

Finn waved them off.

"Don't worry, I said he's *trying*, not succeeding. His team is horribly inept. All they've managed to do is liquefy a few street urchin 'volunteers' in the process. They're nowhere close to having the Xalan science right, and he's smart enough to know that if he tried to bring your Alpha in, the creature would stop building his warship cores or worse out of protest."

Noah had never liked Madric Stoller, but every day he grew to want him dead even more. First the treachery of Talis Vale and now this monster? Sora deserved better. It would be miracle if the planet survived with that sort of leadership.

Noah looked over at Kyra, who was covering her mouth, laughing while chewing at something Erik had said. While she lit up the room with her smile, Noah's thoughts were dark.

She's not one of your Earthborn toys or Soran fangirls, Noah thought, but then he caught himself. *They're just talking. Calm down.* What was wrong with him?

Noah waved his hand over his empty rectangular plate, which disappeared with the last remnants of his grilled barfish into the surface of the table.

"Lunch is over," he said, standing up quickly. He circled around and hauled Finn up by the collar more forcefully than he should have in public.

"But I'm not done y—"

Another jerk and Finn agreed to start walking away from his remaining meal.

"It's only a few more days," Asha said as she split off to head up to the bridge. "Try not to kill him."

Noah made no promises.

But then it was over. The core wound down and Asha's miniature fleet found itself back in the Soran system at last. Noah stared out the viewscreen in the observation deck as the planet slowly grew from a pale blue dot to envelop his entire field of vision. Despite their recent journey to Earth, it was Sora that felt like home. The twisted, ruined place where they'd found Lucas was a dead world, even if the air was breathable and the rain didn't melt your skin. Earth was a husk. A ghost of a planet containing nothing but billions of dead and wretched monuments to war and savagery. Savages like his true father.

Noah watched Finn Stoller's private aeroshuttle whisk him away back to Elyria. It was a relief to be free of him, and Noah hoped they never had to see him again.

"He can't be trusted. We should have killed him," Erik said as he approached Noah and stood beside him, watching the shuttle. Noah looked at him. Anger flashed in his bright green eyes. But also something else. Hurt.

"I know he was your friend," Noah said. "It has to be hard to realize he was capable of this."

With Erik and Noah on separate shifts with Kyra and Finn, they hadn't had much chance to talk about the night of the assassination attempt, or Finn's involvement.

Erik waved him off.

"He's dead to me," he said. "I'm just saying he should be dead to everyone else too for what he tried to do."

Erik was talking tough, but Noah could feel the emotion being masked in his voice as the taillights of the shuttle dipped out of view. This was the first glimpse of the heavy toll Finn's betrayal had likely had on his brother, something Noah hadn't really stopped to consider while fretting over Kyra's safety. Erik didn't have many friends, after all, even at the colony.

"You know we couldn't," Noah said. "His father—"

"His father deserves it even more!" Erik hissed. Noah looked around nervously at the SDI officers milling around. Asha was chatting with Kyra behind them.

"Keep your voice down," Noah whispered forcefully. "Stoller will pay."

"She won't be safe until he does," Erik said, looking over at Kyra.

"This is not your responsibility," Noah said, putting his hand on his brother's shoulder. Erik brushed it off.

"Of course it is!" he snapped. "He was my friend, I brought him here! I brought *her* here!"

Noah was taken aback. Erik taking responsibility for actions? Worrying about the safety of others? Erik stole a quick glance at Kyra again.

Oh.

Noah knew that look. He'd caught himself too many times looking at her the same way.

Kyneth save us.

16

The most powerful people on Sora were in a single room, seated around a massive central holotable in the Grand Palace. There were so many maps and charts and readouts and videos playing, it was hard for them to even see each other through the layers upon layers of holograms.

Madric Stoller was front and center of course, flanked on either side by his cabinet, who were little more than a collection of nodding heads whenever he opened his mouth. Then there were his top military officials who were equally as subservient, though Tannon Vale had also been brought back into the fold for this gathering. Aside from Stoller's government entourage, Asha, Alpha, and Zeta were seated next to each other across from the High Chancellor.

And there was Lucas, though he wasn't actually physically in attendance.

He was locked in a cell with allium walls a dozen feet thick all around him. The room they had him in was a mile underneath Alpha's lab at the Merenes Military Base, and he watched the meeting from a holographic viewscreen that took up the entirety of one of the walls. The three-dimensional image was so crisp and lifelike, it was almost like he was physically attending. Almost.

Lucas wasn't a prisoner. Asha had made that clear. But as his Shadow abilities had begun to manifest, there was no way they were ever going to let him in a room with that many important people. Not to mention there was the Archon's promise to use Lucas as a weapon, which Lucas had relayed to the Stoller administration along with the other details of the conversation he'd remembered with the creature that had twisted his genes and kept him locked away for sixteen years. It was the current topic of conversation in the room, and Alpha had led off with the most alarming piece of new information.

"If Lucas is remembering accurately," Alpha said, "this 'Archon' seems to imply that he is not Xalan. That he is manipulating my people for his own ends, guiding their moves from the shadows."

"What do you mean he's not Xalan?" Stoller asked incredulously. "What the hell is he then?"

"You recently learned that you are not alone in the universe with the discovery of Earth, Makari, and the other colony worlds," Zeta said. "Perhaps there is still more to discover."

"Those were planets full of Sorans," a stone-faced female general said.

"He's probably just another experiment gone mad, like that Desecrator," an admiral chimed in.

"How did he not get a good look at this 'Archon' in over sixteen years? How can we trust anything he says at all?" Stoller's right hand, Viceroy Draylin Maston, spoke with venom. He was a pale man with jet-black hair and a thin, listless face that suggested only the impression of handsomeness. He was Mars Maston's cousin, Lucas had learned, but possessed none of the admirable qualities of Lucas's former friend. He was a political viper, figuratively poisoning Stoller's enemies in the eyes of the public, or sometimes literally, if the rumors were true.

"I told you," Lucas said, his mind much clearer and the psychosis that caused him to attack Noah having left him. At least for now. "My memory is still fragmented, rebuilding. But even then, I may never have actually seen him; I was nearly always unconscious, and he often spoke psychically when he wasn't even present. I only saw glimpses of his shape in shadow, which did seem vaguely Xalan. But his eyes. His eyes were—"

"We don't need a sketch of the damned thing," Stoller said, slamming his fist on the table. "We need to find it and kill it. The war is turning! Their fleets are pulling back across all the colony quadrants. We have them on the run!"

For once, Stoller wasn't embellishing. Alpha had relayed the news that Xalan fleets had pulled out of nearly every colony planet system. Intelligence suggested they were drawing back to Xala, but they hadn't shown up there yet. Also strange was that, while a few planets like Makari had fallen to the SDI, some of the others were still being hotly contested when the Xalan fleets abruptly turned tail and fled. It made little tactical sense, but Sora was celebrating and the Xalan resistance and civilians left behind on the other worlds were welcoming the SDI relief fleets with open arms.

"I would caution against an overabundance of optimism," Zeta said. "It is not necessarily the case that the Xalans' decision to leave the colony systems is a sign of surrender. The broadcasts I have intercepted would indicate some larger—"

"Are you a military tactician, Xalan?" Stoller asked. There was at least one snicker from his men.

"I am a communications officer that has led the Resistance to—"

"You are not," Stoller cut her off. "Do not discount the work our forces have done besieging those planets and breaking the spirits of your friends."

Alpha stood up and loomed over everyone in the room at eight feet tall. The metal claws on his prosthetic hand dug into the paneling of the table.

"I will not have you address her in that way," he growled, "whether or not you are ruler of this planet. And to classify the bloodthirsty Xalan armies who butchered my family as 'friends' is outrageous, and I will not tolerate it!"

The room grew loud with arguments from all across the table. Asha suddenly bolted up.

"Hey!" she shouted. The room quieted. "Can we stick to the most pressing matter at hand?" She gestured toward Lucas. "Why haven't you greenlit Lucas for treatment yet? Alpha needs to get to work reversing the Shadow conversion process before it does god knows what to him."

"Reversing?" Stoller said, a glimmer of something dark in his eye. "Oh no, we must *complete* the transformation," he said, turning to Alpha.

"Complete?" Alpha said, stunned. "You are insane as well as ignorant."

"Do you not wish to win the war, Xalan?" Stoller asked with a hard stare.

"Of course," Alpha said, "But Lucas—"

"Lucas is now the most powerful soldier we have. We've been trying to make one like him for years now, but the Xalans have done it for us."

"I have recently learned of your abominable experiments," Alpha growled. "I will not help you continue them on my friend."

"His abilities are not yet under his control," Zeta pleaded. "It is possible he will never be able to harness them."

"But what if he could?" Stoller said, flashing a greedy smile as he looked at the holographic feed of Lucas's cell.

"One super soldier would not make a difference in this war," Tannon Vale said gruffly, finally speaking up. "The Xalans have dozens of Shadows, hundreds even. What can one man do, even an extraordinary one?"

"What can one man do?" Stoller asked with a smile spreading out under his mustache. "I'll show you what one man can do."

Stoller raised his hands and a video stream floated up from the central table, expanding to almost their entire field of vision.

"This footage comes from the decrypted data your own daughter recovered at the Earth genetics lab," he said, glancing at Alpha and Zeta. "It shows that this *Archon*, whatever he is, has given us a gift beyond compare."

The video started playing, and a jolt ran through Lucas. It was a place he recognized easily: the sky-level bar in the Dubai hotel. He was looking at himself through frosted glass. His eyes were closed. The date-stamp of the security loop said it was the day of his rescue.

Xalan scientists milled about sifting through holographic displays and looking through readouts on Lucas's unit. Armored soldiers patrolled the main floor, and a few were looking out the windows toward the sand dunes that once made up the Persian Gulf. There was audio, and in addition to the noises of machinery and electronics, the Xalans could be heard grunting and growling at each other.

An alarm went off. The scientists all crowded around a flashing console while the soldiers drew their weapons and looked for the threat.

The Resistance raid?

The scientists moved from the console to Lucas's chamber and killed the wailing alarm. The feed zoomed in and Lucas could see that his eyes were wide open, glowing electric blue, his pupils white. He stared straight ahead past them. The Xalans were all growling at each other and gesturing wildly, until suddenly . . .

The Xalans froze and the room went silent. They didn't just stop talking, they ceased moving all together.

What?

Lucas could see Stoller's eyes gleaming wickedly through the holographic display.

With blank looks on their faces, the Xalan soldiers turned and started unloading their rifles into anyone in their field of vision. Most of the scientists were cut down in an initial wave of plasma, and the soldiers turned the rifles on each other. What lab techs hadn't been killed started slashing at each other wildly with their claws or surgical blades. Some picked up dead soldier's guns and began firing them with the same vacant looks. Lucas's eyes were still open in the tank, but he was obviously seeing none of what was happening.

Oh god.

The video feed switched to an overhead view of the hotel lobby where the massacre was amplified exponentially with far more Xalans on the ground level. Xalans stabbed and shot each other at point blank range, and gallons of black blood were spattered around the room. The lobby doors remained barred. No one had broken in. The Archon's research team was simply turning on each other and tearing themselves to pieces.

It seemed like an hour, but in truth it was probably all over in less than two minutes. In the end, there was only one Xalan left wandering around the piles of corpses in the lobby. He held a bloodied metal fragment in one hand and a pistol in the other. There were horrifying slash marks across his chest, and he was favoring his right leg, which had suffered a plasma burn. Tottering awkwardly around the bodies, gaze fixed straight ahead, his pace slowed down until he stood just below the staircase. The metal shard and pistol dropped from his hands, and he simply put his claws to his throat and dragged them violently across it. Blood poured to the floor as he collapsed on the spot. The room was silent and still.

The same could be said for the conference room in the Grand Palace. Mouths hung agape as everyone tried to process what they'd just witnessed. Lucas found himself with the same reaction.

I don't understand.

But another voice.

Yes. Yes you do.

Madric Stoller made it clear for everyone.

"The readouts the scientists were looking at before the massacre were Lucas's psionic fluctuations. Your daughter uncovered a dramatic, unprecedented spike in the data at that precise moment."

Stoller paused. "He did this. Or rather, *he made them do it.*"

"Impossible," Alpha said breathlessly.

Die, Lucas had thought. *And she had.*

Every eye in the room was now trained on Lucas's holographic cell feed.

Asha was now putting together the pieces of what he'd told her about the blackened woman.

"Do you remember?" she whispered to him.

"I don't—" Lucas stammered. "I can't—"

He had no recollection of any of this, though it confirmed a suspicion that had been eating at him since the memory of the woman with the knife. But how? How was this possible? And on this large a scale? Even psionic Chosen Shadows didn't have such an ability, did they?

"You are a new creation."

"Are you alright?" Asha asked him, her face full of concern. And fear.

"You will bring Sora to its knees."

"I need access to him," Alpha said sternly. "Immediately."

"I will find what drives you, and I will use it to make you laugh as you destroy everyone you love."

"This is how the war ends," Madric Stoller said, looking straight into Lucas's ice-blue eyes. "This is how the war ends at last."

"Squeeze," Alpha said, his eyes narrowed, trained on a set of blank readouts on a floating screen in front of him. They were in one of the vast laboratories the SDI had given him in the military base to work on projects for the war effort. Lucas was his latest endeavor.

"It's really not safe for you to be here," Lucas said. "You saw what I did in that video, I could do the same to you without even knowing—"

"I am aware of all possible risks involved with my presence here," Alpha said, his eyes not leaving the monitor. "Now squeeze."

Lucas obeyed. He tightened his grip around the metal cylinder as hard as he could, his black veins bulging from the effort. The allium crumpled inward like tinfoil, and Alpha's empty monitor came alive with data spikes. His gold-ringed eyes widened. He did a few quick calculations in the air and spoke to a floating recorder that was orbiting the pair of them.

"Patient demonstrates eightfold increase in grip strength. Compare to tenfold increase in run speed from previous test."

Lucas had spent the morning sprinting back and forth across the expansive room at speeds so fast it disoriented him. He'd actually failed to stop once and blown a hole through the western wall, which prematurely ended the test.

Lucas looked down at the mangled can of allium in his hand. They made vaults and warship hulls out of the stuff. And containment cells, like the one in which he currently resided.

So this is what being a Shadow feels like.

The sensation was hard to describe. Now that his head had cleared and he wasn't hallucinating imagined enemies anymore, he had time to relish his new abilities. He felt more alive than he'd ever been. The power that flowed through his sickly black veins was palpable.

Alpha suddenly injected him with a syringe full of clear liquid. As soon as he pulled the needle out, the tiny wound closed, healing instantly.

"What was that?" Lucas asked. A chill raced through him and he shivered. It felt like ice water was flowing through his arm and into the rest of his body.

"Stage one of your treatment," Alpha said. "I am no geneticist, but I will do my best to slow or reverse the Shadow conversion process using the data my daughter has recovered regarding the process."

"But I feel great, Alpha," Lucas said excitedly. "Better than ever, actually. My mind is clear, I'm in control of myself. It's the best I've felt since they woke me up."

Alpha looked at him with something resembling pity.

"Your newly enhanced immune system masks the underlying issue with the conversion process. It is automated at this point in its deployment. Left alone, it will fully convert you into a Shadow."

"I don't understand," Lucas said. "I'm an asset like this, I can help. You can change me back once the war is won."

"I cannot," Alpha said sternly. "Once conversion fully takes hold, it is irreversible. But I fear we may not reach that point in any case."

"What do you mean?" Lucas asked.

"Your new immune system is not merely fighting off disease and injury. It is eating into your healthy cells, deeming them too weak for their purposes. If they are not adequately replaced, conversion could eat you from the inside out. It is how many Shadow candidates die, and the data suggests it is simply a much longer process with humans and Sorans."

Alpha paused and looked down toward the floor.

"Your life continues to be in incredible peril as your body transforms, though I worry the more pressing danger is the threat you will become to all of us if you fully convert."

Lucas fell silent at that.

"There are only two paths forward. Either I reverse the conversion process and cure you of this *infection*, or I attempt to increase its speed, allowing you to fully convert before any harm can befall you. The latter path seems appealing due to your present abilities, but I fear it is the far more dangerous option, and should not be attempted for your own good and the good of us all."

Lucas finally found his voice.

"You heard Stoller. He wants me for the effort. He'll kill you for trying to revert me."

Alpha waved his claw dismissively.

"I am attempting to mask my work and forge my data regarding your development for as long as is possible. My intention is to cure you before my true intentions are discovered. The High Chancellor will believe I am forging you into a weapon after witnessing your power, while I am in fact doing the opposite."

"I could help," Lucas said. "As a full Shadow. You saw what the Archon has done to me. What I can do to them."

Alpha glowered at him while continuing to enter data.

"I know you believe this to be true, but you would risk such a transformation? Knowing what you do about your abilities? Who is to say once you reach full conversation, you would not turn into the Archon's slave like this 'Black Corsair'?"

Lucas shuddered. He hadn't considered that.

"So you're not going to test my psionic abilities?" Lucas asked, looking down at the crushed allium and thinking back to the Archon's terrifying crucible with the burned woman.

Alpha finally stopped typing and looked directly at Lucas.

"This new mutation . . . unnerves me. It is a dark power the likes of which I have never witnessed. I worry not for my own safety should I dare 'test' it, but for the lives of everyone on this planet. You do not yet grasp the full extent of what you are becoming."

17

The icy wind whipped at Noah's face as he stepped out of the transport. Winter had come to Colony One.

The buildings, brand new and ancient alike, were buried in a solid two feet of snow along with the forest that surrounded them. Even in a heated thermal overcoat, the chill reached deep into Noah's bones.

The landing platform had been cleared, heat filtering through the pavement to melt whatever ice covered it, and dozens of hooded shapes stood in bulky white coats ahead of them. One figure broke from the others and sprinted to embrace him.

"Noah!" she cried.

"Sakai."

He embraced her and the cold faded from his mind. He'd forgotten the smell of her. Even the wind couldn't whisk it away as his face was buried in her hair.

"I knew you'd make it back," she said. Noah saw tears freezing on her cheeks.

Wuhan strode up beside his half-sister and clapped his hand on Noah's still-aching shoulder. He tried not to wince.

"A trip to the homeworld, huh? You're going to have to educate the children," he said, motioning toward the group, who were all gathering closer. Erik was already surrounded by five female admirers, but he was pushing past them. He was uncharacteristically silent and wearing a grim expression. Something told Noah he wasn't pleased to be back in the "colony cage," as he called it.

Quezon circled around to Noah's other side.

"What was it like?" he asked.

"We're better off here," Noah said, his arm around Sakai. "I'll tell you that."

He turned around as two more hooded figures descended from the ship, one tall, one short. Theta and Kyra.

"Everyone," Noah loudly announced to the group. "This is Kyra. She'll be staying with us a while."

Kyra pulled down her thermal scarf and flashed a brilliant smile at the group.

"Hello," she said, and Noah felt the hearts of every male present stop. A few females as well. She had that power, just like her predecessor.

Sakai hugged her immediately.

"So good to meet you at last," she said. "I've enjoyed our little talks."

"Little talks?" Noah asked, his eyebrows raised.

"We've been sharing all sorts of fun stories about you from when you were little," Kyra said in a teasing tone. Noah hadn't even realized the two had been in contact on the ship.

The returning party was not sharing the fact that Finn Stoller had attempted to kill Kyra on the return trip, so Noah supposed he didn't mind her keeping something much less important a secret.

"Oh gods," he grinned, rolling his eyes. "This was a mistake."

As he looked across the smiling faces of Sakai and Kyra, he knew he might not be joking.

Once they landed, Lucas and Asha shipped out to some undisclosed location, presumably to figure out how to keep his father from turning into the next Corsair. Lucas had been coherent when he'd left, profusely apologizing to Noah for assaulting him. Noah tried to remain bitter about the attack and the secret Lucas had kept about his father, but it was hard to hold a grudge against a man who had not only saved the planet but had been imprisoned and tortured for a decade and a half as a reward. He and Lucas parted on good terms, but Erik's cold good-bye left the impression his brother still saw Lucas as more of a threat than a parent.

There was good news about the war. The Xalans had reportedly abandoned their own colonies and were retreating. At least, that's what the Stream had been blaring ever since they got home. That meant Noah's most pressing problem was keeping Kyra safe at Colony One and getting her some answers about her true parentage. If she had parentage at all, that is. And of course there was Stoller himself to deal with, a monumental undertaking if there ever was one.

Keeper Malorious Auran was still nowhere to be found. The man had retired from his work at the Grand Palace shortly after Madric Stoller took office and had been living a quiet life in Mal Dur'anne, but now he had simply vanished. Noah feared the worst, and he was afraid Kyra did too, though she wouldn't say it.

"She's still in trouble, isn't she?" Sakai said, snapping Noah out of his daze as he unpacked in his quarters. Well, their quarters, more often than not.

"She is," Noah said. "She's here to be kept safe."

It was the best place they could think of. Even if Stoller had butchered a church full of Anointed at the White Spire nearby, there was no way he'd try the same at the colony itself with so many of the Earthborn and their guards around. The soldiers left were all personally recruited and vouched for by Tannon Vale after the revelation that one of the guards had turned and given up Kyra.

"What happened at the spire?" she asked. "Who is after her?"

"We're not sure," Noah lied. He hated how it felt, having to conceal the truth from Sakai. He trusted her, but that sort of knowledge was dangerous to have. "Someone with a vendetta against her family, we're guessing."

That was an understatement.

"I'll bunk with her," Sakai said. "I'll keep an eye on her to make sure she's alright."

"You don't have to," Noah said, lugging a heavy crate across the floor filled with the power armor he'd worn on Earth. "They're putting five of the Watchman's top guards at her door."

"Still," she said. "She'll be lonely. Like a princess locked in a tower." Noah stood up and looked at her. There was a hint of something in her eye. *Does she know?*

But leave it to Sakai to immediately start caring for a girl she barely knew. Noah felt a pang of guilt, but didn't know why. He shook it off and lifted a metal case onto his bed.

"What is all this stuff?" Sakai asked, brushing her hair back. it seemed impossible to Noah that he had forgotten how beautiful she was. Being so close around Kyra had been like staring into the sun for too long. But now his sight was returning and he remembered why this was the girl he cared for more than any other.

"It's a gift from a friend," Noah said as he opened the electronic lock. The lid swung open to reveal his darksteel warhammer, which made Sakai gasp.

"Quite a friend," she said.

"Yes, she is," Noah replied with a smile.

"Let me guess, tall, thin, pale?"

"You're on the right track."

Both of them laughed. They were already falling back into their old rhythm, which was comforting after the harrowing ordeals of the past few months. She was his anchor, he realized now. His touchstone. Noah grabbed her by the waist and drew her toward him.

"You can bunk with her tomorrow," he said, and moved in to kiss her. "Tonight, *I* need you."

It was strange, concentrating on schoolwork after all that had happened. Noah had missed months of lessons and was scrambling to catch up, even with copious amounts of grace from his instructors. He had piles of coursework he was finding hard to care about given everything he'd just endured. Urtorian history lessons and the density of thulium didn't seem like particularly applicable knowledge anymore. The colony was a bubble. Now that it had burst, it was hard to feel comfortable back inside.

Combat training seemed like a sick joke now that he'd experienced real war, killed real people, real Xalans. What had been intense and pulse pounding before now felt like a children's game. Vibro-weapons and pulse blasts crumpled his Earthborn brethren into unconscious little heaps. They didn't sever their limbs or blow off their heads.

Noah had seen so much death recently, it was hard to stop seeing it. The others didn't understand. They couldn't.

Erik was even less engaged than he'd been before he left. He rarely showed up to class and barely even made appearances at combat training, which used to be his favorite activity. They'd often find him wandering around in the woods long after a match ended, not having fired a single shot. When pressed, he simply replied that it was "boring." Compared to Dubai, he certainly had a point.

Noah only saw him light up when he was around Kyra; she somehow managed to breathe life back into his brother. But only briefly, and he would darken whenever she wasn't around.

One day, Erik finally managed to show up to a hand-to-hand training bout, likely only because Kyra was present. The event had been moved indoors on account of the freezing temperatures, though occasionally they'd spar in the snow to "toughen them up," as their instructors put it. A silver-haired ex-Guardian named Celton was their combat instructor and was barking commands to Lyon and Wuhan, who were flogging each other with wooden weapons in the ring. In less than a minute, Wuhan had Lyon on his back with his staff at his throat. No surprise there.

Noah sat in the curved seating that rose out from the ground like a miniature gladiatorial arena. Traditional Soran schools had nothing of the sort on campus, but the Earthborn were a special case. And it wasn't as barbaric as it probably looked from the outside. It served to help the students blow off steam and learn how to dismantle attackers should the situation call for it. And with a newfound promise that they'd get to leave the colony at age twenty, they just might need such training to deal with the dangerous wide world.

Celton called the next pair down to the floor: Quezon, the dark, usually silent giant nearly as tall as Noah, and Kavala, his half-brother by way of their shared mother from Earth's Philippine island chain. Kavala was wide with muscle from his Greek father and was one of the more formidable Earthborn in the ring. Quezon's reach could give him the edge, however. The two began to slowly circle one other. They were fighting without practice weapons, bare fists only.

Noah and Erik were sitting in a row, boxing Sakai and Kyra between them. Noah didn't much care for the pairing implication, but Sakai had assured him that Kyra had no late-night visitors in their shared quarters, be they assassins or his brother. That much was a relief at least.

Celton was just about to signal the match to start when he noticed Erik in the stands. This was his first appearance at sparring since their return.

"First Son!" Celton called out from the floor, using one of Erik's most disliked nicknames. "Nice of you to join us today. Will you be taking part in a match yourself?"

Erik slouched back a few more inches.

"Only if I'm facing you, Instructor," he called back.

"If only I were allowed to give you the thrashing you so desperately seek," Celton replied with a smirk. He'd always disliked Erik, as did a fair number of the teachers. "You're telling me you learned nothing running away from Xalans on Earth?"

Erik's annoyed look turned downright dark.

"Careful, Instructor."

"I'm just saying, if you're some world-hopping warrior now, it would be nice if you graced the rest of us with a lesson."

Erik glanced sideways toward Kyra, who was chuckling at the banter. Noah knew his brother well enough to know that Erik probably took that as her laughing at him.

Uh oh.

Erik rose from his seat.

"I'll fight," he said, turning away from Kyra and slowly marching down the rows of seats toward the floor.

"Ah, amazing! The little prince agrees."

Now *that* was Erik's least favorite nickname. Noah could almost feel the heat pouring off him.

"And who will you challenge?" Celton continued, gesturing outward to the Earthborn in attendance. Kyra looked nervously at Noah and Sakai.

Don't do it, Erik.

Noah didn't want to fight his brother. Not here, not now, not again. Though, as he considered it, he wasn't sure if it was because he thought he'd win, or that he'd lose.

"Them," Erik said instead, pointing toward Quezon and Kavala, who had ceased their circling to witness his exchange with Celton. Both looked surprised. Noah breathed a secret sigh of relief, but then shook his head as he realized what his brother was getting into. His ego was bad enough normally, but to have Kyra around inflating it was making matters worse.

"Fine," Celton said, jovial no more. He wanted to see Erik get demolished as penance for his boasts.

Kavala simply shrugged and looked at Quezon, who was silent and locked eyes with Erik as he stepped into the ring.

"What's he doing?" Sakai asked, her voice low.

Noah looked at Kyra.

"Showing off."

"He can't win, those two are—"

"He can."

He will.

Few people truly understood Erik's fighting prowess when he set his mind to it. Noah was one of them. His father had killed Shadows. His mother had conquered armies. Destruction was in his blood.

Quezon swung first. Erik ducked under the punch and countered with a sharp jab to his exposed ribs. Kavala lunged at him from the side, but Erik rolled over the top of his broad shoulders and kicked the back of his knee when he landed, sending him tumbling. Quezon launched himself over the stumbling Kavala and let loose a lightning-quick series of kicks that Erik deflected left and right until one struck his shoulder. Erik curled his newly reattached fingers into a fist and countered with a hard right to Quezon's jaw.

Kavala regained his balance and ran at Erik full-steam. Noah's brother was barely able to duck the clothesline in time, but as Kavala whipped around on the backswing he caught Erik in the chest with an elbow. Erik flew backward, but as soon as he landed he launched himself up and threw both feet into a dropkick that connected with Kavala's abdomen. Erik hit the ground and rolled out of the way as Quezon tried to stomp down on him with one of his long legs. Erik caught the inside of Quezon's calf with his hooked foot and pulled him down as he got up. He drove the taller fighter into the ground with a crushing punch, but then bent backward to avoid another swing from Kavala. Erik blocked a second punch and a high knee, which lifted him off his feet all the same. He countered with a pair of spinning high kicks, one to Kavala's face, the other to Quezon's arm, which he was using to get back up. Quezon went crashing back down to the earth, and Erik landed a pair of jabs and a hard right cross to Kavala's already bloodied face. His eyes went in two different directions as he fell to the ground.

"*Enough*," Celton shouted, dismayed at the outcome.

Quezon was livid as he scrambled to his feet. Kavala regained his senses and joined him. They wouldn't be embarrassed any more than Erik would. Both dove toward him. Whatever fury was on their faces, it was nothing compared to the expression he wore.

In half a second, he grabbed Quezon's arm and drove straight through it with his palm. The subsequent scream and bone crack were only matched by Kavala as Erik stomped his boot into his shin and splintered it.

There were screams coming from the crowd too at that point. The floor was covered in blood, as were the three combatants, and white bone shards poked out of Quezon's useless arm and Kavala's ruined leg. Kavala was howling in agony while Quezon had apparently passed out from the pain.

"Erik!" Noah shouted, leaping up from his seat the moment he'd heard the first bone crack.

Erik turned to face Celton and mouthed something no one could hear over the cries of the Earthborn all around them. Celton let loose a thunderous punch that Erik made no attempt to dodge. His brother hit the ground between his two victims. Noah looked back toward Kyra. Both she and Sakai had their mouths covered with their hands, speechless. Theta was one row up from them and looked equally horrified.

Noah arrived at the carnage on the floor. His brother was on his back, conscious, but staring blankly at the rafters.

Smiling.

Laughing.

Noah marched through the med bay, where Kavala and Quezon were having their bones set and two Chinese half-sisters were recovering from a bout with the parasite. The door at the end of the bay lifted and he made his way down a series of winding hallways until he reached the area he was looking for: holding.

The cell was covered in dust; it was seldom needed for the normally well-behaved Earthborn. But his brother had managed to land himself there a few times. He sat cross-legged on the ground, drawing shapes in the dust with his finger.

Noah approached the glowing barrier screen that kept his brother locked inside and got as close to it as he could without touching the energy field. Erik glanced up at him. No one had bothered to clean him up, and he was still painted with dried blood.

"What is *wrong* with you?" Noah growled through clenched teeth.

Erik lazily brought himself to his feet and approached the barrier.

"You could have killed them," Noah continued.

Erik rolled his eyes.

"Since when is a broken bone a near-death experience? They'll be mended in a week and you know it."

Bones had been broken in the ring before, but always accidentally, and never out of purposeful savagery.

"What *was* that?" Noah said. "You trying to show off to Kyra? If you think that's the sort of thing to impress her, you don't know her at all."

"Oh and you do?" Erik spat back. "All your late nights on the dreadnought give you some insights into her delicate nature?"

Noah resented what Erik was hinting at.

"We never—"

"Of course you never, gods forbid you betray your nonexistent oath to Sakai."

"She needs our protection," Noah said. "Not your unwanted affection."

"Maybe she wants both," Erik said. "You ever think of that? You weren't the only one spending fourteen hours a day with her, you know. She deserves better than a giant oaf who has delusions of being some sort of saint, despite stealing longing glances at her chest whenever possible."

Noah banged on the screen angrily, and immediately regretted it as his entire arm went numb. He tried to shake out the needles with limited success. Erik was just trying to provoke him now, and he was falling for it.

"This isn't even about Kyra, is it?" Noah said, the feeling beginning to come back to his fingers.

"Of course not," Erik snapped. "It's about going to Earth and fighting in a real war, and now being forced to come back here for playschool."

"We have a duty here," Noah said. "We have an entire species to help train and cultivate so the human race doesn't go extinct."

"You think that's the most pressing issue at hand here? Our dear father is a psychotic Shadow, our entire planet may fall to this Archon asshole, and our High Chancellor has put out a hit on your little platonic clone friend. And I'm supposed to care about exam scores and my combat training KDA? How can you stand it after what we've just been through? It was bad enough before, but now it's just unbearable."

The scary thing was that Noah agreed with everything Erik was saying. The everyday happenings of the colony seemed so insignificant now after all they'd experienced. Was he any closer to helping his father regain his sanity? Helping Kyra escape her death sentence? Winning the Great War? But still he pressed Erik.

"The others look up to you," Noah said. "You're a role model, and it terrifies them to see you like this. What sort of example is that?"

"You're all the role model they need, brother," Erik said with a sarcastic grin.

"Theta looks up to you too. She adores you. You should have seen her today after she watched you tear those guys apart. She was heartbroken."

"Like I give a shit about what Theta thinks!" Erik shot back. "She's useful when she's pressing buttons to let me out of this place or arranging trips to other solar systems. I see those blushing looks she gives me, but someone should tell her that two different species can't mate!"

There was a loud clatter from the side of the room. Theta was standing there and had dropped a tray of bandages and gel vials. Her snow-white face was bright crimson as she scrambled to pick them up.

"I was just . . . I was coming to treat your . . . I volunteered to address your injuries while—" she stumbled over the words, and her claws were shaking as she reassembled the contents of the tray. "My apologies, I will return another time so as not to intrude on your private—" She turned and quickly left before she even finished the thought.

For all Erik's rage and swagger, he looked downright mortified when Noah turned back to him.

"*This* is why you're alone," Noah said, jabbing his finger toward his brother within an inch of the screen. "This is why you'll always be alone."

18

Lucas sat outside in one of the many paved courtyards of the military base. Soldiers marched around in formation, and a pair of prototype aerial fighters were being worked on in the sprawling hangars across the way. It was starting to get cold on the continent, though it would likely never see snow. Thick gray clouds rolled by, but they hadn't unleashed any rain yet. Still, Lucas could hear thunder off in the distance.

It had quickly become clear that keeping Lucas locked up in the sublevels was to no one's best interest when, out of sheer boredom, he had pummeled the walls of his cell until the allium was warped to look like a frozen pool of turbulent water.

He eyed the outer perimeter walls he could easily leap or charge through with his newfound strength and speed. But he had no reason to do so. He needed Alpha's help, and besides, where would he even go? One of his children thought he was a monster—which was hard to refute given his current half-formed Shadow status—and he'd accidentally assaulted the other during a psychotic break. And Asha? At least she had been allowed to visit him. And there she was.

Asha wore military fatigues a few shades darker than the rest of the soldiers in the base. She still had her winged Guardian emblem pinned to her chest, though she hadn't been sent out on a mission with them since the Purge of Makari, as they called it. Since then, Commander Kiati had taken her Guardian squad to assist on Aerias, one of the farthest colony planets, where fighting had been fierce both in orbit and on the ground until the Xalan fleets had fled. Lucas was pleased to hear of Kiati's promotion in the wake of Mars Maston's death. The squad deserved a leader of her caliber. Rumor had it Asha was offered the position herself, but turned it down.

Her hair was long and wild as it always was, and she had to brush it out of her face when the winds began to pick up. It was stunning how little she'd aged, and Lucas felt downright ancient beside her, acquiring more silver hair by the day. At least it was growing back.

He embraced her when she reached him, the engines of her transport winding down a ways off. Soldiers turned to stare at the pair of them. Lucas was used to everyone looking at Asha when she entered a room (or a military base, for that matter), but knew it was him they were gaping at. Lucas was wearing a long, high-collared olive jacket, but black veins crept around the sides of his face. And there was no hiding his electric eyes, which stood out in the grayness of the day as though they glowed. However well trained the soldiers were at the Merenes base, they were always visibly unnerved whenever he surfaced. Even so, all were sworn to secrecy about his return to Sora under threat of imprisonment. Knowing Madric Stoller, possibly worse.

"How do you feel?" Asha asked as she pulled away from him. The pair started walking toward the hangars. The soldiers all snapped to attention and pretended they hadn't been gawking.

"Weaker," Lucas said, smiling stiffly.

"Well, weaker for you these days isn't saying much," Asha replied. Lucas nodded.

"Alpha's charting about a 30 percent drop in my strength over the past few weeks. He believes he's almost fought off conversion completely, and it shouldn't be much longer now."

"That's a relief," Asha said, breathing out a sigh. She eyed Lucas curiously when he remained silent. "Isn't it?"

"Imagine you were given the power to do anything," he said. "And all you were told you *should* do was sit in one place while the gift was slowly taken away from you."

"A gift?" Asha said, wrinkling her nose. "That's what you think the Archon did to you? Ask the Corsair how that's working out."

"You sound like Alpha," Lucas said, the hangars growing large up ahead. "But you don't know until you've experienced it. There's nothing like it."

Lucas made his next step a stomp, and the pavement cratered beneath his boot. Asha was not impressed, and Lucas felt a bit silly.

"I just want you to be rid of this so you can get out of here and we can try to be family again," she said.

"The boys don't really want much to do with me," Lucas said, thrusting his hands deep into his pockets.

"The boys don't know you," Asha said. "And you don't know them. You've been missing for the last sixteen years, and psychotic or unconscious most of the time since you woke up. This is the best I've seen you, and it's because Alpha's treatment is working. Don't you want more days like this?"

Lucas nodded silently. She was right. Lucas's head was as clear as it had been before they'd gone to Xala. Probably since pre-war Earth, for that matter.

"And what about your other . . . *gift*?" Asha pressed.

"The mind control," Lucas whispered. Saying it out loud was bizarre. "It's what Stoller's really after. Same as the Archon, I imagine. Alpha won't test it. I'm too scared to try. Strength and speed I understand, but that? It's terrifying. Even I'll admit that."

"All the more reason for Alpha to continue your treatment," Asha said, putting her hand on the back of his neck. They were in the shadow of the hangar now. Lucas looked up at the fighter hanging suspended from the ceiling. One of Alpha's designs, from the looks of it. It was a marvel of engineering, seamlessly merging Xalan and Soran technology. The other copy of the ship next to it had much of its paneling open, and a team of engineers was performing electrical surgery on it.

"I know," Lucas said. "But what if I can be the tipping point in the war?"

"The war has already tipped, if you ask the top brass," Asha said. "Stoller thinks the Xalans are prepping for one final desperation push, but our homeworld defenses will shred them. They lost too much trying to retain the colony worlds."

Lucas sighed. He supposed they were right. That he should give up these strange, wondrous, horrible powers and return to an ordinary life if the war truly was about to come to an end. He had his family back. What could be more important than that? He needed to remember that was all he had ever wanted.

A few days later, Lucas sat alone in his windowless living quarters, flipping through various layers of the Stream on the mammoth projection that took up most of the wall. The news broadcasters were practically tap-dancing with the news that the Xalans were on the run and saying Chancellor Stoller was due full credit for turning the tide of the war. Lucas scoffed, thinking of how many warship engines Alpha had assembled over the past few years, and how any sort of victory would have been impossible without them.

It had been a few days since Alpha had stopped by to treat and test Lucas. At least Lucas thought that was how long it had been. Often, to avoid the uncomfortable stares of the soldiers, he didn't even leave the sublevels of his chambers. Days and nights passed by with him none the wiser. Lucas probably hadn't even slept in at least two days, though he felt no worse for it. Another Shadow side effect? It seemed there were too many to keep track of. But still, whatever Alpha had been treating him with, he felt himself growing weaker by the day. A few of his black veins had reverted to soft red and blue. His eyes had dulled a bit in color.

Lucas was surprised when the outer doors to his quarters opened and a new face entered. A grandmotherly looking woman in a long silver coat shuffled through the entryway with a smile stretched across her face. Lucas approached her cautiously.

"Hello, Lucas!" she said, beaming. If she was put off by his appearance, it didn't show.

"Um, hello," Lucas replied, eyeing her coat, which was so long it dragged behind her like a train. She had fine white hair threaded into a single thick braid that wrapped around her head. Her moss-green eyes twinkled and deep lines branched out from the corners when she smiled. She looked old, which was a rarity on Sora, meaning she had to be at least 160 or 170.

"It's a pleasure to finally meet you," she said, giving Lucas a short bow. "I've been looking forward to this day for a while now."

Lucas returned the quaint bow, still unsure of what was happening.

"Oh, I'm sorry," she said. "Where are my manners? I am Jahane Stellen Tarla. I used to work with Malorious Auran before he gave up his genetics lab to become Palace Keeper. More recently, we built Colony One together, and I was on the Earthborn project for oh, about a decade I'd say. I've also worked with your friend Alpha from time to time these past few years."

"Interesting," Lucas said. "And where is Alpha?"

"Ah," she replied. "This is the reason for my presence. Alpha has been called away to fix an urgent problem with null core production. It's more crucial than ever we fit the last of our warships to chase down the remaining Xalan fleets, and it is a matter that required his most urgent attention. I am here in his stead, tasked with following his treatment regimen to the letter to make sure you're in fighting shape for when you're needed to help us win the war!"

She was bursting with energy for someone so seemingly ancient. Lucas cocked his head. "You're following his exact regimen?"

"To the letter," she repeated, and produced a white case from inside her coat. She opened it to display a familiar row of syringes. Clear liquid was bound inside the glass: the cocktail that had been slowly curing Lucas over time. If she really was following Alpha's orders, she'd continue to cure him without even knowing it. But still, Lucas was wary.

"Why didn't Alpha let me know about the switch?" Lucas asked. "Not that I resent your presence, of course," he added politely.

"The issue really was quite pressing. But oh yes! I'd almost forgotten. He did record this to pass along to you when I arrived."

The woman pulled out a small chip and a hologram sprang out. Alpha's face rose up in between them.

"Greetings Lucas," he said. The hologram flickered with some sort of interference. "I apologize that I have been called away to deal with this pressing problem. I have hand-selected Geneticist Tarla to continue my regimen to ensure your continued progress. She has assured me that, though Shadow science is past her level of understanding, as is true of all Sorans, she will follow my instructions exactly during my absence. I cannot say how long this problem will continue to draw my attention, so forgive my absence until I am able to return."

Alpha looked briefly off screen then back again, his eyes fixed forward.

"Farewell, brother."

The hologram cut out.

Lucas believed he understood now. Alpha had picked the most amiable geneticist available who wouldn't understand that Lucas was being cured instead of having his abilities amplified, but who was still skilled enough to administer the treatment without botching any of the steps. The forged results would continue to present themselves as fact and the Stoller administration would be none the wiser. Lucas would be cured, and by then hopefully the war would be won and Stoller wouldn't even care about the "failed" experiment. Alpha really was ten times smarter than Stoller would ever be.

For the next week, Lucas took his treatments from Geneticist Tarla, who insisted she be called "Jahane" at all times. She rarely stopped talking, filling the silences between injections, body scans, and DNA samples with stories about her expansive family, which included a hundred great-great-grandchildren. Each and every one had their own list of accomplishments, and Lucas couldn't help but grow fond of the proud grandmother. She rarely asked him any questions outside of those required for the procedures, which was also a welcome switch. Lucas was tired of being prodded about Earth, the war, his imprisonment, his family, all of it. It was nice to simply exist and let someone else spill their life story for a change.

"You're making fantastic progress!" Jahane said one day after Lucas squeezed a can of allium into rubble. The data produced massive spikes on the readout, but Lucas could see he'd done less damage to the allium than he had in previous weeks when he'd been stronger. Or had he? The twisted metal was hard to gauge, actually. Whatever the case, if the tests were showing power spikes, Alpha's forged data was continuing to get the job done. Lucas almost felt bad for lying to the sweet Jahane, however. He hoped she wouldn't get in trouble when the truth eventually did come to light.

"Any word on when I can get in touch with Alpha? Or Asha?" he asked.

Jahane's smile was forever at full wattage. "They should be wrapping up shortly, but Alpha is performing his work at the Thylium orbital hangar. Asha has been sent to guard him in this critical stage of the process. Unfortunately the solar storm persists and they're unable to be reached."

"What about Colony One?" Lucas asked, suddenly thinking of the boys.

Jahane lit up. "Oh, that can absolutely be arranged! Why didn't you ask earlier?"

Lucas couldn't think of an answer. In truth, he wasn't even sure why. Perhaps it was because the last time he could remember his children, they were barely able to talk. Still, it was reassuring that he was able to reach out to at least some of his family. He was growing a bit concerned with Alpha and Asha's silence, but felt more at ease knowing Colony One was still accessible. Everything was fine, right? Though if he couldn't get ahold of Noah or Erik, that would set off some alarm bells.

Jahane was already dialing the colony on her scroll. Lucas felt himself relax when Erik's face appeared in front of them.

"Yeah?" Erik said irritably.

He was fine. Everything was fine.

"Hey, uh, Erik," Lucas said awkwardly. He still didn't feel like it was appropriate to say "son." He'd have been more comfortable doing so with Noah; even though Erik was his flesh and blood, he felt far more distant from his biological offspring.

"What's new, father?"

Lucas's heart momentarily leaped at being addressed as "father," but he quickly realized it was probably sarcasm.

"Nothing," Lucas said. "I'm just undergoing treatment while Alpha and your mother are away."

Jahane was slowly backing out of the room to give him some privacy. Though it was obvious the government would be monitoring anything and everything said.

"They're gone?" Erik asked, rubbing his hand through his hair. "News to me. But hey, that's always how it is with Asha."

Lucas didn't much care for his tone.

"She saved all of us back on Earth," Lucas said. "If I recall, she extracted you from a mess of your own making."

Erik rolled his eyes.

"And if *I* recall, if I hadn't gotten us into that *mess*, you'd still be locked in a tank being probed by the Archon."

Lucas nodded.

"And I am forever in your debt."

Erik didn't know what to make of genuine appreciation. He turned to the side. It revealed a large scrape near his ear.

"What happened?" Lucas said.

Erik swung his scroll projection around a bit, and Lucas caught a view of . . . was that a lightscreen?

"Are you in *prison?*" Lucas asked.

"Well, that makes two of us," Erik replied smartly.

"I'm not in prison. I'm under observation," Lucas said gruffly. "And don't change the subject. What the hell happened?"

"Oh hey, look, Noah's here. Talk to him," Erik said, ignoring Lucas completely. He held the scroll up to the lightscreen and Lucas could see a tall blond shape.

"Is that Lucas?" he heard.

The video feed changed from Erik's scroll to Noah's.

"Hey," Noah said. His hair had been cut shorter·than when Lucas saw him last. His eyes were tired. It was understandable; he'd been through a lot the past few months. More than anyone his age should.

"Just seeing if you two were alright," Lucas said. "But I can see I've missed some things."

He could see Noah was walking, and shortly a door slid shut behind him. The new room was darker, quieter.

"I'm tempted to say it's just Erik being Erik, but I'm worried about him. He went too far this time. Really hurt some people."

"What happened?" Lucas asked.

"Long story," Noah said, shaking his head. "Suffice it to say, what happened on the ship really shook him up."

Asha had told Lucas about Madric Stoller's attempted assassination of Kyra Auran, and the revelation that she was some relation to the deceased Corinthia Vale, if not an exact copy of her. Lucas now knew why the girl had unsettled him when they first met. He had heard every tall tale about clones. But none of this was her fault, and it was hard not to feel for the poor girl. "Has Erik always been like this?" Lucas asked.

Noah shifted his head back and forth.

"To some extent. It was bad when you were gone, but honestly it might be even worse now that you're back."

"Because I'm some sort of monster now?"

"You're just not who he thought you were."

"What do you mean?"

"Yes, he hated that you died and left him alone. But there was a time before he felt that way. When he was little, he adored you. He read every scroll written about you, and was constantly bragging to all his friends in the colony about his father the dauntless warrior, savior of Sora. You were his hero, until your absence finally overshadowed your myth and he got cynical as he grew older. Now? You're back, and you're . . . something else."

Lucas's heart was caught in his throat. His stomach felt frozen.

"And what about you?" he said quietly.

Noah stared straight into the scroll.

"I believe you can be that man again, if you don't die in the attempt. That said, I'd take a live father over a dead hero, even if it's a selfish thought."

With no ability to contact Asha, Lucas found himself sifting through archived Stream feeds of her in the late, dim hours of the night. He found one clip of a parade celebrating the anniversary of when Asha and the others had returned from their mission to Xala. There were open-air hovercrafts stretching down the recently rebuilt Tatoni Square in downtown Elyria, each carrying scores of soldiers and officers who were said to have performed some feat of bravery during the massive aerial battle with the Xalan fleet near the gas planet Altoria. Eventually, the final hovercraft—a massive, pearl-colored, dozen-engined transport—carried Asha, Alpha, Zeta, and Kiati, the remnants of the Xala infiltration team. Alpha and Zeta waved awkwardly at the millions in the crowd; the gesture wasn't common in Xalan culture.

And then there was Asha.

She was born for moments like this, and had trained for them as a model and rising television star on Earth before the apocalypse cut her career short. Her voluminous dark hair floated in the breeze and she dazzled the streetside audience with her smile. She wore a crimson dress laden with gold jewelry. The crowd's cries of adulation drowned out the musical fanfare being played as the hovercraft drifted lazily down the street. The Soran public really did worship her, and even with Asha being out of the spotlight in recent years, polling showed the planet remained united in their love for the beautiful, courageous woman from Earth. No telling what the same polls might show if Lucas publicly returned from the dead in his current grotesque state.

Lucas froze the video and expanded his hands to zoom in. Asha's smile was frozen. Peering closer, he knew her well enough to decipher that it was merely a mask. He'd seen her real smile. Her true smile. *That* smile. And this wasn't it. This was an act, and the resolution of the video allowed him to catch a glimpse of small tears in the corner of her eyes.

Closing the feed, Lucas saw another file on the main page of the scroll. Alpha's message. He poked it idly and Alpha's head rose out of the scroll once more.

"I apologize that I have been called away to deal with this pressing problem. I have hand-selected Geneticist Tarla to continue my regimen to ensure your continued progress."

Lucas watched it once. Then watched it again.

"I cannot say how long this problem will continue to draw my attention, so forgive my absence until I am able to return."

Lucas picked up a tone he'd missed the first time, which was easy to do with Alpha's translator collar. Alpha sounded . . . hollow, almost. He watched it again.

"Farewell, brother."

Alpha wasn't that sentimental. The last time he'd said those exact words, he was leaving Lucas behind to die at the hands of the Desecrator.

Something was wrong.

19

Noah woke from another nightmare. In this one, he had been lost in the flaming Dubai hotel, choking on smoke, ears filled with the screams of the dead. Back in his room, he looked around for Sakai, but she wasn't there. She was in Kyra's quarters, where she had been since he'd returned from Earth. The bed seemed vast without her. Colder. Noah still hadn't gotten used to it.

Checking the time, Noah groaned upon realizing dawn was still hours away. He considered climbing the iced stairs to the White Spire to clear his mind, but he had yet to return to the site of the massacre. Word had it the church was going to condemn the ancient temple as unholy ground because of the horrors that had taken place there. Finally, after thousands of years as a spiritual landmark, the spire would slip into ruin with no one to tend to it.

Half an hour later, Noah's eyes finally started to drift shut again when he was woken by a blaring tone from his communicator. He fumbled in the dark for the device and when his thumb finally found it, an image of Sakai shone out of the display in the darkness.

"Noah," she said, visibly on edge. "Get over here, now."

Noah fled from his room without even stopping to grab his thermal coat. He sprinted through the snow to Kyra's quarters, and a trio of guards clad in ice-blasted armor waved him inside.

Noah's adrenaline kept him warm internally, though his skin was tinted blue even from his brief time outside. Sakai reached him and instantly recoiled at his temperature, but her mind was too preoccupied to comment on his ill-conceived wardrobe.

"What's wrong?" Noah said through chattering teeth. "Is Kyra okay? Are you?"

"We're fine," she said. The inactive guards outside had indicated as much. "But you need to see this."

Noah rounded a corner and saw Kyra sitting on the edge of her bed with Erik beside her. He'd gotten out of lockup yesterday afternoon when Tannon gave up the idea that any punishment he could render would actually affect his brother's behavior. Theta, meanwhile, had fled the colony for some unspecified "errand," assuredly devastated by Erik's inexcusable cruelty toward her. Noah was a little annoyed they had called him, but the tears in Kyra's eyes quickly made him forget anything else.

"What is it?" he asked. She looked up at him and wordlessly floated a video feed from her scroll so that it expanded and hovered in the center of the room.

The video was choppy, and entire sections of it were glitching or blacked out. The audio was distorted and alternated between mute and a high-pitched tone Noah could barely hear. But despite the quality, it was clear who was speaking. Malorious Auran. His bone-white hair had grown out and was wildly disheveled. He looked dirty, or bloody, but it was hard to tell which with the hue of the video constantly shifting.

"Kyra, I am so sorry [static]," he began. "I tried to [static] but they [static] blocking all communications since the [static]. I know what you [static] be thinking if you have [static] truth by now. But there is more than [static] know. This is not [static] secure, and you should not try [static] find me."

Noah and Erik shared a worried look.

"Do not try to find me. I [static] wanted to say good-bye, though I do not [static] when this message will reach you, or if it will. They will find me soon, but I will never let them use me to [static] to you. I will—"

Keeper Auran looked to the side, eyes wide with fear. The feed went white.

"Keep going," Noah said, pointing at the floating blank space in the middle of the room.

"That's all there is," Erik said. "It cuts out there."

"Where did it come from?" Noah said, his mind racing.

"It's encrypted. It almost destroyed the message to even get it to play, and there's definitely no way to trace it to its point of origin," Sakai said.

"Get Theta to—" but Noah stopped mid sentence, remembering she was gods knew where right now, thanks to Erik's crassness.

Kyra stared down at her scroll in shock. She hadn't spoken since Noah had entered. Her voice was soft in the tense room.

"We need to find him. He's clearly in danger, trying to protect me somehow."

She stared vacantly ahead.

"I can't let him die for me. He's all I have left."

Noah ran his hand through his hair, which was just starting to unfreeze after his brief time outside. Ice water trickled down the back of his neck.

"We need to take this to Watchman Vale," he finally said.

Erik shook his head violently.

"No way. Look, I'll get us a ship, we can—"

"We can do *what*, Erik?" Noah snapped. "No one is whispering magic words in our dreams to guide us to wherever he is. We need help. We can trust the Watchman."

He looked at the small, blond girl on the bed. She'd never looked so fragile.

"He needs to meet Kyra, and then he'll understand."

Tannon had just returned to the colony after spending time in the capital to consult with Madric Stoller on what was being called the "Lucas problem." Stoller was firm on using Lucas as some sort of weapon, though Tannon equated the idea to trying to fight a fly with a flamethrower. You might achieve your end, but it was entirely possible you'd burn everything and everyone around you to ash in the process. They had no idea what Lucas was capable of, and poking and prodding him into becoming some sort of executioner's axe to try and finish off the crippled Xalan army was asking for trouble.

Eventually Tannon stormed out of the capital, frustrated by watching his successor celebrate a victory over Xala that hadn't happened yet, but content that Lucas was at least being treated well with regular visits from Alpha and Asha. It was a rare thing that Tannon missed being in power, but Stoller's mix of idiocy and evil made him wish there was still a "High Chancellor" before his name to right the obvious wrongs happening all around him.

Tannon had told all of this to Noah the previous day in a rare moment of candor. The Watchman trusted Noah, and in turn, Noah was ready to trust Tannon with something too surreal to believe.

"Bring her in," Noah said as the two of them were standing in Tannon's office, having said little to him so far other than the fact that a friend needed his help.

The door slid open and Kyra entered the room with Sakai and Erik. She wore a dark forest-green tunic and her hair was hastily wrapped into a loose bun. But even unadorned and exhausted, there was no mistaking her beauty.

Tannon raised an eyebrow.

"So you must be the infamous Miss Auran," he said. "Heard you were given quite a scare up on the spire earlier this year."

"Thank you for seeing me, Watchman," she said, lifting her eyes to meet his gaze.

"I thought—"

But then Tannon's voice caught in his throat. He stood there, stunned, then suddenly weak enough at the knees to grab the edge of his desk with both hands.

"*Gods*. What is this?" he said, breathless.

Noah saw it in his eyes. He knew. He had wondered how long it would take him. Most of the planet only knew Corinthia Vale from Stream feeds, but Tannon had watched his niece grow from a child to an adult, and the adolescent in between.

"You're *Cora*," he said, his voice a little more than a whisper. He walked toward her slowly, reverently. He raised his hand and brushed the line of her jaw with his finger, seemingly surprised she was, in fact, real. The hard, stern man Noah knew had melted away. Tannon's face was like a child's, full of wonder and amazement.

But then suddenly, he was back, rigid and tense, realizing the impossibility of the vision standing before him.

"Who *are* you, girl?"

"I'm Kyra Auran," she said. "Past that, I do not know. The only man who can answer your questions and mine is in grave danger."

Tannon listened intently to everything they told him about Kyra and Madric Stoller's quest to end her life. He had already hated Stoller for a number of reasons, but he was boiling as they finished the story about stopping Finn's assassination attempt on the return voyage from Earth. It was also the first time Sakai had heard the full truth, and she wore a look of shock.

After cooling down with a stiff drink pulled from his desk drawer, Tannon watched Malorious Auran's garbled message three times. On the third, he paused and eyed something suspiciously. Drawing his hands outward, he zoomed in on the frame. It was just before the end, when Keeper Auran looked to the side and feed was cut. Tannon raised his arm and the dark background grew a few shades brighter. He repeated the gesture, and suddenly a small figure materialized over Auran's left shoulder. Kyra let out an involuntary gasp.

"What is that?" Sakai asked, poking her finger through the floating figure.

Tannon made another gesture and the resolution increased marginally. The figure was armored, and had a helmet with two vertical slits running down the length of it.

"Ah, damn it all," Tannon said angrily. "He should have known better than to run there. He should have come to me."

"Where?" Erik demanded. "Where is he?"

"Solarion Station. Their security forces wear those helmets."

The room fell silent. All of them knew about Solarion Station. The whole planet knew, but no one ever liked to talk about it.

Eight hundred years ago, a small mining station owned by Solarion Corporation was built in the orbit of Apollica, a tiny scorched rock planet that sat closer to the sun than any other in the Soran solar system. The station was set to mine superheated asteroid fragments that Solarion believed could be refined and sold as a cheaper form of darksteel, a metal forged from downed comets.

At first they found some level of success, and the new alloy couldn't be harvested fast enough. Solarion Station grew exponentially with new additions to house more and more workers. Many who had taken jobs there tried to complain about the horrendous living conditions on the station, but it was nearly impossible to broadcast messages back to Sora due to Apollica's proximity to the sun.

Eventually, when they could take no more, the workers revolted and took over the station, halting mining altogether. Their overlords hired a mercenary army to invade the station and crack skulls until their underlings saw reason. Unfortunately, just as the army arrived, it was revealed that the company's prized metallic alloy would degrade and become brittle in just a few years' time. The entire operation became useless. In an effort to avoid a total loss, they converted Solarion Station into a private prison. The first inmates were the rebellious workers, most of whom died incarcerated months or years later.

The prison kept expanding, housing the most unstable and violent inmates of Sora outside of the dungeons under the Grand Palace, though eventually constant riots and corruption charges closed it down and Solarion went bankrupt once and for all. Many of the prisoners stayed, however, with nowhere else to go. Solarion became a floating free state, a haven for thieves, smugglers, mercenaries, and all those wishing to escape the law. Last estimates said that nearly two hundred thousand people called the station home, the small mining platform having grotesquely expanded over the centuries into a jagged, massive monstrosity of a city. An angry, buzzing hive orbiting a quiet planet.

Malorious Auran was far from the sort of person who'd normally be within a million miles of the station, but Solarion was notorious for its nooks and crannies where fugitives could hide for generations. Fleeing Stoller's forces had made Auran truly desperate, it seemed.

"So the security forces have him?" Kyra asked. "Will they give him to High Chancellor Stoller?"

Tannon rocked his head from side to side.

"They'll probably try to sell him," he said. "In a city ruled by gangs, Solarion Security is the worst. They used to attempt to enforce the law back when Solarion might have been salvageable, but the years have turned them into something else entirely. They're made up mostly of disgraced soldiers or discharged law enforcement. They wield incredible power on the station, and the 'security' identifier is almost a sick joke at this point; every member, from commander to conscript, is rotten to the core."

Tannon saw the fear growing in Kyra's eyes.

"I'll dispatch a team to the station immediately. They don't take kindly to SDI out there, but I'll have my men in plainclothes, and they'll get your grandfather back."

"When do we leave?" Erik asked.

"Don't start with me, Erik," Tannon sighed. "Solarion is no place for—"

"Watchman, you can send your team, but I promise you I will steal a ship the second they leave and be a hundred miles behind their engines the whole way there."

Tannon and Erik locked eyes. The Watchman knew the boy well enough to know he would do exactly as he said. Noah could already see the resignation creeping into his face.

"Then I'll have to escort you myself."

Sakai followed Noah back through the snow toward his quarters. The sun was just starting to rise and the winds had died down. A fresh layer of powder covered nearly everything but the heated walkways between buildings.

Once inside, Sakai began throwing clothing into a storage crate. Noah cocked his head.

"What are you doing?"

"Packing," she said. "It's what, just a two-day flight? The wonders of wormhole-free, intrasystem traveling."

Noah put his hand on top of hers as she was folding up a gray thermal suit.

"Whoa, you're not going. No way."

Sakai turned and glared hard at him. She pulled up her hair and wrapped it into a quick knot before turning back to continue folding.

"I'm serious," Noah said, this time grabbing her wrist. She wrenched it away.

"You're serious?" Sakai snapped. "Look, I forgave your little Earth trip on account of your brother being psychotic, but you're telling me the three of you are going to run off without me again?"

"Kyra won't stay here when her grandfather is in trouble. She needs protection," Noah said, trying to keep calm. "Erik and I—"

"Erik and you what?" Sakai said. "I'm sorry, but Tannon Vale and his men can protect her better than you. And even so, she already has one brother attached to her, why does she need two?"

"She's my friend," Noah said. "I have to—"

"She's my friend too," Sakai interrupted. "Which is why I'm coming."

"But—"

"But what? I'm not strong enough to protect her?"

"It's dangerous."

"I've had the same combat training as you."

"You don't need to go."

"And neither do you."

They sat in strained silence for a minute before Sakai spoke again. "Or is there another reason you don't want me to come?"

Noah narrowed his eyes.

"Girls talk, you know," Sakai continued. "Kyra told me all kinds of stories about your valiance, protecting her from assassins, Xalans, Shadows, Stollers. When she talks about you, she drifts away. She doesn't even realize it, but I do."

"Are you saying—"

"I'm not saying anything." Sakai's tone softened. "You're incredible. I've always told you that. I knew someday you'd be a great hero like your parents; it was inevitable."

Sakai put her hand on Noah's shoulder.

"But when your hero starts rescuing princesses, it's a little unsettling when they look like her. And when they look at your hero like she does."

Noah clasped both his hands lightly around Sakai's arms.

"When I was out there, ready to die with my bones being snapped by the Black Corsair, all I was thinking about was you. You brought me home again. I don't know what I'd do without you. That's the only reason I want you to stay. Not because you're not capable. Not because of Kyra. But because I don't even want to think about the possibility of losing you."

Sakai sighed.

"And you think I want to lose you?" she said. "That I like seeing you attacked and injured and risking your life? I'll go insane if I stay here. Every minute of the months you were gone, I was in constant fear the next message I received would be the worst kind of news. I cannot go through that again. I *will* not."

Noah sat down on his armor crate and put his hands to his knees.

"You need to know all the combat training in the world doesn't prepare you for what's out there. The real world is brutal, horrible. It's no game. Sometimes I wish I had never left this place at all."

"You can't make that decision for me," Sakai said. "If we're supposed to be this next generation of humans, the *only* generation, we can't just be alive. We need to live."

"But Solarion?" Noah said. "You want to start there?"

"I want to start with being with those I love, helping someone who desperately needs it."

That was the Sakai Noah knew. Why would he ever have expected anything less? He knew they could talk for days, and no matter what, she'd still be coming.

But would she come back? Would any of them?

20

"I must depart," the Archon said, his voice a freezing river pouring through the curves of Lucas's mind. He was back in the Dubai cryotank, a tall, bleary shape lurking outside the frosted glass.

"It is too soon for you to make the journey yourself," the Archon continued, "but Sora's doom is at hand. We will meet again when the planet is ash and I am able to extract what I need from its resting place. Sora believes Xala wants their water, their resources, their oxygen. It is true, Xala does, but I am not Xala. Sora is only a means to an end. To eradication. And you, human, are the key that turns the lock at last.

"I work to restore your Earth, so that it can become another vessel to serve me in the coming purge. Do not fail me, and I may allow you to return to your homeworld someday. To walk among green fields and blue skies. I can allow you to imagine you never lost the life you once had, however meaningless and trivial it was. Your delusion will be more peaceful than the other's, lost in eternal torment, tearing up ship after ship, never finding what he seeks.

"Sora is arrogance incarnate. They think they are the prize, but they merely guard it, unknowingly. I may be only a soldier, but in my millennia I have been able to rebuild weapons they can only dream of. I have fed them to the Xalans like opiates, and in turn they have never deviated from my purpose.

"This last creation, assembled in the furthest corner of black space, will be Sora's end. I don't trust the fools I have tasked with its completion, and must return to unveil its glory myself. When Sora falls, you will be ready. You will lead me to what I seek, and this galaxy will see its lights go out, one by one.

"The Xalans tell tales of you, human. The Shadow slayer. The monster killer. But your destiny is far greater than a victory or two. You are the spark that ignites the wildfire that will burn through civilizations like kindling. And I am the wind, the unseen force fanning the flames."

Lucas felt power coursing through his veins. It was a dull hum, one that made him feel more alive than he'd ever been, unable to sit still in the confinement of his quarters. It was a problem.

Though he felt spectacular, he knew what it meant. Either Alpha's treatment had failed to halt or reverse the pace of Shadow conversion, or his new caretaker, Jahane, had been injecting him with something else entirely. The latter was the most problematic idea. If it were true, than that meant—

"You have a visitor, Lucas!" rang Jahane's sing-song voice from outside in the lab.

A vistor? Was Alpha back? Was Asha? Had he been worried for nothing?

Lucas bolted up from his bed and turned toward the metal wall he'd pummeled full of dents. They didn't allow him mirrors on the base; they didn't think it was helpful for his psychological recovery. Looking at the polished allium, he only saw a warped, concave version of himself, merely a hint of his eyes, filled with blue flame. He stretched out his arms, and saw even more black veins snaking underneath his skin. Shirtless, he could see the blackness threading through his newly muscular torso, like black worms devouring his insides. And every day there were a few more.

When Lucas left his room and saw who was there, he breathed a sigh of relief. It wasn't Asha or Alpha, but Theta. Perhaps not who he was dying to see, but if they were letting her see him, it meant everything was fine. Didn't it?

Jahane had the same permanent smile plastered on her face as she welcomed Theta into the room. Most Xalans looked the same, all gray and stony, but Theta took after her mother with a brilliant white coat that would have made her a beauty on her homeworld. But raised among humans, she was shy, and there wasn't a trace of arrogance about her. Her gold-ringed eyes met Lucas's, though he couldn't read her expression. He thought again of how he must look.

Even though Jahane was still beaming, she looked nervous, with tiny beads of sweat dotting her skin. As Theta approached Lucas, Jahane put a wrinkled hand on her wrist. The young Xalan towered above her.

"Sweetie, can I take another look at that clearance authorization?" Jahane said in a high-pitched voice. Lucas felt as if he could hear her pulse quicken from across the room.

"Certainly," Theta said, and waved a data file from her communicator, which fluttered to the luminescent scroll in Jahane's hands. The woman eyed it suspiciously and walked toward the main doors.

"Lovely accommodations," Theta said, eyeing the expensive lab equipment all around. She was being genuine, it seemed, as Xalans weren't generally sarcastic, but she too seemed visibly on edge.

"What brings you here, Theta?" Lucas asked, his voice masking light panic. "Did Alpha send you?"

Theta glanced back at Jahane worriedly.

"May we speak in private?" she asked.

Lucas knew there was no such thing as privacy in the base thanks to an indeterminate number of obviously placed recorders and cameras, and likely even more secret ones, but he led her around the corner into his quarters all the same. Jahane was speaking into her communicator to someone, but he couldn't make out what she was saying.

"We may not have long," Theta whispered when they reached the room. Or, tried to whisper, at least. All her translator collar did was lower the volume of her voice, so the effect wasn't quite the same.

"What's going on?" Lucas asked. A knot was starting to form in his stomach.

"After an . . . incident at Colony One, I needed some time away. I tried to visit my father who I was told was working at the Thylium orbital hangar. Halfway to the station, I was denied access."

"Yeah, I heard there was a solar storm wrecking havoc out there," Lucas said, eyes narrowing.

"I rechecked all current status reports on Thylium by hacking SDI remote logs," Theta continued, voice wavering. "My father never reached the station."

Lucas started pacing around the room, the knot in his stomach tightened painfully.

"Asha is supposed to be there guarding him . . ."

"Lucas," Theta said. Her black eyes were wet. "I spent the last three days infiltrating SDI off-book servers. Some of the most advanced encryptions your species is capable of. There I found an order. One that issued an arrest warrant for Asha and my father. They have been apprehended and taken to an undisclosed location."

Lucas froze while his insides melted. His mind was racing so quickly it almost hurt.

No.

"The second part of the order is something you should read for yourself," Theta continued. She waved up a data file to hover in between them. "It is from High Chancellor Stoller's Viceroy, Draylin Maston."

Lucas expanded the text.

Attn: GS Jahane Tarla—We've now confirmed Alpha's data on Lucas has been forged since his return. The Xalan is trying to cure him, as we feared. His stats are dropping rapidly, and soon he'll be nothing more than simple flesh and bone, and entirely useless to us as anything but a trophy to trot out to the public. We don't need a trophy. We need a weapon.

I'm securing Alpha and the volatile Lady Asha and sending you in his place with a cover story. Using Alpha's "cure," we've managed to reverse engineer the actual Shadow conversion formula, at long last. I realize you couldn't make your own batch in fifty-odd attempts, but now we finally have it in hand. Data says trials on humans or Sorans could take years, but Lucas is already far enough along to be a current asset, provided we can control him when this is all over.

Report everything he does or says. Send all data by EOD after collection. This could be your finest hour, Geneticist

Tarla. Your greatest work and eternal place in history. Or it could mean your slow and painful execution. Do not make Lucas your latest failure. He is too valuable to lose.

Lucas read the entire document almost instantly, the Shadow conversion having dramatically increased his cognitive functioning. In a rage, he whirled around, his fist moving through the holographic page and slamming into the opposite wall with such force the entire level shook like it had just been hit by an earthquake.

Theta looked terrified, and when she spoke, her metallic voice was shaking. She raised another file from her wrist communicator.

"I forged my own clearance to visit you, and an order for your immediate transfer authorized by the Viceroy himself. I was hoping we might use it to leave this base peacefully, though I do not know if my falsified information is convincing enough. I was forced to draft it rather hastily, given how recently I acquired this information."

Lucas sat down on his bed, chin to his chest. His knuckles were cut, but he couldn't feel the pain. A piercing alarm began to bounce around the metal walls of the laboratory floor.

"There's no peaceful way out of here," Lucas said through clenched teeth.

Lucas stormed out of his quarters, Theta trailing timidly behind. Then, after a blinding sprint forward, he was across the room, his hand around Jahane's soft throat. She grasped at his forearm with a grip stronger than one would think with her supposed years, though infinitely weak compared to his own. A garbled voice squawked out of her communicator.

"What's the prisoner's status?" it shrieked as the long, slow alarm blared all around them.

Prisoner. He had been so foolish.

"You lied!" Lucas roared at Jahane, lifting the tiny woman a solid three feet off the ground. She continued to claw at Lucas's iron grip. Theta finally caught up to the pair of them, long strides allowing her to bound across the room.

Lucas released Jahane, who crumpled down in a heap next to the door, which flashed with red lights indicating total lockdown.

"Can't you see it was worth it?" she choked out, pawing at her neck like the motion would help her find more air. "Can't you feel how strong you've become?"

"You ran Stoller's Soran Shadow trials. How many did you kill? Dozens? Hundreds?"

"To save *billions*!" she wheezed. "You could save us all if you'd only cooperate."

"And this is how you make me fall in line?" Lucas growled. "By kidnapping my friends? Where are they?"

Jahane merely glared at him. Her face was twisted in anger and pain. It was clear that her permanent smile was nothing more than a facade. This was the real geneticist, one who had committed countless atrocities on Stoller's behalf and had slowly dosed Lucas with Shadow serum until he was ready to burst with power.

"You'll never find them," she spat.

"*Where!*" Lucas bellowed, and he knew immediately he'd struck the right note. A piece of his brain felt like it had just touched ice, causing him to wince painfully, but the effect on Jahane was immediate.

Her eyes went vacant. She stared past Lucas and Theta to a blank spot across the room. She was his now.

"Where?" he said more calmly.

"I do not have that information," Jahane said matter-of-factly in a monotone cadence. "The Viceroy will know."

"Where is he, then?" Lucas said sharply, temper spiking again. "Where is Draylin Maston?"

"The palace," she said, her voice still raspy, bruises already forming around her throat. Her stare slowly softened, then she blinked her eyes and glared at Lucas. She was back.

"Your friends will be dead by the time you reach them," she said.

"Stoller and the Viceroy better hope not," Lucas said, darkening her frail form with his shadow. "Or I will burn their entire ruling class to ashes."

"Lucas," Theta called from behind him. "We must go, sensors indicate troops are moments from—"

"Alright," Lucas said, letting out a cough. Then another. Something was in his lungs, burning. Barely visible yellow gas was starting to pour from the ventilation ports in the room. Lucas looked at the door, then down at Jahane.

"Kill me, then," she said. "And be done with it. The monster I've helped create would make for a fitting end."

"No monster," Lucas growled. "Not yet."

He turned away from her as she dissolved into a fit of hacking coughs, and he planted a sharp kick into the double metal doors to her right. They exploded outward, allowing fresh air to rush into his lungs.

"Come on," he said, turning back to Theta. "Stay behind—"

"Lucas!" Theta shouted, as loud as her translator would let her.

Lucas turned and saw a quartet of armored guards sprinting down the corridor, rifles raised. They fired.

The effect his abilities had on his perception of what was happening was strange. Lucas stiff-armed Theta to the side, sending her flying to safety behind a wall. He could see ovals of burning plasma hurtling toward him. Not frozen, but like someone was lobbing a very slow pitch down home plate. A pitch coming at fifty miles per hour rather than the usual 1,500 of a plasma round. He ducked in and out of the bursts with ease, though one did manage to painfully graze the side of his arm.

Lucas wasn't a telekinetic Chosen Shadow like the Council or the Black Corsair, but he only needed their trademark strength and speed against something as fragile and slow as man. He drove his fist into the chestplate of the first soldier, which cracked like ice, then whirled around to shatter the helmet of the next one with his elbow. The two were unconscious before they hit the ground. His next strikes were more precise. He knocked the third soldier's rifle downward so that it fired into his companion's leg. As a shrill cry filled the hall, Lucas wrenched the entirety of the last soldier upward, sending him flying a dozen feet into the ceiling to come crashing back down to earth. The only sounds now were the moans of the shot soldier mixed with the dull wail of the alarm.

"Follow me," Lucas called to Theta, who had a look of complete shock on her face. The entire exchange had taken just a few simple seconds, though it had felt much longer to Lucas. He grabbed one of the soldier's rifles, but there wasn't time to stop and change into armor that might shield him from a shot he didn't have the capacity to dodge. As he lifted the rifle out of the downed soldier's hands, he caught a reflection of his own face in the man's helmet. His eyes were wild, and so blue they were glowing.

They turned the corner to find the lift open with even more guards spilling out. Some fully armored and helmeted, some merely in fatigues, hastily assembled to respond to the distress call.

Lucas's mind raced faster than he ever thought possible. His brain instantly assessed the armor of each soldier, their weapons, their positioning, who was likely to fire first, who had a clear line of sight on him. A flood of data surged through his mind in a single second, and he knew exactly what to do just as the first trigger was pulled.

Though these were Stoller's soldiers, tasked with keeping him at bay, they weren't the enemy. There was a loose threat on base, and they had to contain it. He would have done the same. They didn't deserve to die, and Lucas was thankful he still had enough of his sanity to realize that. For now.

During his instant analysis of the scene, he found his target. Lucas rolled right to dodge a stream of plasma from the first few soldiers, then unloaded a precision shot into the blue stun grenade clipped to the foremost soldier's belt. The device exploded at his waist, sending searing white light and deafening sound through the other half dozen soldiers all around him, who cried out and staggered around, crashing into one another. Lucas took advantage of their disorientation to sprint into the middle of them, cleaving the group in half and sending all six crashing into the sides of the hallway where their armor dug deep gashes in the walls. When none stirred, Theta danced over the downed bodies and entered the lift with him. One unarmored soldier lying prone on the ground tried to raise his pistol toward the pair of them. Lucas stamped down on it with his boot, crushing the gun to scrap and atomizing a few of the man's fingers in the process.

The lift rocketed toward the surface. Lucas stopped to catch his breath, but realized he didn't need to. He'd never been able to fight like this. Think like this. It was exhilarating, terrifying. Theta couldn't take her eyes off him. He was an impossible creation, a horrible one. But his thoughts were fixed on Alpha and Asha alone.

"How far is the palace from here?" Lucas asked as the lift sped past sublevel after sublevel toward the surface.

"8,854 miles," Theta said, seemingly not needing to reference any data to say that with certainty.

"Can you open a connection to the colony?" Lucas asked. He wiped a smear of blood from his chest. He didn't know which soldier it had come from.

Theta fiddled with her communicator. "We are still too far underground. When we reach the surface, I will show our clearance to the local authorities on base and then we can—"

"Theta," Lucas said, stifling a reactive laugh. "We're far past forged clearances."

"Then have you formulated a plan for our escape?" she asked.

"Sometimes you just have to improvise," Lucas said, checking the readouts on his rifle.

The doors opened, and Lucas remembered where this exit went. To a hangar for one of Alpha's many projects: the mech testing grounds.

Problem.

When he saw what was outside, he shoved Theta back into the lift and wrenched the doors shut with his bare hands. He leapt upward just in time for a hail of plasma to pepper the metal. Landing on a precarious catwalk, he surveyed the situation on the ground below. There were dozen soldiers but, more pressingly, there was also a pair of giant mechs, streamlined versions of the exosuit Alpha had designed to fight Commander Omicron's Paragons during their first trip to Sora onboard the Ark. Why did he have to be such a damn good engineer?

The catwalk exploded and Lucas was forced to leap away before the blast arrived. The barrel arm of the dark-red mech was smoking, while the navy-blue one had a shot heating up in the chamber. A second blast, another impossible leap. The soldiers tried to get a bead on Lucas while he darted across the room. The air was thick and hot with plasma, too much to effectively dodge. Lucas took cover behind the torso of an unfinished exosuit and the pings on the metal were fast and frequent. A shot from an unseen mech caused the torso he was hiding behind to rocket into him, sending him sprawling forward, sliding across the ground with fresh pain shooting through his back. Filled with rage, Lucas kicked the mangled, smoking metal piece forward, where it bowled over a pair of soldiers. Lucas got off two shots expertly guided into the shoulders of two other troops—nonfatal, but assuredly painful. He let off a stream toward the mechs, but the plasma merely spattered off the suits. Both the crimson and navy units were sprinting toward him now, gun barrels raised.

He raced forward like a whirlwind to meet them.

The first booming shot whizzed by him and its heat baked the right half of his body uncomfortably. He leapt forward and drove his fist into the headless mech, ripping off the morenthic plating to reveal the flesh-and-blood human inside. The operator's eyes were wide with terror, and Lucas flung him down to the ground before leaping to the adjacent navy mech. He landed on its shoulder and pummeled its gun arm with a flurry of barefisted strikes. The barrel started heating up to fire to try and shake him off, but its housing was now severely bent inward from Lucas's thunderous blows. The stifled explosion inside the arm sent Lucas flying off the exosuit as the mech whirled around and fell on its back with a thud that shook the entire hangar.

Lucas stood up and pulled three inches of shrapnel out of his side. Only five soldiers remained in the room, the others lying on the floor with gunshot or blast injuries. Lucas raised his heavy rifle with one arm. Five other guns clattered to the floor, the soldiers dropping to their knees with hands raised and looks of fear on their faces. Lucas marched the soldiers over to the lift, where they traded places with Theta. She wandered outside to marvel at the carnage. Lucas slammed the doors shut and cratered them with his palm so they wouldn't reopen.

Turning back to Theta, Lucas finally felt something close to exhaustion. He'd fought like a demon, but still had limits. He clenched his side where blood flowed from his ribs and let out a sharp hiss as he bent down to press the superheated barrel of a discarded pistol to his wounds to seal them shut.

Lucas looked forward toward the final obstacle. The hangar doors. He stumbled toward them and found them slowly rising, light flooding in to reveal the destruction inside.

An army waited for them.

Three hundred soldiers. A half dozen mechs. An enormous hovering tank with a barrel the size of a oak tree. Anything that could fire plasma or metal was pointed directly at him. It was too much. Far too much.

"I'm sorry," he said to Theta as he struggled to stay on his feet.

"Perhaps I will see my father again," she said as two burly soldiers approached her. Fifty were now shuffling toward Lucas. A veritable firing squad. One hammered his boot into Theta's backward-bending knee, causing her to fall. The other raised his pistol to the back of her head. There would be no prisoners. No witnesses. Lucas tried to lunge forward but couldn't.

"Stop," he cried. "*STOP!*"

His brain felt like it had been submerged completely in freezing water. He clutched the sides of his head and dropped to his knees as the pain forced tears from his eyes. When his vision returned and the stinging dulled, he saw what was happening around him.

No shot was fired.

The two men froze, then relaxed, arms at their sides. Lucas recognized the vacant looks on their faces immediately. Turning around, he saw the same blank stares across the entire army. Legions of soldiers, unmoving, stares fixed straight ahead with weapons dangling at their sides.

Lucas cautiously walked toward Theta and helped her to her feet.

The silence was eerie. There was no shouting. No gunfire. Just the purr of the hovertank's engine and the distant groan of the alarm.

The entire base was empty, even though it was filled with Sorans.

But if Lucas knew anything, it was that it wouldn't last long. He shook out the remaining splinters from his head and finalized the last leg of his plan in an instant.

"Come on," he said to Theta, and the two of them made their way through the maze of frozen soldiers, who didn't move even when they were brushed or bumped into. Lucas briefly thought of another word, "die," for what they almost did to Theta, but he thought better of it and pressed forward. He was in no way eager to feel that stinging chill in his mind again. There was no pain quite like it.

Another hangar loomed ahead. Two prototype aerial fighters hung from the rafters like sleeping bats. Soon they reached a long rope that automatically hoisted them to the cockpit of the one with its paneling closed up and ready for flight. The sleek pearl-and-gold vessel bristling with unmatched firepower and a miniaturized blue-core drive was Alpha's latest masterpiece.

"Can you fly this vessel?" Theta asked, securing her restraints in the gunner's seat. If she were any taller, she wouldn't have fit. A dome closed up and around them.

"Yes," Lucas said, his eyes and brain analyzing the Soran/Xalan hybrid controls at lightning speed. A thousand menus and settings and options and readouts, and it was all so *simple*. But Lucas's mind was fatigued. Whatever he'd just done out there had taken most of the strength he had left. Once he studied the cockpit, it was all he could do not to pass out.

"Greetings, Lucas. I will be assisting you on your flight today," said a soothing female voice from thin air.

Lucas jumped and looked around for the source of a voice. It took him a moment to realize it was an onboard AI. One that recognized him.

"Mission orders are absent," said the AI. "Please relay destination coordinates."

"The Grand Palace," Lucas said. "But for now, anywhere but here."

The soldiers on the pavement outside began to stir, their minds once again their own. They turned around and shouted, no one realizing where Lucas had gone.

Until the engines fired.

"Have a pleasant flight," the fighter's AI said with a smile in its disembodied voice.

The craft detached from its suspension, violently snapping the cables, and floated out onto the airfield ahead. A hundred rifles and a very long tank barrel turned toward them. But then Lucas clenched his hologram-wrapped fist, and they were gone, a distant dot in a sea of blue sky.

21

The ship stank. Noah hadn't just been sheltered from war up until recently; he'd also grown unintentionally attached to a life of relative luxury as one of the famed Earthborn. He traveled in top-of-the-line military transports and, hell, even his trip to Earth was in Finn Stoller's luxury liner.

No such luck for the voyage to Solarion. A military ship would likely be shot down on sight without prior clearance. An expensive cruiser would be hijacked and stripped for parts. So they were in a confiscated pirate vessel Tannon had ordered from a nearby SDI impound.

And it stank.

Though, to be fair, so did most of them.

While much of Sora was full of the rich and the beauty those rich could afford, Solarion had no such airs. It was a dark, ugly place, and so were the people in it for the most part, far from the wonders of age-slowing genes and thoroughbred family lines. The group of them had to look the part as well as act it, and seventy-four hours in a sweltering tin can without so much as a vapor shower was a good start. The two-day flight had been mercifully short given the ship's conditions.

They'd already docked at the station thanks to a forged ID slip and were ready to head out onto the streets in search of Malorious Auran and his presumed captors. All their communicators were deactivated, lest Solarion Security pick up any unwanted chatter coming from Sora that might give them away.

Tannon's team shifted uneasily in the exit bay as they rehashed their plan one last time. It had actually been Erik's idea, though it was anyone's guess how it would play out in practice. They'd find out soon enough.

Their combat instructor, Celton, was one of the three other soldiers Tannon had brought with them. Any larger of a group and they'd attract too much attention. Celton and Tannon could practically be brothers, with hard jaws and silver hair, but Celton's eyes were amber while Tannon's were mismatched green and blue.

The other colony soldier in the group was Worsaw, a sturdy rectangle of a man with a constant scowl on his face whom Noah recognized as a guard who had always been outside Kyra's tent. His eyes were narrow and angled like Sakai's, but his pupils were midnight blue and he had a long thin scar running down his left cheek.

The third soldier was a specialist they simply called "Key." She was an ex-Guardian from Tannon's days as an admiral, now some sort of intelligence officer who fed information from the current High Chancellor to the former one. She was pale as a ghost and her auburn hair was streaked with black and drawn into a tight braid that tumbled all the way down to the small of her back. Her cheekbones were razors, her nose a sharp point. When she walked, even on rusted metal floors, her steps made no sound.

Tannon's team was a collection of anonymous faces, and they could step off the ship in ragged cowls and patchwork armor plating and look right at home on the streets of Solarion. The rest of them, however, had a higher profile.

Of course Tannon had been the High Chancellor of all of Sora, and was therefore forced to wear a pair of dark goggles that wrapped up and over his head, concealing nearly everything but his nose and chin. An effective disguise, and the various built-in lens filters could do everything from detecting heat signatures to seeing through walls.

Sakai wore her hair down in a way that shielded half her face, and a grimy scarf covered up most of the rest of her features. Erik had opted to brand himself with a demonic facial tattoo that would be all anyone saw when they looked at him, instead of the son of the most famous pair of warriors on the planet. It would fade from his skin in a week, but the effect was unsettling and made him look right at home with the other psychopaths wandering the dark alleys of Solarion.

Kyra had opted for a simple hood, and because she was so small, most passersby wouldn't see her face at all. The coat it was attached to had its sleeves ripped off, and she wore a long mud-brown dress underneath with a bottom edge like a wind-tattered flag.

Noah was clad in a bulky jacket that went from his calves all the way up to the middle of his face. When clasped shut, the high-collared coat covered his nose and mouth completely, which was why the style was high fashion for thieves in the area. The coat had some weight to it with sewn-in anti-blade plating. It amplified Noah's already formidable size to menacing proportions. Though the darksteel warhammer strapped to his back would tell most to stay away by itself. If they didn't try to slit his throat and steal it, that is.

They all had weapons; not carrying one openly on the streets of Solarion was an invitation to robbery, murder, or worse. Kyra had her scattergun slung over her shoulder. Sakai was given a handgun and a thin, jagged short sword. Erik had his laser pistol and an unknown amount of other hidden weapons under his clothes. Noah remembered the pistol had once been part of a set. The pistol's twin hadn't been seen since Earth and eventually Noah realized Erik probably lost his fingers when the second gun overheated in the fight against the Xalans and it exploded in his hand. Naturally, his brother would never admit that.

Tannon and his troops carried larger rifles that looked like they'd been assembled from scrap metal, but were in working order. The four of them alone looked like the makings of a formidable gang, which was the effect they were going for. It was rather odd seeing the usually freshly pressed Tannon Vale dressed like a cross between a bounty hunter and a smuggler.

They were ready. Or as ready as they could be.

A dozen odors hit Noah as he exited the shuttle, ranging from sewage to shellfish and everything in between. Despite their bared weapons and tough facade, they were immediately swarmed by brave merchants, who shoved mutated fruit in their faces or tried to sell them rusted stunguns. Worsaw and Celton pushed them aside, and the group marched down the busy street, avoiding eye contact with everyone and anyone.

Solarion was more or less a giant cube made up of over two hundred or so levels that stretched in all directions for miles. The station slowly spun around Apollica underneath a triple-layered plexishield that filtered the sun to a manageable brightness and kept the replicated oxygen inside. It was odd to see the star looming so large here, a dark bronze because of the shield. Apollica itself was a dusky pink on the horizon, its true color warped by the excessive amount of pollution in the artificial atmosphere. They were at the top of the station. The lower you descended, the worse the floating city was said to become. Rumor had it the last few levels were completely uninhabitable, and the creatures that did live there had transformed from Soran into something else entirely. Thankfully, they didn't need to go down nearly that far.

"Do you know where we're going?" Erik asked Tannon.

"It's been a while, but yes," the Watchman replied, scanning the crowd through his visor.

The sheer hideousness of the people was jarring. Even dressed in rags, hard, smooth, tank-bred faces like Key's and Celton's stood out here, and if anyone ever caught a glimpse of Sakai or Kyra all would be lost. Disfigured prostitutes writhed up against walls as they passed. One was missing an ear; another had an entirely robotic arm and a chemical burn scarring half her face. Gang members flirted with the women, spikes implanted in their bald heads, tattoos covering ashy skin. Enormous blades dangled from their hips while century-old military rifles were slung across their backs. Noah caught a glare from one who sneered at him, revealing a mess of brown metalwork where his teeth should have been.

It was a relief when they reached what was called a "chasm lift," a massive elevator that held hundreds at a time and traveled to every level of Solarion but the last few. On the floor there were jagged metal outcroppings where benches likely used to be, until they were ripped out by vandals. They filed inside and stood around like livestock being transported to slaughter.

Twenty levels down a cry rang out. The chasm lift crowd parted to reveal a man bleeding on the ground, a knife under his ribs. Three thugs with long, oiled black hair circled him, picking off his weapons and credit chips. The assailants were pale and looked half-starved. All wore ragged green garb adorned with the symbol of a white skull split in half. They hurled insults at the downed man as the crowd inched further away from them.

Noah reached for his hammer and started toward them. Tannon gripped his shoulder with his hand and slowly shook his head back and forth.

He was right. Noah knew they couldn't draw attention to themselves, but it took everything in him to stand and do nothing. Looking down, he could see fear and pain in Sakai's eyes. *This is what you signed up for*, he wanted to say, but didn't.

By the time they left the lift at the forty-seventh level, the thugs were laughing and joking with each other, and the man was dead.

They were in the prison wing now, the portion of the station that had been the maximum security facility before it was closed down and a city was stacked on top of it. Here, Tannon promised they'd find who they were looking for.

The entry to the former prison was still protected, just not by traditional guards. The sentries that stood there now were a half dozen men, rippling with muscle and holding a variety of terrifying-looking weapons ranging from rust-bitten axes to modern scatterguns. The central gate they stood before had two giant black leathery wings painted on it. Lucas could see the same symbol tattooed on a few of the scowling men who eyed the lot of them like a particularly delicious breakfast. The wings behind them reminded Noah of an altered version of the Guardian's famed silver feathered wings, pinned to the chests of all its tank-bred soldiers and, on occasion, Noah's mother.

Tannon approached the sentries, chest inflated with the natural confidence he always wore. The tallest guard spoke with thunder.

"Go home, offworlder."

So much for their disguises.

"We're here to see Zaela," Tannon said with authority.

The men moved to encircle them. Noah watched Kyra inch closer to Erik, who had his hand on his pistol.

"I don't think you heard me," the man said, looming over Tannon. His skin was almost pitch black, but his eyes were green in a sea of yellow. He had a jagged double scar across the side of his neck, and shoulders like a mech exosuit.

"You need to—" he began, but a heavily accented voice rang out of the communicator hanging from his collar. A woman's.

"Gods damn it, Razor, let him in. Oi'd know that goat's voice anywhere."

Tannon's mirrored lenses stared the man down, and the accented voice continued.

"Now, ya brute!"

Noah's stomach unclenched as the eight of them were ushered inside the compound. The wings parted and slammed shut behind them once they were inside.

After walking down corridors full of broken lightscreens and more angry-looking men stamped with dark wings either on their skin or clothing, they entered what appeared to be the central dining wing of the former prison. Even more gang members were here, again all men, and the space appeared to be some sort of combination of war room and drinking hall, tall metal glasses of dark liquid set sloppily down on holotables projecting maps and data clusters.

In the middle of the chaos was a lone figure, a woman. She had dark brown skin with long tendrils of jet-black hair clustered together and hanging down her back like tree vines. Her eyes were pools of violet, her face flecked with white scars. She wore light armor plating that covered her chest and legs, and her bare arms were solid muscle. The leather wings from the gate were stamped on her right shoulder, and Noah was surprised to see the feathered ones of the Guardians tattooed on her left. *So that's how she knows Tannon.*

She walked toward them cautiously, like a beast circling prey it doesn't quite understand.

"Off wit' it then," she said, and Tannon peeled the metal goggles from his face.

"Satisfied?" he asked, and the woman suddenly darted toward him, stopping just shy of his face. She only came up to his chin, at most. Her age was hard to determine. She smelled like alcohol and plasma afterburn.

"It's you, ya," she said, stepping back and picking up a cylinder of murky liquid, which she sipped from. "Come to visit at last, Watchman? Or come to take me back?"

"Neither," Tannon said. Noah thought he saw him hiding a small smile.

"Key, Celton, good to see yas," she said. "How's th' retirement?"

"Babysitting," Celton said, nudging his head toward the four younger party members. Tannon shot him a sharp glare, and the woman eyed them curiously.

"Name's Zaela," she said with a quick nod. "Oi knew ya friend here from way, way back."

Noah returned her nod, but didn't speak. Kyra and Sakai each forced a quick smile while Erik remained stonefaced.

"Not much for chattin' ya?" she said to Tannon, jerking her head toward the group. "Well let's talk then, grab a drink from one of th' fellas an' come wit' me."

On the way to Zaela's "office," which turned out to be the former quarters of the corrupt prison warden, Noah's suspicions were confirmed that she was indeed ex-Guardian, as she chatted to Tannon and the others about the unit. What wasn't mentioned was whatever event turned her from SDI soldier to Solarion warlord.

"It's a simple proposal," Tannon said. "It'll make you rich *and* give you more power in your little kingdom of rust here."

"Oi have power, an' marks," Zaela said. "Oi got everything oi need right here," she said, arms extended toward her shabby office piled high with weapons and large vats of spirits. Noah still couldn't place her accent. Was she from the Sorvo Republic? Kashiit? The Sand Plains? It was hard to say.

"Black Wings on top of things these days, ya?" she said. "Don't need no nothin' from ya."

"Not on top of Solarion Security," Tannon said. Zaela frowned and started peeling a fruit with a long, surprisingly clean knife.

"Don't count. SolSec's a fixture. Ain't no one on top of them. They take a piece of all th' gangs in return for not sendin' us into th' sun. That's life on th' Station."

"What I'm offering is billions of marks, and a shot at crippling SolSec," Tannon pressed.

"A shot at death," she said, continuing to skin her fruit. "An' a shot at the boys bootin' my ass outta here for sayin' such nonsense."

Kyra suddenly chimed in, expectedly.

"Why do you recruit only men?" she asked. Everyone looked stunned that she'd spoken, Zaela included. But after a pause she answered all the same.

"All fellas from th' homeland. Can't trust th' girls. Fellas simple. Girls scheme, talk, claw ya eyes out first chance. But not you, starfish, ya? You too nice an' pretty for that," she flashed a glowing yellow smile at Kyra and laughed. "Who this one, then?" she said to Tannon.

"We're trying to find her grandfather," he said. "SolSec has him."

Zaela's eyes narrowed.

"Must be pretty important to drag th' lordly High Chancellor off his throne," she said sarcastically.

"Ex-Chancellor," Tannon corrected, annoyed.

"Whateva, how much ya pay then?" she said, taking a bite from the green skinless sphere in her hand and chasing it with a swig from a nearby bottle.

"I don't pay you anything," Tannon said, "Solarion Security will."

Now that made Zaela curious.

22

The ionosphere was quiet. Despite the early hour, Lucas and Theta could see the dark blue of the night sky, a billion stars winking in the wake of the fighter's engines. Lucas's head had finally stopped throbbing, and Theta was talking to someone on her communicator behind him. Sora rotated beneath them in silence as they hovered on the edge of the planet's atmosphere. The golden tint of the ship's domed viewscreen made everything appear more crisp and constantly highlighted cities below or satellites and space stations ahead. The blue-cored fighter Alpha had designed was blindingly fast, and, even spending barely any time with the ship, Lucas knew all of its ins and outs thanks to his lightning-quick Shadow cognition. The friendly AI kept chattering at him whenever there was more than a few minutes of silence.

"Systems normal, destination twenty-two minutes away," it chimed.

"The Viceroy is not at the Grand Palace," Theta said, finally closing down her communicator.

"What?" Lucas said. Jahane couldn't have lied to him. Not in that state.

"I should clarify, the Viceroy is *no longer* at the Grand Palace," Theta said.

"Where, then?"

"His aide would not tell me, only that he has departed on a pressing off-world assignment for the High Chancellor."

Goddamnit, Lucas thought. *He could be anywhere.*

"Though he requested not to be disturbed," Theta continued, unperturbed, "his aide helpfully gave me his communication frequency in order that I might leave him a message, which he would return at his earliest convenience."

"His comm frequency," Lucas said. "Can you trace that?"

"Ordinarily it is not thought to be possible from a singular piece of otherwise meaningless data, but—" Lucas's heart leapt at the "but." He knew what came next.

"But your mother is the foremost comms expert in the galaxy."

"Correct," Theta said. "She is already expecting us at Orbital Relay Station 117. Mercifully, she was not taken along with my father."

"Orbital Relay Station 117 is five thousand seven hundred and eighty-two miles from our current location," the AI added helpfully.

"Mercy has little to do with it," Lucas said, ignoring the program and manually changing their destination. If Theta was in orbit, it was unlikely Stoller would bother having her apprehended, particularly when Asha and Alpha were already enough to "motivate" Lucas. Though motivate him to do what remained to be seen. They had badly misjudged the ease with which they believed they could manipulate him. They'd never kill either of them and lose any leverage they had on him.

They wouldn't?

Lucas shoved the doubt from his mind. They couldn't. And he suspected Alpha and Asha could handle themselves, even in captivity. Both had proven adaptable in similar situations, from Kvaløya to Rhylos. He punched in the coordinates Theta waved over to him from her rear-facing gunner seat, and the fighter made a sharp turn. Theta had already disabled the fighter's onboard tracking chip, much to the AI's dismay, meaning no one was following them. Not that they could, given their speed.

"Great work, Theta," Lucas said. "Through all of this. Thank you for telling me what had happened to your father and Asha. Who knows how long I might have been tricked into staying at the base, being pumped full of god knows what."

"Oh, you are most welcome," she said from behind him. He could practically hear her blushing. "I did not know who else I could trust."

"Why didn't you tell my sons?" Lucas asked.

"I was already close to your location when I discovered the truth. I thought time was of the essence."

"What made you leave the colony in the first place?" Lucas pressed. "You mentioned some sort of incident? Is everyone alright?"

"Yes, yes," Theta said. "I did not mean to concern you. It was just a . . . misunderstanding with Erik. He . . . interpreted a pattern of behaviors on my part as indicators of . . . romantic feelings."

That made Lucas raise his eyebrows.

"He what? He made a pass at you?" Lucas had heard a lot of tall tales about his miscreant son. But this—

"No. His misinterpretation was that *I* had such feelings toward him. He was . . . thoroughly disgusted by even the suggestion of the idea, which I understand entirely. Xalan and human biology would never allow for—"

"So he was an asshole," Lucas said, shaking his head. The poor girl. Using science to deflect the simple truth of a harmless crush.

"Erik has lived with a heavy burden; an entire race looks to him to lead. He has the potential for greatness, to follow the path before him forged by his parents, and now by his brother, who is more man than boy in recent years," Theta said contemplatively. "Though I fear in consistently lending him my aid for his foolish pursuits, I have only quickened an alternate path to his ruin."

She really did care for him. It was touching to hear, and tragic at the same time. From what Lucas knew of his son, Erik had not done much to deserve such loyalty.

"I also owe you a great debt for looking out for my sons, all these years." he said. "And for helping bring me home to them."

Theta fell silent, uncomfortable with praise.

"Can I ask you something?" she said hesitantly.

The fighter whipped past a news beacon orbiter, broadcasting a Stream feed to the planet below.

"Of course," he said.

"Despite my father's objections, I have studied his decrypted records from the Genetic Science Enclave. There has never been a Shadow specimen to exhibit your unique . . . influence on others."

"Mind control," Lucas said plainly. He shivered.

"How do you do it?" she said. "What is it like?"

"It's just a thought, sometimes a word. And it hurts," Lucas said. "The pain can range from a twinge to something indescribable. And afterward, it feels like I've chipped off a piece of my soul. Sometimes just a shard, other times a slab. I can feel the hollowness inside me. I can feel it now."

"There were so many at the base," Theta said. "How is such a thing possible?"

Lucas shook his head.

"I don't know. It's all new to me. It's . . . terrifying," he said honestly. "The strength, the speed—I understand that, or at least I'm starting to. But the rest of it, it's dangerous, like your father told me. I can see that now."

After pausing to consider what he'd said, Theta spoke again.

"You have something most Shadows do not have," she said. "You possess friends and family who care for you. Who love you. Hold onto them and you will be able to retain your humanity as your power grows."

"Is that in the GSE research you read?" Lucas asked.

"It is not, yet I prescribe it all the same. You would be wise to listen."

That was dangerously close to an order from the pale, timid, teen-aged Xalan. For a moment, Lucas forgot his fear and panic, and was comforted by her words.

The AI jabbered at them for the rest of their flight to Orbital Relay Station 117, one of thousands of hunks of metal orbiting the planet to boost military and civilian communication to distant planets and, more recently, the Xalan colonies. Zeta was stationed with a small team of civilian contractors, whose spines all went stiff with fear as Lucas opened the entry hatch to the relatively cramped outpost. They obviously all recognized him as the famed dead Earthborn, but due to the blackness threading through his skin and clearly unsettled, shock-ingly iced eyes, none so much as spoke to him. Lucas was past caring about keeping his resurrection a secret, but the team were loyal to Zeta, and she said no one would ever know he was there.

Zeta could barely fit in the station, which was little more than a few cramped corridors of fiberfoam and pearlsteel, jammed with aging electronics. It didn't look like it could house anyone comfortably for more than a day or two, which was how long the team had been there. They were trying to extend the comm frequency of the station to interact with others recently set up in deep space, hoping to bounce a strong signal all the way to Earth. A few scattered SDI teams were there, scouring the remains of the Dubai genetics lab and attempting to hunt down more possible hidden Xalan installations on the planet. The giant floating machines transforming the Earth's ruined atmosphere were left alone to be confiscated and studied at a later date.

The Archon's words resounded in Lucas's head.

I work to restore your Earth, so that it can become be another vessel to serve me in the coming purge. Do not fail me, and I may allow you to return to your homeworld someday. To walk among green fields and blue skies.

Zeta regarded Lucas with a short bow as the three members of her crew remained wide-eyed and mute.

"Thank you for bringing my daughter to me," she said, translator flickering with a light purple hue. "My family is ever in your debt."

Lucas shook his head.

"I'm in yours, but I have to ask one more favor."

Zeta nodded.

"Theta already relayed the frequency to me and I have just completed the trace," she said. She drew up a spherical data file from a nearby monitor and the hologram disintegrated into thin air as she spread her claws outward.

"Your craft will now be able to seek out Viceroy Maston's vessel. The data indicates he is heading somewhere within the local solar system."

That was a relief. Lucas didn't want to spend days or weeks chasing him through a wormhole.

"We should depart," Theta said eagerly, moving toward the airlock.

Lucas and Zeta spoke at the same time.

"*We?*"

"Theta," Zeta said. "You are in no way going to attempt to aid Lucas with his mission. What you did at Merenes Military Base was dangerous enough, but you will stay here with me until we receive word your father is safe."

"But I can assist with the endeavor," Theta stammered. "I can—"

"You've done so much already, Theta," Lucas said. "I'll take it the rest of the way from here. I don't know what could happen next, both with the SDI or Xala. Or myself, for that matter, in my current state. I have to do this alone. Your father would never forgive me if I purposefully put you in harm's way."

Theta was sullen, but nodded.

"I have tasted adventure on Earth, and I will admit, it was not to my liking," she said. "But I would never forgive myself if I could have done something more to save my father, and did not."

"You've done more than you know," Lucas said, putting his hand on her shoulder and staring into her watery golden eyes. "I'll bring him back to you, I promise. Get to a safe place on the ground and let me know where you are. The colony, maybe?"

"We shall."

Lucas nodded to Zeta and the frozen crew members and turned to leave.

"Remember what I said, Lucas," Theta called after him. "Remember who you have, even when you are alone."

He would.

Sora was a pale blue dot as Lucas raced toward the gargantuan sun. The tint of his viewscreen had darkened substantially to allow him to keep pressing forward toward the Viceroy's location, and the star now looked like little more than a muddy brown orb with bright cracks of flame poking out of it.

The prototype fighter was three times faster than anything in its weight class, and twenty times quicker than traditional cruisers in open space, facts and figures offered up unprompted by the AI, which relayed the information with a tone approaching pride. The perils of a self-aware ship, he supposed.

Lucas checked his readouts and found that he was gaining on the Viceroy's craft. Maston's intended destination was still unclear, but Lucas was certain the man would never reach it.

Lucas still felt off-kilter after the escape from the military base where hundreds of slack-jawed soldiers had let him pass with ease. The pain had ceased, but it was like a void had opened up inside him. He told himself it was just concern for Asha and Alpha, but he was worried it was something more.

He almost jumped out of his skin when a voice spoke from behind him.

"The irony," it said. It was low and full of gravel, not the smooth, feminine voice of the AI. "The Shadow killer becomes the thing he fears most."

The voice was coming from the gunner's seat behind him. Lucas twisted and turned violently against his restraints, but the rear-facing seat was out of his view.

"So you know now. What the power feels like."

He knew that voice. He'd never forget it.

Omicron.

It was impossible. Lucas flipped up a display of the rear of the cockpit, showing him the gunner's chair. Piercing blue eyes glinted at him, inset in a face of pure black. Lucas's flesh crawled and his chest tightened painfully.

It's just a hallucination. It's probably a side effect of conversion.

"Nothing to say, human?" Omicron purred. "Pity, our last conversation was painfully short."

"You're not here," Lucas spat out. "And I have bigger things to worry about."

"Bigger things?" Omicron scoffed, waving his claw in the inlaid viewscreen feed. "You race to rescue two souls when the fate of your entire species hangs in the balance? You embarrass the Shadow name. Our very purpose."

"I am not one of you!" Lucas said loudly, checking to make sure the oxygen levels were still normal in the ship. If they weren't that could explain what was happening.

"Not yet," Omicron said. "But you have tasted our power. And now you drink from it like a man dying of thirst."

"I want to be rid of it!" Lucas cried.

"You do not," Omicron replied coolly. "Though you waste your time thinking otherwise. You squander your potential with this menial task. If you were wise, you would be using your gifts to slaughter your enemies in battle."

"Like you?" Lucas said. "Look where you ended up."

"Dead, yes, but having lived as one of the finest warriors the galaxy has ever known. I conquered worlds. I brought savage civilizations to their knees." Lucas could hear the fierce pride in his voice. "I regret nothing."

"Get out of my head," Lucas said. "I've had enough delusions to last me a lifetime."

"You think this a delusion," Omicron said, his voice amused. "Of course you would."

"What do you mean?" Lucas asked cautiously.

"It seems you have reached an advanced enough stage in conversion to breach the Circle."

"The Circle?" Lucas asked.

"All Shadows are linked psionically to their creator, the Archon, and therefore tethered to each other as well."

Lucas blinked, trying to process that.

"But you're dead."

"Death eliminates the body, not consciousness. Not for us Shadows, anyway. We all live on through him."

"Through the Archon."

"Indeed. It is through him I have found my son again, at last. A welcome gift after centuries of devoted service to his cause. Though I did not know the truth until after my demise."

The Desecrator. Lucas shuddered even thinking about the monster that was Omicron's mutated offspring.

"What is the Archon?" Lucas pressed.

"He is Xala, and we are him. By design."

"What does that mean?"

"You will learn, in time."

Lucas fell silent before his racing mind formed another question.

"The Other. The Black Corsair. Is he in the Circle?"

Omicron nodded in the viewscreen window.

"Yes, but that one is . . . disturbed. You will not find him if you seek him. He is the Archon's unchained beast, a hound chasing after prey he will never catch."

"I don't want to seek any of you," Lucas said, pressing his hands to his temples. "I don't want to be in this Circle."

"You dishonor it with your presence. But many here are in awe of your power. It is like nothing that has come before. The Archon believes you humans of Earth are the next stage. Some mutation allows you this influence on the mind. Personally, it sickens me. A warrior should need nothing but his claws to tear nations asunder. As I did. As my son would have, had you not ended his life."

Lucas was dizzy. Was this real? Was this some sort of fever dream? His vital readouts were being monitored by the ship and oddly said all was well, but he couldn't believe it. They'd drugged him at the base. Something. Anything.

"Continue your tedious fool's quest," Omicron said, looking out the viewscreen to the stars around them. "Find your lost souls, and then force them to witness the devastation you will bring your race."

And then, he was gone.

It took Lucas a solid half hour to even remember where he was, or what he was doing. He jerked back into focus at the sight of a dull red planet and saw blue engine lights floating up ahead. His readouts were flashing, the AI telling him he'd caught up with his target.

Pull it together, he thought. *Think of Asha.*

He blinked and pushed the ghostly Omicron's words from his mind. His viewscreen highlighted the Viceroy's dreadnought, and the six fighters flanking him. An escort bristling with firepower.

This isn't going to be easy.

201

23

Solarion Security headquarters was on the very highest section of the station, level zero, meaning nothing was above them except the barely visible dome that kept them all breathing. From there they could see the top half of Apollica and one of its bright, rocky moons, the name of which Noah couldn't recall, though it had likely been a question on a solar geography test at some point in his colony education. Theta would know. He was glad she wasn't here, that she hadn't gotten caught up in this newest dangerous scheme.

Most SolSec guards wore the double-slitted helmets they'd seen on Keeper Auran's tearful good-bye broadcast, but some of the men and women went without them. At a casual glance, the lot of them did look like something resembling an actual security force. On closer inspection, something was . . . off. Their armor was a little too tarnished. Their boots a little too bloodied. Tattoos crept up the necks of the helmetless. The walls of the SolSec compound were thick with fresh paint, halfhearted attempts to cover up graffiti. Their headquarters was in far better shape than anything else they'd seen on Solarion, but still in a state of disrepair compared to official military bases or security HQs on Sora. There was no order to the troops inside. They laughed and joked and cursed and fought like all the other gangs they'd seen. They simply had the best armor, the best weapons, and a fortress that literally kept them on top of their little world.

Noah's cuffs were starting to itch.

He marched with his hands clasped behind his back. Next to Erik. Next to Sakai. All three of them were restrained. Following behind them were Tannon and his three soldiers, along with Kyra, Zaela, and her man Razor, all unbound and prodding them forward with rusty energy rifles. The masked Tannon had Noah's darksteel warhammer slung across his back and Erik's laser pistol on his hip. The SolSec soldiers stopped in their tracks to stare at the strange procession.

The plan was insane, so it was naturally something Erik had concocted. The biggest shock was that Tannon had not only listened, but filled in the blanks to make it work. Well, it hadn't worked yet. Not by a mile.

Their faceless SolSec escort led them to a towering building with most of its front-facing windows blown out. There was an inscription on the metal as they entered, but it was in Ba'siri and Noah couldn't read it. He had a deepening sense of foreboding as the massive metal doors shut behind them.

The main lobby of the building had likely been just that, a lobby, at some point in the distant past, but now it had been transformed into something vaguely resembling a throne room. What once was a stone fountain in the middle of the sprawling space was now bone dry, and a central tower now had a metal staircase in front of it that lead up to a platform where a group of men surrounded another figure sitting in a wide chair.

The man was blond with narrowed amber eyes, which regarded them distrustfully. His armor plating was black and could possibly have been darksteel, which would have made it very valuable indeed. On his chest, as with every other soldier in the facility, was stamped a flaming red sun. *Just another gang.*

The man ran his hand over a rather long rifle that lay across his lap. It looked newer than anything in the room. It was the sort of weapon Finn Stoller would have a story for.

The man's face was practically handsome and mostly free of scars, a rarity in the area. As he approached, Noah realized the young man might not be more than a few years older than he was. His voice further betrayed his youth.

"Alright, Zaela, how are you going to waste my time today?" the leader said, rolling his eyes before the group of them even came to a halt.

"Commander Hayne," Zaela said. "No time wastin' today. Have an offer for ya."

Noah looked over at Erik, his brother forever wearing a scowl. The faux demon tattoo had been scrubbed off his face.

Now that they were closer, Hayne could see them more clearly. Conflicting expressions of recognition and confusion crossed his face.

"Is this is a joke, Zaela? Are the Black Wings really that desperate you're going to try and pull something like this?" Hayne laughed, a few of his men joining in.

"No jokes, Commander," Zaela said, unsmiling. "I offer ya th' Earthborn. Fellas snatched 'em up just yesterday. Came to th' station to score some Paradise, they say. Can't get it nowhere else these days."

Hayne shook his head, still chuckling under his breath. He rubbed his gloved hand through his straw-colored hair and stood up, slowly descending the steps in front of them.

"You mean to tell me the two most famous brats on the planet came to our little kingdom here to score halos?"

Paradise was an extremely potent hallucinogen that caused intense pleasure reported to last for days. But the aftereffects included hopeless addiction and severe blood clotting. Regardless, the high was so intense, and it was so expensive to make, it was nearly impossible to find, except for in a charming place like Solarion. But as Hayne eyed them with intense suspicion, Noah realized perhaps this was not one of Erik's better plans. The young man arrived at the ground and walked toward them. Noah had a solid five inches on him, but his armor made him just as wide. Hayne panned over the two of them to look at Sakai. His breath was rotten.

"Who's this one, then?" he asked, lifting Sakai's chin forcefully with his hand. Noah lunged toward him, but Worsaw was holding him in place.

"One of th' colony tykes," Zaela said. "Siki, Saka, somethin' like that. She a pair wit' one of them, Stream says."

"You do look familiar," Hayne said, squinting at her. "Though you were prettier in the feeds. You two certainly look the part, but how do I know you're not a pair of those Earth-worshipping surgery freaks?"

"That's exactly who we are," Erik growled, playing his part. "You really think the Last and First Sons would be dumb enough to come here?"

"They disagree," Hayne said with a smile, "about their identity. What do you say to that, Zaela?"

"What do oi say?" Zaela said, swinging her braids over her shoulder and thumbing the handle of her knife. "Oi say check th' genome ya? Th' shit's public record."

It was true. The genome of the Earth strain of Sorans, the humans, was available for all to see in the interest of science. There were certain markers in their DNA that couldn't be forged or replicated.

Hayne waved a pair of guards over. Lucas, Sakai, and Erik all flinched as the tips of knives ripped into their forearms. Blood droplets were collected and fed into a nearby machine run by an unarmored man dressed in a dirty silver coat.

The test only took ten seconds to process, but it felt like a hundred years.

"No shit," Hayne said, eyes widening as he surveyed the results on a scroll.

"An' check th' Stream," Zaela said. "Them boys be missing for days now. Missing cause they here."

Hayne stopped to consider what he was seeing and hearing. The results couldn't be faked. It was indeed human DNA floating in front of him, helix spinning slowly in midair. Zaela continued.

"Figure th' SDI would pay a mad mark to see them safely returned," she said. "A mighty mad mark."

"Then why didn't you just ransom them yourself?" Hayne asked, handing off the scroll to the silvercoat. "What have I done to deserve such a tribute?"

"Oi ain't foolish," Zaela said. "Oi ain't gonna pull something like that without talkin' to you an' cutting SolSec in. Oi enjoy keepin' my head on. Plus me an' SDI got history," she tapped her left shoulder tattoo.

"You're not foolish," Hayne said, eyebrow raised. "Then what's to stop me from killing you and your men right now, and simply taking these three for myself?"

Zaela smirked.

"They poisoned," she said. "Gotta mursotoxis compound in they system, mixed wit' some other lovely stuff. They gotta few days at most. Cure ain't easy to find 'round here, 'cept one vial I got hidden away somewhere. Deal done, an' ya get it. Healthy Earthborn. Mad marks comin' your way. Stoller ain't gonna risk embarrassment wit' these ones. He's got more money than Kyneth and Zurana. He'll pay right quick."

The gears were turning in Hayne's head, that much was clear from looking at him. Finally, he said something that told Noah that Zaela had won.

"How much?"

Zaela gave a wide, yellow smile at last.

"Twenty bill for each of them ya? Five bill for the girl, Siki."

Hayne burst out laughing, and once again, his men followed suit.

"Twenty billion each? And you said you weren't a fool."

Zaela shrugged.

"When Fourth Order snatched that Asha up, they asked for fifty trill. They was tryin' to feed a whole continent. Oi have smaller aims."

"Fourth Order got atomized not long after that."

"They went too far. Gods made 'em crazy. But still, ya can turn 'round and sell 'em back for ten times that much easy, and ya know it. Oi just want my fair share for th' opportunity."

Hayne turned to speak in hushed tones with some of the men around him. Noah and Erik eyed each other. Sakai kept her head down.

"Eight bill for each, and girl for one bill."

Zaela threw up her hands.

"They die then. That's an insult. Fifteen bill each. Siki for three bill."

Hayne was starting to get visibly annoyed, but he realized the value in front of him. The corner of his mouth twitched.

"Final offer. Thirty billion for the set. And let me see that other one you've got hidden under there," he motioned toward the hooded Kyra. Noah froze.

Zaela hesitated, but finally nudged Kyra forward. Tannon gave Zaela a hard stare through his goggles and Key and Celton whispered nervously.

"She ain't one of them," Zaela said. "She Soran. My new lovegirl. Fresh from th' homeworld. Cost me a major mark."

"Hood down, darling," Hayne said in a velvet tone that made Noah's temperature rise.

Kyra obeyed. She was sweat-soaked and filthy, but stunning as ever. They hadn't trusted Zaela's "fellas" with Kyra or Sakai alone, so they were forced to be integrated into the plan. But this, this wasn't part of it.

"Amazing," Hayne said, obviously seeing far more than he was expecting under the hood. "Where did they grow this one? What agency?"

"If ya have to ask, they won' talk to ya," Zaela said, folding her arms.

"How much for her?"

"She ain't no ransom. No one be lookin' for her." Noah could hear the nerves starting to creep into Zaela's voice.

"I have no intention of resale with this one," Hayne said, Kyra desperately avoiding his eyes. "So I'll say again, how much?"

"Not for sale, Commander."

"A hundred mill, just for her," he said. That made Zaela's fall silent. *No,* Noah thought. *This is not how this is supposed to happen.*

But Zaela had marks in her eyes. Despite lending her aide to them, she was a warlord, through and through. And a businesswoman as well.

"If you'll pay a hundred mill, you'll pay three," she said confidently. "If not, you got plenty of tail elsewhere here."

Hayne glared at her. In a flash, he took Kyra's cloak in his hands and tore her jacket and dress wide open, revealing smooth skin and form-fitting underwear. Kyra let out an involuntary gasp of horror, but remained still. Both Erik and Noah struggled in their restraints, but their appointed guards cuffed them before they made a scene. They were supposed to have no interest in this girl, this stranger, after all.

"I'm sure you know how hard it is to get choice meat here," he said, running his eyes up and down her shaking frame. "Unlimited helpings of slop is still slop." He cast a glance toward a collection of grimy prostitutes in the rear of the room, clinging to SolSec armor plating.

"This . . ." he said, grazing his gloved hand against the side of Kyra's tear-stained face and down her neck to her collarbone. Every muscle in Noah's body tensed as Hayne briefly cupped her breast, a cruel smile on his lips. Erik was downright rabid, struggling against Worsaw's unrelenting grip. "This is like a ten-course meal at the Golden Leaf," he finished.

Hayne met Zaela's eyes.

"Two hundred and fifty million. That must be a hundred times what you paid for her. You're lucky I'm in a generous mood. I also just so happen to have a delivery for another SDI customer waiting, so this Earthborn ransom will be well-timed."

"Done," Zaela said without hesitating. Noah burned with anger. "But my guards stay wit' all 'em till deal's done. No messin' with th' merchandise before cash in hand. Try anythin' an' they all die an' we all outta luck. An' you out your new toy too," she said, nodding toward Kyra who had her hands clasped behind her back and was unable to cover up from the leering faces all around her.

"Agreed," Hayne said, a sick smile crossing his lips. The warlord and the soldier shook hands. Finally losing control, Noah lunged toward him, and something cracked across the back of his head. Stars gave way to darkness.

When the light returned to his eyes, Noah felt a splitting pain at the base of his skull, and realized he was being dragged across a sticky metal floor.

"Thank gods, he's awake," came Worsaw's voice. "Now he can walk by himself."

Worsaw and Celton pulled Noah to his feet and he wobbled to find his footing. He was in a corridor facing a long set of stairs, ending in a room with a pale golden glow. He steadied about halfway down and marched the rest of the way. When he arrived at the bottom, he saw Kyra, Sakai, and Erik all gathered in the middle of the space, cuffed and surrounded by Tannon, Key, Razor, and a handful of SolSec guards. Zaela was gone. The dungeon was lit only by the glow of the lightscreens holding other prisoners at bay.

"Block's full from the recent round-ups," a fiery-haired Solarion guard said, motioning to the men and women in cells all around them. The prisoners were all stripped of armor and weapons, clad only in rags. Tattoos of what appeared to be rival gang symbols were etched on their skin: forked lightning, horned animals, crossed blades, and the like. Some were unconscious or sickly, but many looked suitably threatening, pale yellow eyes hungry for both food and blood.

"Throw them in with the old man," one of the helmeted guards said. "He's harmless, and it'll be one nice little SDI package for when our guest arrives."

"Even the girl?" the helmetless soldier said. "She ain't part of that deal."

The other man shrugged.

"The Dark Wings bitch will get paid soon, then we'll just haul her up to the Commander's quarters so he can start his party. These lot won't try nothing in the meantime, will you lads?"

Erik glowered at the men as Noah spoke.

"Of course not," he said. "We're not animals like you."

That earned him a blow across the face from a metal glove. Blood trickled from his nose down his lip.

"Take them, then," the helmeted guard said to the rest of his unit. "Keep an eye on this lot," he said, nodding to the prisoners. "And especially these ones," he continued, motioning toward Tannon, Razor, and the others. "If this deal goes sideways, the Commander will have all our heads on pikes at the gates."

"If you try anything, we're here to make sure they ain't no use to nobody," Razor said so convincingly Noah wondered if he didn't mean it.

Tannon took off his cloak and wrapped it around Kyra's torn clothing as they rounded the corner in the dungeon.

"Why bother covering up the whore?" a Solarian guard asked.

"She's for your boss," Tannon said gruffly. "Not this rabble, right?" He motioned to the other prisoners.

The red-haired guard tilted his head back and forth.

"Yeah, but I wasn't minding the view, eh?" He nudged his companion, who chuckled beneath his helmet. Tannon's mouth was a thin frown, but he said nothing further, and secured the garment around a grateful Kyra.

The Solarion guards led them around a corner past another patrol into a corridor that housed only one cell along its wall. The lengthy containment area was mostly empty, save for one man.

Noah had known Keeper Auran since he started forming memories. He remembered him from his playdates with Kyra, and a long time ago he was in charge of the colony itself, always keeping a careful eye on how the Earthborn he'd helped create were growing. But eventually he retired, and his last visit had been at least five years ago. The colony had turned from a science project into a miniature society. The need for geneticists was replaced by the need for true leadership, and so Tannon stepped in as Watchman. But during the time Noah did know him, he was always full of warm smiles and kind words, dressed in ornate robes signifying his lofty place in Soran society.

The old man in the lightcell was almost unrecognizable. He was gaunt, and whatever robes he'd once worn were soiled and could be smelled from across the room. His normally close-cropped white hair was wild, his eyes almost empty. His body was covered in bruises and scrapes, and he sat huddled on a small stone bench. Though he'd looked disheveled in his video message, seeing him in person was heartwrenching, knowing how regal he'd once looked. Noah's chest tightened and he watched fresh tears stream down Kyra's cheeks, though the guards thought she was mourning her predicament, not the state of her grandfather. Noah wondered if SolSec even knew who Auran was, or if they were just happy handing him off to Stoller's agents without realizing his identity or why he was being sought.

The lightscreen flickered briefly, then faded, and the group of them were shoved inside the cell. Auran's eyes widened now that he could see them up close.

"Oh gods," he whispered. "What have I done?"

24

There was no sound in space, but Lucas's cockpit was alive with flashing alarms and the AI announcing impending doom in the calmest voice possible. The firefight he found himself in was pushing every limit he had, even in his newfound Shadow state. Six heavily armed escort ships wove around him as the Viceroy's dreadnought sped away as fast as its dozen colossal engines would carry it. Lucas had had a few hours of training inside a fighter that wasn't even officially listed for service yet. Flying circles around him were men who likely had been in flight school since they could walk, piloting the best ships Sora had built for the war.

Lucas could feel his mind coming apart at the seams as he twisted the ship through the blackness of space to avoid never-ending streams of autocannon plasma and antimatter missiles. His temples were on fire where the neural connectors were interfacing with his mind. His brain felt as if it were roasting on a spit.

Stop! Eject! Die!

Lucas tried to summon his dormant influence on the unseen pilots buzzing like hornets all around him, but to no avail. Either they were too maneuverable for him to target, or his brain simply didn't have the capacity to mold their minds to his will, far too preoccupied with a hundred different other tasks that would ensure his continued survival.

As glad as Lucas was Theta was safe, he wouldn't have half minded someone in the gunner's seat other than the ghost of Omicron, but even he had departed for the fireworks.

Lucas finally caught a break when one of the enemy ships lobbed a volley of shots toward him. He veered hard right and the plasma ate into the wing of another passing fighter, causing it to spin wildly out of control. A rare green success indicator lit up in his holographic console amid a sea of red.

"Target damaged," the AI sang cheerfully as Lucas shifted upward to avoid a missile spiraling toward him. Sweat was dripping into his eyes and his discolored veins were bulging in his arms. A new fighter was on his tail now, its pilot hidden behind mirror black glass.

"Air mines," Lucas said, finding the listing in the ship's interface.

A shower of sparks shot out from the rear of his prototype ship and spattered harmlessly across the viewscreen of the pursuing craft.

"Ah, shit!" Lucas cried, realizing his mistake. "Those were flares!" When he did find the mine release a half second later, the ship had already spun out of the way.

All his evasive maneuvering was causing him to lose the Viceroy's ship, which was racing ahead, well aware it was under siege. The blue engines grew dimmer in the distance.

"Goddamnit!" Lucas said as he stopped spinning and drew the throttle to full force, racing after the dreadnought. While he wasn't out-shooting his rivals, he could certainly outrun them, and in a flash he had caught up to the Viceroy's craft, a polished diplomatic vessel thick with armor plating, but no outer defenses, hence the escort. Lucas targeted the engines with a stream of precise shots. Five engines of twelve were struck, and three went out completely. The ship involuntarily lurched starboard, slowing dramatically, but Lucas couldn't fire another volley as the fighters had caught up with him. He dove under the ship and banked left, taking the firefight away from the craft. He needed the Viceroy alive, after all.

In between spitting out proximity warnings, the AI suddenly said something puzzling.

"In the event your assigned gunner is absent or deceased, it is recommended you cede control of autocannon targeting and ordnance launch to the discretion of the ship."

"What?" Lucas exclaimed, veering right as a splinter-shaped missile nearly grazed his hull. "You can take over the weapons systems yourself?"

"That is correct," said the AI.

Lucas suddenly realized this was the sort of AI that had been permanently banned after the Machine Wars on Sora, but either Stoller had ignored such laws or Alpha had gone off-book by himself.

"Why the hell didn't you tell me that before?" Lucas asked.

"The system requires a short period of time for calibration in order to properly assess the present threat."

"I've been at this for ten minutes. How long do you need?" Lucas said, exasperated.

"This is a prototype vessel. The system has never been used in real-world combat scenarios." The AI sounded mildly annoyed, though Lucas could have been imagining the tone.

"Alright, fantastic," he said, spinning twice to dodge two separate plasma volleys coming at him from opposite sides. His mind felt like it was melting. "Engage! Activate! Do it!" he shouted.

"Very well," the AI said, this time sounding pleased.

The first missile launched wasn't deterred when the enemy fighter spun out of its way. It looped upward and plunged back toward the retreating ship, accelerating in the process. It plowed straight into the body of the aircraft and blew it apart in silence.

Lucas barely had time to blink before he realized that on the other side of the ship, an enemy fighter had just had its cockpit breached by a precision plasma blast, catching it square in the glass despite both crafts' blinding speeds.

"Jesus," he said breathlessly, marveling at the AI's handiwork, and veered around toward the remaining fighters. The damaged one from earlier still hadn't managed to catch up, and was likely free-floating fifty thousand or so miles behind them.

Lucas fired his own burst of shots while the AI took control of another pair of missiles, launched from the underside of the ship. Lucas missed his target, but the other two fighters split left and right, and the missiles followed. Suddenly, each cylinder exploded into shards that flew out at odd angles. The first ship tried to dodge the shrapnel, but caught two metal spikes in the wing. Electricity crackled and the ship lurched and turned belly up like a dead fish. Lucas turned to find the other ship had at least a dozen of the shards stuck into it, including one through the cockpit itself. No electrical overload required. The last remaining fighter was fleeing.

"Remaining enemy craft no longer poses a threat," the AI reported. "Abandon and proceed to target dreadnought?"

"No," Lucas said. Any ship that could fly was a still a problem since he needed to board the dreadnought. "We need to take it out."

Much to Lucas's surprise, the AI assumed control of the engine itself and raced toward the escaping fighter. A pair of bright gold lasers shot out from under the wings of the prototype vessel and tore into the last ship. The explosion was colorful and quiet.

"Relinquishing control," the AI said, sounding disturbingly forlorn. The ship was Lucas's once more. His mind ceased racing, and he breathed a sigh of relief as he steered toward the crippled dreadnought. Debris from the destroyed fighters was scattered in space around them.

"Um, good work there," Lucas said as the ship went quiet. "Did Alpha give you a name?" He felt a bit foolish after he'd asked the question, and was surprised when the AI responded.

"I am prototype N4T-11E. Codename 'Natalie,' as designated by my creator."

Lucas smiled for the first time in weeks.

As his nerves slowly cooled down after the firefight, it seemed fairly obvious to Lucas that he was going to have to blow a hole through the docking bay doors of the dreadnought and board through a gaping wound in the hull. So he was unnerved as he circled around the side of the vessel and the doors opened automatically, seeming to welcome him inside.

The bay was empty. There were no other fighters waiting to unload on him. No manned auto-turrets hurling plasma toward him. No soldiers floating in zero G aiming ordnance his way. Lucas sat staring at the opening, unsure of what to do next. It had to be a trap, didn't it?

"The ship is hailing us," AI Natalie announced. "Patching the feed through to your viewscreen."

The pale face of Viceroy Draylin Maston greeted him. The man smiled, revealing flawless teeth behind his dark, groomed beard.

"Welcome, Lucas. I know why you are here, and I find myself clearly outmatched. I surrender."

"Give me a good reason why I shouldn't blow you out of the sky right now," Lucas growled.

"You already know that," the Viceroy said. "I believe you have two reasons, in fact. Come aboard and we'll discuss things further. I mean you no ill-intent. Though even if I did, we both know I would not succeed in any attempt to contain or destroy you. I am no fool. Dock your vessel and meet me on the bridge."

"Where are they?" Lucas asked, but the feed was already black and the ship had faded back into view. After a minute's pause, Lucas guided the fighter into the open bay.

The dreadnought was an eerie maze of empty hallways and blank holoscreens. Despite its size, Lucas hadn't run into another soul as he navigated himself toward the bridge, which he was beginning to suspect might not actually exist.

At last, he found the proper lift and found himself racing up the last few levels of the ship. He was tense, as if the elevator could explode at any second, or the doors would open and he'd find himself riddled with plasma. He tried to ready his mind in case he needed his unseen power of influence, but part of him was frightened, realizing he still didn't quite know how to control the ability. His muscles were coiled springs as the door opened.

He found the crew.

The bridge was enormous, as tended to be the case with vessels of this size, but everything here was covered in luxurious, lavish platinum and gold trim with plush seats and even what appeared to be a fully stocked bar on the starboard side. But it wasn't the opulence that caught Lucas's attention. On the deck stood at least a hundred men and women lined up in neat rows, standing stiffly at attention. Some were armored, clearly soldiers, others were not—navigators, engineers, pilots. None were armed. Their hands were clasped behind their backs, and none had so much as a pistol or knife on their hips.

Lucas slowly lowered his own weapon, an automatic handgun clipped inside the cockpit of his fighter for emergencies.

The crew was split in half, one group facing the other, forming a narrow pathway to the main captain's chair and viewscreen. Most tried not to catch his eye, but a few couldn't help themselves. Lucas could see a few unarmored officers outright shaking in barely bridled terror.

Walking down the living corridor, Lucas saw a figure at the end standing in front of a jewel-encrusted captain's command seat, arms open wide. The Viceroy wore a slim, high-collared suit with tails that reached his ankles. His chest sparkled with meaningless awards, and his dark eyes glittered in a similar manner. Lucas saw that he was the only one in the room armed, and his eyes widened as he realized the Viceroy's hand was on the pommel of Asha's black-bladed darksteel sword, slung loosely off his hip.

"Lucas, welcome to the *Endless Dawn*. Isn't she lovely?" the Viceroy said. "The High Chancellor bestowed it upon me for a decade of loyal service to his administration."

"What the hell is this?" Lucas asked, eyeing the crew as nervously as they eyed him, still clutching his pistol.

"Word has spread about what you did at the Merenes base," the Viceroy said, lowering his voice. "I have no intention of seeing myself or my men come to harm by attempting to stand in the way of you, our . . . unstoppable force."

"Should have told that to your pilots," Lucas said, nodding toward a visible debris field outside the viewscreen. A wing of a destroyed fighter was drifting lazily into view.

"Yes, well, the Royal Air Battalion has a rather high opinion of themselves and wouldn't listen to me."

"Bullshit," Lucas said. "You thought they'd kill me before I reached you."

Draylin Maston shrugged. "Believe what you will, but we are here now. And judging by the surprising lack of casualties at Merenes, I suppose you haven't completely lost your mind."

"No," Lucas said. "But you have, if you thought you'd be able to control me by threatening the lives of Asha and Alpha."

The Viceroy frowned.

"Damn, I thought it a rather inspired idea. Though it appears the High Chancellor and I have misjudged the depth of your incredible power, even with your conversion incomplete."

"You've misjudged a lot of things," Lucas said, immune to the Viceroy's flattery. "Like that I won't tear you and everyone in here to shreds if you don't tell me what I need to know."

A shiver ran through every single crewmember present, Maston included. He found his voice.

"I will trade you the information you seek for the lives of everyone you see here, myself included, of course. I will straighten all this out with the High Chancellor and we can forget this whole ordeal ever took place, as it's just a great misunderstanding. We both want to end this war with Xala, wouldn't you agree? We just had different ideas on how to go about it."

"Stoller will lead Sora to ruin at this rate, even with Xala wounded," Lucas said. "What sort of man is he to threaten innocents this way? Scientists, women, little girls."

The Viceroy let out an exasperated sigh.

"Your definition of 'innocent' is a strange one. Your Alpha is the greatest mind of this war, and his inventions have contributed to the deaths of millions on both sides. Your Asha could not even count the number of heads her black blade has taken," he patted the sword on his hip. "And if you reference the young, lovely 'Miss Auran,' you'll know she isn't really a person at all. A ghostly abomination, more like. Your boys are in quite a predicament, attempting to defend her honor at Solarion Station. I was just heading there now to retrieve them."

"What?" Lucas said. "What's happened to Noah and Erik?"

"They are in the hands of some very bad people hoping to make a large sum of money. You are more than welcome to accompany me to liberate them. After you've seen to Asha and Alpha, of course."

"If the next words out of your mouth don't tell me where they are, you and your entire crew will start tearing each other's eyes out with smiles on your faces." Lucas's tone was molten.

A low murmur rippled across the nervous crowd. Lucas didn't even know if he could do such a thing at will, but if they'd heard what he'd done at Merenes . . .

"They are here," Draylin Maston said suddenly, a touch of panic in his silky voice. "Locked in the hold. I would not trust anyone else with them, even after I was tasked to bring additional prisoners. I was on my way to building quite a collection, I must say."

Lucas blinked.

"They're here? On this ship?" His heart soared.

The Viceroy nodded. "I will have someone escort you to—"

"I'll find it," Lucas said, his pulse racing. "Though if you try anything, you will all die painfully, mark my words."

"Implying we will *not* die if we comply. You are most generous, Lucas. I knew you were a man of honor." A nervous smile crossed the Viceroy's lips.

Lucas ignored the man's groveling and stormed out of the room, the crew breathing a collective sigh of relief behind him.

Lucas tore through the corridors of the ship at speeds he couldn't comprehend. He'd taken one look at a floating schematic of the ship on the bridge and had memorized its floorplan instantly. Reaching the hold in under a minute, he ripped the thick door off its hinges and threw it behind him down the hall.

In a room full of cells, only one lightscreen was active. Lucas raced to it and jammed his fist through the controls so that it sputtered and died in front of him. He dropped to his knees when he saw what was inside, and his racing mind almost made him collapse on the spot.

Asha, clad in black rags, smiled at him. Alpha's gold-ringed eyes were wet with emotion.

"We knew you'd come," Asha said as he threw his arms around her. She met him with a kiss, and he felt Alpha's claw on his shoulder.

"It is incredible to find you here, Lucas," Alpha said, his translator flickering faintly. "Though my thanks must wait. What of my family? Are they safe from the clutches of these madmen?"

Lucas nodded.

"It was Theta who told me where you were. She walked onto the Merenes base like she owned the place and helped me escape. Brave girl."

Alpha's chest inflated with pride. Lucas continued.

"I left her with Zeta on an orbital station, but they should be heading back to Sora."

"My thanks, Lucas," Alpha said, attempting to mask the emotion in his voice. "Now, what of our host?"

"I'll kill him," Asha said, blinding rage in her eyes.

"I left Viceroy Maston alone for now; his crew surrendered after I took out his fighter escort with one of your prototype ships, Alpha. *Natalie*, I believe it's calling itself?" Lucas hid a smile.

Asha ignored the reference.

"He's still alive? Time to change that. Take me to the bridge."

Lucas rested his hands on her shoulders.

"He said Noah and Erik are on this place called . . . *Solarion*? He implied they were captured, and that he was on his way to collect them. Do you have any idea what's going on?"

Asha shook her head and looked confused.

"What the hell would the boys be doing on Solarion Station?"

"If you don't know, we may need the Viceroy to shed some light on what's happening. Alpha, can you repair this ship and get us there? I'll make sure the crew doesn't give us any trouble. These cells down here look like they're just begging to be filled."

"Of course," Alpha said. "I will assist in any way I am able. We must head to the bridge to assess the damage to the vessel."

The three of them stumbled as a muffled explosion rocked the ship somewhere above them. Asha and Alpha were pitched against the back wall and Lucas struggled to keep his footing on the grated floor.

"What the hell?" he said. "I swear, if Draylin Maston thinks he can try me right now . . ."

Lucas brought up his communicator and shouted into it.

"Maston! What's going on? What are you trying to pull?"

The feed was soft static.

"Viceroy?"

Silence. A garbled sound. An abbreviated scream. More silence.

Fear crept up Lucas's spine. He flinched as he heard Omicron's unmistakable voice in his head.

"Well, this will be interesting."

25

Malorious Auran nearly died from the shock of seeing Noah, Kyra, and the others sharing a cell with him. He was inconsolable.

"I should have never sent that message. I told you not to look for me. I told you I was *protecting* you. And now, I have brought ruin to all," he said with tears in his eyes.

"Grandfather," Kyra said, putting her hand in his. She was clearly unsettled seeing him in such a state. "It's alright. We and the others have a plan," she nodded toward Tannon and the rest of the team, who were conversing with the Solarion guards out of earshot.

"A plan?" Auran said, mouth open in shock. "I know little of the vile men who run this place, but I know enough to say that no matter what you think you are doing here, all of you are in incredible danger. Noah, Erik, how could allow poor Kyra and Sakai to put themselves in harm's way like this? And for what? An old man?"

"For the truth," Erik said bluntly. "You owe Kyra that much. Whatever secret you planned to take to your grave, you need to share it with her, now."

"Ah," Auran said, looking crestfallen. "I am revealed at last, then. It was only a matter of time."

"We came a long way, Keeper," Noah said. "And for what Kyra has had to endure throughout her life, and the last few months in particular, you owe her the truth."

Kyra looked into her grandfather's eyes. "Please," she said, voice breaking. "Please tell me who I am. And who Corinthia Vale is to me."

It was a long time before Auran spoke again. They could see the wheels turning in his mind, trying to deduce the best way to explain the impossible.

"There are two types of clones," he began at last. "Torn clones and birthed clones. Both are illegal, but one is far more dangerous than the other.

"Torn clones are the ones you hear stories about. Their creation is, and always will be, an abomination of nature. A torn clone is grown in full adulthood, taken from the genetic material of another. Torn clones can be grown from live subjects, but were commonly created from the dead. It was an attempt to give a second life to a soul taken from the world. For loved ones to regain their lost, exactly as they were.

"Torn clones are the same person as their originals. Exactly so. The DNA is an obvious mirror, each clone's appearance and age the exactly the same as their original. But more importantly, even memories can be transferred from the subject to the clone. At first, it seemed like the cure for mortality. A person killed before their time would simply find themselves alive in a new body. It was a revolutionary discovery."

"Why haven't we heard of it then?" Sakai interrupted. "There's nothing in the scrolls about such a breakthrough."

Auran shook his head.

"Nor should there be. It is dangerous to give the public hope about such a thing. Especially given the end result, why the findings were destroyed and made illegal, and stories of clones turned into nothing but myth and legend.

"Torn clones would have the memories of their originals, but after a period of months, the side effects were disastrous. Clones created from the living would try to hunt down and kill their originals with fervor. Clones created from the dead would slowly see their memories fracture and distort. Their realities would become unstable, unlivable. Their physical bodies suffered no ill effects but their minds were shattered beyond repair. There is nothing so tragic as to watch a mother regain a lost son through torn cloning, only to have him turn into an unrecognizable monster before the year was out. I have tried to wash my hands of those experiments for many years, yet I still find them stained. It may have been the arrogance of youth that led me to believe I could masquerade as the gods, but I cannot blame such things for what led me to you, Kyra."

Kyra was silent, tears etched on her cheeks.

"You are not a torn clone, Kyra. You are a birthed clone. Though the stigma is still present, birthed clones suffer no such ailments as the torn did. They are created from embryos as all children are, not grown into already mature bodies. They simply have the exact same genetic sequence as an existing individual. This allows them to be perfectly healthy and sane, unlike their torn counterparts. For that, I am thankful, but I am still a fool."

"Why?" Kyra said finally. "Why was I . . . created?"

Auran swallowed a practically visible lump in his throat and continued.

"Corinthia Vale was the pinnacle of my entire life's work as a geneticist. After Talis Vale's husband was killed in the war, she wanted a child to remember him by. She wanted his legacy to live on. He deserved a perfect child, she said. One without equal. With an unlimited budget, I was finally able to genetically engineer a Soran as close to perfection as had ever existed, using both Vales' DNA as a template. Ten years and a trillion marks later, Corinthia Vale was born. She was a Soran without equal, though none of you are old enough to remember.

"I did not understand why Talis Vale came to me once I was Keeper, some years ago, and demanded I create another Corinthia. An exact replica. Though now the answer is clear. It was when the young Miss Vale was en route to Vitalla, a trip she could not be convinced to avoid. As we now know, Talis Vale had conspired with the Xalans to make a sacrifice of her father and our chancellor, Varrus, along with a sizable portion of the Rhylosi population. Though Corinthia would be protected fiercely by Commander Mars Maston, Talis knew there was every chance she too might die in the endeavor. Too late to call off the entire scheme with the Xalans, she simply commissioned me to make a second Corinthia, should the first not come home. She said that she wanted her daughter to have a sister upon her return, one as perfect as her, though I should have suspected her true motives.

"Mercifully, Cora did survive Vitalla, and when she returned unharmed, Talis contacted me and said to destroy the child I was in the process of creating. It was then I should have realized I had not been creating a sibling for Corinthia, but a potential replacement. But I was blind by my devotion to the Vale family.

"And yet, this was one order from her I could not obey. My own daughter had struggled for years to conceive a child. But she had a rare genetic disorder even we were powerless to heal, and it resulted in stillbirth after stillbirth in the birthing tanks. She was devastated. I believed if the Vales deserved a perfect child, so did my own family. Why should I not have such an offspring to call my own? And so, my daughter's next child lived, a beautiful blond girl with eyes of sapphire blue instead of sparkling prism, one of only a few minor differences between the two. They treasured Kyra as I knew they would, and I was satisfied that, for all my misdeeds, I had done something right and good for my family.

"My pride blinded me to the potential repercussions of my actions. That someday, despite her common birth, Kyra would live up to her potential and the truth would be uncovered. Talis Vale never knew what I did, but I fear her successor, Madric Stoller, uncovered my actions through extensive data reassembly in my old genetics lab upon taking office. Kyra wasn't a present threat to his power, but a future one, if she was anything like Cora. When he ordered the death of my daughter, her husband, and the child, I realized what I had brought down upon my family. I hid Kyra away in the hopes he would never find her again. I knew if she could outlive Stoller, she still might real- ize her potential for greatness. And yet, here we are, and I have failed miserably."

Everyone waited for Kyra to speak. She finally did.

"So I *am* a clone, then," she said softly.

"Only in the bare sense of the word," Auran said quickly. "In truth, you are Corinthia Vale's twin, merely born much, much later than she. You are your own person, and though you share her exquisite, invaluable genes, you are free from her memories, her life. Looking at you now, though I regret the position I have put you in, I would never, ever regret your existence, your presence in this world. The gods helped shape you through my own hand, and you are every bit the woman Corinthia was. More, in fact, with treasured friends and guardians who want nothing but the best for you," he gestured to the group of them in the cell. "Though I fear I no longer fulfill that role in your life, as I have brought you nothing but misfortune at every turn."

Kyra shivered and pulled Tannon's dusty cloak around her. Both Erik and Noah were at a loss for words, though Sakai had put a hand on her shoulder. It was true then, what they all suspected. Kyra was a clone of Corinthia Vale, though as Auran described it, more of a sister. The larger shock was how she'd come to exist in the first place, against the better judgment of her grandfather, the proud geneticist.

"What's past is past," Kyra said at last, her eyes hard and dry now. "And no matter what blood runs through my veins, I shall forever be an Auran, not a Vale. It *was* selfish what you did, Grandfather, to steal a child for your own line, but everything you've done for decades now has been to safeguard me, and I thank you for that. I hope in turn to protect you here and now, so that we may move forward with no secrets between us. I cannot blame you for the actions of a tyrannical madman, who is the true cause of all the misfortune you speak of."

Noah watched her in awe. After everything she'd been through, everything she just learned, she forgave her grandfather in an instant. Her entire existence was shattered, and she barely blinked, concerned only for *his* feelings. Noah now knew what it meant when the history scrolls said Corinthia Vale was "born to rule." If only every matter of life could be handled with such grace. In the dark and grimy cell, Kyra shone with an inner beauty that outstripped even her outward appearance. Noah was blinded by it, and could form no words.

His thoughts were interrupted by a Solarion guard, who had walked to the lightscreen with Tannon and the others in tow. The barrier faded and Kyra was roughly yanked to her feet by an armored glove. Erik and Noah bolted up.

"Deal's done," came the voice inside the helmet. "The Black Wings bitch got her marks."

Tannon was on his communicator.

"Everything set, Zaela? The transfer went through like they're saying?"

A garbled voice spoke through his comm.

"Yes, th' money's here. Ya ready for th' next?" Zaela said.

"Indeed," the towering Razor said, his voice rough gravel. "We'll see you shortly."

"Fantastic," said the red-haired guard, taking Kyra's other arm. "Now we get this one to the Commander's chambers and wait for the SDI to scoop up the rest of these wretches."

He stopped, eyeing Kyra hungrily. "But maybe we can have a little fun with her first, eh?" he said, looking toward a stone-faced Celton and Worsaw. "What, you never wanted a taste of your lady's girl? Let's see if she likes boys just as well."

"Let's not," said Tannon, his voice flat. He leveled his pistol at the back of the guard's head and pulled the trigger.

26

The halls weren't empty this time as Lucas, Asha, and Alpha raced back toward the bridge of the *Endless Dawn*. Lucas had to keep his speed in check so as not to lose the others. The group kept running into fleeing crew members, covered in blood, looks of terror on their faces.

"What's happening?" Lucas asked as they sprinted past them, but none answered. They rounded the corner and found a dead soldier facedown in the hall, gnarled pulp where his arm used to be. His fellow guards hurdled him like he wasn't even there.

"We should consider departing," Alpha called out. "The ship is under siege."

"We need the ship," Lucas said. "And we need the Viceroy, come on!" He motioned toward the bridge doors. "Just stay behind me."

The doors opened, and Lucas understood why the crew was fleeing.

The bridge was painted in blood, and there were more pieces of bodies than whole ones littering the floor all around them. Legs, arms, heads, and unrecognizable bits that barely even looked like they'd once been part of a living thing. Ahead of them was a dark figure. No, the man *was* darkness.

The Black Corsair.

A few brave soldiers had stayed behind and were firing weapons at the shape, apparently not as unarmed as they'd initially seemed. But Lucas watched in horror how their courage was rewarded. The Corsair wove around their plasma blasts with ease and raised his hands slightly. A pair of guards vaulted into the air, dropping their guns and screaming. The Corsair expanded his fingers outward, almost casually, and the soldier's cries were replaced by the cracking of bone and tearing of tissue. Both men lost the majority of their limbs, and then were dropped to the floor in a bloody heap. The remaining soldiers who still held guns threw them down and sprinted toward the exits.

The Corsair ignored them and turned to the central holotable. He ripped it out of the ground and hurled it into the outer wall, revealing a cowering Draylin Maston, shivering in his blood-stained suit, holding out Asha's sword with shaking hands like it was no more than a tree branch.

"Please," he said, his voice quaking. "I told you, he's in the hold. Take him. Take this ship. Take everything. Please, just let me go."

Lucas, Asha, and Alpha took careful steps toward the turned back of the Corsair. Asha had pulled a rifle from a detached arm on the ground, and Alpha had found a damaged submachine gun that didn't look like it would even fire. Lucas kept his pistol trained on the Corsair.

"Hey," he called out. "Looking for me?"

The Corsair turned toward them, and Viceroy Maston collapsed to the ground, overcome with relief.

"You," said the Corsair, speaking for the first time. "It is time for you to face justice for your crimes." His voice was a host, a thousand speaking all at once. It shook the room like an unsettled volcano.

"You're his slave," Lucas said loudly. "Don't you realize that? You serve the Archon, but for what? You can be free of him. Free of whatever influence he has over you."

"I am free," the Corsair growled. "Free to exact vengeance. Free to roam the galaxy until all the traitors are extinct. Free to search until I find him."

"Until you find who, me?" Lucas called. The Corsair threw out his arm and telekinetically flung the Viceroy sideways into a pile of bodies.

"The Archon says you are valuable. That you will lead me to him, as a traitor yourself."

Lucas thought of Omicron's words.

"He is the Archon's unchained beast, a hound chasing after prey he will never catch."

"Who?" Lucas asked. "Who are the traitors? Who do you think you're looking for?"

The Corsair was no more than twenty feet away now. He snarled with unbridled rage, words that carried the force of a hurricane.

"I hunt the Fourth Order! I seek the monster Hex Tulwar, who will pay for extinguishing the only light in this world, my Cora! You will help me find him or you will suffer a thousand fates worse than death!"

No.

Standing close, Lucas could see it now.

His curled hair was burned away, replaced by a black scalp.

His dark eyes were now lit with blue flame.

His olive skin was charred into darkness.

But the line of his jaw. The angle of his nose. The way he strode toward them with purpose. It was him. But how? How?

Asha's barrel dropped as she slipped into shock, coming to the same realization as Lucas. Her voice was a whisper in the strangely silent room.

"Oh god, Mars."

27

The cheers of the damned echoed throughout the halls of the prison facility at Solarion Security headquarters. The imprisoned banged on the walls and floors of their cells as they watched Tannon and his team butcher the patrolling guards as the final stage of the plan was set in motion. Five Red Suns were dead mere seconds after Tannon's first shot went off, put down instantly by Celton, Worsaw, and Zaela's man Razor before any could react. Key had disappeared somewhere into the darkness.

Tannon stepped forward and wiped some blood from a shocked-looking Kyra's cheek. The red-haired guard's head had exploded right in front of her, and even after all she'd endured, it was a horrifying sight. Noah even felt nauseous as he surveyed the carnage.

Malorious Auran had some spatter on him as well, and was clearly terrified.

"This is your plan? To take on an army on my behalf? We will never leave here alive."

"We will if we have an army too," Razor said sharply. "Up, old man, it is time to go."

Tannon turned to Noah and Erik, pulled the metal goggles off his head, and tossed them to the floor. No need for disguises anymore. He unslung Noah's warhammer from his back and unclipped Erik's laser pistol from his hip. He offered each to their respective owners.

"You know the rest," he said. "Go straight for the gate, and don't look back."

"If we really wanted to cripple SolSec like you said, we'd leave here with Hayne's head," Erik said darkly.

"We'll hamstring them plenty as is," Tannon said, glaring at Erik. "This may be a prison break and a robbery, but it's not an assassination."

"But what he did to—" Erik looked over toward Kyra, who was being handed a pistol by Celton. Sakai already held one.

"While I tolerate your insubordination at the colony for some reason, the time for that is over," Tannon interrupted. "This mission is balanced on a knife's edge. This is no time for debate, and no place to disobey."

Erik could do nothing but frown. Tannon's comm chirped. It was Key.

"Two dead in the tower," she said metallically. "All good to spring the doors?"

"Affirmative," Tannon replied into his collar.

There was a brief silence, then the lightscreens started to go out one by one. Each cell lost its glowing door, and the eyes of every prisoner lit up as the forcefields were snuffed out. When all the cells were open, the dirty, dazed gang members wandered out into the halls. It was Razor who spoke next, after clasping forearms with a dark-skinned prisoner with a Black Wings tattoo.

"Brothers," Razor said. "Though we come from different factions, warring ones even, the time has come to unite for a common purpose. To tear down the tyranny of Solarion Security!"

A rousing cheer from the group indicated universal support for the idea.

"Arm yourselves with whatever you can find," Razor said. "You have been in the dark too long, and the light will find you soon. Once it does, make every Red Sun you see bleed crimson."

There was a louder shout than the first, and the prisoners set upon the dead SolSec guards, stripping them of their armor and weapons. Noah barely had time to grab a submachine repeater off a nearby guard before the dead man's other armaments were torn from his body.

"Let's move," Tannon said, and the rest of the haggard group didn't need to recognize him as the former High Chancellor to listen to his command.

The light pierced Noah's eyes when they reached the surface level. He could only imagine what it felt like to see the sun, however dim and tinted red, after years underground like some of these men. There were no female prisoners; Noah suspected Hayne had an entirely different purpose for them.

The SolSec guards manning the ground level didn't have a moment to react, nor a prayer of survival. The mob rushed over them like a wave, and they were torn to shreds by hands and teeth and improvised shards of metal. Guards closer to the exit were mowed down by gunfire before they could even raise their weapons. Noah tried to level his repeater for a shot, but there were too many friendly bodies in the way. "Friendly" was a relative term in this case; the group was as savage and rabid as a pack of wild dogs. Fortunately, they were running down a common enemy.

Noah looked behind him, making sure not to lose sight of Kyra or Sakai. Both had avoided being crushed by the stampeding mob so far. Behind them was Auran, hands to his ears. The screams of the guards and the roar of the released prisoners made it hard to hear anything else.

Until the explosion, that is.

Noah had just made it out of the building when the front gate erupted in an enormous blue fireball that ripped the metal doors open and took the two adjacent guard towers down with it. That brought another victorious cry from the prisoners, who must have thought Kyneth and Zurana themselves had orchestrated this miraculous day. But really it was Noah's brother and Tannon Vale.

Almost as soon as the flame dissipated, a dark blur shot through the smoke. An aircycle raced into the yard and swerved hard right, unleashing a torrent of piercing ionic metal rounds from side-mounted cannons, shredding the armor of the SolSec troops now suddenly caught between the prison mob and the breached gate.

It was Zaela, her braids whipping in the wind spirals exhaled by her engines. She reached over her shoulders and brought back two energy rifles grown men wouldn't have the strength to dual wield, but she unloaded them all the same, arms tense with steel muscle, unheard laughter on her lips drowned out by booming gunfire.

Two more aircycles sped through the smoldering remnants of the gate, and behind them came four hundred Black Wings, armed to the teeth and racing to support their leader. Zaela had now directed her attention toward the remaining guard towers on the wall. Rockets with pink-tinted booster flame shot out from the rear of the aircycle and spiraled toward one of the obelisk-like towers. One guard dove fifty feet to the ground before the missile hit, but whoever remained inside was instantly incinerated. A second missile hit another tower midway up, and the metal groaned until it snapped, sending the entire thing crashing to the ground.

The prison group had finally spread out enough to the point where Noah could breathe again and, more importantly, contribute to the effort. He cracked off a stream of shots at a nearby guard, who spun around wildly as the plasma ripped through his plating at close range. Up ahead, Noah could see Razor hacking at the legs of a SolSec mech with his battleaxe. Key had reappeared and was slicing through Red Suns with a curved blade, her normally stoic face now lit with fury. Worsaw had a rusted scattergun he was using as a club now that its energy cell was dry. He bashed in the face of a SolSec helmet before driving it into the abdomen of another passing soldier. A thunderous high knee appeared to break the man's neck when he doubled over.

Behind Noah, Kyra and Sakai walked with pistols extended, but they weren't firing. This was Sakai's first real taste of actual combat, and though she'd trained for the concept of war, nothing could have prepared her for the pandemonium that surrounded them. Finally, a Solarion guard got close enough that Sakai was forced to unload a shot that hit him square in the neck. Her face was expressionless as he toppled over ungracefully, clutching at the wound.

"The gate!" Noah yelled over the din, and motioned them toward the opening in the wall Zaela had created. He'd lost track of her aircycle now, but could still hear the whine of its engine somewhere nearby. One of the other cycles had been destroyed by a fresh group of SolSec that had emerged from a nearby barracks. A single-engine microjet zipped overhead and unloaded spinning twin barrels into the crowd, a red sun stamped on its nose. Three more jets appeared behind it, and the Black Wings were forced to turn their fire toward the flying craft.

There was a reason SolSec ruled the station. Their firepower was unmatched and their numbers were massive. More and more troops streamed out of nearby buildings, and even some of the more blood-thirsty prisoners began to flee toward the ruined gate as well.

Noah caught up with Erik and Tannon, who were firing into a disorganized unit of Solarion soldiers. Tannon's shots landed between the horizontal eye slits of two men while Erik's pistol cut what might have been an armored woman completely in half. He spun around and planted a knife into the skull of another guard wrestling with Celton nearby, and Erik gave his instructor a quick wink, which was met with a scowl from the silver-haired soldier.

Erik's head snapped to the right as something else caught his attention. Bobbing around in the fray up ahead was a shock of blond hair. It was Hayne. The young warlord was screaming orders to his troops while he slowly backed away toward the main doors they'd been escorted through earlier. He was falling back with a contingent of guards, the battle more evenly matched than he liked, presumably. Even at a distance, Noah could see the veins throbbing in his neck as he shouted at his men.

And then, Erik was gone. Before Noah could blink, his brother bolted into the chaos ahead, racing after Hayne as he made his way to the door. His pistol fired golden death at anyone in his way, and his knife cleaned up the rest. Too fast to be caught, anyone he wasn't actively cleaving through found only empty space when they turned toward him.

"Erik!" Tannon shouted, and ran a few steps forward. He turned back to Noah. "Get the girls and Auran out of here," he said, then ran into the sea of light and metal ahead of them.

Noah turned to see Zaela's aircycle park itself next to them. The gust of hurricane wind that accompanied it unsteadied him.

"Time to go, ya?" she said, violet eyes motioning toward the strafing microjets above. The Black Wings had only managed to shoot down one so far, and were starting to be decimated by the rest.

"Money in th' bank, lotta SolSec corpses. Day is won," she continued. "Oi'll give th' girls and ya a ride."

Noah nodded, hoisting up the feather-light Auran into the aircycle; he was stiff with shock. Sakai and Kyra took each of Zaela's hands, and she pulled them up so both were seated behind her. She lowered her hand again to Noah, who stared at it, then back toward the central building.

"I have to get Erik," Noah said, looking back and forth between Kyra and Sakai. "He's my brother, I can't leave him here."

"The Watchman will bring him back," Sakai said, nodding for him to take Zaela's hand. Kyra stared at him with a pained expression, like she didn't know whether he should stay or go. Would she be as indecisive if it were him who had run off and Erik who stayed? He locked eyes with her and saw her mouth a single word, "*Please.*"

Please what? Come with them to safety, or bring his brother back to her?

"No time for this," Zaela said, and the aircycle blew back Noah's hair and stained cloak as the four of them raced away from him toward the gate. The decision was made, but he knew he never really had any other choice. He took the hammer from his back and threw himself into a wall of bodies.

When Noah finally reached the towering doors of the central hall, nursing a fresh plasma graze and some shallow stab wounds, Tannon was surrounded by a protective ring of Black Wings holding back the SolSec hordes. The Watchman was banging on the door in frustration with an armored glove. He looked disappointed to see Noah.

"I told you to get them out of here," he said, giving the door one last pound for good measure.

"They're out," Noah called over the din. "I'm here for my brother." Tannon shook his head.

"Now that your father's alive, I can't have his kids dying on me. I don't need two of them taking stupid risks. One's enough."

"You need to get that door open, don't you?" Noah said, ignoring Tannon's persistence. The Watchman glared at the tall metal doors.

"Stand back," Noah continued, and Tannon reluctantly obeyed.

Noah curled his hands inward on the hammer's grip. The two metal spheres lit up on the side of the head, glowing the same blue as his eyes. He planted his right foot and hurled his entire body forward into the swing.

The shockwave was visible as dust shook off the metal in circular waves. A millisecond later both doors were torn from their hinges, dancing into the hall like playing cards tumbling in the wind. Noah's ears were ringing and every one of his bones felt like it was vibrating.

Tannon raced inside and Noah followed, attempting to stop his teeth from rattling inside his jaw. Down the hall, the roar of the battle outside grew quieter, but was replaced by the gasping of a Solarion soldier, clawing at a slit throat in the darkness. Erik had indeed come through there. They ran toward a light at the end of the hall, and the sounds of gunfire echoed off the stone walls ahead. They leapt over two more fresh Red Sun corpses before they made it to the larger antechamber.

Ahead was Erik, engaged in combat with Hayne, clad in his matte black darksteel armor. There was one more dead guard draped over the edge of the dry stone fountain, blood pooling where water had once flowed freely. Erik had apparently lost his pistol somewhere, and was deflecting blows from Hayne with only his knife. Hayne was wielding a larger blade, a short sword glimmering with a thousand colors of oil. Noah noticed his expensive rifle split in half near the foot of the stairs. Tannon and Noah raised their energy weapons at Hayne, but the pair were dancing around too quickly for either to get a clear shot.

Erik slashed upward with the knife, but Hayne rocked back so the blade missed him cleanly. He countered with a series of blindingly fast swipes at Erik's ribs, but his brother managed to twist out of the way of each of them. Erik swatted Hayne's sword hand away with his left wrist and stabbed downward with his right arm, but the blade was deflected by the plating on Hayne's forearm, which sent sparks showering to the floor. Hayne countered immediately with an upward swing of the sword. Erik dodged it, but caught an armored fist in his gut that followed it. There was a malevolent glee in Hayne's eyes, but his next decapitating blow missed as Erik spun right just as the blade came down.

Noah began to charge toward the pair of them, but a group of four guards rushed in from the right side of the room. Pulling out his repeater, Noah hit the first one square in the chest, and winged another. They returned fire and Noah was forced to roll behind a nearby pillar as the plasma took chunks out of the stone. Tannon fired his hand cannon, which plowed through the red sun painted on one of the soldier's chests, and his second shot detached the arm of the man Noah had grazed. The remaining soldier pulled the trigger of his rifle, but the gun detonated in his hand as Tannon put one more round directly into its power cell. The soldier staggered backward, somehow managing to dodge subsequent fire from Tannon, but Noah spun out from behind the pillar with his warhammer. The horizontal blow to his side sent the man flying into the wall to their right, and Noah followed it up by spearing his chest plating with the spike on the hammer's head. If the man had survived the initial strike, he was surely dead now. Blood pooled on the inside of his nearly opaque helmet. There was a moan from the Red Sun on the ground with no arm, but he wasn't moving.

Noah turned his attention back toward Erik and Hayne, who had danced further away from them. Tannon fired a dangerous shot that hit Hayne's shoulder plating and threw him momentarily off balance. Erik used the opportunity to send his knife racing toward Hayne's eye, but the young commander's sneering face and blond hair disappeared behind a double-slitted helmet that clamped down over his head an instant before the knife landed.

"You fight well for a child," Hayne jeered from inside the helmet. Suddenly, blue jets shot out of his back and he launched himself into the air. The flames disappeared and gravity slammed him back down to earth, with Erik barely having time to lift his knife in defense. Hayne's sword cracked it at its base, and the useless blade clattered to the floor as Erik tossed away the handle and rolled right. Hayne rocketed himself forward as Erik barely dodged thrust after thrust. Finally, one swing caught him across the breastbone, and a thin red line parted fabric and skin. Erik grimaced and clutched his chest.

Noah sprinted toward the pair of them, and leapt toward Hayne with warhammer cocked and starting to glow. In an instant, he learned what happened when darksteel met darksteel.

The armor didn't splinter, and the hammer didn't shatter. Rather the two of them were thrown apart as the force plowed Hayne all the way through a stone pillar and flung Noah into the crumbling staircase behind him. The rock bit into his barely protected legs wrapped in leather instead of metal armor. He heard a sickening crack and dropped to the floor in agony, pain radiating through his right leg.

As Noah tried to recover, Erik launched himself toward the dazed Hayne, who was picking himself up from the bits of marble strewn around him. Erik lunged for Hayne's sword, which he'd dropped beside him, but Hayne's leg found him first. The armored kick slammed into Erik's side. Hayne flew to his feet and spun around with another kick, this one landing across Erik's cut chest. Erik was flung backward, but Hayne flew after him, propelled by the jets on his back. One final punch connected with Erik's jaw, and even at a distance Noah saw his brother's teeth eject from his mouth.

Erik hit the floor groaning, holding his chest and bloodied face. Noah tried to stand, but his broken leg completely collapsed from under him. He grimaced as he pulled himself up to the foot of the stairs. He tried to toddle, supported by his hammer, toward Hayne who was approaching the downed Erik with his blade drawn.

"Killing little boys, raping little girls," Tannon called out from the center of the room, his pistol trained on Hayne. "King of this floating ruin of shit and death."

"You'll regret this day, grandfather," Hayne spit out, turning toward him. "You have no idea what you've done here. You don't know what sort of wrath this will bring down on your head. I will kill you and your two charges slowly. It might take weeks, months, years even. And I will make you watch as I ravish those delicate girls you brought with you over and over."

"You will die, here and now," Tannon said, gun arm steady. "I am Tannon Varrus Vale, First Watchmen of the Guardians, Grand

Admiral of the Soran Defense Initiative and former High Chancellor of the planet you fled from."

Hayne's face was hidden inside the helmet, but his silence said he knew exactly who Tannon was, now that the man had stepped into the light, face free from his old disguise.

"If that is true, all that will happen today is that my legend will grow ever larger," Hayne said finally.

"Then earn it," Tannon said. He fired his pistol.

Hayne rocketed toward him, jets spewing flame behind him. He dipped right so Tannon's first two shots spattered off his indestructible armor. Tannon didn't get off a third as Hayne smashed into him and dragged him across the floor and into the opposite wall.

Noah staggered toward the mess of dust and smoke, using his hammer as a crutch. He could feel the bones grinding in his leg, his femur snapped in two. Erik was picking himself up, his mouth drooling blood onto the ground. He tried to wipe it away with the back of his hand, but it just kept flowing.

Tannon and Hayne had extricated themselves from each other after their collision and were circling one another. Tannon was a large man, but Hayne towered over him in his suit of armor. Tannon had lost his pistol, but Hayne still had his sword, which Noah was horrified to see was coated in dark blood. Tannon was favoring his right side, and Noah could see blood running down his left leg, seeping through his clothes from an unseen wound. Hayne lunged, and Tannon dodged, but he wasn't as sprightly as Erik. Still, even after being cut, he grabbed Hayne's wrist and spun him off balance, tripping him with a swift kick the suit's stabilizers couldn't recover from in time.

"Watchman!" Noah cried, and he used the last of his quickly draining strength to heave his black hammer toward Tannon. The old man caught it in midair and immediately brought it crashing down on Hayne's chest. His body smashed into the floor, creating a vast spiderweb of cracks in the stone.

"Your story ends here," Tannon said as he raised the hammer again. This time, it smashed into Hayne's visor, shattering glass and detaching the housing from his collar. The young man's eyes were unfocused and Tannon pried the rest of the helmet off with his hand.

"Face your death like a man," Tannon said, flipping the hammer around in his hands so the rear spike was facing forward.

"We face death together," Hayne said with a red smile, amber eyes glinting madly. Tannon drove the hammer down just as Hayne brought up his oiled blade. Noah couldn't scream. He couldn't do anything.

After a deafening crash, Hayne was dead, his head a red ruin on the floor with the hammer sticking upright out of the shattered stone. But Tannon clutched his side, the short sword lodged between his ribs. He crumpled to the floor wordlessly.

"No!" Noah finally shouted and he hobbled toward the fallen Tannon. Eventually he lost his balance and hit the ground painfully. He dragged himself toward Tannon's body. Erik was staggering toward them as well, a look of horror on his bloodied face.

Tannon was groaning, his armored hands around the blade. Just as Noah reached him, he pulled the entire sword out with long gasp that might have been the most painful sound Noah had ever heard.

"Little shit," Tannon said, wheezing like he had a new hole in his lung. And it seemed he might, judging by the angle of the blade. Gripping Noah's forearm weakly, Tannon held out the blade with the other arm.

"Analyze it," Tannon said, choking on blood. "Save your brother."

"What?" Noah said frantically. "What are you talking about?"

"Poison blade," Tannon said, holding the sword aloft in the light. It was red with his blood, but still had an oiled shimmer to it. Noah looked over at Erik who was still stumbling toward them. He dropped to his knees when he found his lost laser pistol, discarded on the ground, but as he gripped it, he vomited up a stream of blood and foam.

"Oh gods," Noah whispered. Up ahead in the corridor they'd come from, he could hear the iron march of soldiers coming to greet them. In the distance, he could make out the faint outline of red suns. Erik spewed another torrent of liquid misery across the floor, and clutched his chest wound. He collapsed on the spot.

Tannon looked at Noah with stern, mismatched eyes, a brilliant green and blue. Each breath was a painful wheeze and both his mouth and torso wound were emptying his body of blood, which filled the cracks in the stone below him.

"Three wives, you were the only kids I ended up with," he said, his voice far away. "Could have done worse, I suppose."

"Watchman," Noah said frantically, looking toward the approaching soldiers. "Get up, we have to try and go out the rear." He tried pulling Tannon up but the man's face contorted painfully. Noah set him back down.

"I'm tired, son," Tannon sighed. "I've earned a rest. A long one."

Noah's mind raced with a silent prayer. His lips moved involuntarily. *Kyneth save us.* The clomp of metal boots was closer. *Zurana protect us.* He could see the glowing eye slits of the SolSec helmets in the darkness ahead.

"Take care of Cora," Tannon said, delirious. "She'll save us all someday."

And with that, his body relaxed, and his breathing stopped. Erik lay motionless a few feet away. The thunder of footsteps stopped. Noah's vision drifted into darkness.

The whine of an engine.

A wave of screams rippling toward them.

Autocannon fire.

Noah's eyes sprang open. A microjet was strafing down the hallway, unloading a firestorm of plasma on the approaching troops who were trapped in the narrow corridor. The guns stopped firing as the jet burst into the room and flew over Noah's head. It spun around in midair and resumed firing into the hall. The remaining live troops were fleeing the way they'd come, though most were being torn to shreds by another round of cannon fire.

Once the hallway was clear, the engines spooled down and the jet landed behind them. Noah pulled himself off Tannon's lifeless body and spun around as the cockpit opened. Out jumped Razor and Celton, who ran toward the three of them.

"Oh shit," Celton exclaimed after seeing the carnage in the room.

"Get them all inside," Razor said. "We must go."

A door on the side of the jet opened to reveal a cramped compartment where missiles were likely once housed. Celton and Razor lifted Tannon and Erik inside and came back for Noah. Both of them dragged him to the opening and lay him sideways next to his brother. Erik was coated in blood and vomit and didn't appear to be breathing. The last thing Noah heard were the engines firing as he lost consciousness.

28

It wasn't possible.

Lucas had watched Mars Maston die. During their mission to Xala, the man had hauled a Shadow into a cramped escape pod by the blade of his knife, and the two butchered each other as they rocketed through space. Lucas saw the blood pour from Maston's neck in the pod's video feed. He watched the data readouts, devoid of all life signatures. Maston had saved all of them from the Chosen Shadow's wrath, and it had cost him everything. This was a sick joke. A mind game of the Archon. The demonic figure before him was not his former friend.

Though part of him wanted to believe it was. And so did Asha, it seemed.

"Mars," she called out weakly, "it's us."

The Corsair stared at them blankly. It was hard to tell where his thin black armor plating ended and his obsidian skin began.

"What do you remember, Maston?" Lucas said. "What has the Archon done to you?"

Mars Maston's eyes narrowed. His voice sounded as if a thousand souls were trapped inside him.

"You speak as if you know me, traitors."

Lucas lowered his pistol as slowly as he could manage.

"Just tell us what you remember. *Who* you remember."

Maston's dark face looked momentarily confused.

"There is only the pair of them. Him and her. Tulwar and Cora. I will find him and kill him, and when I do, the Archon will bring her back to me."

He didn't remember them at all, then. The Archon had carved up his mind and memories to give him a single focus, to turn him into a whirlwind of destruction.

"Who have you killed? On all those ships, in all those systems?" Asha asked slowly, attempting to understand. All of their guns were now lower than they probably should have been. Draylin Maston looked at his cousin in awe as he propped himself up, his fine robes soaked in the blood of his dismembered crew.

"The Order," the Corsair Maston replied. "Their agents are everywhere. They've died screaming, as they should. As you will, once your purpose has been served."

God, Lucas thought. He'd been butchering SDI and civilian convoys thinking they were Fourth Order, thinking he was hunting down the already dead Hex Tulwar.

"Who is the Archon?" Lucas pressed, determined to find an answer from at least one of his creations.

"The Tomes of the Forest were wrong," Maston said. "The Archon is our god."

God of the Shadows. And still unhelpful.

"Tulwar is dead, the Order is scattered," Asha said, a pleading look in her eyes. "The Archon is not a god, and can't bring Cora back, no matter what he's telling you."

"The words of a liar mean little," Maston mumbled, inching toward them. The viewscreen showed a vast expanse of space behind him. The stars drifted sideways as the crippled *Endless Dawn* was floating dead in the vacuum. "Why should I believe the fabrication of strangers, desperate to save their own lives?" he continued.

It was Alpha who spoke next, for the first time.

"You know us, Commander Maston. Some part of you does. Why else would you take the time to speak openly, rather than slaughter us and be on your way as you have done on so many ships, so many times before?"

Anger flashed in Maston's unnaturally blue eyes. They'd been a rich brown once, Lucas recalled.

"This one is needed," he said, pointing to Lucas. "The rest are expendable."

Hallucination? Memory alteration? Deep psychosis? What was this new version of Maston suffering from?

"But cousin," Viceroy Draylin Maston finally said, getting to his feet, every one of his limbs shaking with fear. "We are blood, family. I am elated to see you alive! The other cousins will be so pleased. We all thought—"

Maston turned toward the Viceroy. He extended his hand, and Asha's darksteel sword detached itself from Draylin's hip and shot across the room and into Mars Maston's hand. Maston pulled his arm forward and the Viceroy flew toward him, a look of shock on his face as he appeared to be pulled across the room by his belt. Maston whipped the sword straight through his cousin's midsection as he passed by. Asha kept her blade sharpened to the last molecule, and it made a cut so clean the Viceroy didn't even collapse until he was five feet on the other side of Maston. Each half of him hit the ground with a wet thud, and the three of them were speechless at the sight, even in a room full of similar carnage.

"Another Fourth Order agent," Maston growled. "Expendable."

He turned toward them.

"And now you."

This wasn't Mars Maston. This was a weapon. This was simply the Black Corsair.

"You will come with me, or your friends will die in a much slower manner. I would relish the opportunity."

Corsair Maston was itching for a fight. He might have forgotten that Lucas was a weapon too. Lucas clenched his fist and raised his pistol again.

There was a sound from behind them. The rear doors slid open and in marched a unit of armored Xalan Paragons, Maston's crew aboard his impossibly fast ship, the likes of which Lucas and his sons had fought in Dubai.

"And what of them, Commander Maston?" Alpha said, gesturing to the soldiers whose gray faces were hidden behind dark oval helmets. "Who is your . . . unusual-looking crew?"

The soldiers lined up behind the three of them and pointed a collection of energy weapons at each of their backs. A quick glance behind him and Lucas saw there were ten of them.

"Do not dare mock the Guardians, Xalan," Maston seethed. "Over the centuries they have killed more of your kind than there are stars in the sky!"

"Jesus Christ . . ." Asha said, trailing off as she realized what Maston was saying. As the Black Corsair, the Archon had Maston killing SDI troops thinking they were Fourth Order, while using a Xalan crew he thought were Soran Guardians.

"Your counterpart is a useful weapon," the Archon had told him. *"Destroying fleets on a whim on his imagined quest for vengeance, but he merely improves upon existing constructs."*

Existing constructs. A Chosen Shadow. Whatever this facsimile was, it truly was just a shadow of the man he once called an enemy, then a rival, then a friend.

"This ends here," Lucas said with confidence that surprised even him. "Either you can cast off the Archon's influence and join us, or you can die here and now."

"I serve my god willingly," Maston said, fully indoctrinated, it seemed. "And your threats are empty, traitor."

Maston raised his arms. Alpha and Asha shot up into the air, propelled by psionic force. Asha held on to her rifle, but Alpha's weapon was sent tumbling to the ground. Asha tried to fire but found the gun torn from her grasp and flung across the room.

Lucas's pistol was wrenched away from him as well. Maston the Corsair was able to perform multiple psionic actions simultaneously, a talent Lucas had never seen before.

Lucas dropped to his knees, and the Paragon unit to his rear advanced toward him. Asha and Alpha strained in the air, their bodies starting to contort in painful ways.

"I surrender," Lucas said loudly, raising his arms over his head. Blood seeped into his clothing after his knees hit the wet metal.

"No!" Asha choked out from above.

Maston eyed him curiously and took a step forward, as did the Paragons behind him.

But Lucas had a talent he bet the Corsair had never seen before either.

"Fire!" he screamed.

Lucas's mind was engulfed in a freezing inferno as the Paragon troopers all turned their weapons toward Maston and simultaneously fired.

In a moment of apparent shock, Maston lost his telekinetic grip on Alpha and Asha, who went tumbling to the ground. Asha landed on her feet, but Alpha hit the ground squarely on his back. Maston barely had time to leap away from the execution squad before him, and he backflipped over the stream of plasma headed his way. His own troops fired shot after shot as he flew around the room and took cover behind a mound of corpses he'd created earlier. They began to circle around the hiding place, continuing to unload as the pile of bodies was reduced to charred carbon.

Maston rose, and the Paragons flew upward with him.

"Enough!" he bellowed, as his own soldiers were launched twelve feet in the air, most losing their grip on their weapons before crashing back down to the ground.

Die! Lucas thought with all his might, directing his mind toward the snarling monster in front of him. The man flinched, perhaps for a millisecond, but then he rushed forward past his dazed troops directly at Lucas, Asha's sword in his hand, unfazed by Lucas's attempt to control him.

So much for that, Lucas thought as the black shape raced toward him.

In the corner of his eye, Lucas saw Asha flick her wrist. There was a small metal cuff around it, one the Viceroy hadn't thought to strip from her, even when taking her famed weapon for his own. But it was an essential part of the package.

The electromagnetic tether wrenched the sword from Maston's grip a second before he arrived. It shot across the room and landed in Asha's outstretched hand.

Course-correcting, the airborne and now swordless Maston lowered his shoulder and barreled into Lucas. The two were flung into the starboard wall, which cratered from the impact. Through the shooting pain that followed, Lucas could see the confused Paragon troopers regaining their senses after his influence faded. Asha knew well enough to not let them collect themselves, and she'd already decapitated three before a single one could turn to fire on her. Alpha followed her lead and was unloading into the group with one of the Paragon's own energy rifles. They began to return fire and he was forced to dive behind the upturned holotable.

Lucas had larger problems. His body was racked with pain after the collision with Maston, who was now two feet away and swinging a black fist toward his face.

Time slowed, and this close it was easy to see it was indeed Mars. The skin and eyes were terrifyingly transformed, but it was clearly the face of the man he once knew; faint traces of his former good looks could be seen under the monstrous facade. He was even swinging the same punch that had struck Lucas more than once years ago.

While Lucas was able to deftly dodge even hypersonic plasma rounds in his own current Shadow state, Maston's fist was moving even faster. Lucas didn't have time to block and took the strike across the temple, which dislodged him from the wall and sent him flying to the hard metal floor. Maston's speed matched his own, if not exceeded it. The Paragons, Alpha, and Asha seemed to be fighting in slow motion out of focus across the bridge. Maston was moving at lightspeed, however.

Lucas barely had time to roll out of the way as Maston's knee slammed into the spot where his head had been a fraction of a second earlier. Lucas tried to get to his feet, but felt himself wrenched upward by an unseen force, and then caught a roundhouse kick in the chest, which propelled him into the viewscreen of the ship. He was yanked forward again by Maston's telekinesis and met with a stiff clothesline that sent him pinwheeling around twice before he crashed into a communications console. Ignoring the pain, Lucas picked himself up, bringing a nearby rifle with him. He took aim, but Maston flung his arm sideways, and Lucas involuntarily swung the rifle outward with one hand and let out a stream of rounds that whizzed dangerously close to Asha's head a few dozen yards away. She barely had time to turn and scowl at him before having to refocus and skewer an encroaching Paragon.

Lucas dropped the gun as soon as he was able, terrified he couldn't even control his own body in the face of Maston's awesome power. He lunged toward the man again, but Maston brought his palm down and psionically slammed him into the ground before he could reach him. There was something resembling a sneer across his cracked lips, just above his dimpled chin.

He's just toying with me, Lucas thought. The idea was terrifying. *I can't win. We can't win.*

Alpha and Asha had won, however, and had just finished cleaning up the remaining Paragon troops across the bridge. They ran toward him, but Lucas held out a bloody hand to stop them.

"Wait, wait," he said hoarsely, but it was too late. Maston's eyes flashed with an electric charge, and he seized control of Asha's arm, causing her to whip her blade around to stop within an inch of Alpha's throat. The Xalan froze in his tracks, then his own arm was pulled upward, and he held a pistol aimed at the side of Asha's head. It was clear neither one of them could move a muscle, completely under Maston's control. Both looked uncharacteristically terrified.

"Wait!" Lucas shouted. "I'll come, I'll help you find Tulwar. But only if you let them go."

Maston turned toward Lucas, his hands raised like a puppetmaster.

"I knew you were a liar," he said. "I should execute these two as a lesson for your treachery."

"If you do, you'll never find him," Lucas said. "The Archon will be most displeased, and you'll never see Corinthia again."

He had to play along. Maston would butcher Alpha and Asha where they stood if he didn't. Lucas couldn't kill him. It was impossible. All the stories about the Black Corsair's prowess in combat were true, it seemed. As were the Xalan scientists who thought a Soran Shadow could be more powerful than a Xalan one. Even one made out of a dead man.

Maston shifted his head slightly and dropped his arms. Asha and Alpha relaxed, their weapon arms dropping to their sides. Lucas ran to meet them, pain coursing through most of his body. Something told him if he wasn't half a Shadow, he'd have died instantly from any one of Maston's strikes.

"What are you doing?" Asha said, visibly shaken from being immobilized. "You can't go with him."

"You'll die if I don't," Lucas said, putting his arms on her shoulders.

"Lucas, you cannot—" Alpha started.

"The Archon needs me alive," Lucas interrupted. "This isn't like Xalan central command. You're not leaving me to die. If I go, I can find out what he wants, and who or what he is. And there may be some hope for Mars. He claims not to know us, but he has no real reason not to kill either of you and drag me out of here with all my limbs broken. Maybe there's still some part of the true Mars left inside him."

"There isn't," Asha said fiercely, casting a hard stare at the statuesque monster behind Lucas. "I won't let you go, not again."

"Nor shall I," Alpha said, his translator properly conveying his grave tone, which was matched by the determined look in his gold-ringed eyes. Both gripped their weapons tightly, and were clearly ready to die in his defense.

"I know you won't," Lucas sighed. "Which is why I'm sorry for this."

"For what?" Asha asked, eyes narrowed.

Listen, Lucas thought. His mind was still in pain from turning the Paragons against Maston, and another invisible icy knife drove through his skull.

Asha and Alpha's faces relaxed. Tears welled in Lucas's eyes when he saw their blank, dead eyes staring past him.

"Listen to me," Lucas said, voice cracking. "You're going to leave. Take the fighter in the hangar bay and go to Solarion Station. Find Erik and Noah. Get them back to Sora. I'll find you. One way or another, I'll find you."

Lucas concentrated as hard as he could. He mind was screaming in agony. He had to make sure they did what he said. That they wouldn't come running back through the door in twenty seconds, his influence having worn off. When he could take no more, he broke off his mental focus, taking his head into his hands. It throbbed in time with his pulse.

Without saying a word, the tranquilized Asha and Alpha simply turned and walked out of the bloodied bridge. The door slid shut behind them. Lucas hated what he'd had to do to them, but hopefully it had saved their lives. It was clear Maston could eviscerate them with a look if he wanted to.

Lucas turned back to the blackened figure. Maston's light armor plating didn't have so much as a plasma burn from his sacking of the ship and their fight. He really was a new kind of monster.

"Wise choice, traitor," Maston growled. The multitude of voices that made up his speech was unsettling. Lucas wondered if any of them were actually his own. Was this what Lucas was destined to become once his transformation was complete?

"Now what?" Lucas said, rubbing his temples, which still felt like they were being jabbed with a thousand tiny needles. His ability would not work on Maston; that much was made clear from their brawl.

"I take you to him," Maston said. "And we watch the rest of the Order fall."

Lucas's gaze darted to the viewscreen as a ship rose into view. The gold engines of Alpha's fighter glowed hot against the darkness of space, then flickered as the ship shot out toward the stars and a tiny red planet in the distance.

Thank god, Lucas thought. *At least they're away from him.* His eyes went back to Maston.

The Black Corsair raised his hand with two fingers extended. Lucas felt a slight pressure in his neck. A nerve cluster constricting. Dark spots appeared in the corners of his eyes, then consumed his vision entirely, and he collapsed to the blood-soaked floor, almost thankful for the respite.

29

It was the end of summer, which in recent years had been the hottest time. Noah, desperate to get away from the endless noise of the Colony One construction crews, wandered through the woods, swatting at imaginary enemies with a broken branch. Eventually he stopped swinging the piece of wood around and tossed it aside as he realized he was working up something of a sweat in the heat. The wind momentarily rushed through the trees, offering a bit of relief, but it was gone as quickly as it had come.

Noah didn't really like his new home, and hadn't quite adjusted even in the year he'd been there so far. He didn't understand why they had to keep moving. But they told him that now, this place would be where he'd stay until he was grown. His mother was being sent back out to fight the Xalans, and she promised to visit often. But mostly Noah was left to his own devices, running around playing with the smaller, younger kids. He was nine years old, but was as tall as some of the teenage caretakers at the colony. He felt like some sort of mountain giant from a fable. But some were nice, and he was told they were special, like him. They were all from the planet Earth, and as such they had to stick together. Noah asked why the colony wasn't on Earth then, since there were colonies on lots of planets, but Keeper Auran just laughed at him. "When you're older," he said.

Noah bounced on some flat rocks embedded in a stream. He slipped on the last one and frowned as his foot plunged into the shallow water, soaking his shoe. He soon forgot his misfortune when he heard soft crying from up ahead over the grassy ridge. He trudged up the hill and saw a little boy sitting on a stump.

"What are you doing out here, Erik?"

Erik looked up at his brother. He'd just turned seven the previous week, and his light green eyes were brimming with tears. Noah immediately saw that his black hair was tousled, full of bits of twig and leaves, and he had caked dirt and a small scrape on his face.

"Nothing," his brother said sullenly and turned back toward the ground. His lip was stiff and he was pretending he hadn't just been crying.

"Who was it this time?" Noah said, walking over and sitting down on the forest floor next to his brother, arms folded over his knees.

"No one," Erik said, staring straight ahead.

"Heraklion? Lyon? Penza?"

Erik looked at him sharply.

"I said no one!"

"Alright," Noah said, staring out into the trees. Bird calls rebounded all around them and the sun was just starting to go down. "What did no one say, then?"

Little Erik became alive with anger.

"They said daddy didn't kill the Des'crater! They said it was all made up and just a story to make people happy! Like how Kyneth and Zurana give us gifts every solstice even though they're not real!"

"Dad was real," Noah said. "He did all those brave things. You can ask mom. She was there."

"Mom's gone," Erik said, downcast.

"What did you do when they said that about dad?" Noah asked.

Erik wiped his eyes with the back of his hand.

"I said they were wrong and they said I was a liar. Herak—Someone pushed me into a bush," he said, touching his hand to his scratched cheek. "And everyone laughed."

Erik was a year older than the kids at the colony, but smaller than many, including some of the girls.

"I wish daddy was here to tell them all what he did," Erik said. "Then they would *have* to believe it."

"Everyone believes what dad did," Noah said. "The whole world does. The other kids are just teasing, you can't let it bother you."

"I hate it here!" Erik cried out, slamming his tiny fists into the sides of the stump. "All the kids are so mean. I miss Kyra. She was nice."

Noah hadn't seen Kyra for a long time now. Keeper Auran said he couldn't any more, and Noah had been upset about it for a long time.

But slowly, he was almost forgetting about her with so many new kids around. Noah was surprised Erik still remembered her.

"You have to get used to it," Noah said. "The kids here are like our new family. We're all from Earth. Like mom and dad."

"*You're* from Earth," Erik said forcefully. "*I'm* from Sora. I heard the guards say Earth is a bad place. They say that Earth did *that* to you."

Erik pointed at the scar on Noah's arm and shoulder.

"We're from both places then," Noah said, itching his arm. "And we're brothers, so you have to listen to me. Don't let the other kids bug you."

"I'm going to run away and make my own planet," Erik said matter-of-factly. "It will be better than Earth or Sora. Only nice people can live there. Like mommy and Kyra and Keeper Auran."

"What about me?" Noah asked with half a smile.

Erik took a minute to deliberate, and finally rolled his eyes.

"*Fine*," he said, "but only if you let me be leader."

Noah chuckled.

"Alright, well, if you want to be the leader that means *you* have to be nice too. So no fighting with the other kids, no matter what they say or do."

"If they're mean, I'll be mean," Erik said grumpily, kicking at the dirt with the sole of his boot.

Noah just sighed and shook his head. His brother was silent for a while.

"When I grow up I'm going to do brave things like daddy," he finally said. "Everyone will remember me too."

"I'm sure they will, Erik."

"*Move!*" a thin, dark man with a dozen rings through his ears shouted at Noah as he pushed him aside in the dimly lit room inside the Black Wings compound. Noah grimaced as he hopped on his good leg; his other one was currently being held together by bent steel and cloth, and his head was swimming from a blunt syringe full of painkillers.

Erik was laid out flat on a table, coughing in fits, spitting up congealed masses of blood, his eyes darting around in terror. Tannon's corpse was on the floor in the corner, covered by his own bloodied cloak. Despite the supposedly mellowing effects of the medication, Noah's heart was racing while he watched the earringed man they called "Wax" try to stitch up his brother's wounds with gel. He was the gang's resident combat medic, it seemed. Celton was next to him, running analysis on the poison blade they'd brought back.

Noah looked around for his hammer and saw it discarded on the floor like a piece of scrap. He tried to reach for it, but his sense of balance was warped and he almost fell over. He looked back toward his brother, who started convulsing on the table like he was possessed by a demon.

"Seizure!" Key shouted as she tried to hold him down by the legs. She was missing the top of her ear, but didn't seem to notice. Noah hobbled over to press down on Erik's shoulders. His brother's eyes were white, completely rolled back into his skull. Foam and blood erupted from his mouth again like a clockwork fountain. The alleged medic grabbed his jaw and turned his head so he wouldn't choke on the mixture.

"I'm reading some sort of clorixine compound," Celton said loudly over the din of the room, looking at a stream of floating data.

"Clorixine?" the medic asked, dark eyes flitting back and forth. His fingers ran over an array of needles laid out on a nearby side table. He finally picked one and plunged it into a spot just under Erik's armpit. The syringe clicked and shot a mixture of pale orange liquid into his brother.

"What is that?" Noah asked, words slurring.

The medic withdrew the needle and tossed it back on the table. Erik's convulsing stopped, his eyes closed. Blood tricked down from the corners of his lips, but was no longer erupting from his mouth.

"Coma," the medic said, looking at the digital scroll Celton placed before him.

"You put him in a coma?" Noah asked. The medic glared at him like he was an imbecile.

"Slows the spread of clorixine. Buys time to mix up a proper cure."

"Will . . . will he be alright?" Noah asked, looking down at his unmoving brother.

"Ask the gods," the medic said, waving his hand dismissively. "I cannot say."

As Tannon lay dead and his brother was possibly dying in the medical wing, the rest of the camp was celebrating. Despite heavy losses, the theft, prison break, and subsequent attack on Solarion Security headquarters had destabilized the organization's hold on the station. Zaela was boasting to her troops about all the new equipment she was already procuring with the billions of marks pilfered from SolSec before the attack, and news was spreading that Commander Hayne himself had been killed in the assault. Rival gangs were now taking down SolSec outposts on their own initiative, and a few were even showing up to pay tribute to Zaela, the new presumed leader of Solarion. The noise of the party being thrown in the main hall was louder than the actual battle had been.

Using his hammer as a makeshift crutch, Noah shoved his way through legions of raucous Black Wings, many trying to thrust a drink into his hand. His part in the day's events was well known, but he was in no mood to celebrate anything. Tannon Vale was dead. His brother could follow him soon. It was all he could do to keep from coming apart at the seams.

Noah ducked into a hallway and pushed a wooden door out of his way. He slammed it shut behind him, which only muted the noise slightly. The room was a mess, and on the stained foam mattress sat a shivering figure covered in soot, dirt, and flecks of blood. Sakai was whimpering, and raised her head as the door shut.

Her eyes were angry.

She ran up to Noah and struck him across the face so hard he could feel it even through the meds for his leg. When he looked at her, stunned, she did it again. He caught her hand on the third attempt.

"What are you doing?" he cried, rubbing his face and releasing her wrist.

"What are *you* doing?" she shouted back, tears in her eyes. "You would risk everything for . . . *him*? For that little psycho?"

"He's my brother," Noah yelled, his temper spiking. "And now he could be dead in a matter of hours!"

"Well, that's what having a death wish will do to you," Sakai shot back. "He could have had the decency to go off on his fool's quest without dragging you and Tannon along! He's dead! The man is dead now because of your stupid brother, and you could have died trying to save him too!"

"I had to—"

"You had to do *nothing*," Sakai said with steel in her voice. "You say he's your brother, but aside from the fact that he just physically is *not*, what has he ever done for you, other than almost get you killed? Why would you feel like you owe someone like that anything? Why would you turn and leave me to go after him?"

"You were safe," Noah said. "Zaela was taking you out of—"

"We were safe, huh? Tell that to SolSec soldier who jumped on the back of the aircycle who I had to stab through the eye. I was far from safe. But that's fine, I can take care of myself. But what I can't do is deal with the fact that when it came down to it, you chose him over me. You chose the 'brother' who would risk *all* our lives to get revenge on some nobody who disrespected his crush. You chose him over me, the girl who loved you more than anyone has ever loved you, even your own family."

That pierced Noah like a poisoned sword.

"A great man is dead because of your brother," Sakai continued, "and you're still apologizing for him. I'm done with the both of you. You're just as bad as he is if you can't admit that if he'd just gone with the plan, all of us could be alive and well right now, him and Tannon included. Now you tell me he's dying? Well whose fault is that? Maybe your beloved gods are punishing him for his collective sins at last. Or maybe he finally got his wish to die the hero. Hopefully Kyra will appreciate that."

Before Noah could even open his mouth again, Sakai shoved him aside and flung open the door. She stormed out into the crowded hall, and he lost sight of her in the mass of dark bodies.

His shock soon boiled into anger of his own. He shouldn't have gone after Erik? Not to save his brother? Not even to try and help Tannon? Erik had done many terrible things, but he was family, blood or otherwise. And despite his recklessness, he'd rescued their father *and* Malorious Auran, and helped kill a warlord responsible for the murder, rape, and torture of untold thousands. He deserved to die for that? What right did Sakai have to say such a thing, even in her grief?

Noah punched the closed door, which cracked and sent splinters into his fist. He couldn't even feel them. His hammer fell to the floor with a metallic thud, and he sat down on the mattress, burying his face in his hands.

Or was Sakai right? Was his brother just a reckless, vengeful idiot who had gotten a great man killed? One that had been more of a father to both of them over the years than any supposedly dead war hero? Noah didn't know what to think, but he certainly didn't want Erik to die regardless. Sakai hadn't seen his suffering from the clorixine poison, shaking and vomiting and during brief moments of consciousness, looking terrified. No one deserved that. The coma was a mercy.

Noah shivered as the edge came off his painkillers. He blinked, and nothing felt real. He'd lost Tannon, possibly his brother, and certainly Sakai, it seemed. It was a nightmare. But he couldn't wake up.

He shook his head violently and rose to his feet. His broken leg was tender, but stable with the makeshift bracing. Picking up his hammer, he wobbled to the door and threw it open. This time, when Noah reached the hall he took the first drink handed to him and drained the entire thing, ignoring the liquid fire that burned as it tumbled down his throat. It tasted like hovercraft fuel smelled. He grabbed another, and contorted his face into a forced smile as a trio of Black Wings smashed their cups into his in celebration. The liquid sloshed and he downed the remnants quickly. He tossed the clay container over his shoulder and had picked up another before the first one shattered on the ground.

Hours later, Noah had no idea where he was, nor how long it had been since he had stumbled out of the Black Wings compound. He squinted to try and read the signs to at least figure out what level of the station he was on, but the numbers were blurred beyond recognition, as was most everything else around him. There was yelling and screaming, and something that very much looked like fire coming out of the windows of a building ahead. The warhammer that he was still using to brace himself stopped when it hit something metal. Noah looked down and saw an armored body with a red sun on the breastplate, resting in a shallow pool of blood. The figure was missing a head, and Noah gingerly stepped over it, almost losing his balance in the process. He remembered enough of the events of the day to realize there was some sort of rebellion in progress, a backlash against SolSec. He didn't want to remember anything that had happened. What good was drinking if he still remembered?

Whatever he'd consumed paired with his cocktail of pain meds was wreaking havoc on his coordination. He kept almost losing his grip on his hammer, but catching the handle just at the last second. The entire station was in chaos. Figures ran by too fast for him to see what they looked like, but he supposed he looked no more out of place than anyone else.

"Hail, offworlder!"

He supposed wrong.

Noah wheeled around to where the voice had come from behind him, nearly falling from the sudden movement. Ahead of him were three human-like shapes. His eyes were unfocused, and he could only make out milk-colored skin, long, stringy black hair, and the color green.

"That's an awfully nice hammer to be used as what, a cane?" the middle man said, his voice nasal and tinged with a slight East Kullan accent. The others snickered. Noah opened his mouth and no words came out, just a jumbled collection of vowels. More snickering.

"Tall, pretty boy like you looks tank-bred. Maybe one of those boy toy jobs from Dakarian?" the man said, leaning toward him.

Another unfortunate memory hit Noah. Three pale, long-haired men in green, stabbing a man to death in the lift. He had no idea if this was the same group, or simply other members of the same gang.

At present, their faces were blank spheres of nothingness, his eyes too bleary to focus on them.

"Earthb—" he spat out. "Earthborn."

Why are you telling them you're Earthborn? his mind snapped at him.

"Did you say 'Earthborn'?" the man said, and the other two were now doubled over with laughter. "Well, nice to meet you, I'm Madric Stoller," he said, roaring hysterically.

One of the other men stopped laughing.

"Ya know, he does sorta look like the one of 'em."

The first man waved him off.

"You're high, Yassa, let's just gut him and see what we can get for that hammer."

Noah's eyes caught the flash of a silver knife. On instinct alone, he whipped the hammer around toward the man wielding it.

The swing was a lot faster in his own mind. The lead thug looked surprised as he jumped back, the hammer missing his face by a solid foot. Unfortunately, its primary purpose was keeping Noah upright, and as the hammer came around, he toppled to the pavement like a felled tree, fresh pain shooting through his caged leg.

"That was a lively attempt," the thug said, standing over the downed Noah. "But I'm bored now."

Noah reached for his hammer, but he'd lost it in the fall, and it was a few inches outside of his reach. The pale assailant raised the knife with both hands and stabbed downward forcefully. Noah did the only thing he could, and raised his hand. The knife slid through his palm, and the shock was too great for him to even scream. The hilt hit his fingerbones and the blade stopped half a foot from his chest. Noah forgot about the pain, already masked by whatever was in his system, and grabbed the man's dirty cloth collar. He wrenched the thug downward so his face smashed into the pavement and he lost his grip on the knife. Noah pulled the blade out of his palm with his other hand, and jabbed at the neck of the now-dazed man. His diminished motor skills missed the intended plunge into the thug's throat, but he sliced along his skin, right through a black cracked skull tattoo. Blood shot out of the cut like a geyser.

"Hey!" one of the other men said, realizing what had happened. Noah lunged for his hammer and grabbed it, then swung it around so the rear spike caught the approaching man in the hip. He howled in agony as his friend raced toward Noah. He couldn't pull the hammer free, and made a hasty attempt to throw the bloody knife at the other man. It wobbled wide left, and the man's boot struck Noah's face, making his world dissolve into stars. A second later, his sight returned, and he saw the vacant eyes of the man next to him, having already bled out from a severed artery. Noah barely had time to react to another kick, and this time grabbed the man's foot and twisted it sharply with all his strength until he heard a stiff crack. More screaming. Noah was reeling as he sat up, and found the other man swinging his own hammer at him, blood gushing from his side. Noah rocked backward to dodge the darksteel blur, and the momentum of the swing caused the man to stumble. From his seated position, Noah caught the man's belt in his good hand and pulled, causing him to fall and land on top of his friend with the broken ankle.

Noah fumbled to catch the dropped warhammer, but it eluded his clumsy grip and clattered to the ground. The man who had just wielded it was trying to get up, but Noah slammed him back down with a punch that hit him square in the forehead instead of the nose. Once again, he landed on top of his friend. Noah shook his hand out. His other one was bleeding profusely from the knife wound, and he discovered most of his fingers wouldn't bend.

Noah finally found the warhammer and used it to get to his feet. As soon as he did, he brought it over his head and slammed it into the back of the downed man. Bone cracked, the hammer glowed, and the force threw him a solid five feet backward into the middle of the street. Picking his head up, he saw all three of the men were still. He looked up and found a bright halo hovering around every source of light. The smell of smoke was heavy in the air. He felt pain, though not nearly as much as he should, he knew. His chest rose and fell rapidly as breath escaped him.

A hot wind blew over him, accompanied by the whine of an aircycle engine. A pair of boots hit the pavement next to him. The figure was out of focus. A woman's voice.

"*Gods*, Noah . . ."

He woke up on a beach. Noah lay back in the sand, and crystal clear waves reached the bottoms of his heels before retracting back into the sparkling sea. There wasn't a cloud in the sky, and the ghosts of two moons could be seen opposite the brightly shining sun.

Tropical greenery swayed behind him, and there wasn't another soul in sight. Colorful birds darted in and out of the trees, and to his right and left, the shoreline stretched out to infinity. It reminded him of a place he, Asha, and Erik had once lived when he was very small and their family was still hiding from the public. Even so, that island had never been quite this beautiful.

Noah looked down and saw that his arm was completely free of his famed burn. His broken leg and stabbed palm no longer hurt. His other scars, from accidental injury and battle alike, had evaporated.

"Noah."

A voice, and then she appeared out of thin air.

Kyra's blond hair was longer than he'd ever seen it, and it flowed down over her shoulders with a purple-and-white flower tucked behind her ear. Her eyes sparkled, even bluer than the perfect ocean behind her. She wore a wispy coverall masking a bright swimsuit. She kneeled in the white sand, a look of concern in her eyes.

"Noah, where are you?" she said.

"I'm right here, of course," he said, his voice sounding strange in his head. He moved his arm to touch her cheek, but it seemed to take ages to get there. She put her hand on his fingers and slowly lowered the hand. Every inch of his body felt like it was being bathed in sunlight that was warm, yet refreshing at the same time. He couldn't stop smiling. *This must be what plants feel like*, he thought, not comprehending his own strangeness.

"Where are you?" Kyra repeated.

"The island," he said slowly. "Kin-tai? Kin-toi? I can't remember. It's beautiful here. You're beautiful."

"No wonder they call it Paradise," Kyra said under her breath, looking away.

"What?" Noah said, confused. "What are you . . . What are you talking about?"

"The drug, Paradise," Kyra said, staring into his eyes unromantically, like she was looking for something. "It's in your system, along with four different types of liquor and three classes of narcotics. I just did a blood test."

Noah furrowed his brow, which again seemed to take ages. Paradise?

"I didn't take any . . . I was . . ." He was speaking too slowly to finish the sentence.

"It was probably mixed into something you drank. Its effects were delayed by the other compounds in your system."

"Just relax," Noah said, waving her off. "Enjoy the sun. It's so nice here."

"It's not real," Kyra said softly.

"But I can feel you," he said, his fingers grazing the back of her hand.

"Feel this," she said, taking his hand and placing it on the sand. She dragged it forward. The sand moved, but it felt like cold, rough metal.

"I don't understand."

"You're in the Black Wings compound. They told me you wandered away, so I went to look for you. I found you in the street next to a pile of bodies."

"Robbers," Noah said. "They weren't nice. This is a planet where only nice people can live."

Kyra shook her head.

"You're not making any sense. But it's alright; I mixed up something that should ease you back into reality soon. Just don't try to move."

"No," Noah said, shaking his head as violently as he could manage. "I want to stay here."

The sun was starting to go down now, and the sky was a brilliant painting of pink, red, orange, and yellow. The tide was falling away from his feet, pulling sand with it.

"You can't run from what happened today, Noah. No matter how badly you want to. Wherever you think you are, it doesn't change the fact that people need you here in the real world."

Noah pressed his palms into the sand, feeling only cold metal. His head hit something invisible behind him. The island was dimmer now. Darker. Not quite as pretty.

"Make it stay," he said frantically. "Make it stay."

"It will be gone soon," Kyra said. "But I'll still be here with you. Don't worry. You'll always have me."

Noah felt like bursting into tears as the island continued to fade. Instead, he lunged forward and kissed her. He felt her whole body tense in shock. He kept his eyes closed. He didn't want to open them. But he did.

He pulled back, and saw Kyra looking at him with wide eyes, face flushed scarlet. He was in a dark, dingy former prison cell that was so old it still used metal bars. Dirty blankets and cots were spread around on the floor, the central light flickered. The walls were painted with rust and glowing graffiti. His leg was wrapped in a bloodsoaked bandage, as was his stabbed hand. Kyra wore a tightly wrapped leather tunic with a retracted hood, and a look of complete confusion. He could still feel her lips on his. The sensation lingered. That much wasn't a hallucination then.

"I'm . . . sorry," he said, unsure of what else he could say.

"Sakai . . ." she whispered.

"Hates me."

"Erik . . ."

"Deserves a better brother," he said, putting his face in his hands. "And you deserve someone better than me. I don't even know what I'm doing anymore."

His head was finally starting to clear, and every part of him hurt, both inside and out.

"I don't deserve any of you," Kyra said, her voice starting to break. "Not Tannon, not Erik, not a Guardian escort to protect me, not a small army to save the family *I've* endangered. I'm not worth it. I don't know why everyone thinks I'm worth it."

"You are," Noah said quietly. "Everyone knows it but you. You're what this world needs."

"And what I need," she said. "What I've *always* needed . . . is you."

This time it was she who leaned forward to meet his lips with her own. It was Noah's turn to look shocked when she pulled away.

"That may be the most selfish thing I've ever done," Kyra said. "With any luck, you won't remember any of this tomorrow."

Even in a delirious stupor, Noah knew he'd never forget it the rest of his life.

"I will," was all he could manage.

"Get some sleep. Dream of the island. Dream of the planet with only nice people. Just don't leave this room. I have to go check on Erik."

She got up and exited through the open doorway, leaving Noah alone with his reeling head and an unsettling avalanche of emotions.

I love her, he finally admitted to himself. *Gods damn it, I love her.*

30

When Lucas came to, he didn't understand where he was. He expected to wake up in some dark torture chamber onboard the Corsair's ship. Instead, he found himself still on the bridge of the Viceroy's vessel, nearly in the same spot he'd fallen. Standing above him was none other than . . . Alpha?

"You are awake, excellent," Alpha said, his translator flickering orange. He glanced toward the viewscreen full of stars. A few odd objects appeared in the distance, but they were too small to be identified. "Your assistance is required."

"What?" Lucas said, getting to his feet and rubbing his head. "What the hell happened? Why are you back here? Where's Maston? Where's Asha?"

Alpha let out a snort.

"After your . . . *influence* wore off of the pair of us inside the fighter, I intercepted an incoming transmission. One side was scrambled, but from the sound of it, Commander Maston was being called away by the Archon, presumably. Despite your attempt to force us to flee, we returned to this vessel and were curious, and elated, to find he had left you behind."

It didn't make any sense. "Why go through all that trouble just to leave me here?"

Alpha shook his head. "I do not know, though I am certainly wary. I have scanned you for any toxins or explosive devices, but you appear to be untouched."

"Where's Asha, then?" Lucas asked, looking around the bloody bridge for her.

"As I fixed the ship's engines and we waited for you to wake, I convinced her I could manage your care here while she flew to Solarion

Station to find your sons. The late Viceroy indicated they were in imminent danger, after all. She left reluctantly, but with the speed of that
fighter, she should be there shortly, and will let us know when she arrives."

Lucas winced. He felt hungover, something he hadn't been in close
to two decades. Everything on the bridge had a strange tint to it.
Alpha looked nervously at the viewscreen.

"Alright, so let's go to Solarion then," Lucas said, trying to blink
away lingering spots in his eyes.

"Upon fixing the ship's engines, I made the decision to activate the
core and jump to a location outside the star system, should Commander
Maston return to collect you. Unfortunately, I seem to have worsened
our predicament."

"Alpha, what are those?" Lucas said, squinting at the shapes in the
viewscreen scattered among the stars.

"It appears I inadvertently jumped to a Xalan communications
relay. Those are a pair of motherships, and a listening post. Our
engines are overloaded from the core's activation. The stealth drive is
drawing too much power to keep us hidden for long. We are drifting
closer, and will soon be visible to them."

Lucas's head was swimming. It was unlike Alpha to screw up this
badly. He jumped them right into a Xalan comm station? It must not
have been on the military intelligence maps.

The two ships were growing closer, and Lucas could clearly make
out their jagged Xalan architecture. The listening post was a wide-
spoked wheel of metal with long antennae protruding from the top
and underside of the center. What system were they in? All the readouts were glitching and scrambled.

"What's the plan, Alpha? You always have one," Lucas said nervously.
Alpha looked forlorn.

"In this case, I do not. It is why I must ask something of you with
an enormously heavy heart."

Lucas looked at him, confused.

"What are you talking about?"

"Our power is failing; we will be visible in minutes, if not seconds
when the stealth drive gives out. After which we will be promptly

destroyed by the vessels you see before you. It would not be a fitting end for either of us, as I am sure you would agree."

Lucas's chest was starting to constrict. The lights began to flicker in the room. The engines groaned painfully. The ship was starting to shut down completely.

"What . . . what am I supposed to do?"

Alpha looked at him with stern golden eyes.

"Though I fear your strange new power, I must ask you to call upon it now. Turn those ships against one another, and the station they protect. Only then will I have the time required to fix our own vessel and jump to Solarion."

"My power?" Lucas said. "I can't do that. I can barely control a room full of people I can see for more than a few seconds."

"A few seconds is all that is necessary," Alpha said, voice suddenly cold. "And the minds of the crew on each ship's bridge."

Lucas shook his head.

"I can't do it. They're too far away. There are going to be too many of them. Too many commands to issue."

"You overthink your own ability," Alpha said. "There will be no more than two dozen men on the bridge of each ship. You only need to send them these firing coordinates."

He pulled up a long column of ten character numbers that Lucas memorized instantly.

"I can't . . ." Lucas repeated. "They're too far away and hidden inside their ships."

"You do not need to see them," Alpha said. "You only need to draw on their energy, their presence. Sight is a sense you only think you require. You can feel them, can you not? Concentrate."

Lucas did, closing his eyes. There was nothing at first, but a sensation slowly tickled his mind. Like little pricks of warm light. Clusters of them. In the ships. In the station. Some were moving, some were still.

"Power at 1 percent and dropping," Alpha said as the lights kicked out and faint emergency fixtures painted the room a ghostly blue. "We will be visible at any moment."

Alpha put a claw on his shoulder.

"You are capable of this," he said. "I know you have the strength within you. Believe in your gift as I do."

Gift?

An alarm sounded. The words TARGET LOCK shone in bold across the viewscreen. The two ships were turning toward them.

"We are revealed," Alpha said, with a sigh.

Lucas closed his eyes. He focused on the two most dense clusters near where the forefronts of the ships would be. His lips rifled through the list of numbers.

Suddenly, his brain caught fire. The cold burned so sharply he dropped to his knees, holding his head in agony. His screams echoed around the room. It was like an unrelenting hailstorm of frozen daggers in his head. No other pain had matched it.

Lucas forced his eyes open, and was stunned by what he saw. The two massive warships had in fact opened fire on the listening post, not them. Missiles spiraled out of their launch bays and collided with the slowly rotating structure, which blew apart silently. The next volley of ordnance was fired at each of the ships themselves. As they exploded, Lucas could feel the little warm lights in his head going out all at once. The area soon became a massive debris field, the vacuum of space extinguishing the flames instantly. Lucas's head was throbbing so violently it felt like a drum was being beaten in his ears. He tried to get to his feet, but stumbled back, his head still engulfed in freezing pain.

Tears wormed their way out of his clenched eyes and ran down his face. There was only darkness. No more little lights. He blinked open his bleary eyes and saw Alpha's claw extended out in front of him.

"I didn't know I could do that," Lucas said, stunned, his voice hollow. He took Alpha's claw.

"*I did,*" a voice said. Lucas's spine stiffened. The voice wasn't Alpha's, and it came from inside his own head. The claw hoisted him up. Lucas blinked.

The claw wasn't gray, it was black, and had four-pronged fingers, not three.

Lucas stumbled backward as he saw the figure in front of him.

"My creation," the Archon said. "Returned to me at last."

Lucas couldn't form words; he could only stare at the creature before him.

Though the Archon had the same general shape of a Xalan, there were distinct and immediately noticeable differences. His skin was black. Not charred like the Shadows, but oiled and glistening. He wore no armor, but was covered in patched plating with the same wet shimmer as his skin. There were stiff, sharp ridges extending up his back and covering his joints.

And his face. His snout was shorter than that of most Xalans, and devoid of an actual mouth, with only smooth skin in its place. His dark eyes had no rings, and were merely thousands of points of light in a black field. *Eyes like galaxies.*

Lucas's heart was racing. He looked around and suddenly was aware of where he was. On the bridge of a ship, but one that was distinctly Xalan. Gone were silver floors and walls stained with the blood of the Viceroy's crew. Everything was matte metal with hundreds of holographic displays, all seeming to function autonomously with nary a crew member present.

It was all a lie.

Alpha, the ship, the threat. It was the Archon in his head. Or was it? Lucas turned to look out the viewscreen. There was still a wide debris field of metal confetti floating in the distance. His head still pulsed with icy pain.

"What . . . What did I do?" Lucas said frantically. He lunged at the Archon, who merely took a step back and he stumbled forward, grabbing only air. His Shadow strength was gone, as was his speed.

"Manners," the Archon said, glittering eyes narrowing. "The serum in your veins has disabled the physical aspects of your gift."

Gift. Lucas should have known something was wrong when Alpha referred to his previously abhorrent powers as such. And instructed him how to properly use them. Lucas spoke again through clenched teeth.

"What *happened* here?"

The Archon spoke, his voice reverberating in Lucas's mind.

"You destroyed the Soran solar system's most advanced listening post without Xala firing a shot. They are now scrambling to figure out what sort of disaster caused the station to combust. Our ship was never seen."

The Soran solar system?

"It was the only station that may have had even a chance of detecting our approach at such a close range. I thank you for your service."

Lucas's mind was racing. Had he just unknowingly killed thousands of Sorans? He scanned the debris for any traces that could tell him. This was another of the Archon's tricks. It had to be.

"Detecting what?" Lucas said, turning back toward the creature, who seemed to effortlessly blend into the darkness that surrounded him.

"Why, the invasion of Sora, of course."

The Archon raised his hand and the ship pivoted around. The debris field disappeared and was replaced by a bright blue, white, and green orb. Sora.

Oh god.

From the corners of the viewscreen, Lucas could see other Xalan ships of every shape and size come into view. Motherships, transports, and colossal titanic cruisers he'd only seen in orbit around Xala itself. The radar of their own ship was alive with lights, each indicator a Xalan vessel. There were thousands.

This is it. This is their entire fleet.

They were racing toward the planet, which was growing larger.

"What are you doing?" Lucas said. "The planetary fleet defenses will shred you before you're within a million miles."

This was the all-out assault Madric Stoller had been warned about, but it was always dismissed as impossible. The SDI had thousands of ships spread out in the system, guarding Sora from such an attack. But what role was the listening post supposed to play?

"You can't tell me you fixed a cloaking drive to every ship in your fleet," Lucas said, trying to understand. The Archon blinked, his lids closing sideways.

"I do not need a thousand cloaking drives for a thousand ships. Only one."

What?

"And you are riding inside of it."

The ship passed by an SDI dreadnought, which acted like they weren't even there. The planet was getting closer and closer.

A ship that cloaked an entire fleet? It was impossible.

"This last creation, assembled in the furthest corner of black space, will be Sora's end. I don't trust the fools I have tasked with its completion, and must return to unveil its glory myself."

Lucas remembered what the Archon had told him before his departure in Dubai. This was it. His final weapon. A ship, a mobile cloaking drive to render an entire fleet invisible. The Sorans couldn't be within a thousand years of developing or detecting such a thing. There had to be a way to warn them. Lucas's eyes raced around the room, a hundred consoles were executing a million different tasks. It occurred to him that the Archon was controlling all of them with his mind, even as he gazed out the viewscreen. Lucas ran to one of the consoles and started trying to read the flurry of Xalan symbols and appropriate it for his own use somehow.

His body seized up, and he was wrenched across the room, slamming into the viewscreen.

"You force me to wreath you with chains as well as strip you of your strength?" the Archon said, annoyed. He turned the immobilized Lucas to look out the window. Sora loomed large, and they were passing more and more SDI ships.

"What *are* you?" Lucas choked out. "Another Shadow mutant? Some general or scientist or covert operative who rose up to fill the void left by the Council?"

The Archon turned to look at him. The lights in his eyes grew brighter.

"Amusing," he purred. "But insulting. I am not one of these wretched creatures. I am a dragon commanding ants, to use terms of your world. The time has come for me to be silent no more. Xala exists because *I built it*. The Xalans live because *they serve my will*. I am their god, their creator. And yours, do not forget."

"You're psychotic, delusional. The Sorans made the Xalans," Lucas said with certainty. "And you didn't create me, only warped me into . . . this." He looked down at his black veins. "I do *not* serve you."

"Perhaps the weight of the thousands of Soran lives you just ended has not found its way to your soul yet. But it will, in time, perhaps once you realize you helped kill billions more. You are more difficult to manage than the other, but you show much promise."

"The other. What did you do to Maston?" Lucas asked. "What did you do to my friend?"

The fleet passed a glass-domed space station, and cloaked Xalan ships split out of the way to avoid it.

"The Sorans were poor test subjects. Useless bags of faulty genes and weakness. But him. The one who killed not one, but *two* of my own Shadows, even a further evolved psionic variant. When I discovered his body orbiting our planet, I would have been remiss not to attempt to reforge him into a warrior of my own."

Lucas struggled against his invisible bonds as the Archon continued.

"The first thirty clones were dismal failures, but the last one survived conversion, by some miracle. A fractured soul, still clinging to life, it seemed. The clone's mind was unstable, with memories exceptionally easy to mold and shape. His power was unmatched, and only needed gentle prodding to kill thousands of his own kind on what he imagines to be a noble quest."

The Archon turned to him.

"But you. The first *human* subject. The last of Earthkind. You were an unmatched success with exceptional power not seen in eons. Some subtle mutation that allows it. I *must* have more of you, after seeing what you are capable of. I have sent the other to collect more specimens as the invasion commences."

The colony. His sons. Asha. The Earthborn, the only humans left in existence. He wanted them all now after seeing what Lucas could do. His heart was racing and sweat was pouring down his face.

"But first, you serve a more important purpose. As Sora burns, we will have work to do."

Lucas had no idea what he meant, but was fuming. "Stay away from my family. Turn and leave Sora while you can. The SDI will tear you to pieces if I can't first!"

"You cannot," the Archon said. "And neither can they. You fail to understand. The war between Sora and Xala ended when you destroyed that sensor station. It was the planet's only hope of possibly detecting this fleet early enough to mobilize their defenses. Now, they investigate a presumed accident, not what was the first shot in this, the last battle of the Great War."

Sora was huge now, a giant ball of life and hope. Tears started to well in Lucas's eyes. The Archon suddenly released him from his psychic grip, but he couldn't move regardless. He just stood, transfixed as the cloaking ship pulled up in front of an SDI warship and came to rest. Scattered Soran ships were everywhere around them, and a holographic map of the solar system showed the Xalan fleet was spread all over, nestled up next to unsuspecting military targets. Their every move was guided by the Archon's inaudible orders.

"Witness the fall of Sora," the Archon said. "The beginning of the end of your entire species."

Lucas looked around the bridge. Every console, every display was glowing orange and flashed with a single Xalan word. The symbol for FIRE.

The darkness of space erupted with silent, brilliant, blazing chaos.

31

Less than a dozen people were present for the funeral of a man who once governed a planet of a hundred billion. Tannon's body was rotted and warped from Hayne's poison, and so his metal casket, fashioned from the housing of a defunct missile, remained closed. Solarion Station mostly burned their dead or sent them tumbling down the elevator shafts to feed the feral creatures on the lowest levels, but everyone agreed Tannon Vale deserved something more dignified.

They were in orbit around the station aboard Zaela's warship, the *Skysplitter*, a stolen SDI interceptor and a legendary pirate vessel in its heyday. Only a small group of them had assembled to see Tannon off, including Asha and Alpha, who had arrived at the station in a bizarre-looking military fighter with no recollection of the journey. Noah listened as they recounted their entire harrowing tale of being abducted by the Viceroy and the SDI and rescued by Lucas, only to be boarded by the Black Corsair, who they discovered was their late friend, the legendary Commander Mars Maston. Or at least some twisted version of him. Malorious Auran quickly deduced the signs of the Corsair version of Maston being a "torn clone," one grown at full adulthood from a dead body, with the distorted memories and psychosis typical of the process.

There was no trace of the Viceroy's vessel when they tried to locate it. Likely the ship had been destroyed and Lucas and Maston were lightyears away. Asha and Alpha were already panicked when they arrived, and their mood was certainly not improved when they learned that their old friend Tannon Vale had died, however heroically. Both stood with stone gazes, looking out into the field of stars behind his casket.

Erik was alive, and the clorixine had been purged from his system over the past few days. He'd barely spoken since he'd regained consciousness, and now stood at attention more rigidly than he ever had when Tannon was alive and barking orders at him. Noah wasn't sure if it was luck or divine favor that Erik had survived the poison, but his brother had emerged from the ordeal looking less like a boy and more like a man.

Noah's head ached severely; he still hadn't fully recovered from the night he'd drunk himself into a stupor and almost been murdered on the streets of the station. His hand and leg were on the mend, and a constant stream of questionably legal meds kept the pain at bay.

He'd mostly avoided the girls over the past few days. Sakai was still bubbling with quiet rage and neither of them were anywhere near apologizing to each other. She cast hard glares at him whenever they passed in the compound, but had nothing to say. It hurt Noah to have her so angry at him, given how loving and kind she was normally. But he didn't know what to say to fix things. Really, he didn't know if he *wanted* to fix things.

It was impossible not to think about the moment he shared with Kyra, the only part of that night he wanted to remember. She blushed when she saw him and gave him shy smiles, a welcome change from Sakai's frowns, but mostly spent her time looking after Erik once he'd woken up. They hadn't had more than a spare moment to talk about what happened, not that Noah would know what to say if they did.

Solarion was about the most unromantic place imaginable, and death was in the air all around them. Zaela was slowly solidifying her newfound power as SolSec officers fought to assume Hayne's command, their troops being torn apart by rival gangs as they did so. The violence appeared to be settling down somewhat at last, as more and more SolSec troops were defecting instead of fighting back.

Zaela, Celton, and Key were taking turns sharing old Guardian war stories with the group as their way of memorializing their old commanding officer. Some were actually quite funny, including one about a young, newly minted Tannon ordering a raid on a Kulvath rebel outpost that turned out to be a whorehouse. Rather than reorganizing and relaunching the mission, Tannon declared the following week "shore leave," much to the dismay of the Grand Admiral at the time, his father Varrus.

It was good to laugh, even on such a somber occasion, and the entire affair was a much more fitting tribute to the man than some buttoned-up state funeral at the Grand Palace with Madric Stoller giving a meaningless eulogy full of false flattery. In the end, nearly everyone shared a story or two, including Noah. He managed to get through one about Tannon's first day as colony Watchman without choking up.

Noah had won a race through a forest course soon after military training had started for the young Earthborn, but was chastised by Tannon when he reached the finish line and forced to run the circuit twice more. Noah was confused. He hadn't just won, he'd beaten everyone by a mile due to his age, size, and strength.

"Why am I being punished, Watchman?" he asked.

"Because what good is being fast and strong if you leave the ones struggling behind?" Tannon said. "Selfish soldiers will either run ahead to get themselves killed, or leave everyone else to die in their wake."

The next race, Noah came in last, carrying an injured Sakai, who had twisted her ankle on a root, and Tannon had nodded in approval. Noah swore he saw a smile briefly flicker across Sakai's face as he finished the story, but only for a moment. It wasn't long after that they'd become a pair.

Erik refused an opportunity to speak, only staring blankly at the casket. He leaned against the back wall, shoulders now slumped, his usual confidence sapped from him completely. He looked hollowed out, and older. Much older.

Asha stepped forward to circle Tannon's metal tomb. It seemed like she hadn't slept in days. She ran her hand over the metal, and turned back toward the group.

"What can I say?" she said. "Tannon Vale found us drifting in the black of space, believed our story, and gave us the training to become soldiers, not just survivors. He worked to clear our names when the whole planet thought we were liars, murderers, and traitors. He essentially raised our children when I . . ."

Asha trailed off and looked at Noah.

". . . when I could not. I am honored to have called him a mentor and friend, and if Lucas were here, I know he would say the same. This galaxy has seen few better men, and Sora should be lucky to see another ruler like him."

And with that, there was nothing more to say. The *Skysplitter* pivoted around until the shaded sun engulfed them all in its red-and-orange radiance. Tannon's coffin was loaded into the launch bay and, as they all watched, was shot into the sun, faint fiery engines carrying it toward the glowing mass.

The next few hours were spent debating how best to try and locate Lucas, but no one, not even Alpha, had any useful ideas. Maston and Lucas could be anywhere now, given the insane travel speeds of the Corsair's ship. For all they knew, Lucas was already in the clutches of the Archon himself. Their only consolation through it all was that they knew the Archon wanted Lucas alive. Though it would be à fate worse than death if the Archon was trying to transform Lucas into a leashed monster like the Corsair Maston.

It was a while before Noah noticed that his newly silent brother had disappeared from the room altogether. Noah left the comms bay where they all were gathered and headed back up to the bridge of the ship, which was now docked at the station. He found Erik alone, slouched in the captain's chair in front of the viewscreen, gazing into the tinted sun.

Noah walked around the chair and saw his brother was holding a pistol in his hand. Not Stoller's laser weapon, but Tannon's hefty hand cannon. He hadn't realized Erik had picked it up during the fight at SolSec.

"What are you doing up here?" Noah asked.

Erik turned the gun over his hand. It was old, scratched, and flecked with dried blood.

"That should have been in his coffin," Noah continued. "I think it was his father's."

Erik didn't look at him.

"I forgot I even had it," he said, raising the gun up, holding the barrel with two fingers. "Here, feel free to tape it to a missile and fire it at the sun."

Noah exploded with anger.

"You asshole! Do you have any idea what you've done?" he shouted, he spun the chair around to face him, but was stopped by what he saw. There were tears in Erik's eyes. He hadn't seen his brother cry since they were children.

"Go on!" Erik yelled back, sitting up straight. "Let's hear it! Let's hear all about how much I screwed up and how I got a man killed who's worth a hundred times what I am."

Noah was struck mute. His anger froze, then faded. Erik went on.

"Let's hear about how I finally went too far this time. About how I'm a danger to anyone and everyone. I've heard it from you a thousand times already. Sakai blew up on me yesterday, and Asha nearly took my head off a few hours ago. And even Kyra is thinking it, though she'd never say it out loud. I get it! And you're all right!"

Noah just looked at his brother's grief-stricken face.

"I wanted Hayne dead more than I wanted anyone else alive. And for what? To impress a girl by handing her his head? A girl who is peace and grace and kindness incarnate? I'm a godsdamn fool."

Erik looked down the sight of the pistol, aiming at nothing in particular.

"I'm well aware the Watchman died because of me. I know you could have too. The only real justice would have been for me to die as well, but these witch doctors pulled me back from the brink somehow. I was close. I was close to the other side, and there was nothing there. No one. I was alone. And now that I'm back, that feeling hasn't left me. I don't think it ever will."

Noah finally spoke up, the rage gone from his voice.

"You're not alone. You know that. As much as you seem to want to reject us, you have a family. You have the Earthborn. Hell, you have an entire planet who adores you."

"Being a celebrity isn't being a hero," Erik shot back.

"It's not," Noah said, nodding. "But you're well on your way to graduating. You have the talent. You have the heart. But you lack the restraint."

Erik shook his head.

"Gods, you sound like the Watchman. He gave me this same speech a hundred times."

"Well, maybe now that he's dead, you'll finally take it to heart," Noah said quietly. "You want to make this right? Be the man he always knew you could be."

Erik was silent. This wasn't the lecture Noah had envisioned. He couldn't yell and scream and threaten his brother when he seemed so broken. Finally, Erik stood up from the chair and attached Tannon's hand cannon to his right hip. His laser pistol was on his left.

"I'll never be you, you know," Erik said. "*You're* the hero of the pair of us. You're the one they'll build statues of and sing songs about."

"Not likely," Noah replied. "But you don't need to be me, or Lucas, or anyone. Just a better version of yourself."

Erik scoffed.

"I just want to be someone she can look at without fear in her eyes."

Noah knew who he was talking about.

"Kyra's been through a lot," Noah said.

"And I put her through most of it," Erik said. "I know."

"Just don't put her through any more. Change for her, too."

Noah felt guilty giving that sort of advice given what had happened between the two of them just a few nights ago. But the last thing he wanted to do was to throw down the gauntlet with Erik about Kyra right now. His brother moved toward the exit.

"What do the gods tell you, Noah?" Erik said, his back turned. "What do they say is going to happen to us?"

"They don't say much these days, but I suppose I don't either," Noah said.

"Don't lose your faith," Erik said. "One of us needs it at least."

The next day, Noah was nearly all packed up for the short trip back to Sora and Colony One. In the wake of Tannon Vale's death, Malorious

Auran would resume his duties shepherding the Earthborn as he had a decade earlier. Celton would oversee all the military training. Celton swore that no matter what his orders, he wouldn't let SDI agents get within ten miles of either Keeper Auran or Kyra. There were likely to be some sparks to come, but the colony was defendable, at least. And Noah realized it might be time to call in a favor or two with Finn Stoller.

The elder Auran posited that perhaps it was important to start thinking about closing down the colony for good in a few years, allowing the present and future Earthborn a more unstructured life. Noah was practically a grown man, and the rest of the Earthborn were only a few years behind him. Life without the colony's guidance would have been unthinkable a few months ago, but much had happened since then. The other Earthborn besides Sakai and Erik had remained in the bubble, however, and might have a harder time adjusting to such an idea. Were they really ready to start their own society? To have families? Noah wasn't sure. It was hard to imagine Penza and Wuhan as parents, but it wasn't as difficult to picture others in that role.

Noah looked across the Black Wings main hall at Sakai, who had her nose buried in a scroll. He did miss her. He wanted to talk to her about what Erik had said, but she still wanted nothing to do with him. And gods knew he shouldn't discuss those kinds of things with Kyra.

The blond girl sat next to Sakai, idly watching Wings spar with each other on the cracked stone floor. Kyra lightly tapped her foot to some grainy, blaring music with only the barest semblance of a beat that was bouncing around the hard walls of the room. Her expression was a permanent half-smile, even as the room stank horribly of sweat, alcohol, and vomit. Even in a place as vile as this, she made it just a little bit better by being there.

Noah did love her, to the point where it actually hurt, but what sort of future could he have with Kyra? If Erik or Sakai didn't murder him first, the two could never have a family with Sora and Earth's inexplicably incompatible biology.

She would be enough, said a voice in his head.

His thoughts were interrupted as Alpha came to sit next to him.

"Greetings, Noah," the Xalan said. "Have you prepared yourself for departure?"

Noah nodded.

"I have. Though it's going to be an uncomfortable ride home," Noah said, looking across at Sakai, whose head was still down.

"Yes, I hear the ships we have access to are quite sub-par," Alpha replied, missing Noah's meaning as he often did.

Kyra had her chin resting in her hand, and was watching Razor brawl with two stout Wings who only came up to his shoulder. They were testing out shiny sets of power armor, purchased by the newly rich Zaela. Word had it she was about to close on the biggest warship docked at the station for a cool five billion marks. Other gang members shouted praise and obscenities at the men who were fumbling around, getting used to fighting with mechanically amplified strength. Noah had been trained to use such armor since childhood, and forgot just how far behind the rest of civilization Solarion was. He was sitting in the mess hall of a six-hundred-year-old prison, after all.

Asha was pacing around the room looking eager to leave for Sora. The other Black Wings stole glances at her. At all of them, really. Now out of their disguises and with the arrival of Alpha and Asha, their presence on Solarion had become conspicuous. Rumors were flying through the station that the Earthborn were in Zaela's camp and had somehow instigated the uprising. Even with the neutering of SolSec, they were targets and needed to leave as soon as possible.

"It'll be good to be home," Noah said.

"Agreed," Alpha nodded. "Zeta and Theta have made their way back to Colony One and will be there to greet us when we return."

"I hope Theta and Erik sort things out," Noah said, freezing immediately after the words had left his mouth. Alpha cocked his head.

"Is there some problem between your brother and my daughter?" he asked.

Noah's mind raced.

"Uh, they were just . . . fighting about . . . Earth," Noah said in stutter step.

"Is that so?" Alpha said, eyes narrowing.

"Yeah," Noah continued, saying whatever came into his head. "Erik . . . swears that Earth will stay uninhabitable, but Theta says those Xalan terraformers showed real promise in transforming the climate."

Alpha scoffed.

"For as much regard as I have for young Erik, he should defer to the scientific wisdom of my daughter. I've done cursory analysis on those orbital devices and the readouts are indeed encouraging. What an odd topic to cause a conflict between them."

"Someone should tell her that two different species can't mate."

Noah cringed even just thinking about how deeply Theta had blushed.

"Yeah, odd," Noah said, but realized he'd accidentally broached an interesting subject. "Wait, so you're saying Earth could be fully habitable again?"

Both Noah and Alpha jolted when one of the Wings crashed to the floor in his power armor with a loud bang. The laugher of the rest of the men rebounded around the chamber as the other two in metal suits helped him up. Razor was simply shaking his head.

"I would require more data to say that with certainty," Alpha continued. "At the very least, Earth could start producing enough water to be a useful planetary outpost for the Archon, which I am assuming was the purpose of the experiment. A dying planet like Xala may be too far gone for transformation, but perhaps there is hope for Earth yet. Why do you ask? Are you eager to return to your homeworld?"

Noah shook his head vigorously.

"It wasn't exactly much fun the last time. But I'd rather see a Soran settlement there than a Xalan one, that's for sure. Errr, no offense."

Alpha ignored him and brought up a hologram of Earth on his scroll. Old Earth.

"It was an amazing planet in its prime," he said. "Even though I was there as a punishment, I enjoyed my time scouting the civilization before the war began. For all its faults, it was a place of great beauty, rich culture, and a population that overwhelmingly wanted nothing more than better lives for their children. Earth's final age lacked many would-be conquerors or warlords. Their wars were small. Microscopic when compared to our own."

Alpha paused, then continued with a sigh.

"I despise what we turned your planet and your people into. A bare wasteland full of killers as vicious as we were. In Earth's last days, I saw savagery I had never fathomed possible."

"From savages like my true father, the cannibal," Noah said darkly.

"Yes," Alpha said plainly. "Though there is nothing 'true' about the father you reference. Other than your size, you share nothing with that monster of a man. You are a product of your adoptive parents, through and through."

"Also killers," Noah said, eyeing Asha, who had given up pacing and sat down next to Kyra and Sakai.

"Sadly, we live in a time where good men and women must be as such. This war has made us all do things we never would have fathomed in another life, has it not?"

Noah thought about how many men and Xalans he'd killed in the past few months. He suddenly realized he wasn't keeping track anymore. And he couldn't see their faces.

"It has."

"And I fear there is more we still must do."

They were silent for a while, with the cheers and jeers of the Black Wings echoing around the antechamber.

Soon they were all onboard the ancient pirate vessel they'd arrived in, but this time they had an outgoing escort. Zaela knew how to pay her debts, and though she'd originally been doing them a favor by providing them aid, the rewards she'd reaped from the downfall of SolSec far surpassed her wildest expectations. As such, she was sending three of her best mid-range ships with them, and Alpha's prototype SDI fighter was tucked inside their own craft as a last resort. They weren't anticipating having to spar with any of Stoller's forces, as they were likely trying to sort out what had happened to Viceroy Maston and his ship. As a precaution, their mini-fleet was purposefully avoiding that sector entirely.

"If anyone's not here yet, they're getting left behind," Asha called out to the group assembled on the bridge of the pirate ship.

"All necessary parties are accounted for," said Alpha, leaning over the rusted central holotable, which only worked when given a few sharp kicks.

Noah rounded the chair to see his mother. She'd arrived at the station wearing little more than rags and now wore a frayed leather jacket and flight leggings Zaela had given her. Her sword hung over the back of the chair. It shook as the engines fired. Asha's look of grim determination was broken as Noah came into view.

"We'll find him," he said, putting a hand on his mother's shoulder. She looked up at him.

"God, when did you get so old? It feels like just yesterday we found you outside our ship in your dead nurse's hands."

"Probably for the best I don't remember that," Noah said with a stiff chuckle.

"I know you didn't ask for all this. I thought the colony would give you some semblance of normalcy while I fought demons worlds away, but . . . it seems there's no way to escape this kind of life for us."

"I don't know," Noah said. "But I'd rather be here than a pile of dust and ash on Earth in any case. I have a home. I have a family. I have . . . friends," he said, glancing over at Kyra who was talking with Key in the corner. She flashed him a brief smile mid-conversation as he caught her eye.

Asha glanced over her shoulder.

"Someday you'll have to explain to me why she's worth all this trouble."

"Someday she'll probably show you herself."

Their attention was diverted when the viewscreen began to flash with an incoming transmission indicator.

"That's an SDI hailing frequency," Celton said, eyes widening. "I wouldn't—"

Asha's patience snapped. "I'm done with this bullshit," she said as she waved her hand through the receiver controls. An SDI captain Noah had never seen before appeared onscreen. He was male, but that was about all they could tell as the transmission was heavily distorted from the nearby solar radiation.

"I don't know who or where you are," Asha shouted into the viewscreen. "But if you're here on Stoller's orders, I have an entire space station full of firepower ready to reduce you to a million tiny satellites spinning around Apollica, and a population itching to declare war on the government!"

A voice crackled through the feed. The figure was moving, as were many shapes behind him. Noah was perplexed to see that the transmission data indicated the message was being broadcast not only to their ship, but any and all in the vicinity.

"Please," he said, his voice desperate. "You have to [static]—"

Asha leaned in toward the flickering image.

"The fleet is—"

More static. The picture went black completely, but the audio kicked back in. Someone screamed in the distance, and there was a low rumbling that slowly grew louder.

"It's over," the voice said, a strangled whisper.

"Xala is here. Xala is everywhere."

32

Xala was everywhere. Lucas watched as nearly the entire SDI planetary defense fleet was reduced to scrap in a matter of minutes. For centuries, millennia, the Soran solar system had been safe under their watchful eye, but now the Xalans flooded through them like they weren't even there.

At such close range, the decloaking Xalan ships were destroying entire vessels before the Sorans knew what was happening. Lucas's eyes darted over the readouts on the bridge of the Archon's ship and saw the only SDI vessels that had even managed to fire back were in the outer rim of the system, where presumably they had a few seconds to react as the fleet surrounding Sora itself was destroyed. But even so, the data showed a huge casualty rate for Sora and only miniscule losses for the Xalans. It was utter decimation.

The readouts didn't do the carnage justice, but Lucas knew what he was seeing out of the viewscreen was happening a thousand times over all over the system. Titanic SDI ships were ripped open bow to stern by unrelenting missile volleys. What few fighters had been scrambled were now in pieces, their pilots drifting frozen through space, rigid and dark against the shining sphere of Sora. There were so many bodies it was hard to tell them from the debris, and Lucas's heart was caught in his throat. He hadn't spoken and barely moved as everything unfolded before him. The Archon stood silent in a sort of trance, mentally directing his troops all over the system. Though he couldn't directly control them the way Lucas could forcefully influence others, he commanded them all the same. The remaining Xalans who hadn't rebelled after the revelation of Alpha's father's message served the strange creature without question. And why shouldn't they? He'd won the ten-thousand-year-old war for them at last.

Lucas thought of Asha, Alpha, and his sons on Solarion. He had barely heard of the outpost, but knew it was close to the sun and that the SDI wouldn't go anywhere near it. That meant they could still be alive, as Xala was clearly targeting military craft in preparation to invade or destroy Sora itself. Still, it was clear the Xalans wanted to wipe their race out completely.

But Sora. Sora was the last hope. They'd held the wolves at bay for thousands of years. Was this how it ended? And had Lucas really contributed to the planet's downfall? He hoped the destruction he saw out of the viewscreen was just another vision from the Archon. That the fleets were fine. That it was another mind game. But he could feel in his bones that it was real. Untold numbers had been butchered in the last few minutes alone. The galaxy had never seen destruction on such a scale. It was over. It was all over.

The Archon met Lucas's hard gaze. Neither of them said anything. What could be said? He had won.

"What now?" Lucas finally asked. There was no point calling the Archon a monster, a murderer, or any other such insult. The creature was far beyond such things. He was in the midst of slaughtering millions and looked entirely unfazed.

"Now I take Sora for my own. And we journey to an ancient place where you will find the answers you seek."

"I seek nothing," Lucas said. "You've destroyed my second home now. What good would answers be?"

The Archon shook his head slowly.

"I will not destroy Sora as I did Earth. That was a . . . tactical error. It would be unfortunate to poison such a prize as this. We will invade, and the extermination of the Sorans will be a long, painful process. I will take no shortcuts with world-ending, atmosphere-corrupting ordnance. Xala's bombs and Earth's nuclear devices ruined that world nearly beyond repair. I would not relish repeating the same process here, on a planet worth ten Earths. Cities will burn, lives will end, but the planet will live on to serve my glory."

That was cold comfort to Lucas. While it was good to know the planet wasn't about to be immediately carpet-bombed into ruin, the

Archon systematically hunting down all its Soran residents wasn't exactly a welcome alternative.

Lucas was exhausted, he suddenly realized. He felt constantly weak and on the verge of collapse. Though his Shadow-enhanced strength and speed were gone, he felt less than even a normal man. He was a child, powerless to do anything to stop the rampaging nightmare before him.

They were moving slowly toward Sora, and from the left side of the viewscreen, a damaged SDI dreadnought came into view. It was plunging straight toward the planet, venting oxygen and crewmen from a hundred fissures in its hull. Lucas could only see the tail end of the name embossed in gold on its side, as the other letters had been burned off by plasma fire. The "—ION" fell slowly until it began to glow red when it met the atmosphere. It broke apart into three enormous pieces, which tumbled toward a continent in the southern hemisphere of the planet. Lucas felt more tiny lights in his head go out. It was too much to bear. Lucas slumped down against the cold metal back of a console. The Archon stood before him, a dark shape silhouetted against a soon to be burning Sora.

All the rage had left Lucas. Only shock remained. Everything he'd done on Earth and Sora and Makari to survive and fight back was all for nothing. This was the end.

"Remove him," the Archon said. Lucas looked around. Two dark shapes materialized and approached him. "I must prepare for our descent to the surface," the Archon continued.

Four blue eyes glinted in the darkness. Two charred black Xalan Shadows in plated power armor grasped him by the arms and hauled him upright as if he weighed nothing. The tips of their claws dug into his arms and thin trickles of blood tumbled down his already stained and torn clothing. He struggled for a brief moment, but their iron grip tightened to the point where his bones felt like they were about to fracture. The Archon regarded him with a featureless face and eyes alive with piercing stars.

Lucas was used to cells at this point, though the room he was locked in was clearly meant to serve an alternate purpose on the cloaking flagship.

He'd hung around with Alpha long enough to know what the life support system of a starship looked like, and he was staring at a large pair of gravity generators twice as tall as he was. The ship was clearly not meant to house prisoners, so the Archon had locked him in the most secure room on hand. The controls, like the door, were locked, and the displays in the room were a mix of Xalan text and unfamiliar symbols Lucas couldn't place. He heard the tapping of bone claws on metal outside, meaning the Shadows were on the other side of the sealed door, keeping an eye on him as the Archon did god knew what elsewhere. Lucas was thankful the room had no windows, and there was no more destruction to see. But he could feel it. He could feel the death all around him.

He paced around the room for the twelfth time. It was spacious enough to house the enormous gravity drive, but there was no way to tell how big the ship itself was. He waved his hand through the locked holocontrols once more. There was no hope of hacking them; they didn't even seem to notice he was there. The room was thick with allium, darksteel, and a litany of other indestructible materials. An improvised prison, but an effective one.

He had nothing.

No strength.

No speed.

No influence.

No Natalie.

No Asha.

No family.

No home.

Lucas eyed the metal edge of the base of the control unit. In a room full of smooth surfaces, the corner was sharp. A dark thought struck him, then stuck in his mind for an hour, then two, until it was all he could think about.

Could he do it? The Archon wanted him, needed him for something. Probably to manipulate him to kill more Sorans as he began his purge of the planet. Probably to become the next Corsair, and fight alongside Maston, where he would be just as brainwashed as the shell of his former friend.

Could he end his own life to avoid such a fate? It would be worse than death, after all. He couldn't save his family, and they would be better off at least if they didn't eventually have to fight against him as well as the Archon's Xalan hordes. He'd been dead for years, and they'd survived, thrived even. Perhaps this time his death would motivate them to find the victory that he couldn't give them.

He carefully placed the bare flesh of his wrist against the metal corner. It was cold. He was cold. Could he really—

"Spare me such an embarrassing place in history," came a rumbling voice from behind him. Lucas jumped back from the control cluster and spun around.

"That I would be killed by a warrior who would become little more than a mewling coward in the end."

The towering shape wandered into the dim light from behind a generator.

A dozen feet tall, natural armor from head to toe. Crimson skin. Infernal eyes.

The Desecrator.

The vanquished mutant Xalan dragged his claws along the allium drive plating. They left no mark, made no sound.

After a moment, Lucas's heart slowed from its sudden furious pounding.

"The Circle," he said. "You're there too. Your father said you were."

The Desecrator chortled.

"It is a wretched place, locked up with so many I despise. As welcome as it was to find my father again, the other Shadows banished there make it most unbearable."

"Why are you here now?" Lucas said, rubbing his wrist and shoving his sleeve down over it, now almost embarrassed about what he had been considering.

"To save you from your own idiocy," he growled. "Self-inflicted death, just as the war commences? Shameful."

"The war is over," Lucas said. "You won."

"I won nothing," the Desecrator snarled, flinging his claw out derisively. "You killed me, as you may recall."

"Yet here you stand."

"As little more than a shade, trapped on a useless plane of consciousness."

Lucas circled the creature slowly. He was tense, even though he had no reason to be. Still, he'd seen the beast before him end more lives than he could count. His visage alone was terrifying enough, even without a tangible physical form. The Desecrator's insect wings twitched periodically from inside their housing on his back.

"Why do you care what happens to me? To Sora?" Lucas said.

"I do not," the Desecrator replied. "Though it appears you are my best hope for both vengeance and release."

"What are you talking about?"

"I do not begrudge you defeating me in battle. That my father and I share. But what I despise far more than death is being controlled. Chained. Used."

The Desecrator's eyes burned into Lucas.

"The Archon has made fools of us all, something we only know now that death has locked us away in the prison of his mind. We are still the slaves we were when we were small and docile as Sora's pathetic creations. Nothing has changed. The Archon controlled the Council from the shadows and, in turn, pulled my father's strings— pulled mine. He is the one who sacrificed my brothers and sisters in pursuit of the perfect warrior. Killed my mother with grief. Killed my father and me by provoking you and your companions to action. He turned our entire race into little more than his own sword and shield."

"What is his end game?" Lucas asked. "What does he want, if not the destruction of Sora?"

"Oh, he does want that," the Desecrator said. "But place your trust in me when I say that this war you believe is ending is only just beginning if he is not stopped. Though I care not about such things. I want his head for what he has done to Xala. To my family. And if he dies, the Circle breaks. I will be trapped here no longer and will pass on to what lies beyond. Here the chains are not physical, but they hang just as heavy around our necks."

"What about the other Shadows in the Circle?" Lucas asked.

"Few have actually died in battle over the centuries, as you well know. The Archon slaughtered a number who turned against him after your friend's dissemination of the truth across the colonies. A few stray rebels eluded his wrath, but most remain blindly loyal, even those who know his true aims. They are lost forever to his madness, and will not be swayed by the bitter voices of the dead."

Lucas leaned against the oxygen tank as the Desecrator brushed past the locked doorway. His footsteps were silent.

"What are his 'true aims'? What is he planning? Who, or what, is he?" Lucas fired off the questions he still couldn't understand.

"The secrets bound in his mind must stay there, and I cannot break free of that constraint," the Desecrator said with a snort. "Though I imagine you will discover his intentions soon enough. Provided you allow yourself to live that long."

"Even if I believed all this," Lucas said, locking eyes with the beast, "that you're trying to help me, what can you actually offer? You're little more than a ghost of what you were. You can do nothing."

"I can sway you from your course of idiocy!" the Desecrator bellowed. "You have slain many monsters. Live to slay one more."

"How?" Lucas asked.

"Reclaim your gift. Realize your full power. It may surprise even him."

Lucas shook his head.

"He injected me with something, a serum. Everything is gone. Wiped away completely."

"A lie," the Desecrator said. "It is a mental block, not a chemical restriction. Such a thing would not even be possible."

Lucas was confused.

"What are you saying, that he's psionically cutting off my power?"

"Yes. It was one of the first things the Council did to rein in my own strength all those years ago. A tactic taught to them by *him*, no doubt."

"But it didn't work."

"My father trained me to resist their influence. Once the battlefield was level, restricted to physical power rather than mental tricks, I was without equal. As you saw."

"Wait," he said, a realization dawning. "You can resist psionic influence *completely*. It's how you defeated the Council. What did your father teach you?"

The Desecrator's eyes narrowed, like he was considering sharing some great secret with a man who by all accounts should be his mortal enemy. Finally, he let out a long sigh. His breath should have washed over Lucas, but he felt nothing.

"My father made a point of studying the psionic Chosen when their powers started to emerge. He even befriended a select few. He discovered their power, all our power, comes from a deep, pure pain. Pain that must be controlled, managed, turned outward. It is why the transformation process is so agonizing and grotesque, with few surviving the ordeal."

Lucas thought of the icy torment inside his mind every time he tried to exert his influence, pain which grew worse with each new use. Did this happen to all Chosen Shadows? Was it something they learned to overcome, or manage?

"Pain is more than a feeling of physical discomfort. It is one of the purest things someone can experience, and it has no equal, not even in its opposite, pleasure. Pleasure is fleeting, but pain is everlasting. Pain can span an entire lifetime. In ancient times they used to say that only through true, pure pain can you see the face of God."

Lucas heard the Shadows growling to one another out in the hall.

"What does this have to do with the Chosen?" he asked.

"The Chosen draw their power from their own pain at first, but the truly formidable draw it from others. To resist, you must embrace *your* pain. To know it, use it, so they cannot. And if you can master that, you will be free from their control."

"I don't understand," Lucas said. "You want me to hurt myself?"

The Desecrator shook his head.

"No, you fool. Have you not been listening? Pain is eternal. It is not a simple cut of the knife. It builds over time. An instant of pain is nothing, but cumulative pain is a wellspring of unmatched power. *That* is what you must tap into."

Lucas blinked at the creature that towered above him. He wondered if the Circle was even real. If this was just him slowly losing his mind. Whatever the case, the Desecrator seemed to know his thoughts.

"Doubt me if you will, I care not. But if you heed my counsel, you may save the lives of trillions, including the precious few you still hold dear. I want the Archon dead for my own purposes, but we share a common goal. There is no cause for me to mislead you here. If I could tear him apart myself, I would, though I must rely on you to bring about his downfall. A worrying thought."

"Pain," Lucas repeated. "How will I know when I've done what you're telling me?"

"You will know, as I did. We are both cursed and blessed to have known so much pain, so that we may have so much power."

And with that, he was gone, and Lucas was alone in the room again.

Lucas was restless, unable to comprehend what the Desecrator had told him. Suicide was far from his mind now, and his pacing had increased in speed as he tried to understand the "pain" he was supposed to find.

Calm down, he thought. How could he tap into a wellspring of anything when his heart was beating like a hammer in his chest?

He stopped, took several deep breaths that filled his lungs to capacity, and felt his pulse slow. He walked over to the pair of enormous gravity drives and tried to understand what he was supposed to do next.

Pain. He'd endured an incredible amount over the years. He could remember every bruise, every break, every bullet, every blade. Was that what he needed? Was that what would be required to "embrace" his pain and free himself?

After a moment's consideration, Lucas began to strip. He pulled off the tattered remains of the formerly pearl-white flight suit he wore and tossed it aside. His body shivered as his bare feet touched the cold metal floor. He wore only a pair of fitted black pressure shorts.

It was only now he realized that the sickly black veins threaded through him were gone, reverted to their muted shades of red and blue. The Archon's mental block had made him completely human again, something he would normally celebrate, but right now as a simple man he was of no use to anyone. He needed those oiled veins and those ice-blue eyes that he saw had now dimmed to slate gray as he stared at himself in the reflection of the polished floor. He needed his "gift" back.

He sat down and folded his legs in a way that seemed appropriate for something resembling meditation. He looked down across his skin. It was as smooth as it had been before the Xalan invasion of Earth. The countless scars he'd amassed since were all gone, healed after the Archon pulled his burning body from underneath the corpse of the Desecrator. They'd grown him an entirely new suit of skin, and the injuries he'd sustained since had been healed by accelerated Shadow-like regeneration. For the first time in nearly two decades, he was flawless.

But it didn't matter. Lucas didn't need physical marks to remember the horrible things he'd had to endure.

"How do I do this?" he said out loud to empty room. He figured he might as well start from the most recent horrific trauma he'd endured. Since becoming a Shadow he'd felt pain, but only a fractional amount of it. His body was so much more resilient after emerging from his psionic chrysalis, and the brief flashes of momentary pain in battle paled in comparison to what had come before.

The first thing that returned to his mind was what it felt like to be almost entirely engulfed in flame. The Desecrator's corpse was heavy, crushing, the fire seared his limbs and scalp and he could smell his flesh burning in the aftermath of Natalie's explosion. He was barely conscious at the time, but could remember it clear as day. The burning felt so real he snapped his eyes open to pat down his arms.

A good start?

He drifted backward further. In his mind's eye he watched the blood pour from a gaping wound in his ribs from a metal shard planted there by a Council Shadow. The flow never stopped, never slowed. He could feel again the life draining out of him.

He remembered the pure hell that had been the jungles of Makari, running a massive fever, being stung and bitten mercilessly by insects. He remembered how badly the pounding in his head had gotten, like something was trying to beat its way out of his skull. He clutched his forehead in imagined agony.

The voyage there had been even worse. Maston had commissioned two beastly soldiers to beat him as close to death as they could manage. He could feel every wound open, every bone snap. He cringed, and his eyes were forced open again. It took him a moment to catch his breath.

Before that, an iron kick from a towering metal behemoth that detached his ribs. An explosion at the Grand Palace that singed the inside of his lungs and wrenched his vertebrae out of alignment. Lucas rubbed his spine instinctively.

Further back. To the Ark. To a time when he could remember nothing but the giant black claws of Omicron tearing mercilessly into his flesh. Being thrown across the room into metal walls like he was nothing to the horrible creature in front of him. Lucas brushed his hand across his chest, but the scars were gone.

And then, the plasma blast that had blown through his midsection, just as they were ready to celebrate Alpha's rescue. He'd shielded Asha and Noah, but at a heavy cost. Alpha had hacked up a spare human to replace half his vital organs, and recovery had been nightmarish. Lucas traced his finger along his body where the long, curved scar had once been.

He thought of the one-eyed man who dug a knife into the meat of his thigh at Kvaløya. He thought of the woman he now loved who had initially put a bullet in his shoulder and left him for dead in the Georgia heat. He winced as he remembered the sheer torment of when he'd had to fish the slug out by hand.

But in the end, what he remembered most was the hunger, the constant, horrible gnawing in the American wastelands that felt like his insides were eating him alive. It was constant pain, constant agony. Enough for ten lifetimes.

Lucas's eyes sprang open. He was dripping with sweat, panting profusely. All of his nerves tingled, like the pain he remembered had flooded back through them, if only for a millisecond.

As he settled himself and stood up, he slowly walked around the room. *Did it work? Was that it?*

He didn't feel different. He looked down and saw a stray vein or two that could look discolored in the right light. He peered into the floor and found one, maybe two microscopic flecks of blue among the sea of gray.

Whirling around, he drove his fist into the allium tank, then cried out. The noise was loud, and his fingers throbbed. He shook out the fresh pain and peered at the spot he struck. A dent, but only a hair deep. He remembered how he'd pummeled the allium walls of his cell into jelly back on Sora. This, this was nothing in comparison. It wasn't enough. It wasn't nearly enough.

"That was everything!" Lucas yelled into the empty room. It was a lifetime of the worst physical pain imaginable. "And this is all I get?" He gestured at the tiny dent. "It's not enough!" He realized that he was trying to summon the Desecrator to explain, but the creature didn't appear.

"Goddamnit!" Lucas yelled, almost hitting the tank again, but thinking better of it at the last moment. He collapsed to his knees breathing heavily once more, almost on the verge of hyperventilation.

What was he doing wrong? What had the Desecrator suffered through that he hadn't?

Really, how had the Desecrator suffered at all, other than the horror of the initial transformation process? The creature was practically indestructible. Lucas had seen him shrug off what should have been fatal injuries like he couldn't even feel them. What pain was he drawing from then?

"Pain is more than a feeling of physical discomfort," he'd said. *"Pain is eternal. It is not a simple cut of the knife. It builds over time."*

Cultivated pain. What sort of injuries don't heal?

"He is the one who sacrificed my brothers and sisters in pursuit of the perfect warrior. Killed my mother with grief."

Lucas imagined what it must have been like for the Desecrator to have watched all his older brothers and sisters killed in the Shadow transformation process. To watch his mother dissolve along with her family. The misery. The agony.

That was pain. True pain.

"I understand," Lucas said aloud, calmer.

He sat down once more. This time, he searched for no exact memories. Almost immediately, he slipped out of one plane of consciousness and into another.

Lucas found himself in the throne room of the Grand Palace, before it had erupted in flames from a Fourth Order bomb. It was dark, lit only by the moons outside, and seemed five times as large as when he'd been in it previously. The ancient stone seat of power looked like it was a mile away from where he stood.

And then they appeared. Three figures, cloaked in wispy white streams of fabric, hoods raised. They shifted around the room making no sound, moving across the floor stripped of all furniture.

Lucas shivered as a breeze blew through the open doors on either side of the room. The silence was deafening.

"What is this?" he finally said. The wisps turned toward him. He took one step toward the throne end of the room, but then sprang back as one of the figures materialized before him. Its hood fell, and Lucas stared into a pair of prismatic eyes.

Corinthia Vale.

Her expression was solemn, almost stern. Her golden-blond hair was wrapped tightly in a series of interwoven braids behind her head; the white robes she wore floated like she was underwater. Lucas couldn't speak, he simply stood silent, transfixed. Her beauty was legendary, but here her perfection was sharp, unsettling.

"I am the horror of Sora," she said at last, the pitch of her voice twisted slightly into something that made his skin crawl.

"I am the madness and mayhem you found on this planet, and in your service to it. I am the murdered girl who perished at a feast in your honor."

Lucas remembered the light going out of those multicolored eyes after the bomb exploded. The burns coating her face and neck. Her pretty blue dress, fully ablaze.

"I am the lost brother-in-arms, forever at rest in an alien jungle."

Something caught in Lucas's throat as he remembered Silo's death in the Makari wilds. The trigger he had to pull. The red mist. The jungle's screams. His first real friend from another world.

"I am the martyred commander. The man who saved you. The friend they twisted into foe."

Seared into his mind was the look of acceptance on Mars Maston's face as he ejected the escape pod with him and a Shadow inside. Lucas watched his body lying still on the ship's monitors. And now, the new creature. The Corsair. The monster of darkness and insanity some version of him had become.

"You will know my pain. Let it be the mortar of your bones."

And with that, she was gone.

Lucas looked around, and saw the other wisps had disappeared. He stumbled toward the throne end of the room, which still seemed so far away. His stomach was a solid knot.

Something brushed past him in the dark. A whisper. A flash of light. He turned to follow it, and found himself staring at another shade.

Her hair was platinum waves, spilling down her shoulders as the ethereal cloth billowed around her. Eyes of emerald green stared through him, piercing like blades. She was a photograph brought to life, and he knew why she was there.

"I am the horror of ruined Earth," Natalie said with ice in her voice. "I am the constant despair and oppressive darkness of the world's last days."

Lucas shivered as he remembered his years-long trek across the country. The loneliness. The destruction. The hopelessness.

"I am the mountain of bodies you created and climbed to find life, the sea of corpses you crossed for a new beginning."

How many had he killed? Had he ever really counted? There was the atrocity at Kvaløya, but the trail of bodies he'd left across America was endless. He told himself they deserved it. They were all evil. Lucas remembered the sound of bone snapping as he broke the neck of the army captain who butchered his group of survivors without quarter. The man with Natalie's photograph. The man who etched her name on the rifle.

All my love.

But there were so many more. Robbers, cannibals, murderers. But were they? Were all of them? Weren't some just trying to survive like him? That's a question he was forced to stop asking himself back then, before it drove him mad. But here it was again as he stared into the accusing jeweled eyes before him.

"I am the billions of dead, crying out from the dust for vengeance," she continued.

Before the wastelands, the war was quick, but horrific. Before he'd started killing, there were so many dead. He watched cities burn as the sky was swarmed with terrifying spacecraft. He remembered seeing the mushroom clouds that seemed to linger for eons. How many souls did each represent? A whole world dead. His family dead.

"You will know my pain. Let it race through your nerves like fire."

His head swam, he felt sick and miserable. Natalie was gone, and he knew who the final shade would be.

She came from a long way off down the empty hall. It felt like years until she reached him. Her hood was folded down revealing a third shade of blond, a touch darker than both who had come before. Deep blue eyes, but no smile. An implacable look that existed between disgust and unending sorrow.

Sonya spoke, and his wife's warped voice caused him to tremble.

"I am the horror of your wretched life, before this all began."

All the breath was gone from his lungs, and he couldn't find it again.

"I am the devoted partner who offered kindness and care in return for neglect and betrayal. I am the lost little boy forever in search of an absent father. I am the life never truly lived, drowned in an unending well of poison drink."

Nothing before the war even felt real. But he couldn't run from it. Couldn't bury it forever. Here it was, staring at him in the face.

He thought about every terrible thing he'd ever done long before a worldwide invasion had given him an excuse. He remembered how much he'd once loved the woman in front of him, and how poorly he'd treated her once she was his. How she and his son witnessed the beginning of the apocalypse as he was three thousand miles away, drunk and in the arms of another woman.

"I am the disappointed father, a useless, selfish wretch for a son. I am the martyred brother, who died while those far less worthy lived."

Fathers shouldn't hate their sons, but his did. But looking back, it was hard to blame him. It's no wonder he had wanted Sonya's brother as his own. The poor young man killed in one of Earth's own pointless wars, long before the interstellar one began. Adam should have been the one to live through it all, not Lucas. He didn't deserve to.

"I am the forgotten tragedy of a half-formed man, only forged into a finer one by the fires of death and destruction. You will know my pain. Let it flow through your veins and nest in your heart."

She was gone, and Lucas fell to his knees and cried out. The sound echoed around the empty hall.

Lucas raised his head and found himself at the foot of the great stone throne. He'd crossed the endless span of the room without noticing.

"No more," he whispered. But a figure clad in pure darkness sat on the monolithic seat before him.

"Rise," she said. He didn't want to look.

Her hair was coal black, her light-green eyes blazed in the dark. The shadows floated around her like orbiting spirits as she stood up.

Asha spoke with unbridled rage, her face twisted into something terrible.

"I am the horror of extinction," she said. "I am the end of this new world. Of all worlds."

"I haven't lost you," Lucas choked out as he reached out to touch her.

"Not yet," she said, and she took his hand. Her expression softened. She grazed his cheek with the backs of her fingers.

"But you will. You will lose everything, everyone you have left. That pain will consume you wholly, and there will be no returning from it, and no escape, even through death itself. It will follow you into eternity."

Lucas was speechless. He was shaking all over.

"You will know the pain of losing me, like you have lost so many others. Take that wretched thought, plant it in your mind, and let its roots spread through every inch of you. Only then will you be free, and able to avoid this fate."

A supernova of light, sound, fire, and ice exploded in Lucas's mind. Tears wrenched themselves from his eyes, and every muscle in his body contorted unbearably. The pain was everywhere. Every cell. Every atom.

His eyes sprang open. They glowed electric blue in the reflection of the polished floor. His oil black veins hummed with power and fury.

33

Though Solarion Station was full of hardened, violent criminals, mercenaries, and murderers, a hush had fallen over the entire floating city. Every citizen was glued to viewscreens full of frantic news reports from the homeworld, or they stared out into the stars, seeing distant blue-and-white explosions almost immediately snuffed out by the vacuum of space. For all the chaos that had come after the fall of SolSec, the station now was quiet, terrified. Gang territory disputes and old vendettas meant next to nothing now in the face of nearly certain death.

With no military remotely near the station when they arrived, the Xalans spread out throughout the system hadn't paid them any mind yet. Rather, they'd appeared at every defensive outpost at once, seeming to materialize out of nothing. Some were saying they found a way to pinpoint core jumps to a thousand precise locations at once, but scientists like Alpha said the initial evidence pointed to some sort of mass cloaking capability, though even he didn't understand the technology that would allow for such a thing.

Noah walked briskly down the street toward the damaged Solarion Security compound, which Asha and Zaela had taken over after their flight home had been cut short by the invasion. It was far better outfitted than Zaela's Black Wings base, and ex-SolSec gang members were all either in the wind or had joined up with her.

On the side of the road, people were gathered in clusters, staring at giant holographic viewscreens showing terrified reporters covering the invasion. Pieces of wrecked SDI ships were hammering Sora like micro-meteors, and the first Xalan landing parties were heading down to the ground after planetary surface defenses had mostly been reduced to rubble.

The headline on the glitching, fuzzy screen currently read "WHERE IS CHANCELLOR STOLLER?" The supposed ruler of the planet hadn't been seen or heard from since the Xalans appeared. Most thought he was dead, but Noah suspected otherwise.

Asha had issued a coded distress beacon advising any and all SDI ships to rally to Solarion, as most of the Xalan fleet was giving up on the stragglers and heading to form a protective ring around the planet itself to prepare to bomb and invade. So far only a few SDI ships had shown up, with no officer onboard ranking higher than corporal. Scores of civilian vessels had arrived as well, but were largely useless in a tactical sense. Fortunately, word had it that the fleets guarding or laying siege to the Xalan colony planets were nearly home, most having departed soon after the Xalans disappeared. It was clear now where they all went. Whoever this Archon was, this invasion was a masterpiece of military strategy and impossible technology. The war seemed over. But yet, they lived. Though who knew for how long.

Noah walked through the gaping hole that used to be the SolSec main gate past a collection of Black Wings guards chatting nervously with one another, pointing to lights in the sky. He made a beeline for the refurbished comms hub, one that Alpha had been working tirelessly to clean up, cleansing the solar radiation from the broadcasts so they could more easily receive and transmit messages to and from the remaining SDI and Xalan resistance forces. Noah had a call of his own to make, one he suspected wouldn't be quite so long distance.

Alpha was frantically trying to reach Zeta on the surface of Sora. Asha was talking to a group of shell-shocked SDI officers, freshly arrived at the station. Noah sat down at a console and tried the hailing frequency he'd gotten from his brother. The comms here were the newest on the station, but that meant they were still about six decades old. Noah swore he smelled smoke coming from near his feet.

Finally, an answer. A narrow pair of blue eyes underneath a mop of reddish brown hair appeared before him. Finn Stoller looked stunned to see who was on the other end of the line.

"Godsdamn, Noah. How did you get this frequency?"

"Shut up, Finn," Noah replied, "and listen to me. Are you with your father?"

Finn Stoller looked around nervously. He was clearly on a ship and Noah recognized the plush luxury of a supercruiser lounge behind him.

"I, uh . . ."

"It's time for you to live up to your end of the deal we made when we didn't slit your throat for what you tried to do to Kyra. I know your father isn't dead like the news reports are saying, and my guess is that you're both trying to flee to some secret satellite hideaway you own, am I right?"

"No, we just . . ."

"Shut up, Finn," Noah commanded. "Your father panicked. Losing a ten-thousand-year-old war is a lot to handle, I understand. But think about this. Where will you go, really? Whatever haven you think you're headed to, how long will you last there? Months? A year or two with your supplies? In the meantime, every Soran in the galaxy will be exterminated, and you'll die starving and alone in the middle of space."

Finn averted his eyes from Noah.

"We'll live long enough."

"And Sora will die."

"What are you asking me?" Finn snapped back.

"Tell your father to turn your ship around and meet us at Solarion Station."

"Solarion?" Finn said, scrunching up his nose. The feed dissolved in static, then reappeared. "What the hell are you doing there?"

"It doesn't matter, but for now it's safe. The remnants of the defensive fleet are rallying here, and hopefully the rest of the SDI from the Xalan rim planets will arrive soon. Your sister included."

Finn looked around again and lowered his voice to a whisper.

"You don't understand. My father is useless. He lost his mind the second the Xalans showed up. He's acting like we're going on vacation or something, and he hasn't stopped drinking since we got onboard."

Noah shook his head.

"Whatever state he's in, the Soran people need to know he's alive. They need to know that the government is still functional, even when facing annihilation. He needs to at least *try* to coordinate a response to this."

Finn rubbed his forehead.

"I'm telling you, it won't do any good. Can't you track down that old bastard Tannon and tell him he's in charge?"

"Tannon Vale is dead," Noah said stiffly.

Finn paused.

"Well, I guess that makes sense given the state of the fleet."

Noah didn't want to bother explaining that the exact circumstances of Tannon's death were in no way related to the invasion.

"Just tell your father what I said. If he doesn't agree, chain him up and drag him here if you have to. Prove you're not the coward we all think you are," Noah growled.

Finn glared at the screen, but nodded.

"I'll get him there."

Noah had no choice but to trust him.

"I'll believe it when I see it," Erik said, folding his arms across his chest.

"He said he was coming," Noah said. "I think he'll pull through."

"I might have to kill him when he gets here then," Erik replied.

"Finn or the Chancellor? Never mind, it doesn't matter, you're not killing anyone. I know you've learned enough to know that."

He didn't say it, but Tannon's death still hung over both of them. Erik's face darkened, but he remained silent.

"I can't reach Colony One at all," Sakai said, trudging up the last few stairs to join them on the roof of the main hall. The cloudy dome protecting the station showed winking stars, but no more distant explosions. The massacre of the SDI fleet had stopped, or at least was slowing.

The crisis had forced Sakai to speak to both of them again, though her usually cheery demeanor was gone, possibly forever.

"I tried all my brothers and sisters, everyone I could think of. Even the guards. No one is answering. Alpha says Theta and Zeta are there too, and if *they* can't get comms working . . ."

She didn't have to say it. They were all fearing the worst already.

"We'll find them," Kyra said, turning back toward them from where she'd been stargazing. "Alpha's reestablishing new comm links every few minutes with the homeworld. I'm sure it's only a matter of time."

Forever the optimist, even in the face of armageddon. Sakai did not look comforted.

"Where do you think Lucas is?" Erik asked. There appeared to be genuine concern in his voice.

"It's pretty clear the Archon wanted him alive. He's probably in the eye of this storm somewhere, if I had to guess," Noah said.

"He'll fight his way out," Erik said confidently. "He'll be back and probably bring the head of the Archon with him." He momentarily sounded like the young boy from a decade past who enthusiastically told endless stories of his father's famed battles to anyone who would listen.

"Let's hope so," Noah said.

"I can't believe Asha and Alpha survived the Corsair," Kyra said. "And that he's some twisted shade of Mars Maston. What a terrible thought."

"And that he's killing us all in the hopes it will bring Corinthia back," Erik added.

"That would almost be romantic if it wasn't so horrible," Kyra said, a visible shiver running through her. Though she'd never met either Maston or Cora Vale, Noah realized she probably still felt tied to their story. At least she was the "right" kind of clone, while this neo-Maston was the very, very wrong kind.

Sakai tapped her wrist communicator.

"Something's up. I think someone just arrived."

"Stoller's here already? There's no way," Noah said. "Not unless he was hiding under the station."

"No, it's . . ." Sakai slowly shifted her gaze upward. A load of small specks were visible through the cloudy viewscreen. They grew larger as they came into view from the dark side of Apollica. There were dozens.

Fear seized Noah. The Xalans had found them. It was only a matter of time.

But the ships grew closer. The cubic hulls and golden engines were clear now. Sorans.

"More remnants of the defense fleet?" Kyra asked.

"I don't think so," Noah said as he tried to block out the dull sun with his hand to get a better look.

After another few minutes, the lead ship slowed down and turned to dock near the top of the station. Painted letters on the side of the dreadnought were crudely drawn, not the usual precision stencils on every other ship. It read "MOL'TAAVI."

Another ship docked next to it. This time, it was more easily recognizable. The SDI *Genesis* had the silver wings of the Guardians stamped on its nose.

"It's the Makari fleet," said Noah breathlessly, and the four of them darted toward the stairwell.

Noah thought she was the most imposing woman he'd ever seen, and he'd grown up with the realm's greatest warrior for a mother. Commander Kiati, First Watchmen of the Guardians, was as tall as he was, one of the finest tank-bred Guardians in existence. With genius level intelligence and unmatched physical prowess, she was the only survivor from the mission to Xala outside of his parents and Alpha and Zeta. Rumor had it she'd saved both his father and mother's lives at one point or another, which explained the warm greeting from Asha. A smile and a salute was more than most got from her. Key and Celton were pleased to see their old squadmate again as well.

Kiati's hair was the color of dark flame and stood out starkly against porcelain skin. Her eyes were leaf green and filled with anger. Who knew how many of her SDI compatriots had died that day.

"We burned through our entire null core collection to get here as fast as we could," she said, voice sharp like glass. "Almost ruptured a few hulls in the process."

"Well, we're all glad you're here," Asha said. Zaela eyed Kiati curiously. Noah guessed their time in the Guardians hadn't overlapped.

A bald man stood next to her; he was tall and lean. His power armor looked new, but he had white tattoos on his face, and a bone necklace hanging over his plating. There was an enormous black-tipped spear on his back that looked like it was from another millennium. Suddenly, Noah knew who he was.

"They gave you your own ship, Toruk?" Asha said with a raised eyebrow, confirming Noah's suspicions.

"The skyship was easy enough to learn in time," Toruk said. "I have mastered all the machines of your world by now."

"And the Soran language too, I see," Asha said. "You get more eloquent each time I see you."

"A necessary requirement of command," Toruk said. "I have armies to lead now, not only a tribe." His accent was unlike any Noah had ever heard, but he spoke Soran well.

"How bad is it?" Kiati asked. "The reports coming in are all over the place."

"It's worse than whatever you've heard," Asha said. "We've scavenged what ships from the fleet survived the initial assault, along with a few pirate craft from the station itself, for all the good that will do."

Kiati nodded.

"We've directed our fleets to take up defensive formation around the station. The Xalans have to know you're here by now, but they can't surprise us again with the same trick. With our ships this should be fortified enough while we figure out the next course of action. Where is the High Chancellor?"

Asha shook her head.

"He's coming," Noah chimed in. "Though I'm told he may not be fit for command."

Kiati turned to him. "He never was," she said with obvious disgust. The SDI officers present exchanged wary glances, but stopped when she glared at them.

"Are you really the boys? Gods, it's been years," she said, eyeing him and Erik. "Bigger than you look on the Stream. Heard you can fight too."

"We can," Erik said plainly.

"I don't doubt it," she said. "Where is Lucas? I should probably tell him I'm somewhat relieved he isn't dead."

"Captured," Noah said. "But not for long," he added, echoing his brother's earlier confidence.

"I don't doubt that either," she said, her face expressionless.

She turned back to Asha, and Toruk strode toward them, examining them like zoo animals.

"The god-children, sons of Saato and Valli," he said, motioning to Asha with a flick of his head.

Noah had studied the religion of the Oni, but only knew a trivial amount about it. He was aware of the strange parallels between their gods, the First Man and Woman, Saato and Valli, and their own, Kyneth and Zurana. Both were fond of forests too, it seemed. Asha once told him that Toruk believed she and Lucas were reincarnations of the gods.

"God-children, huh?" Erik said with a tone that made Noah elbow him.

Toruk smiled more widely than a man as formidable as him normally would.

"I have learned much these last years. I know about skyships and electrics and planets full of other Oni. I am no savage. But still, my gods are out there, keeping me strong. If they are not embodied in the flesh as your mother and father, then they at least fill their souls with great courage. And yours as well."

"We're just glad you're here," Kyra said with a wide smile of her own. "It's a pleasure to meet someone from Makari at last. I've studied so much about your culture."

"Ah, a scholar!" Toruk said. "I too forever seek knowledge. War satisfies the body, but rarely the mind. We shall, how do you say, compare notes when the day is won."

"I'd love that." Kyra beamed. Sakai rolled her eyes so fast Noah almost didn't catch it.

"Toruk," Asha called out from the holotable where she was gathered with everyone else. "There will be time for tea parties later."

Toruk gave all of them a quick wink and headed over to join the group.

311

"I hope he's not that nice on the battlefield," Erik said.

The dozens of Xalan claws threaded through the necklace clattering on his armor seemed to indicate he was not.

It wasn't until about six hours later that Stoller's ship did arrive. They were all summoned to come onboard his craft; Noah caught something in his transmission about him not wanting to "step foot in that disease-ridden shit satellite."

In the hours since the Guardians and Toruk had arrived, more incoming fleets had made it to the station, including Stoller's own daughter. Maeren's command was a respectable thirty or so warships. She resembled her father uncomfortably, and had forever shrugged off the gene therapy or cosmetic surgery that was the norm on Sora in an endless pursuit of beauty. She was military through and through, and cared little about such things. Her jaw was iron and her hair was a darker shade of brown than her little brother's. The two barely looked related at all, and their personalities couldn't be more dissimilar. Finn was twitchy and irritating, while she was stoic and largely silent. She was Noah's favorite Stoller already, even if she hadn't spoken a word to him.

One final figure had joined their group, one more imposing than anyone else present, even Kiati or Toruk. He called himself General Tau, and he was a full-fledged Xalan Shadow. He commanded nearly the entire Xalan resistance fleet, and had brought much of it to the station with him. Tau was one of the few Shadows who had defected from the Xalan homeworld after Alpha's father's revelation about the true origins of his kind. There had been other Shadows who had turned, but according to Tau, the Archon had made a point of hunting them all down over the years. Tau was one of only a handful of surviving Shadows that fought on the side of the resistance, while the vast majority remained loyal to the Archon out of idealism or fear. Tau was old, one of the original Shadows, not one of the new Chosen, and had fought alongside Commander Omicron centuries ago. But he remarked that the Council's lies had eaten away at Omicron and, had he lived, he likely would have joined Tau in his defection. Tau remained firm in his belief that he still fought for Xala, but *his* Xala.

Not what it had been twisted into by the Archon's lies and deceit. As such, he and Alpha had gotten along swimmingly over the last few years, as both had the same goals in mind for their homeworld.

Even if Tau's motives were pure, his presence was menacing. Noah and the others had gotten used to Alpha's tall gray frame hanging around, but Tau was a Shadow. His midnight-black armored skin and his blue-flamed eyes were enough to send a chill down anyone's spine. He towered over everyone as they marched toward the docking bay where the Chancellor's ship was parked. The citizens of Solarion regarded him with gaping jaws and more than a few ill-advised insults, but he paid them no mind.

Stoller wouldn't even dock his ship at the station itself, so the group had to cram in a short-range shuttle and fly to where he was parked, in the middle of his daughter's fleet, which formed a protective shell around his vessel.

Noah shook his head as he saw his luxury supercraft was called *The Stoller*, because what else would he have named it? It was sprawling and gaudy, all pearl and gold. A floating castle surrounded by menacing warships for bodyguards.

Once they arrived, they surrendered their weapons and walked down hallways full of portraits of past Stollers, all different shapes and sizes through a few dozen generations. They shared few features, but there was a general haughtiness to them all that seemed to be passed down as a forever dominant gene. The end of the hall revealed a massive three-dimensional model of Madric Stoller himself, clad in military finery, holding a ceremonial sword pointed at some unseen (and certainly imaginary) enemy.

The large doors opened and Finn Stoller snuck out before closing them behind him. He regarded the group nervously, particularly Kyra, and Noah and Erik inched toward her protectively.

"I got him here," Finn said. "But I'm telling you, I don't think this is a good idea."

"We need to speak with him," Asha said sternly. "The public needs to hear from him. He's still the goddamn High Chancellor, even if he is a criminal and an asshole."

"Just let us in, Finn," his sister Maeren commanded. "I saw him at his worst dozens of times before you were even born."

"Nice to see you too, sis," Finn said, before stepping aside. "Don't say I didn't warn you."

The group moved past him and the doors opened inward. Finn pinned himself to the wall as Erik glared hard at him when he passed by. Kyra ignored him completely.

The inside of the main hall of the ship was as opulent as the outside, if not more so. A sprawling, elaborately carved table sat in the center and marble pillars lined the circular room. In between the pillars were ornate, two-dimensional paintings that created vast murals that wrapped around the space. The ceiling was as if it didn't exist at all; it was a skylight open to the stars. All of it was a stark contrast to the squalor of Solarion, and all of them, dressed largely in shabby, unwashed clothing, looked extremely out of place.

Stoller stood at the end of the table, surrounded by masked, heavily armored guards. His personal security detail. No one knew who they were or how they were recruited, but they served him blindly. Some said they were actually prototype AIs, highly illegal machines he used to ensure complete loyalty. They never spoke, never showed their faces, so it was impossible to tell.

Holding a long-stemmed crystal glass, Stoller focused on drinking its ruby-colored contents before glancing in their direction. He swayed as he stood and his eyes were unfocused. His royal finery was dotted with red stains from the wine, and there were a few shattered glasses on the table in front of him, along with a large collection of other bottled drinks.

"Why did no one tell me the fleets were gathering near Apollica?" he barked immediately as soon as the doors shut behind them.

"During the attack, there was no way to get in contact with you, Chancellor," Kiati said diplomatically.

"I called them here," Asha said. "It seemed like the safest place to regroup within the system."

"You have no authority to do that," Stoller snarled. "And safe? We are dangerously close to an annihilating force of wretched Xalans," he shot at glance at General Tau and Alpha. "We should be six systems away by now, which is the exact protocol I was following before your incompetence dragged me back here!"

"Run?" Asha scoffed. "You have to be joking. You want us to flee as Sora burns? As billions die?"

"And you want to smash our remaining fleet against the rocks by attacking? Utter insanity. We have millions safe here, we can leave. We can go to . . ." he trailed off.

"Might I ask where you are planning to settle once you depart?" Alpha said. "I can think of no worlds that would be both habitable and unreachable by the Xalans. They would find you at any of the colonies, or even Earth. We would be forced to rely on the discovery of livable planets we are not certain even exist at this point."

"We have findings," Stoller said. "Classified findings of other worlds. There's one beyond the outer rim I was just briefed about. Where is the Viceroy? He would know the details."

"The Viceroy is dead," Asha said, and she saw Stoller's eyes widen. "I saw him torn apart by the Black Corsair as far away from me as you're standing now. A Corsair who is likely hunting down and murdering thousands on the surface as we speak. Every moment we delay is another when countless Sorans die!"

"Every moment we stay at this wretched station is another when the Xalans could mount an assault and wipe us out," Stoller shot back. Glancing around the room, it was clear he was outnumbered. "Tell them, Maeren! Tell them I'm right."

Maeren looked around uncomfortably.

"I . . . am not certain retreat is the best tactical maneuver, however appealing it may sound," she said, surprising everyone in the room. "The Xalans have demonstrated they have long-range core and cloaking capabilities far beyond our own. We would fare better in open combat than being hunted down in deep space."

Stoller looked at her like she'd just shoved a dagger in his ribs.

"How dare—"

General Tau cut him off, his voice a muted earthquake.

"We have more power than you imagine at our disposal. More Xalan resistance ships arrive by the hour. My command alone is a quarter of the total of the Xalan invading force. We have enough strength to mount an assault to reclaim your homeworld."

"So, what, so you can have it for yourself?" Stoller sneered, forever distrustful of Xalans, even those that had proved loyal for decades. Tau simmered with a rage that made Noah's hair stand on end, but he said nothing. Toruk spoke instead.

"The SDI forces are few, but you have allies. The Xalans, the Earthborn, the Solarion, and my Oni would be proud to fight at your side."

"Abominations, freeloaders, pirate scum, and savages will save us? That is your plan? *These* are my advisors now?" Stoller swayed so much a guard was forced to step in and catch him with lightning fast reflexes.

"And what about you?" said Erik suddenly. "All we've heard from you for months is how the war has been won. What great advice were you given by your SDI lackeys that you never saw this coming? You were too busy orchestrating the assassination of teenage girls as the Archon was plotting to invade your homeworld! You've kidnapped or attempted to kill nearly everyone in this room!"

Those who didn't know Kyra's tale or of Lucas's imprisonment looked around confused. Hatred burned in Stoller's eyes.

"You allow these children in a high-level tactical meeting, and to spout lies nonetheless? This is utter madness, and I will have none of it. I am following protocol and will be re-exiting the system immediately. It was a mistake to come here and try to talk sense into those beyond the grasp of reason!"

"No," Asha said coldly. "You can't leave. You have to address Sora. They're lost. Leaderless. They think they've been abandoned. They *have* been abandoned."

"Careful Earth girl," Stoller said, his voice dropping. "What you're saying is dangerously close to treason, and this is starting to feel a lot like a coup. Both are punishable by death without trial."

"Lotta things are punishable by death wit'out trial in Solarion airspace," Zaela said menacingly. "And we don't recognize your crown here." The guards shifted in their armor plating, fingers dangerously close to the triggers of their weapons.

"Sir," Kiati interjected. "We can use a portion of our forces to draw them out, then use the opening to send a splinter fleet in behind them to re-establish a surface presence on Sora and trap a large section of their fleet between us. We've been drawing up combat scenarios for hours now and just need your approval to—"

"You won't have it!" Stoller shouted, knocking over a glass as he swung around. "I will not throw away the rest of our fleet on some foolish quest for glory. I will not have my authority questioned by those with no legal right to do so! Who among you dares to challenge my right to rule?"

There was a long stretch of silence, but Noah had had enough.

"It should be her!" he shouted, pointing at his mother, who looked stunned. The words spilled out of him. "Asha can lead Sora. The public has faith in her, far more than they have in you. They will follow her into battle even as you run from it. She will give them hope while you spew nothing but fear and lies!"

Stoller had reached his limit. His voice dropped an octave.

"I am assuming full command of the fleet effective immediately, and all of you are under arrest for collusion and treason. Guards!"

"Father," Maeren said, shocked as a guard clamped an arm around her. "You can't . . ."

He couldn't.

What happened next was blur, as was to be expected when a simple, silly man tried to arrest a room full of the most formidable warriors across four different planets.

There was a mad scramble. Punches were thrown. Weapons changed hands. Claws sank into flesh. Cries of agony rebounded off the walls. It was all over in a matter of moments, and everyone froze, daring the other side to fire a shot.

Stoller's guards were fast, but definitely not machines. The best evidence of that was the blood oozing from their armor from puncture wounds sustained from Tau's claws. Alpha found himself staring down the barrel of an energy rifle, as did Kiati. Toruk had managed to draw a small, hidden knife and had it at the throat of a squirming guard. Zaela and Asha were now holding rifles wrested away from guards, and kept a cluster of them at bay. Erik was on the ground with a guard's boot on his throat and a rifle resting on his forehead. Sakai and Kyra were hiding behind the towering form of Tau, while Noah had taken an armored punch to the gut and was staring straight at a pistol pointed between his eyes. Madric Stoller held the gun, which swayed from side to side.

Suddenly, his eyes widened. Something clicked, and Noah shifted slightly to see the trembling form of Finn Stoller holding a gun to the back of his father's head.

"It's over, father," he said, whispering. Maeren stood next to him, unarmed, clearly distraught.

"With one word, I can kill everyone in this room," Stoller said, slurring.

"With no words, I can kill whoever I choose in this room," Tau growled. A bloodied guard let out a moan from down near his feet.

"Stop it!" came a small voice from behind him. Everyone turned to watch Kyra come out from behind Tau's armor and walk through the frozen stand-off. Erik squirmed under the guard's foot, but he couldn't move. Their blank faces regarded her with curiosity. Asha and Zaela stood aside as she moved past them to stand beside Stoller and Noah. The gun was an inch away from his forehead, and Madric's hand was starting to shake.

Kyra's voice was calm.

"No one wants a coup, High Chancellor. That's not why we're here."

"The situation would seem to say otherwise, you daft girl," he growled.

"We all want Sora to survive. You in your way, and us in ours. We can both have our wish."

Stoller remained silent, which suggested he was listening.

"Appoint Asha emergency Chancellor in a public broadcast. Transfer military authority to her in order to mount a reclamation effort on Sora. Show that Sora is not forgotten, and the government is still functional with you making the decision to step aside."

"I will not relinquish my power to—"

"*You*," Kyra continued, undaunted, "will lead the evacuation of all civilian ships at Solarion Station, saving millions of lives as you take them far away from the coming conflict. When the battle is won, you will return to Sora. If, gods forbid, we fail, you will lead our people in search of a new home. Your daughter's fleet will escort you to ensure you and your civilian charges are kept safe."

The room was stone silent. Stoller's expression was unreadable.

"If there were ever a time to put past differences and personal ambitions aside, it is now," Kyra said with calm authority. "We do not wish to be remembered as usurpers. You do not wish to be forcibly deposed. All of us want to see Sora live through this final stage of the war. Power means little if there is nothing left to rule. Let Asha shoulder that burden while you secure the civilian fleet by executing the evacuation you were planning in the first place."

A moment passed. Then two. Then ten.

Stoller's arm slowly drifted downward. His guards followed suit.

"And they wondered why I thought you were so dangerous," he said somberly to the girl in front of him.

Noah stepped toward Kyra, now that the gun was out of his face.

"Asha may lead my armies," Stoller said. "I will save what remains of Sora as the rest of you throw your lives away. So be it."

Now everyone lowered their guns, and Erik wrenched himself out from under the heel of the guard. Stoller's troops stood at attention, even the injured, and the boarding party began chattering with preparations for what came next.

Asha approached Noah and whispered in his ear.

"I understand now," she said, glancing at Kyra who was talking to Finn, of all people.

Noah was too stunned to speak. He couldn't stop staring at her. Like there was no one else in the room.

Some time later, the war room had been moved completely to Stoller's ship, which was full of far more updated technology than anywhere on Solarion, SolSec included. Stoller was rehearsing a speech with Finn as a test audience while Alpha was drawing up battle plans with

Asha, Kiati, Tau, and all the rest. The room was alive with activity, but Noah suddenly realized that Kyra was nowhere to be seen. He asked Erik but he could only shrug. He didn't feel much like asking Sakai, who was chatting with Zaela in the corner of the room.

Noah set about searching the ship, which he soon realized could take a while given its size. His journey led him to a lot of locked doors and lavish open areas that looked like museum exhibits filled with paintings, sculptures, and holographic art. Finally, on the top level, his calls for Kyra were answered.

"In here," she said to his left. A door opened, then shut as Noah stepped inside.

His breath was taken away instantly.

Kyra stood wearing a long, flowing white dress. It shimmered with starlight, absorbing and reflecting it through the massive windows behind her.

"Where did you get that?" Noah managed to get out.

Kyra rolled her eyes.

"Call me a prat, but I'd been wearing those old clothes for days and was tired of looking at blood and dirt stains. I found this hanging in a wardrobe here, along with about fifty others like it. I assume the Stollers have many female visitors on a ship like this. And now that I'm thinking about that, ew."

They both laughed, which felt foreign.

"I'll admit I hadn't thought to go hunting for clothing. Though I'd be careful wandering around here. The Stollers—"

"I have nothing to fear from the Stollers," Kyra said confidently. "Not anymore."

"How did you do that?" Noah asked, unable to look away from her eternally deep blue eyes. "How did you talk Stoller back from the brink?"

Kyra shrugged.

"Everyone likes to talk, but few listen. High Chancellor Stoller was afraid, not angry. Afraid of death, hence his attempted escape, but then afraid of losing face once he was forced to return. He'd have sooner died than see his regime forced away from him."

"But if he could *give* his power away . . ." Noah said.

Kyra nodded, and played absentmindedly with the ends of her hair. Noah couldn't remember the last time he's seen her wear it down. It had grown long since they first reunited at the White Spire. Every day she looked more and more like Corinthia.

"This way," she continued, "he's free of the responsibility of the war, free of the legacy of a coward, and is allowed to view himself as a hero as he leads the civilians in the escape he always planned to make. He gets to flee, head held high. Asha and the others have their armies and the legal authority to command. Sora has hope when they see their government united and working together to come to their aid."

"The man killed your parents and has been hunting you for years," Noah said, shaking his head slowly. "And you're willing not only to see him live, but have him lauded as a hero? After all he's done?"

"What is more important," Kyra asked, staring out the window at the distant blue speck that was Sora. "My need for vengeance, or the fate of an entire planet? The fate of everyone I love?"

She glanced toward him, and turned the slightest shade of red.

"Stoller will find his reckoning in this life or at the Oak Thrones, but what we do now in these next few moments is far more important than the agendas any of us have as individuals. If our world survives, if you survive, that's all I could ask for."

They stood there, locking eyes for what felt like hours. Finally the last wall broke away.

Noah rushed toward Kyra. He took her into his arms and kissed her deeply. He pulled back and didn't see shock in her eyes this time. Only passion. Only love. She wrapped her arms around his muscled back, pulling him down toward her. They kissed feverishly. Clothing pulled away effortlessly. Her dress fell to the hard stone floor, revealing next to nothing underneath. She turned and walked slowly toward the deep, plush bed, pulling Noah by the hand after her. He followed, hypnotized by the sight in front of him, unable to fathom how it was possibly real. How this was actually happening. He thought of no one. Not Erik. Not Sakai. There was no war. No invasion. No death. No destruction.

Just her. And she was perfect.

They lay in each other's arms a long while later, ignoring pages from their communicators, which still lay on the ground. Eventually, a holographic viewscreen flung itself off the wall toward the end of the bed. Noah's heart jumped, but he realized it was a broadcast, not a comms request. It was an emergency broadcast, one apparently being beamed to every Soran who could view it. It was the tail end of a conference that showed Chancellor Stoller, Asha, Alpha, Kiati, Maeren, and the others, dressed in military uniforms pulled from the ship no doubt, staring stonefaced at the camera. The broadcast was nearly finished, it seemed.

"I'd like to thank High Chancellor Stoller for placing his faith in me to lead you in these dark times," Asha said, her hair tamed into something presentable for the occasion. "You all know me by now, with all we've been through together. Though I am not Soran by birth, your home is my home, and I will defend it at all costs. We have not abandoned you. The Xalans took us unaware, but we are not beaten. Do not lose faith. Sora will survive. You will survive. *We are coming for you.*"

The transmission ended with Asha's green eyes staring intensely into the camera. Noah felt chills run down his spine. His mother had been born for this. This was her war now. She would end it. One way or the other.

"She's a great woman," Kyra said, hugging the soft sheet in front of her. "And she raised a great man." She lay her head down on Noah's broad chest.

"I always thought I wanted to fight in this war. To be the hero. But I don't. I'm selfish. I just want to stay here with you, and let someone else win it for me. I don't want to risk losing you."

"You'll never lose me," Kyra said. "I'll be with you every step of the way, no matter what happens next. We have to reach the colony. Find the Earthborn. Find Theta. We have to find your father, too."

"I know," Noah said, running his fingers along the side of her face, staring into her crystal eyes. "I just . . . don't want this moment to end."

"All moments end; you simply have to live long enough to repeat them," Kyra said with a half-smile. "And after this war, I'm yours for as long as you'll have me. That I promise."

"After the war, huh?" Noah said, eyebrow raised. "Well, that's motivation if I've ever heard it."

Kyra smiled.

"I'm here with you before then too, but perhaps it would be wise not to share that fact given . . . the complications."

"Erik loves you," Noah sighed. "We both know that."

"And you know Sakai loves you."

"Yet here we are."

"I guess we're both selfish. I'm not as perfect as everyone seems to think. I just can't see myself without you. When you left as a child, it felt like part of me was torn away. When I got you back, even through all the death and madness, I finally felt whole again, though that probably sounds silly to say."

"It doesn't," Noah said, and he drew her in close. "I tried to escape it, deny it, avoid it, but I've felt the same from practically the moment you told me who you were."

She smiled and sank deeper into his arms. In that moment, Noah couldn't see Corinthia Vale at all. Only Kyra. Only a girl in love.

If only this could last. If only they could make it through.

He suddenly realized Asha's message was broadcasting on repeat on the holoscreen.

"Do not lose faith," her image said again. "Sora will survive. You will survive. *We are coming for you.*"

34

Lucas felt his whole body shaking with power and rage as he zipped up his ragged flight suit. He had no way to tell how long he'd been in an altered state of consciousness, and it could have been minutes, hours, or even a day. The Desecrator was right. The ghost of the fallen monster had shown him the way to reclaim his strength by drawing on a lifetime of past, present, and even future agony. Now it was time to make the Archon pay, and to find his family again.

The door might have been two feet thick, but Lucas tore it away from the frame like it was cardboard. At the sound of shearing metal, his two still-present Shadow guards whirled around, eyes blazing blue. The moment they saw him, their arms thrust outward.

From the gesture it appeared they were trying to psionically tear his arms off or fling him into the opposite wall. But his feet remained planted on the ground. Lucas didn't move an inch as they waved their claws around in pantomime, trying to exert their power. On the third attempt, something crept across the faces of the Shadows that looked a lot like fear.

"Impossible," one said in his mind, turning to the other. *"We must—"*

Lucas didn't give him time to finish. Newly immune to their psionic control, he lunged at the leftmost Shadow. The two of them crashed into the wall as the other Shadow looked on in shock. Regaining his senses, the Shadow pulled a pistol from his armor, but Lucas slammed his wrist to the floor and the gun shot wildly down the corridor. Feeling the hairs on the back of his neck stand up, Lucas wrenched the Shadow's arm up and pulled the trigger of the pistol with his thumb. The weapon unleashed a deafening blast directly behind him, right into the chest of the other Shadow, who was attempting to smash Lucas's head with the butt end of a bladed staff. The plasma spattered off the chest armor of the Shadow and the force propelled him away from them. Lucas caught the downed Shadow's free arm just as he was pulling a second pistol, one with a shorter barrel and a wide spray that unloaded into the ceiling as Lucas desperately held the creature's wrist away from his face. The gun overheated after five rapid shots that sent debris raining down from the ceiling onto his back. Lucas smashed his forehead into the noseless face of the Shadow before leaping to his feet and flinging the creature by his wrists into the damaged ceiling.

Lucas barely had time to duck as the bladed edge of the staff whipped toward his neck. He knew the Archon wanted him alive, but these Shadows had quickly realized they were fighting for their lives, their psionic abilities useless. Lucas blocked another swing of the staff with his forearm, just inches below the darksteel blade. Using the counter to get inside the reach of the creature with the damaged chest armor, he plowed a fist directly into the weakened portion of the plating. The air was expelled from the Shadow's lungs and Lucas hit him with a stiff uppercut that caused him to lose his grip on his staff.

Lucas grabbed the weapon before it hit the ground and spun it around instinctively. He sliced the barrel off the pistol being pointed at his head by the other Shadow and the gun misfired. The second pistol did not.

Trying to spin out of the way, Lucas felt a hot spray of plasma rip across his lower torso. He flew back into the wall, grimacing in pain, and only stopped a second shower by flinging the staff toward the Shadow's throat, forcing him to dive out of the way.

The other, now staff-less Shadow tried to crush the downed Lucas with a massive clawed boot, but he rolled out of the way just in time. The metal floor cratered, but Lucas was only free and clear for a half second. A second spin kick from the Shadow caught him across the face, and he felt like he'd just been hit with a sledgehammer.

Both Shadows were up now, throwing lightning-fast strikes his way, aiming for organs and arteries. Lucas blocked as best he could, nearly matching their incredible speed, but he felt their coarse claws rip into his ribs and shoulder, which made the plasma burns in his abdomen seem downright pleasant.

Stop! he thought violently as he deflected further blows. *Die!* But even with his power returned, he had no influence over these Chosen Shadows. They too knew their pain. Their blue eyes remained blazing with fury, each swipe more savage than the last.

Finally, one massive front kick caught him square in the chest and propelled him twenty feet down the hallway and directly through a large door that broke open as he struck it. The new area was cavernous compared to the cramped hallway, full of light and sound, but Lucas didn't have time to take in the scenery. The Shadows had reacquired their weapons and were charging at him with blinding speed.

Lucas leapt to his feet, ignoring his injuries, and ducked under a hail of plasma from the hand cannon. The second Shadow reached him first, and Lucas spun over the dark blade of the staff, catching the rear collar of the creature's power armor with his hand as he landed. He wrenched the Shadow downward, and he hit the ground with an echoing thud. Lucas grabbed the now upright staff from the creature's claws and spun it around overhead. Before the Shadow could recover from his skull cracking against the floor, Lucas drove the bladed staff straight through the hole in his chest armor. The darksteel cut through flesh, bone, and the creature's heart without a sound. A silent scream was frozen on the Shadow's face.

Another pair of shots, and Lucas felt more boiling plasma singe his left arm. He dove behind a large console planted in the center of the room, which ate a few plasma blasts before expiring in a fireworks display of sparks and electrical fizzling. The plating cracked, and something glowing within shot streams of light through the room. Alarms began to sound, and holographic control clusters changed from a tranquil blue to an enraged red.

With a frustrated roar, the remaining Shadow sprinted toward him and leapt over the top of the ruined device. Lucas caught him in midair and flung him directly into a large metal object that looked a lot like the housing to a massive engine. Lucas suddenly realized what area of the ship he was in; he was standing in front of what appeared to be a damaged null core. It glowed a sickly yellow, a color he'd never seen before. Its ruptured casing spit out energy so hot he actually felt his hair and skin being singed. The ship lurched uncomfortably, and Lucas almost lost his footing.

A series of shots came his way from the recovered Shadow, and Lucas dodged so they hit the exposed null core instead. No world-ending explosion followed, but the lights in the engine bay flickered and Lucas felt the gravity drive momentarily give way, his stomach crashing into his lungs for a split second.

Lucas charged the Shadow and kicked him straight into the damaged engine housing. This time, the armored creature broke through completely and plunged into a mess of exposed wire and machinery. The Xalan lay stuck in the engine. Smoke streamed from a thousand metal wounds in the massive unit. The ship veered hard, and felt like it was falling before the gravity drive compensated. Alarms escalated their frequency and pitch, screaming for attention from engineers who were nowhere to be found. Xalan symbols were flashing everywhere, indicating some sort of imminent catastrophic failure. The central core was now so hot it was melting through its own protective shell, which was pooling onto the floor as molten metal.

The Shadow recovered from his nest inside the engine, and was at Lucas's throat almost instantly. Lucas tried to avoid him, but the creature's claws sank into his collarbone, mere inches from his windpipe. Lucas had both his hands clasped around the powerful forearms of the much larger creature, and was desperately trying to keep the dagger-like claws out of his chest cavity

"Abomination," the creature growled in his mind.

Dark blood was streaming down his body from his collection of wounds and he felt himself growing faint, darkness encroaching on his vision. As powerful as he was, it was too much. Two Chosen Shadows was more than any man should be forced to face alone.

And yet, he didn't want to die. Not again. Sora needed him. His sons needed him. Asha needed him. And he needed them.

He let go of the Shadow's right arm and drove his palm upward with all his might into the creature's other wrist. He heard bone and armor snap from the powerful blow, and the creature let out a painful howl, recoiling and stumbling backward. Lucas reached out and grabbed the energy pistol from its holster on the Shadow's chest. The creature lashed out with his good arm and knocked the weapon downward, which caused it to fire directly into his thigh. The Xalan dropped to one knee instantly, his other leg nearly blown completely off with his armor useless at such close range. Lucas drew the gun up to the creature's lowered head, but a claw instantly reached up and crushed the snub weapon into scrap.

Lucas knocked the Shadow's arm away with a sharp backhand and brought a fist down across the creature's jaw, which sent him sprawling on the bloody floor. Leaping on top of the heaving mass of metal and flesh, Lucas pummeled the broken Xalan with alternating blows, sending gray teeth scattering across the ground, replacing electric blue eyes with pools of black blood. Lucas felt the creature's life slip away, the Xalan's light extinguished in his mind, but he kept punching until his knuckles were split open and he could barely lift his arms.

His gaze was bleary, and he felt like he was about to pass out. For the first time, he noticed a large porthole in the engine bay. One that revealed they were much, much closer to Sora than they had been. He could see smoke rising from the surface of the planet, and spaceships whizzing by like panicked insects. The massive cloaking ship was falling, getting closer and closer to the surface. A hellish orange glow on the windows indicated they'd breached the atmosphere. His melee with the Shadows had done serious damage in the engine bay. Everything had dissolved into smoke and noise and heat. His lungs were filling with noxious fumes from a cracked engine and a ruptured null core.

And then, a voice in his head, like needles and glass.

"*Enough!*" the Archon said sharply.

Lucas rolled off the dead Shadow and he saw the long, powerful form of the Archon silhouetted in the open doorway. Lucas felt a particularly deep gash in his side, and blood flowed freely from the majority of his wounds. He was in no shape for another fight.

"While you may be my greatest creation," the Archon said, "you are far more stubborn than the other. You seek death the way most seek life. Though I require your wretched existence for at least a little while longer."

The Archon was clearly concentrating, attempting to quell a hundred different angry flashing readouts with his mind and stabilize the ship's rapid and disorienting descent.

"You can't control me," Lucas spat out. "Not anymore."

Sharp laughter cut like blades in his mind.

"You have no idea how mistaken you are."

Lucas summoned the last of his remaining strength and raced toward the Archon, grabbing the bladed staff from its resting place in the heart of the downed Shadow as he went.

The Archon didn't flinch as the blade dove toward a point between his star-filled eyes. At the last possible moment, he swatted the polearm away with one hand and raked his claws up Lucas's already bloodied torso with the other.

Lucas felt nothing as he stumbled past the Archon, holding the staff. But looking down, he saw blood streaming from neat, fresh slices, and the Archon's claws were bright red. They had tips so fine he didn't even feel the cuts, a far cry from the jagged nails of the Xalans that had gored him too many times before. The pain suddenly hit him and burned in his midsection, but he pushed past it with gritted teeth.

He swung the staff around again and again, but the Archon weaved out of its way like it was no more threatening than a strong breeze. Finally, another slash from his claw sliced the bladed head from the staff, and Lucas was left holding a useless metal pole. He swung that.

The Archon finally grabbed it and pulled. Lucas was flung across the room and landed just a few feet from the sparking, sputtering null core. He crumpled to the ground in a heap, panting profusely, a worrying amount of blood draining from his wounds. The intense heat from the damaged core washed over him like a wave.

Lucas had just gone toe to toe with two Shadows and survived, but the Archon was another level of power, strength, and speed entirely. He truly was a god, and fear wormed its way inside Lucas's chest. The core's hellish heat was sapping away the last of his strength. His blood that had pooled on the floor was mixing with molten metal and literally starting to boil in front of his eyes.

Lucas got to his knees, sweat pouring down his face. The Archon was walking toward him, lit up by the glow of the core. Razor claws glinted in the darkness. Ancient constellations revealed themselves in his eyes.

"If you need me," Lucas said, his mouth filling with blood, "come and get me."

Lucas reached over and grabbed the top of the white-hot null core, the pain so searing it felt oddly cold. He wrenched the unit out of the ground completely and hurled it at the damaged engine behind the Archon across the room.

By the time it struck its target, Lucas was already sprinting toward the nearest porthole, the Archon's attention split between him and the core, unable to stop either in time. His eyes were wide with surprise. The shockwave of the explosion shattered the porthole's viewscreen, and Lucas jumped into the void.

Lucas drifted in and out of consciousness during his long descent to Sora. He spun slowly in the air, ice-cold winds tearing at his tattered flight suit. He saw land and water below, an unfamiliar coastline on an adopted planet he'd actually explored very little of before he nearly sacrificed his life for it. He saw the smoking hulk of the critically damaged cloaking ship above him, and now from the outside could see it was a bizarre collection of curved armor plating and sputtering engines. Xalan and Soran ships raced through the sky in every direction, all ignoring him completely.

He blacked out. When he came to, the ground was much closer. There would be no Asha to swoop in and save him this time. *Trees.* He thought. *Water.* He was desperate to hit one or the other, as he had to imagine, even as half a Shadow, dry land would kill him. Maybe he could survive. Maybe he could cheat death just one more time.

A pair of Xalan fighters tore by him, dropping ordnance on the remnants of some Soran city below. The sun was shining brightly, and the only clouds were pillars of smoke rising from the surface. The massive cloaking ship was moving away from him, locked in a flat spin. The ship had about as much control over its descent as he did, it seemed. Flames were pouring out of its every orifice, and it left a meteoric trail of black smoke in its wake.

Maybe he's dead, Lucas thought as he closed his eyes. *Maybe at least I did that right.*

Darkness found him in the air once more, and didn't let go.

The salt stung.

He could taste it as the water lapped into his mouth. He could feel it seeping into the wounds scattered across his body. Opening his eyes, there was clear sky above him. A flock of birds flew by, cawing angrily. Far above them, a formation of Xalan fighters streaked past, too high for their engines to make a sound.

Another small wave washed over Lucas's body. He struggled to sit up, elbows digging into the wet sand that clung to most of his body. Everything ached, his head pounded, and though he knew there were broken or fractured bones lurking somewhere inside him, he could at least move all his limbs. And he was alive, no matter how insane that was given a five-mile plunge into the ocean.

He looked around the beach for the first time and realized he wasn't alone. There were many bodies washed up on shore, their blood turning the water dark. Most were Soran, though there were a few Xalans in full armor plating scattered around as well. None were bloated or disfigured; they hadn't been dead long.

In the water ahead, bits of wrecked ships poked out of the surface of the ocean. Lucas scanned the wide horizon for any sign of the Archon's cloaking ship. There were plumes of smoke everywhere from downed craft, but he couldn't find the ship itself, which could either be a thousand feet under the water by now, or back in the air searching for him. More fighters screamed overhead, these much lower.

Lucas got up and faced the land. Immediately ahead, a hundred feet off the beach, was a stretch of jungle. Behind that, he could see tall buildings poking out of the brush. A city. A small one by Soran standards, but enough of a target that the Xalans had clearly included it in their initial invasion plans. Lucas wondered if a military base was nearby. He needed a ship. He needed to break through the Xalan fleet and reach Solarion where Asha, Alpha, and his sons should be. Provided the station hadn't been destroyed already.

No, he thought. *Impossible.*

He tried to reach out to them with his mind, the way he'd done so unconsciously on Earth. *Noah,* he thought. *I'm—*

But he didn't know where he was. The climate was hot, the trees were tropical, and he was by a massive ocean. But on an alien planet the size of a half dozen Earths, he had absolutely no idea where he was.

I'm safe, he finally said, not knowing if the telepathic message had gone anywhere beyond the echo chamber of his mind.

He looked down. His damp flight suit was hanging off of him in strips. He pulled the rest of it away completely and marched through the sand barefoot. His deepest wounds were still bleeding a fair amount, but the salt had helped, and his Shadow biology had already erased a few of the most minor cuts. The sharpest pain actually came from his right hand, and he looked to see it covered in angry red burns. He'd touched an overloading null core so hot it was melting metal. He was lucky to still have a hand at all.

Had the Archon really survived the blast? After seeing what the Xalan's leader was capable of, the answer was likely yes. Until the Archon's lifeless head was on a spike before his eyes, the creature would be a threat.

Lucas used a piece of his ruined flight suit to wrap up his injured hand, and caked some of his deeper wounds with sand to help stop the bleeding. His muscles burned as he trudged across the beach toward the jungle.

This wasn't Makari. The jungle here wasn't a nightmare. It was a thin strip of greenery separating a section of the beach from the coastal city. Lucas wouldn't have been surprised if the entire thing was artificially grown. In barely a half hour he had nearly made it through to the other side. Along the way he stopped to dress himself in the power armor of a dead Soran soldier who lay sprawled in a muddy puddle on the forest floor. The man had apparently succumbed to his wounds fleeing the city; Lucas hadn't spotted a live Xalan in this area since he crash-landed. Lucas pulled on whatever plating was still functional and armed himself with a long-barreled, scoped rifle that had been strapped to the man's back. He would have to shoot with his left given his maimed hand, but it was better than nothing. Lucas had been around enough Soran military to know the stripes and badges on the dead man's armor meant he had been relatively low-ranked. He tried the man's communicator, but it was half dissolved by plasma.

There were muffled thumps of explosions ahead through the last row of trees. Distant gunfire and screams followed. Lucas stepped out of the brush.

The city was a ghost town. The sounds of war continued, but they were elsewhere, bouncing off collapsed buildings and crater-ravaged roads. Lucas was at the edge of what used to be a park with the downtown ahead. There were more bodies visible now on the streets. Dozens, and as he moved further in, hundreds. Nearly all Soran. Nearly all civilians. Some blown apart, others with still-smoking plasma wounds. A lump formed in Lucas's throat when he found the body of the first child. He went completely numb soon after when he found the twelfth. And then he stopped keeping count.

It was the invasion of Earth all over again. The tropical city even reminded him a bit of Miami, where he'd been when the shooting started all those years ago. Though this metropolis was far larger, with every other building made out of smooth white stone. Some of the more ornate structures suggested parts of the city were very old. Eventually Lucas saw enough signs to deduce its name, Kun-lai. He'd vaguely heard of it before, but had no idea where on Sora it actually was.

Lucas froze when he heard a familiar voice.

"At the time of this broadcast, I am transferring all military authority to Asha the Earthborn while I coordinate the evacuation of civilians out of the system."

It was Madric Stoller, speaking on a holoscreen five stories high, flicking intermittently on the side of a still-standing whitestone skyscraper. Lucas's heart soared when he saw that Asha was standing next to him, along with Alpha. And was that Kiati? And Toruk? What was going on? Flooded with relief, Lucas smiled uncontrollably as Stoller continued.

"Asha will serve as acting High Chancellor effective immediately, and would like to say a few words."

Asha nodded curtly, staring daggers at the irritated-looking Stoller, and addressed the camera with a grim, but determined face.

"I'd like to thank High Chancellor Stoller for placing his faith in me to lead you in these dark times. You all know me by now, with all we've been through together."

Lucas realized they must all be rallied at Solarion, or outside the system somewhere. He needed a long-range communicator.

"Though I am not Soran by birth," Asha continued, "your home is my home, and I will defend it at all costs. We have not abandoned you."

How the hell had Asha convinced Stoller to give her control of the entire planet? Still, Lucas could think of no better symbol for Sora to rally to in its blackest hour. He could see the message was playing on every visible holoscreen in the area, large and small. But there was no one around to watch other than him.

"We have not abandoned you. The Xalans took us unaware, but we are not beaten. Do not lose faith. Sora will survive. You will survive. *We are coming for you.*"

"Soldier!" came a voice from behind him. This one was flesh and blood. Lucas turned around slowly, keeping his grip on the rifle. He found himself facing a platoon of roughly two dozen soldiers on foot with a few more in an armored hovercraft with engines so quiet they'd actually managed to sneak up on him. Sorans. SDI, all wearing the same style of armor as him.

"What unit are you with?" their captain barked. He removed his helmet and strode toward Lucas. He was a tall, middle-aged man with tan skin who looked distantly Asian, if Lucas had to classify him using an Earth race. Lucas began to speak, but realized there was about to be a problem.

"What the—" the captain said, the words trailing off once he got close enough. No doubt he could see Lucas's Shadow blue eyes and the black veins snaking up his neck and down his right arm where the armor plating had been too damaged to use. The man raised his pistol halfway.

"What happened to you, Initiate?"

The rest of the soldiers started to raise their weapons behind their commanding officer, all pointing directly at Lucas. Lowering the barrel of the rifle to the ground, Lucas took a step forward, which made everyone twitch. The captain's gun went all the way up.

"I said, what unit are you with, and what happened to you?" the man repeated.

"No unit," Lucas shook his head. "This isn't my armor."

Perhaps he could have phrased that better.

"Down on the ground!" the captain said loudly. He motioned to the cracked pavement with his pistol. The enormous barrels of guns on the hovercraft swiveled toward Lucas.

"Calm down," Lucas said, taking another step toward him. "*Calm. Down.*"

Lucas felt a twinge in his brain, a sharp, cold prick. The man's eyes unfocused; he clipped the pistol back into his belt. His men became more at ease, but still were pointing all their weapons in his general direction. Lucas approached the man and stood within a few feet of him.

"Do you know who I am?" Lucas said, the man regaining control of himself once more. He looked confused, but left his weapon at his side. "Look at my face," Lucas said.

"It . . . can't be," the captain said, slowly shaking his head. "You're . . ."

"I don't have time to explain. I need a communicator, and I need a ship. You all look like you need an escort to somewhere safer."

The man cocked his head at that.

"*You're* offering to escort *us?*"

"Just trust me," Lucas said. "What's your name?"

"Captain Ozar Torwind, commanding officer of the remnants of SDI battalion 2.903," the man replied mechanically.

"I'm Lucas."

"I'm not sure how that's possible."

The man's narrow green eyes stared into his own and searched his face. Lucas could tell he believed who he was, and he didn't even need to force him to. The two exchanged a stiff Soran salute. Captain Torwind turned back to his men who had now all lowered their weapons.

"You're not going to believe this," he called out.

Lucas turned back to the viewscreen and saw that Asha's message was repeating itself. There was no way to know when it had originally aired.

"We need to get off the street," Torwind said, and Lucas turned to follow him.

"Jus' came out of nowhere. Lost comms with the defensive fleet almos' immediately. Everyone starts running 'round with their heads cut off."

Lucas was talking to a young female soldier with her head wrapped in a bloody bandage. The unit was holed up inside a building that apparently used to sell high-end personal hovercraft. The two military vehicles were parked in the center of the showroom floor as everyone scooped rations out of plastic cans. The sun was setting. The first day of the fall of Sora was nearing its end.

"Orders started comin' in from twelve different places," the woman continued. Her nameplate read "Wisher."

"No one knew where the hell the damn Chancellor was. Everyone figured he was dead until he showed up on the Stream a few hours ago and said he was transferring power to your, uh, missus."

The rest of the group couldn't take their eyes off Lucas. He was a legendary figure in Soran culture, and supposed to be very much dead. And now that he'd reappeared, he looked terrifying between his eyes, veins, and injuries, most of which had been wrapped up by the unit's surviving medic.

"Now that Miss Asha's in charge, orders comin' in more clear now. More or less sit tight. They're plannin' something with the rest of the fleet. Everythin' that didn't get blown to bits when Xala showed up. Suicide, if you ask me."

Several soldiers nodded in assent. Lucas was listening, but fiddling with the best comm unit the platoon had, trying to boost its signal to possibly reach Solarion, or wherever Asha was now. Old Lucas would have no idea how to do such a thing, but Shadow conversion allowed his mind to understand every bit of the technology inside the unit, and how it had to be rewired and amplified in order to reach further than outer orbit, its current max range. The other soldiers watched in silence as the fingers on his left hand nimbly danced around the circuits and wiring, with the other still wrapped in cloth. They almost moved independently of his mind.

"Trust Asha," Lucas said finally, looking up. "From the looks of it she's assembled quite a rescue squad out there. They'll be here soon."

The woman nodded, though looked unconvinced. Her hair was caked in dirt and it was hard to tell what color it had once been. Her eyes were a pale brown, and stared far past wherever she looked. If she'd been stationed in a remote place like this, it was clear neither she nor any of her unit ever dreamed they'd see action like this. The invasion of Sora. It was still unthinkable, even while it was happening all around them. The distant explosions and gunfire never stopped, even as the sun dipped behind the horizon.

"Mind if I ask where you been the last fifteen years?" she said, saying what everyone was thinking.

"Sixteen," Lucas said, turning his attention back to the comm unit.

"That's classified," Captain Torwind said gruffly, just getting off the shortwave radio and returning to the group. Lucas raised his eyebrows.

"You know what happened to me?" he asked.

"Gods no. But I know it's sure as shit classified. And these grunts don't need to know."

They certainly didn't. Lucas didn't want to spook them with a lengthy tale about being half-converted into a Shadow, held prisoner by the decidedly non-Xalan Archon, and then by the High Chancellor himself.

"I was captured on Xala. Taken to Earth. Rescued by my sons a few months ago."

A true, but infinitely shorter version of his tale.

"They do that to you there?" the woman asked, gesturing toward his eyes.

"That's enough, Initiate," Torwind said sharply. "Man's been shot and stabbed more times than I've ever seen. He's earned a bit of peace."

Lucas remained silent and snapped the cover plate back on the comms device. The machine hummed.

"There we go," he said quietly. He got up from the circle of soldiers and wandered behind one of the armored SDI hovercraft. He punched in a lengthy frequency code Alpha used for emergencies. This certainly qualified as one.

A chime sounded once, twice, three times.

Alpha looked as surprised to see him as the moment he'd been found alive on Earth.

"Lucas!" he exclaimed, gold-ringed eyes wide. "I knew you would wrench yourself free of the Archon's grasp! What is your location?"

"Good to see you too, Alpha," Lucas said with a grin. "I'm not sure how secure this hacked-together line is, so I'll just say I'm on Sora. And you all?"

"In . . . space," Alpha said, unable to think of a more specific identifier that wouldn't give anything away to any Xalans listening. "What of the Archon?"

"I destroyed that cloaking ship," Lucas said, something that had been confirmed by the squad who saw the massive vessel plunge into the water shortly before they found Lucas. "The Archon could be dead."

Alpha's face lit up.

"But I doubt it."

And darkened.

"He's definitely not Xalan, Alpha. I don't know what he is, but he acts like he's been controlling Xala all along. Not just recently, but since the birth of your race."

"I do not understand that claim," Alpha said, the picture fuzzing for a moment.

"Neither do I," Lucas said. "He needs to take me somewhere on Sora. Needs me alive. I don't know what he's planning, but it's somehow more of a priority than the invasion itself."

"Holy shit, is that Lucas?" came a female voice from offsceen. "Jesus Christ, Alpha, give me that thing."

Lucas's smile widened as Asha appeared in the frame.

"Greetings, High Chancellor," he said, smirking.

"Thank god you're alive," she said breathlessly. "I knew you would be, but I didn't know if you could get away from Maston and the Archon. Where are you?"

"Sora," Lucas repeated. Asha nodded, understanding he could say no more.

"Want to tell me how the hell you convinced Stoller to make you Chancellor?"

Asha shook her head.

"Your son's girlfriend is a piece of work," she said.

"Which son?" Noah asked.

"I don't even know," she said. "It's all very confusing. But she talked everyone out of a bloody coup and into a peaceful transfer of power. I swear if we put that girl in front of the Corsair she could talk him into slitting his own throat for us."

"It's good you're in command. I saw Kiati and Toruk up there too. Should I expect to see you soon?"

Asha nodded.

"Don't try to reach us," she said. "After . . . what comes next, meet me where they moved Project 11."

That was code for the colony.

"We need to find Zeta and Theta, and we think they're there."

Lucas remembered something the Archon said on the ship.

"Ah shit," he muttered. "I think the Archon is sending Maston there. He said something about collecting more humans because I was such a 'success.'"

Asha ran her hand through her hair and looked away.

"That's all we need. But maybe that means that damned ship of his won't be in the air at least. Trust me, we're kicking things off soon. Just get there as fast as you can and maybe you can head him off."

"I'm trying to find a ship here, but there isn't much that isn't in ruins."

"You'll figure it out," she said. "You always d—"

The transmission went dead. Lucas tried to reconnect a half dozen times before giving up. Either it was being blocked or, if they were on Solarion, natural interference had knocked it out. Eventually he gave up and wandered back toward the group. There was nothing more to say. Except that he loved her. Maybe he wouldn't get another chance.

"You get through?" Torwind asked, looking hopeful.

"I have a feeling tomorrow this war will be over, one way or another."

"You're not as good at speeches as your woman, you know," Torwind snorted.

"Well, that's why she's in charge," Lucas said with a weary grin. Exhaustion was setting in to his aching muscles and he felt lightheaded.

"Sir," the young medic said, approaching him nervously. The kid didn't look older than Erik, and also had dark curly hair. "Probably should get that changed."

He motioned to Lucas's right hand, still wrapped in the rags of his flight suit.

"Oh right," Lucas said, and started pulling the cloth away as the medic dug into his back for a fresh bandage.

Once the first patch of skin was revealed, his heart stopped.

"Kyneth save you," the young female soldier from earlier said. "That don't look right."

Lucas furiously tore off the rest of the bandage as the medic, Torwind, and the rest of the group gaped.

His right hand was pitch black. Charred and dry skin camouflaging the dark veins underneath. It wasn't a burn any longer. Not in the same sense. The darkness had even started to creep up his wrist past where the original burn had been. His skin was dark, rough ash, the way Maston's entire body had been when he'd seen him last. He thought of the burned, disintegrating woman in Dubai. The pool of charred bodies.

His power was starting to consume him.

Full Shadow conversion.

The final stage had begun.

35

Noah had never seen so many ships. They stretched far and wide out into space on either side of him. Ahead of him. Behind him. If this was their crippled, hacked-together fleet, Noah wondered what the scene might have looked like if the Xalans *hadn't* destroyed the vast majority of the system's SDI force upon their arrival.

And still, no one was sure it would be enough. Sora was a blue dot in the distance, and though they were too far to see it, a Xalan fleet at least three times their size was waiting for them out there in the blackness.

Noah had turned off comms chatter. He already had his orders. "Find a gap and go through it," his mother had told him. They'd gotten a hold of Lucas, who said the colony was in imminent danger. Noah was to reach the surface as fast as possible and report what he found. For absolutely no reason was he to engage the Corsair or any other enemy force before back-up arrived.

All of this was provided he could make it through the hordes of Xalans that stood in his way.

"This godsdamn ship won't give me full access to all the ordnance," came a voice through his local comm. It was Erik, seated behind him in the gunner's seat of the prototype, technically illegal, AI-infused ship called "Natalie" after their father's famed rifle.

"Alpha said it might do that," Noah said. "Try asking nicely."

When it was revealed that the rag-tag force actually had more working ships than live pilots, Noah pleaded with his mother to let him fly one. He'd scored well in flightsims at the colony—the highest in the group, other than his brother. Asha only agreed to the idea when Alpha suggested they take the prototype fighter. Alpha promised the AI assist would keep them safe and allow them to contribute substantially to the fight in the process. If any light craft could punch a hole in the Xalan fleet and race through it, it was this "Natalie."

"I've got autocannons and two types of missiles, but I'm pretty sure this thing is full of firepower it's keeping secret."

The other condition was that Erik would be his second. His brother wanted his own ship, but there was no way that was going to happen.

"Is there something you're looking for?" chimed the friendly AI. It sounded like a female newsreader from the Stream. A real person, but a bit . . . rehearsed.

"What is this ordnance labeled EH-130?" Erik asked impatiently.

"I'm sorry, that's classified," replied the AI cheerfully. Erik let out a long groan.

Noah's personal comm chirped. He muted Erik so he could speak privately.

"How are things going out there?"

Kyra. Noah smiled automatically.

"Erik's arguing with the ship, but otherwise pretty good."

Noah kept the fact that his insides were all but permanently frozen with fear to himself. He was terrified of the void in front of him, and what it contained. He didn't want to think that he'd possibly seen Kyra for the last time.

"That ship is supposed to be far smarter than either of you," she said, "so listen to it."

"That's the plan," Noah said.

Kyra, Sakai, and Malorious Auran were all inside Asha's command ship, a Guardian dreadnought called the SDI *Colossus*, which was the most heavily armored craft in the fleet. Asha wanted to pilot an interceptor or fighter, but her advisors convinced her that she had to stay aboard and coordinate the assault. She and Alpha were commanding the entire fleet from the bridge. Noah could see the craft out of the corner of his eye behind him. He imagined Kyra was at the viewscreen looking out at him.

"How is she?" he asked.

"Asha is a rock," Kyra replied. "They'll tell stories about what she did here today until the end of time."

"Unless the end of time is today for all of us," Noah said, choking out a laugh.

"You'll make it through. So will we. Sora is our home, and nothing will keep us from it."

"Well, then I'll see you at the colony," he said. "Provided you're right."

"I'm rarely wrong," she said with an unseen smile.

Noah paused.

"Can you put Sakai on for a minute?"

"Of course," Kyra said without hesitating. There were footsteps and distant voices.

"Hi," came a quiet voice finally. Sakai's.

"Hi."

Noah let the silence after that drag on for too long. He didn't know what to say. The two of them hadn't spoken privately since the night he'd almost died on Solarion.

"I'm sorry," was what finally came out.

"It doesn't matter," Sakai said with a sigh. "All of it stopped mattering the moment the Xalans showed up. You have to know that."

"I know, but I just wanted to say—"

"Noah, if you ever did care for me, just make it to the colony. Find the only family I have in this world. Make sure they're safe. That's more important than your brother's insanity. More important than me watching you fall for another girl right in front of my eyes."

Noah froze.

"I—"

"You don't need to explain. Like I don't understand Kyra's effect on people. Her effect on you. It's . . . I just . . . I'm fine. There are much, much larger issues at stake than my feelings. And that's the last thing you need on your mind right now. I love you enough to let go of you, and I can tell she loves you enough to hold on no matter what. Take that with you into the stars, and nothing else."

Noah was speechless. Sakai deserved better than him. How he'd treated her.

"I will," he finally said, and he meant it. Something dissolved in his chest and he could breathe easier. Still, he didn't feel like he'd earned that relief.

"Here she is."

Kyra came back on.

"Things are starting up here, you should have orders any minute."

"I'll see you on Sora," Noah said.

"I know."

She didn't say she loved him, and neither did he. If she was next to Sakai, she didn't need to have that thrown in her face. But it was implied in every word they'd spoken.

The comm went quiet. Ships were starting to move into formation with one another. A massive squadron of a hundred or so fighters closed in around their own ship. This was their unit. No one was flying solo.

Noah reached down to unmute his brother's comm, expecting to hear him continuing to shout at AI Natalie. Instead there was silence.

"Good to go?" Noah asked.

A long pause.

"Yeah," Erik said sharply. And that was all.

Noah's main comm line squealed and overrode his mute.

"Time to take this goddamn planet back," said Asha's voice. "You all have your orders. Move out."

Despite the comfort Noah had received talking to Kyra and Sakai, as Sora grew bigger in his viewscreen, the fear rose up inside him, filling his stomach, lungs, throat, and eventually flooding his mind completely. He wasn't ready for this. No one could be ready for this. Erik had been similarly quiet, and since even thousands of engines made no noise in space, it was eerily silent.

"You alright back there?" Noah finally called, content to let autopilot keep him in formation with the squadron.

Erik was motionless in the cam feed floating to Noah's right. He was simply staring to the side at the line of warships that seemed to stretch to infinity.

"I'm ready," he said, overcoming his recent quiet streak. "This ship could have been to Sora and back three times already. You wouldn't believe the specs I've found in the internal logs."

"As long as it gets us there once, that's good enough for me," Noah said. He thumbed through a collection of data readouts, most of which he didn't understand in the slightest.

"Just so you know, there's no one I'd rather have back there," Noah said.

Erik snorted.

"Well, I'd take a fighter pilot with about twenty more years of experience up there, if I really had a choice."

They both laughed at that. Fear was momentarily forgotten, but surged through Noah again as a collection of golden readouts turned burnt orange.

"Proximity alert," AI Natalie said in the most urgent tone they'd heard out of her yet.

Noah's lips moved in rapid fire, spitting out whispered prayers to gods he wasn't sure were there anymore. But as the readouts flashed with incoming death, the gods were all he had.

"Kyneth give us strength that we may prevail here today. Zurana give Asha the wisdom to lead us. Hear the last billion prayers of mankind, and guide us out of the darkness."

"Stay in your formations," came Asha's voice over the comm, broadcasting to the entire fleet. "It's about to get loud."

"Kyneth forgive my transgressions. Against my friends, my family. Forgive my lack of faith. Forgive me for only turning to you when staring into the abyss."

"Spearhead is on point," said Kiati's voice, flat without a trace of fear. "Guardian fleet, brace for first contact."

"Zurana greet those who die here today with open arms. Keep the souls of heroes in your embrace. They die to serve you. Your world. Do not deny any of the fallen here today entry into the Forest. Reunite them with the ones they've already lost."

Sora was growing large. Its normally tranquil blue-and-green surface was scarred with swirling storms of smoke, jagged cuts of bright, burning fires sweeping across continents. The glowing orb was peppered with black specks. The massive Xalan fleet was waiting for them.

"Protect my brother. Protect my parents. Protect Kyra and Sakai and Colony One and everyone still left alive down there."

The specks buzzed angrily ahead. They grew larger. Ten times their number were hidden in the darkness of space surrounding Sora. All were rushing to meet them.

"But most of all, kill the damn Archon."

"Engage!" Kiati shouted, the order a battlecry.

Noah watched the Guardian-controlled warship squadron ahead of him unleash so many missiles they seemed to dwarf the stars. He felt a moment of elation until a volley three times as large rocketed out from the Xalan's dark ships back toward them.

A ripple of silent explosions shot through both lines, and then the two fleets were on top of each other. Noah's squadron veered upward, and he followed them, the prototype ship's controls more responsive than any he'd ever used. He almost shot ahead of the group because of the craft's blinding acceleration. His heart pounded and he wiped away a line of sweat from his hairline.

"Frontline hits, at least a dozen of theirs destroyed. Twice that crippled," said Kiati over the comm. "Too close for missiles, switching to autocannons."

Noah's squadron veered around to face Asha's ship, the *Colossus.* Their primary objective was to protect the vessel at all costs, but Noah was supposed to look for a hole to break through to Sora itself to reach the colony and establish a surface presence. In the opening moments of the battle, the opportunity had clearly not presented itself.

Enormous dreadnoughts fired their entire payloads at Xalan motherships, which broke apart silently in the wake of red-tinted explosions. SDI carriers were ravaged by Xalan missiles that seemed to burrow into their hulls and explode after a short fuse. Among all this, fighters from both fleets strafed each other, cannon fire tearing through wings and engines and cockpits in horrible silence.

"Missile volley, take 'em down," came Celton's voice through the comm. He was leading their fighter squadron, and had been an ace

Guardian pilot in his day. A stream of spiraling antimatter missiles were racing directly toward the *Colossus*, already identified by the Archon's Xalans as the primary Soran threat. A few were blown apart by the ship's defensive turrets, but too many still remained.

Noah veered away from the battle ahead and, on cue, Erik released a stream of plasma at the line of missiles, as did two wingmen on either side of them. Six erupted, and another eight were blown up by Celton and his attachment of four fighters up ahead. Three evaded all of them, and collided with the hull of the *Colossus*. Explosions ripped into the armor, but the mammoth ship stood resolute.

"Gonna have to do better than that, boys!" Asha yelled through the comm. Noah wasn't sure if she was talking to the Xalans, or to them for failing to destroy the last few missiles.

Three Xalan motherships had veered toward them to target the *Colossus* directly now, after seeing how well it was being protected. They unleashed three dozen more missiles, these even more erratic than the last bunch, and nearly impossible to target.

Instead of heading toward the *Colossus*, the missiles all split at the same moment, and Noah realized what they were tracking.

"They're targeting us!" he screamed into the comm, but by the time he'd gotten the words out, five Soran fighters were already in pieces.

Noah jerked the ship hard right to dodge a pair of missiles threatening to collide with their rear engine.

"Erik?" he said in a strangled voice. His nerves were racing and his temples were burning from where he was connected to the ship's neural interface.

"We've got it," Erik shot back, apparently having come to an understanding with the AI. The autocannons on the ship flipped around and the first missile detonated well behind them. The second surged forward and was what seemed like inches from their tail.

"Recommend evasive maneuvers," AI Natalie suggested.

"You think?" Noah yelled back, looking at the missile in a floating viewcam. He'd lost all track of where he was in the fight, twisting and turning so that he was now pointed toward the distant sun with Sora nowhere to be found.

"Ship destruction imminent, assuming control," Natalie said. Noah saw the holocontrols shimmer for a moment, wrapped around his wrists, and the fighter suddenly jerked to what seemed like a mid-air stop. The missile shot past them, its engine nearly blinding Noah as it passed inches from the cockpit. By the time the missile realized it had missed, Erik had put a precision shot into its rear stabilizer. The missile spun crazily out of control until it slammed into a passing Xalan fighter.

Noah pivoted the ship around just in time to see the motherships turning toward them to release another barrage. His readouts showed more than half his squadron had been destroyed, though Celton and his escorts were still orbiting the *Colossus* behind them.

Suddenly, the tops of the three Xalan ships erupted in quickly extinguished flame and their hulls dissolved into debris. A Soran ship streaked over the top of them. Noah recognized the haphazard lettering on the side.

"All clear," came Toruk's accented voice over the comm. "Returning to support the Guardians." The *Mol'taavi* veered toward Sora, shooting plasma from all sides at passing fighters as it left the three crippled motherships to float like dead fish.

There was almost no time to process any of this. Noah was constantly dodging plasma and missiles and what looked like jagged shards of dark ice with engines so dim they could barely be seen in the starlight.

After one particularly large aerial loop, Noah found six Xalan fighters streaming toward them, bathed in the light of Sora itself.

"Let's see what this does," Erik said behind him, and a pair of long, thin projectiles shot out of the prototype ship. Each broke apart and sent a flurry of long metal spears directly into all six ships. Noah zoomed through the center of them, dodging cannon fire, and turned back just in time to see all of them explode as the embedded ordnance erupted.

"Holy shit," Erik said. "That was—"

One more missile shot out of their ship and its explosive daggers ripped into a trio of fighters attempting to flank them from the side.

"Nice work," Noah said, catching his breath at last for a half-second.

"That was the ship," Erik said. "She's a hell of a lot better at this than we are."

"Your feedback is appreciated," said the AI with noticeable pride.

The breath escaped Noah's lungs again as he dove down to pass underneath a wrecked SDI cruiser with gaping holes all over its hull. The airspace in Sora's outer orbit had become a maze of live and dead ships. Noah circled the vessel's floating corpse and veered back toward the *Colossus*, which was now quite far away. Noah found a gap in the melee and clenched his fist to max out the fighter's engines. It tore across the distance so quickly it felt like they were teleporting. Alpha hadn't told them what kind of core was in this thing, but it was like nothing Noah had ever felt before.

"Alpha should have built about a thousand more of these, and we'd be in pretty good shape," Erik said.

A thousand ships that fast and powerful with AIs that intelligent would probably spark another Machine War, Noah thought. But he was grateful for the assistance at the moment.

To Noah's right he saw a Xalan ship bigger than nearly any other in the air being swarmed by a Soran squadron that looked like it was assembled from scrap metal. There was only one new ship in the bunch, and Noah knew who was flying it. He patched into her comm.

"Th' engines, fellas, shoot the engines!" shouted Zaela. "They in the back in case ya forgot."

The pirate fleet engaged fighters leaving the destroyer like angry wasps from a hive, and a few ships, including Zaela's newly christened *Sundancer*, circled around to pelt the enormous rear engines of the craft with everything they had. The bright white lights flickered out as the Xalan ship slowly lost propulsion. That didn't stop it from continuing to shoot at the flurry of pirate ships, and Zaela led the rest of the fleet back toward the *Colossus* to regroup out of the crippled destroyer's range.

In fact, more and more Soran ships were heading toward the *Colossus*, away from Sora itself. The air was filled with Xalan ships chasing after them.

Noah's attention jerked back to a flashing danger readout floating inches from his nose, and found he had two fighters behind him. He dodged right to avoid their first barrage of plasma. There wasn't a second. Before the AI could even wrench the controls out of his hands to save their skin yet again, a missile tore into one of the Xalan ships and caused its carcass to rocket into the other one. Both cartwheeled backward until they collided with the darksteel nose of an SDI dreadnaught and were atomized.

"You're welcome," came a voice on the comm, and a Soran fighter soared over them. "Top of my class in Elyria Air Academy, thirty-eight confirmed kills my first year, and they give you two that ship? Godsdamn spoiled Earthborn . . ."

A contagious laugh followed. Whoever it was, they sounded young. Noah barely caught a glimpse of the name on the side of the ship. "Cpt. 'Skyfire' Silo."

"Keep that beauty in one piece," was the last thing the voice said before the ship danced out of sight.

"Prick," Erik said. Noah didn't have time to dwell on their savior further.

"We're pulling back," said Kiati on comm. "Lost nearly half the squad. My ship's venting oxygen and most of us frontliners are out of ordnance. I think it's time."

"Copy," said Asha. "Phase two commencing. All units, full retreat."

The *Colossus* lumbered around and slowly showed the Xalan fleet its taillights. Hundreds of other Soran ships around it followed suit. The chaos organized itself into a steady stream away from Sora, toward the sun. The Xalans streaked after the fleeing forces, and the battle had turned into a footrace.

Noah knew it wasn't time to despair. The battle wasn't lost. Not yet, anyway. What happened next would decide that for good.

"The Archon's fleet has pulled far enough away from Sora," Alpha said on the comm. "Initiate second phase."

"As you command," came the deep, dark voice of General Tau, which sent chills surging through Noah involuntarily.

"Xalans, prepare to annihilate your lost and wicked brethren."

Tau's fleet surged upward from the void of space under Sora. Countless Xalan ships piloted by the sizable Xalan resistance filled the widening gap between the Xalan fleet and Sora. In giving chase, the Archon's ships had left their rear flank exposed, and the resistance fleet raced into it from below. It was Asha and Kiati's plan, but Alpha had put the icing on it.

"Scrambling in effect," said Alpha. Noah could hear the nerves in his voice, even through the translator collar. The entire battle could hinge on whether or not his idea worked.

The Archon's Xalans were stunned to see the resistance Xalans swarming into their midst. Thousands of jagged black ships threaded in and out of each other, the newly arriving craft lost among the pursuing fleet.

"Hold fire," said Tau. "Continue integration."

The Archon's Xalans fired at the first few ships that arrived, but were soon overwhelmed by the flood of new craft that looked identical to their own. Normally they'd be able to easily detect the enemy craft regardless, but that's where Alpha came in.

"They have ceased fire," said Tau. "I believe it is working."

"Excellent," said Alpha with pride.

Alpha had temporarily scrambled the Xalan's ID signals. Friends were enemies, enemies were friends. Only the resistance Xalans would know which ships were hostile, until the signals were uncrossed. But by then, it would be too late.

"Open fire," commanded Alpha, scientist turned admiral for a day.

Just as the Xalans had torn apart the SDI defensive fleet at close range during the initial invasion, the resistance Xalans ripped into the Archon's ships before they could sort out what was happening. They returned fire, but they were destroying their own ships in the process, unable to decipher which Xalan craft were on their side.

The entire Soran fleet ground to a halt and allowed the scrambling Xalans to slam into them. The remains of Kiati and Zaela's fleets combined and tore through the center of the Xalan maelstrom, picking off the Archon's ships while leaving the resistance fighters untouched. They'd likely overridden Alpha's hack already, but it was too late. Noah watched as Toruk's bomber surfed over the cockpit of their prototype fighter and dropped antimatter headsplitters onto the largest enemy ships in the fray.

"This your shot, boys," Asha said to them directly. "Find that hole. Make it to Sora. We'll clean this up and meet you at the colony." There was no mistaking the elation in her voice. The aerial battle was all but won, the tide completely turned despite their enemy's numbers. Xalan squadrons were already starting to flee back toward Sora in droves.

"Affirmative," Noah replied.

"Kill them all, Chancellor," Erik said with a thin smile.

Noah pulled his arms backward and the fighter accelerated to blinding speeds. He wove in and out of ships too quickly to even process how close he was to hitting them. He knew Natalie was helping navigate, but the neural connectors still felt like they were cooking his mind.

"Unlock the goddamn lasers," Erik said.

"The what?" Noah said.

"Access granted," chimed Natalie.

Golden beams of light shot out from underneath the ship, tearing into Xalan armor as they surged past. By the time the ships they were carving into exploded, they were thousands of miles away.

"Gods . . ." Noah said, in awe of the firepower they were barely controlling.

The wall of Xalan ships ahead of them was only growing thicker, however. They could barely see Sora, space was so heavy with fleeing Xalan craft. When the Archon's ships spotted the pearl-and-gold fighter, missile locks popped up in Noah's vision one by one. Erik's lasers slashed through more metal and the AI was firing every remaining projectile they had, but it wasn't enough. The Xalan fleet was collapsing in on them.

"Get behind us!" came a cry through the comm. It was Celton, their squad leader, who zoomed underneath them with a contingent of a dozen other fighters. They locked into a V-formation ahead of the prototype fighter and began shooting down incoming missiles.

"What are you doing here?" Noah said, slowing the ship down to keep pace with their new escort.

"Making sure you reach the colony, what does it look like?"

One of the protective fighters exploded from a stray autocannon barrage.

"Your orders are to protect the *Colossus*!" Erik shouted into the comm.

"My orders are to protect you, you ungrateful little shit," Celton spat back, punctuated by a disturbing laugh.

Another pair of the protective fighters exploded, shielding their own craft from incoming missiles. The rest of the formation started speeding up, and Noah matched them. There was too much ordnance flying through the air to even process. The fleet of remaining Xalan ships was coalescing into an solid mass to stop them.

"Heat up everything you have left, boys," Celton said to his squadron. "And hit your marks. Make sure they make our statues out of darksteel," Celton said. "None of the cheap stuff."

"What—" Erik began, but couldn't finish his thought.

The nine remaining ships broke formation and accelerated into the wall of Xalan ships. White-and-orange explosions ripped through the blackness and consumed Noah's entire field of vision, the cockpit glass dimming to block out the blinding light. Every missile and the engines themselves erupted. In their wake, when the vacuum extinguished the flames, was a gaping hole showing Sora shining through the damaged fleet. Noah regained his composure and blasted through it as fast as the ship could go. Noah guided the fighter around the last few crippled hulks, and sped toward the glow of Sora.

Within minutes, they'd broken through the atmosphere, and the fighter slowed to a fraction of its former speed. Above them, Xalan ships of all shapes and sizes were migrating across the sky toward what appeared to be a specific point somewhere over the horizon. There were still many left, and apparently the Archon thought it best to retreat and regroup after being caught unaware by the surprise assault from the resistance force. If he hadn't, it was possible the entire war would be over already.

Not until he's dead, said a stern voice in Noah's mind. *Only then.*

The fighter rocketed around the curve of Sora until the oceans gave way to greenery doing battle with endless forest fires. Noah tried again to hail Colony One now that they were barely a few hundred miles away, but it appeared distance wasn't the problem. There was still no answer.

"We're through," Noah said when he finally reached Asha. "What's happening up there?"

"They're rallying somewhere on the other side of the planet," she said. "Even with losses, it's still a lot of ships. Have you reached the colony yet?"

"Nearly," Noah said, and felt a lump in his throat. "Celton and his squad died to make sure we made it."

Asha sighed.

"He had discretion to do whatever was necessary to keep you safe. I hoped it wouldn't come to that."

"We could have made it ourselves," said Erik from behind him, though both of them knew it wasn't true. Erik and Celton hated each other, but there had always been an underlying respect below the surface. Noah had known the man for nearly a decade since he retired from the Guardians and took up teaching at the colony. They weren't exactly friends, but he'd taught Noah and Erik most of what they knew about live combat, both on the ground and in the air. It was hard to think he was gone.

"I'm going to send the girls down to meet you with a large detachment of SDI," Asha said. "I'll be there when I can. Your father should be heading to the colony as well, if he's not there already."

That would be a welcome bit of protection.

"Do not engage, no matter what you come across down there," Asha said forcefully.

"Mmhm," Erik said on the comm, the sentiment less than convincing. Noah felt the same way, for a change. Asha signed off and Noah increased the fighter's speed to max in-atmosphere conditions.

At first Noah didn't think much of the columns of smoke he saw rising from the forest ahead amid the mountains. They were everywhere, after all. But panic began to rise in his throat when he looked at the ship's navigation and realized where these particular plumes where coming from.

"No, no, no, no," he said, finding it hard to breathe.

They sped over the mangled remains of the autocannons that had once lined the perimeter of Colony One and then came the facility itself, a mix of old and new structures, many now collapsed and burning.

"Scanning systems are being jammed," said AI Natalie, sounding worried. "Unable to detect life on the surface."

Life. Either the lives of their friends and surrogate family, or the lives of whatever had come through here and ravaged the colony. Noah's eyes darted between the ruined structures, looking for signs of anything, living or dead.

As they descended, it was only corpses that came into view.

"We're too late," Erik said.

Noah made a slow pass over the ruined grounds of the colony, earth scored by plasma, buildings aflame and crumbling. After seeing no movement, Noah lowered the ship until it gracefully landed on a patch of blackened grass. The sky was an infernal orange as the sun began to set.

The cockpit glass slid open and Noah retrieved his weapons from the storage bay in the nose of the craft before leaping over the side. His warhammer was on his back and he held an SDI assault rifle in his arms. Erik joined him, hands grasping two pistols, one his, one Tannon's.

"Enjoy your day!" AI Natalie chimed as the cockpit closed, oblivious to their horrifying surroundings.

Neither of them spoke as they took in the destruction around them. It was silent other than the soft rush of wind-blown flames. Noah crept toward a pile of bodies near the barracks entrance. They were all armored, all guards. A few were in pieces, torn apart with immense force and unspeakable violence. An explosive? But there were no burns marking any of the visible flesh.

Erik was scouring more bodies a few yards away. One of them was Xalan.

"Paragons," Erik said, kicking the creature's leg plating. "Had to be the Corsair and his crew like Lucas said."

Noah found more dead. Guards and a few unarmored teachers. He gasped as he saw the body of his former history instructor was missing her lower half.

"No Earthborn. It's all staff," he said.

"Theta and Zeta should be here too," Erik said, sounding worried. "I don't—"

"There," Noah said, pointing to the technology nexus. The pyramid-shaped building had suffered damage and several dark holes were ripped into the metal. It had likely been on fire at one point, but the flames were extinguished now, and it was merely smoking. It was the only building around where a few lights still flickered inside.

"If they're here, that's where they'll be," he said. He tried his comm, but the signal was being scrambled. The Xalans must have left something behind to screw with their tech. At least he hoped that was the explanation as to why he couldn't detect a single life form in the area.

Noah and Erik walked cautiously across the grounds, occasionally coughing from the smoke and ash blown their way, looking at every shadow shift in the dead buildings and scorched trees. Noah's heart ached seeing the colony in its current state. He'd spent most of his life there. The classrooms and training grounds were his home. The corpses were his teachers and his former caretakers. Now they were gone. Celton was gone. Tannon was gone. It was too much to process. He had to find Theta, Zeta, and the Earthborn.

When they reached the nexus, Noah had to use his hammer to pry open the fused-shut doors. After a series of sickening groans and a bit of help from Erik's laser pistol, the metal parted and smoke rushed out to greet them.

"Up top?" Erik asked as they entered.

"Too exposed. We should head down," Noah replied, waving the smoke away from his watering eyes. "This place has at least half a dozen sub-basements."

Almost on cue, a door ahead buzzed, its indicator switching from red to blue.

"Did that just . . ." Erik said.

"Unlock," Noah said, his heart beating furiously. "Someone must know we're here. Someone is alive."

"Or it's a trap."

Noah suspected that if any surviving Xalans were in the area, they would have been sniping at them from the jungle the moment they landed. This felt like a friendly gesture. At least he hoped it was.

Reluctantly, Erik followed him through the newly open door and down a hall where an elevator opened up of its own accord.

"Theta, is that you?" Noah called out, directing his voice toward a dead-eyed security camera that didn't look functional. There was no response.

"Only one way to find out, I guess," Erik said, and strode into the elevator. Noah followed.

The holographic display popped up and automatically selected sublevel seven before they could even touch it. The ride down felt like it took hours rather than seconds. Noah and Erik raised their weapons toward the doors. A chime sounded as they opened.

Xalans.

Pure, snow-white Xalans.

Their barrels fell.

"Oh thank gods," Noah said, rushing forward to embrace Theta. Behind her stood her mother, Zeta, and a scarce handful of Sorans with various injuries. Most appeared to be civilian staff, but there was a gravely wounded guard propped up in the corner of the room. They'd apparently been using the cramped laboratory as a bunker, and it seemed to be one of the few places in the colony that still had power.

"I could not believe it was you when I saw the ship arrive on the monitors," Theta said, her lanky arms around Noah in an awkward hug. She released him and turned to Erik. Noah's brother walked up to her and planted a kiss on her forehead.

"Never thought I'd be so glad to see you," he said. She immediately turned a fierce shade of scarlet.

"I . . . you . . . as well," she got out, her eyes smiling.

"It is a relief to see you safe, but who have you come with?" Zeta asked.

"We're alone," Noah said. "But Asha is sending more troops down. The SDI and resistance fleets just broke the Xalan barricade. They're in retreat."

A brief rush of exhilaration spread among the weary souls in the room.

"What happened here?" Erik asked. "Is this everyone that's left? Where are the Earthborn?"

Everyone in the room exchanged nervous glances.

"They're gone," said a woman who Noah knew as a chef from the cafeteria.

"The Corsair arrived in a ship of pure darkness," Zeta said. "Xalan Paragons landed and engaged the guards. The colony's protectors put up a valiant fight until—"

"Until that demon came down with them," wheezed the injured guard behind them. He was clutching his bloody midsection and his face was as pale as Zeta's.

"The Corsair tore apart the remaining defenses of the base," Zeta continued. "He and his troops systematically hunted through every building and every inch of the surrounding forest until they found all the Earthborn."

"What happened to them?" said Noah, stomach churning. "Where are they?"

"I saw blue flashes," Theta said, the pink on her skin fading back to white. "They used stun rounds to incapacitate every human. Every Earthborn. Everyone else was deemed expendable."

Noah finally did a headcount. There were only nine people in the room, the Xalans included. There used to be a staff of hundreds here, not to mention three dozen Earthborn.

"They were pulled up into the ship, unconscious," Theta continued. "I saw it on the monitors."

"How did you all survive?" Erik asked.

Theta looked away.

"When the Corsair came, I raced here to ensure the defenses of the base would be secure. I tried to re-arm the cannons that had been knocked offline. I tried to call for reinforcements. I tried to tell the guards where the Xalans were moving. I tried to do everything I could, but it was not enough. The Corsair destroyed everything, was killing everyone. My mother left to try and pull more people to safety underground. By that time, the Earthborn were gone."

"And we were all that was left," said a man behind her wearing a bloodied silvercoat. One of the newest colony physicians.

"I'm sure you did everything possible," Noah said, lightly touching her arm. Her gold-ringed eyes were wet. He wasn't sure he'd ever seen a Xalan cry before. He thought they couldn't.

"I saw . . . I saw," she stammered, "I saw something in the system near the end of the assault."

"What do you mean?" Erik asked.

"The Corsair was accessing the colony's central data tree. He went deep, deep into the roots, further than I even knew existed. He was accessing files that I had never seen before. There were data packets flagged at a level that even outstripped Watchman Vale's clearance."

Noah cringed; he didn't want to relay the news of Tannon's death to her. He supposed he could put that off a while.

"What do you mean?" he asked. "What was he looking for?"

Theta looked to her mother nervously.

"The last file he accessed contained a set of coordinates. I believe that is where he is heading next."

"Where?" Erik asked breathlessly. "Where can we find him?"

"On Sora," Theta said. "Roughly 3,200 miles northwest."

"Sora?" Noah asked. "Why would he stay on the surface?"

Theta raised her hands and brought up a three-dimensional image of an enormous structure bathed in sunshine, surrounded by lush pine greenery.

"What is that?" Noah asked, peering at the picture.

"The files say little, I still do not understand what is there, but—"

Noah's heart stopped as he saw a small tag in the upper right corner of the frame.

It read "Colony Two."

36

"Wait, like ship-ship? On water?"

Lucas shaded his eyes from the sun as he rode on top of the hover-tank making its way through an old dirt side road somewhere along the outskirts of Kun-lai.

"That's what I said," replied Captain Torwind, spitting something offensive and black off the side of the tank. "You said you wanted a ship, and this city's full of 'em."

"I need to get there *fast*," Lucas said. "A lot of innocent lives are in danger."

"We're all in danger, Earthfriend," Torwind replied, smirking. The rest of the unit was jogging alongside the tank, everyone soaked in sweat from the oppressively humid climate. Periodically, Xalan ships streaked overhead, all moving east to west, but none paid them any mind, and they were mostly shielded by foliage on the long-forgotten road.

"Waterships are plenty fast," Torwind said. "And where you say you want to go is just a few thousand miles up the coast. Speedy trip for a skimmer."

"There's nothing in the air we can use?" Lucas asked. Every minute delayed was another the Corsair could be tearing up the colony, or Noah and Erik.

"Unless you can pull a cloaking ship out of your ass, anything you throw up in the sky is going to be classified hostile and shot to pieces by the Xalans. How much Soran metal do you see in the air right now?"

He was right. They'd seen nothing but Xalan ships for hours now. All moving the same direction. All moving to meet Asha, no doubt.

"They won't pay no mind to something bouncing along the water up the coast," Torwind continued. "Especially not a civilian craft. This is a biggest port city in the hemisphere, since you don't seem to know your Soran geography."

"Haven't been here all that long, technically," Lucas said.

Lucas stared at his comm. There had been no word from any of them, Asha, Alpha, or his sons. He figured they must not want to risk any communication whatsoever with the reclamation attack imminent.

Traveling by boat seemed ridiculous, but Lucas had to get to the colony somehow, and without a cloaking drive or a lightning-fast prototype fighter, Torwind was probably right about getting shot down as soon as he took off. The sky was dense with Xalan armor, but he had to trust Torwind that something as innocuous as a sea-bound freighter might slip away unnoticed.

The captain's comm chirped.

"Sir, sensors are picking up something ahead. Xalan signatures, ground-level. Around that next bend from the looks of it."

Torwind raised his hand and the entire unit came to a halt. Lucas's stomach churned, containing only paste-based insta-rations the soldiers had given him. Everyone on the ground stood at attention as he and Torwind dismounted, but some were clearly fading in the heat. Lucas noticed the young woman he'd been speaking to before, Wisher, supporting herself by her rifle, the fibers of her armor slick with sweat.

"If we can see them on the scanner, they can see us," Torwind said. "Ready positions."

The unit snapped to a secondary formation, weapons facing front. Lucas felt the rumble of the tank next to him activating its primary weapons systems.

"They're moving away from us," the comms officer said, rechecking his readouts. Torwind snatched the holographic pad out of his hand.

"I'm reading Soran contacts as well here, how did you miss that, boy?"

The soldier looked horrified, his milky face turning even more pale.

"I—I didn't expand the filtering, I thought that—"

Torwind waved his hand.

"You screw up, people die, soldier," Torwind interjected. "And from the looks of this sensor data, plenty of people are dying right now if the Xalans are right on top of them. We have to scout this before we round the corner and run straight into an ambush. We need our fastest. Lulta, Wisher, Raa'li, that's you."

The three soldiers rushed forward, two men and Wisher, who looked like she was on the verge of collapse. But she stood at attention as stiffly as she was able.

"Sir," all said with a quick salute.

Lucas turned to Torwind.

"Send me with them," he said. The soldiers eyed him nervously.

"You're fast, eh?"

"You won't find faster."

"All them stories true, then?"

"You can see for yourself. But as you said, people are dying."

Almost on cue, a muffled series of explosions boomed in the distance, and a few shrill screams pierced the air.

Torwind waved the four of them toward the brush on the side of the road.

"I need a full report in six minutes," he said. Everyone nodded, Lucas included. The unit watched them disappear into the greenery.

The journey was short. Lucas naturally had to slow down to keep pace with the other three, and somehow the clearly fatigued and sickly Wisher had pushed aside her issues and was keeping up with all of them. The other two men were among the most healthy of the unit. Raa'li was tall and lean and moved gracefully through the brush. Lulta was shorter, but still agile. His tan face was marked by old, deep scars.

It wasn't long before they caught up with the screams.

A Xalan force had set upon a long caravan of Sorans stretching down the dirt road. The creatures had two armored hovercraft that were strafing the ground-bound vehicles of the Sorans, sending up periodic explosions whenever an engine core detonated. Xalan troops on the ground were unloading into the swarms of Sorans fleeing up the road or into the jungle. A few of the civilians had weapons and were fighting back, crouched behind wrecked metal vehicles, but most were either dead or hysterical.

"Shit!" Raa'li said. "They must have all been trying to make it to the port. How many Xalans are there?"

Lucas's Shadow-enhanced mind flipped through every single Xalan he could see, and he calculated the angle of plasma coming from locations that were obscured. A tally instantly sprang into his mind.

"Thirty-seven on the ground, six more in those hovercraft."

The three soldiers turned to look at him like he was crazy, having made the count in under a second.

A woman lay not ten feet away from them on the road. She wailed and cried until a tall Xalan, armor streaked with red warpaint (or blood) in swirling, runic patterns, came by and smashed her head in with an armored boot. He growled something to the rest of the Xalans who spread out to chase down the rest of the Sorans. The road was starting to become paved with bodies. The Xalan leader snorted and strode calmly toward the chaos ahead, directing the hovercraft to fire on what few occupied Soran vehicles still remained on the road.

All Lucas could think of was Earth during the brief war with the Xalans. He'd seen horrifying scenes like this for weeks as he scrambled from hole to hole, trying to survive through staying hidden. He watched the Xalans slaughter hundreds, thousands, as he ran. And hid. And ran. And hid.

It can't happen again, he thought. *Not here. I won't let it.*

He didn't have to hide anymore, he realized, snapping out of a thousand flashbacks playing simultaneously in his mind. He was sitting there, frozen, when he finally had the ability to fight back.

"Actually, give me that," Lucas said, taking the comm from the bewildered Lulta, who had just given his troop estimate to Torwind.

"Torwind, tell the tank to fire two shots at these coordinates," he said.

Lucas eyed the two hovercraft, studying their current trajectory and their position on the road. He calculated how far away the Soran hovertank was to the south, and how fast an armor-piercing round would arc through the sky at the properly aligned angle. He took into account the eight seconds it would take for Torwind to believe him and follow his instructions.

"What the hell are you talking about?" came Torwind's predictable reply.

"Shot one at 1.904/3.332, shot two at 1.905/3.321. Do it now."

Silence.

"Now," Lucas repeated, his tone carrying a weight Torwind respected.

"Alright, firing."

"Now bring the unit around and hit them from the back, I'm going in here."

"You're wha—"

But Torwind was interrupted by the firing of the tank. Two blasts. Eight seconds later, exactly.

Lucas looked toward the faint booms that had come through the jungle behind them, and back to the three soldiers who were staring at him, transfixed. He scratched his blackened arm.

"In about four seconds, start shooting any Xalan you see."

"What is—" Lulta began.

"Three."

"You're crazy, Earthb—" Raa'li said.

"Two."

"Yessir," Wisher said, readying her rifle without question.

"One."

The hovercraft drifted into the path Lucas predicted just as two rounds rained down from the sky, smashing through their armored roofs and detonating inside. The screams this time were Xalan.

"Fire."

Lying on their stomachs on the wet forest floor, the scouting party unloaded on the scrambling Xalans who didn't understand why their supporting armor had just spontaneously combusted. Many had been knocked to the ground. Many never got up again, smoke rising from holes in their heads.

Lucas fired into the fray, but shooting with his left, he found it hard to precisely hit sprinting targets, even with all his newfound abilities. He had one Xalan in his sights, his right arm ablaze with bright flame.

Stop, he thought, and his mind went cold. The Xalan came to an abrupt halt, standing idly even as his arm burned. Lucas finally hit his shot, and the creature dropped where he stood.

Lucas tried to focus, spitting out more mental commands at the remaining Xalans. But the winds had changed and they were blinded with smoke from the wrecked vehicles. Ash was sucked into his lungs, and Lucas and the other soldiers started hacking and coughing uncontrollably.

Die, Lucas thought, and through the smoke could dimly see two Xalans tear their own throats out with their claws. But his eyes burned and the other creatures went on shooting at civilians, full of fresh rage. The smoke cleared a moment and Lucas saw a contingent of armored Xalans pointing toward their vantage point off the road.

"Shit, they're coming," Raa'li said, bolting up to retreat. Lucas saw the plasma round heading directly for his chest, and yanked the man downward so fast he heard bones crack. Raa'li cried out in pain, but the plasma round had grazed the top of his helmet instead of plowing straight through his chest. He winced, but looked at Lucas appreciatively.

"Stay here," Lucas said, turning to Wisher who was the only one of the three who appeared to trust him completely. "Cover me."

"Absolutely," she said with a weak smile. "I'll tell my kids 'bout this sum'day."

Lucas was already gone, sprinting through the brush at full speed. He twisted out of the way of the plasma being unloaded at him and smashed into the collection of Xalans who had discovered their position. They were flung into the air from the impact, and Lucas broke the necks of two of them before they hit the ground. He wheeled around his rifle to put down one who was trying to get to his feet, and then spun to kick an energy weapon into debris as it was being raised toward his midsection. The remaining Xalans noticed his presence and turned their attention from the screaming Sorans to him. They raised their rifles, but two went down from headshots fired from the scout team in the brush. Even at a distance through the smoke, Lucas swore he could see Wisher wink.

Lucas turned to unleash a thunderous punch into a Xalan who was running at him with a long, thin blade. The blow took the creature's jaw clean off, and Lucas grabbed the short sword before it touched the dirt. He flung it behind him into the neck of another Xalan who had just reached his feet.

More of the creatures turned his way. They raised their weapons.

Miss, he thought.

Every one of their shots was wide by five feet, and a few of them dropped from the scout team's sniper fire. Lucas casually raised his own rifle and leveled the rest with ease.

Lucas smiled.

Careful, said a voice in his head, but he shrugged it off.

It was funny though, in a way. They were all just so *slow*. Two more Xalans charged toward him as the entire unit was now letting the Sorans flee to try and take him down. He flung his rifle onto his back, dodged their shots, and ripped through their armor and flesh with his bare hands. The Xalans behind them looked horrified, right before a thunderous explosion liquefied half of them and maimed the rest. Lucas turned around and saw the smoking barrel of the hovertank up the road, Torwind and his unit sprinting full-tilt at the remaining Xalans.

Lucas turned back to the stragglers who hadn't been killed by the blast and dispatched them before the SDI reinforcements could even get shots off.

Lucas chuckled.

So slow, he thought. He'd killed *Shadows*, what could these *ants* possibly hope to do to him?

And they were all dead now. There was no one even left to kill. Except—

The smoke cleared and Lucas saw the tall Xalan again, armor covered in patterned paint and blood, bits of brain tissue still sticking to his boot from where he'd smashed in the woman's head. He'd caught a string of shrapnel across the right half of his body, but he strode toward Lucas with purpose, raising an enormous energy rifle with glowing coils threaded up the sides.

Lucas raised his blackened arm, the skin now dark well above his elbow.

Stop.

The numbing feeling in his brain returned. It was almost becoming pleasant now, not painful. Refreshing.

The Xalan complied, face changing from angry scowl to a blank stare.

Kneel.

The leader dropped to the ground on backward bending knee joints. Losing his grip on his weapon, it tumbled onto the dirt road.

Bow.

The Xalan stared absently ahead, and lowered his face and claws to the ground.

Lucas laughed to himself.

No, out loud.

Quite loudly.

Crawl.

The Xalan inched forward along the road, clawing chunks of earth out of the ground as he slowly crawled toward Lucas, his nose barely inches from the dirt.

Lucas couldn't stop laughing, he was almost doubled over.

What are you doing? came the voice again, but he could barely hear it, and paid it no mind.

The Xalan finally reached him, and Lucas didn't hesitate, stomping down on the creature's downturned head, exploding it into pulp.

More laughter. He couldn't stop.

Look around you! boomed the voice in his head, so loud now it actually hurt. The voice was his own; it was the laughter that didn't feel like him at all. He blinked, and his eyes cleared.

In front of him was a large group of the surviving Sorans. They were looking at him with wide eyes, horrified, mouths agape. Lucas turned around and saw Torwind and the SDI soldiers whispering to each other, looking at him with a mix of disgust, awe, and terror.

Lucas turned to the jungle and saw Wisher standing there, her hand on her mouth, tears in her eyes. She wiped them away as soon as he caught her gaze, but the fear in her face couldn't be masked.

Torwind approached him, clutching a pistol with white knuckles, but he kept it aimed at the ground as he walked, stepping over Xalan corpses on the way to reach him.

Lucas wasn't laughing anymore. He stepped backward, removing his foot from the headless body of the Xalan leader.

"What *are* you, boy?" Torwind asked, his narrow eyes growing narrower. "Because you're sure as shit not Soran, or human."

"I—I am," Lucas stammered, but the words came out as if he was trying to convince himself.

Torwind lowered his voice.

"Look, everyone here is grateful for . . . whatever the hell you just did here, but you should go. Get your ship, and get wherever it is you're going. You're a hair away from losing it, from the looks of it, and you can't be around my unit or these people when you do."

Lucas looked around at all the silent stares. The injured were moaning, and slowly the crowd was dispersing to attend to them. But still, many couldn't look away from him. Lucas stooped down and pulled a ragged cloak out from the storage hatch of a half-wrecked ground vehicle. He flipped the hood up so it covered most of his face. Torwind saw only two bright blue flints burning in the dark shadow across his face.

"Thank you," Lucas whispered, "for everything."

Torwind put a hand on his shoulder.

"Don't lose your way, son," he said, and Lucas knew he wasn't talking about getting to the port. With that, he turned and fled into the forest.

Just hold it together, he thought as he raced over downed trees and shallow bogs. *This will all be over soon.*

He felt the odd urge to laugh again, but swallowed it. It sat in his gut and prodded him like a knife.

The sky lit up just as the sun went down.

Lucas was still bounding through the forest toward what he prayed was the direction of the port when the great reclamation battle began. The trees began to thin out and he saw a host of colorful lights join the winking stars in the heavens. The aerial war was being waged hundreds of thousands of miles away, in complete darkness and silence. The bloom of an erupting dreadnought seemed like a distant candle being snuffed out of existence. In the small flashes of light, millions were dying. Lucas wanted nothing more than to leap up, grab one of the passing Xalan fighters out of the sky, and ride it into battle. The last few Xalan reinforcements racing overhead with black hulls and blue engines would likely find nothing but debris when they arrived. But whose debris? Asha was incredible, and everything to him, but did she have this in her? Could she command a fleet of this magnitude? At least she had Alpha. Between the two of them, Lucas believed there wasn't much they couldn't do. With no way to help on the ground, he would heed Asha's advice to try and meet his sons once they pushed through to Colony One.

When Lucas finally reached the sprawling port, it was packed tightly with Sorans, all watching the dancing lights in the sky with reverence and terror. There were armored guards posted at the mouth of the mammoth wall barring entry into the docking area, and a line of civilians holding their last worldly possessions waited to get in. Lucas kept to the forest and scaled the fifty-foot wall with ease, leaping down on the other side before a patrolling guard could spot him.

Inside the compound it was complete chaos. There were so many people jammed into the docking platforms it was hard to move. The smell of sweat and blood and filth was overpowering, and even if most were silently watching the stars, the air was still noisy with the crying of children and grown men alike. Lucas watched Xalan ships soar overhead. He realized that if any of them deviated from their orders to meet the Sorans out in space, a single bomb could kill the eighty thousand or so civilians bunched up within the walls in an instant. It made it all the more urgent to find a departing ship and get the hell out of Kun-lai.

Lucas pushed past the crowd with his hood still masking his face. It was dark, and it was unlikely anyone would either recognize him or see the black veins snaking their way to the edges of his jawline and the ice-blue eyes that now plagued him. He suddenly realized he'd left his rifle back on the road, but there was no use for it here anyway.

He made his way to a terminal and brought up the data cluster list of the remaining ships at port. His fingers flew through the holograms as the crowd gasped at a particularly bright flash of lavender light in the sky. In an instant, Lucas had every ship's manifest memorized, and quickly calculated that the remaining craft could carry at most fifteen thousand more souls. There were at least five times that many in the loading area, with double that waiting outside. Lucas found the fastest ship left and hacked into its navigation system to shift its course to run as close to the coastline as possible, three thousand miles north. From there it was a short jog to Colony One, nestled in the mountains that walled off the forest from the sea. Lucas searched for an airship, but there were none in the facility. The boat would have to do.

Lucas danced through the crowd like a shadow, only slowing when approaching a line of guards preventing the Sorans from entering the ships themselves. Behind this line was the vessel he was searching for, a freighter called the KLS *Stormcrasher* that had only been built six months ago, according to its spec data. The guards were only letting passengers in one at a time after scanning their ID chips. Lucas waited for the next artificial supernova in the sky and slipped past the guard line superhumanly fast, diving into the water without so much as a splash. The approved Sorans moved up the docking ramp to his right, but Lucas quickly plunged deep into the freezing black water and swam alongside the starboard side of the ship. He surfaced a few minutes later, not remotely out of breath, and scaled the side of the craft like a spider, hoisting himself up over the railing behind a cargo crate. His hood clung to him like a wet rag, but he left it on and made his way toward the bridge. It was lit, and he could see the officers inside from the deck of the ship, which was crowded with shivering civilians sitting on moldy blankets, watching the largest battle in their civilization's history like it was a holiday fireworks show.

Lucas looked back toward the crowd where Sorans were still trickling through the guards to board the boat.

There's no time, Lucas thought, trying to ignore the monstrously cruel thing he was about to do.

Lucas watched the officers scurry on the bridge a hundred feet above him. He closed his eyes, and felt their little points of light.

"*Leave*," he said.

They stopped moving, then started again all at once. Lucas was too far away to see their faces, but he was used to the vacant stare by now. It was haunting. He noticed that he barely felt any cold in his mind that time.

The massive engines of the freighter shook the entire vessel and there was a small cheer from those on deck as the ship slid away from the dock. But it was drowned out by the collection of screams coming from the port as the refugees broke through the guard line in an attempt to catch the boat, which still had room for a few thousand more passengers. Hundreds of Sorans were pushed into the water, with a few jumping in to swim toward the boat. They swarmed the loading ramp like termites, and a few of the most desperate and athletic leapt onto the ship as it departed. Many were less fortunate, and once the ship separated from the dock, those leaping bounced awkwardly off the hull or fell straight into the dark waves below. Seeing the ship was gone, the Sorans split and started flooding toward the few remaining craft still taking on passengers.

The ship slowly picked up speed as it made its way into the open ocean. The Sorans onboard started to make their way below deck as Lucas imagined no one wanted to be caught topside when the ship starting hammering its way through eighty-foot waves at nine hundred miles an hour. Lucas had learned a lot in the six seconds he'd searched through the port's database.

Lucas was about to head into an open hatch on the deck when something caught his eye in the air. It wasn't the battle, though that still raged far away overhead. It was a formation of three Xalan cruisers that had altered course. Instead of heading out of the atmosphere, they were slowly lumbering around to face the surface. To face them.

Are they targeting the ship? Lucas thought, but then saw which direction they were pointing. Toward the port itself.

While his own ship was bouncing over the waves, leaving the thousands on the shore behind, it was too much for Lucas to bear.

"No," he said aloud, but there was no one on the deck to hear him.

"No!" he shouted as the weapon bays of the ships started lighting up with the now panicked mass of bodies trapped between the sea and the walls. Lucas heard distant screams carrying over the water, even as waves crashed around him. It was a civilian installation. They had no defensive capabilities. The guards who were starting to shoot at the looming ships might as well have been throwing rocks.

No, he thought, raising his arms above his head toward the ships. The cold was back. He pushed through it to find the tiny pricks of light in the sky—the captains, the navigators, the engine crew. As he brain iced over, sending chills rebounding through his bones, he thought only one word.

Fall.

The three hulking ships didn't fire at the sea of Sorans on the ground. Instead they slowly tilted forward on their noses, like an elephant attempting to stand on its trunk. When all of them were nearly perfectly perpendicular to the ground, the lights of their engines flickered and died. The great jagged pieces of metal slowly plunged down into the water like great black birds diving for fish. But as they disappeared under the water and the ocean swelled around them, they didn't resurface. Lucas felt the impact as they struck the ocean floor.

Waves four times as high as normal crashed over the edges of the docks, drenching the crowd, but causing far less damage than the Xalan ships would have. Lucas collapsed, panting, his mind recovering from what he'd just done. The pain was fading more quickly than ever. He choked back the sick laughter that had found him back on the road. He loved the power, and hated it. His mind felt like it was being torn apart, and he was afraid to see how much of his body was now charred black.

The new surge of waves reached the boat as Lucas opened a hatch. The wall of water washed over the deck, but Lucas kept his feet and saw that clouds were now obscuring the battle above. Lightning flashes and thunderclaps replaced the celestial war. Lucas headed into the blackness of the boat and slammed the hatch shut behind him.

37

The fighter screamed over the forest, just a few yards above the tree-line, as they raced toward the mysterious installation known only as "Colony Two." Erik and Noah had taken the AI craft to try and reach the location as soon as possible while Zeta and Theta followed in a much slower ship, one of the few that had survived the razing of the colony. The remaining Sorans stayed behind to see to the dead.

Noah had told the SDI squadron Asha was sending to head to the new coordinates they'd uncovered, but was worried now that he was hearing bursts of chatter through the comm.

"Arrived [static] black ship [static] ground forces," said the squadron leader. "[static] engaging, request assistance immedi—"

And that was the last they heard. Noah couldn't reach the squadron again, nor Kyra and Sakai on their personal comms. He should never have agreed to have them come to the surface yet; it was still too dangerous.

"Can't this thing go any faster?" Noah asked the air. The air responded.

"We cannot increase our speed further lest we rupture the core," Natalie chided him. "I am sorry my performance is unsatisfactory, would you like to file a report?"

Noah just rolled his eyes and shook his head.

"Why would they make another colony without telling us?" Erik said. "What's the point of keeping us all secret and segregated?"

"I don't know," Noah said, raising the ship to hurdle a mountain range.

"There could be dozens more for all we know."

"Theta said there wasn't any further information, even after she decrypted the entire core. Just this second installation."

It was a worrying thought all the same. Malorious Auran would know more. He founded the original colony, and surely another one couldn't have sprung to life without his knowledge. Though he had been retired and in hiding for years now. But whoever was there, they needed help, and so did the already captured Earthborn of Colony One.

Noah swerved around a cliff face and found himself staring at their final destination.

"Gods . . ." he exclaimed.

The black, disc-like ship of the Corsair was cutting through the air, engaging a host of SDI interceptors. Below the aerial fight, he could see bright sparks of plasma fire on the ground. As the fighter raced closer, he saw that the Xalans were hunkered down on top of a large hill where the massive compound of Colony Two sat with high sloping walls and shattered windows. In the valley below were Soran forces trying to push their way up while under heavy fire. They were failing.

"Shit!" Noah exclaimed. "Why are they shooting at that ship? The Earthborn have to be in there."

"Probably because it's shooting at them," Erik replied, flipping through the various weapons systems, preparing to engage.

Noah surveyed the battlefield, trying to figure out what to do next.

"I am detecting that craft is under automated control, set to a defensive posture," AI Natalie said, unprompted.

"Automated?" Noah said. That had to mean the Corsair was already inside. There was no sign of him among the cluster of Xalans on the ground. He could be butchering everyone as they spoke.

"Alright," Noah said, a plan snapping together in his mind. An insane plan, but a plan nonetheless.

"Natalie, listen up. You're going to lay down some fire and drop us at the top of the hill. Then you're going to disable that ship *without* destroying it. Just target its weapons and propulsion. Can you handle that?"

"Of course," the AI said haughtily.

"Did you say the *top* of the hill?" Erik asked from behind him. Noah looped the ship around for another pass.

"We need to break their line so the SDI can push through. Got a problem with that?"

"Hell no," Erik said. "Maybe you are my brother after all."

Noah nodded and checked his readouts. They were making a bee-line straight for the fight again.

"I'm giving you control, Natalie," he said, secretly guessing he barely ever had control in the first place.

"Orders locked, the enemy craft will be neutralized shortly."

Such confidence. Noah hoped the computer was up to the task.

"Releasing pilots in three . . ."

They sped toward the Xalans, and a few turned their way.

"Two . . ."

A missile shot out from underneath the fighter, and dove toward the Xalan soldiers.

"One . . ."

Noah barely had time to remember to grab his hammer from the cargo compartment. As soon as he did, the floor beneath him opened and he was falling. Erik was floating next to him a split second later.

The missile exploded, and the air turned into a furnace momentarily as flames leapt toward them from the ground. The Xalans in the impact zone were vaporized, and those around them were scrambling to recover or full of mortal wounds.

The fall was over three hundred feet, and Noah had never tried anything over a hundred in power armor. The data said the shock absorbers should do all the work, but the data wasn't comforting as his stomach rose into his throat.

As he approached the ground, he turned the grips on the warhammer. The spheres in the sides of the head glowed. He raised it over his head.

He looked over at Erik who was already shooting at Xalans with both of his pistols. The ground rose to meet them at last.

Noah and his hammer slammed into the ground with meteoric force. Three Xalans disintegrated immediately and a dozen more were knocked over by the ensuing shockwave. Erik's armor formed a smaller crater nearby, and he was upright and shooting again within seconds. Noah's legs throbbed with pain, but he could stand. He could fight.

The rest of the Xalan line had recovered from the blast and turned their attention toward the new arrivals. Noah recognized the sleek, black armor of the Paragons, their faces hidden behind demonic helms with glowing eye slits.

Noah plowed into them, determined to keep close to avoid rifle fire. A few tried to get off shots, but the weapons, and their arms, were cracked and broken from his next few hammer blows. He drove the top spike of the hammer into an armored chest, and bent down to send hydraulic kick into the helmet of a Paragon behind him.

A gold laser shot by, cleaving another Xalan in half. A pair of booming shots from Tannon's hand cannon decapitated two Xalans taking aim at him from behind. His brother was a blur, dancing through creatures who were all nearly three feet taller than he was. They couldn't touch him.

Noah cried out as a blade was driven into his shoulder. He spun around and snapped off the shortsword at the base with his armored palm, then erased the Xalan's jaw with a thunderous uppercut from the hammer. He looked down and realized he'd taken a plasma shot near his ribs, and once he saw it, felt the hot burn eating into his flesh. He saw Erik take a savage claw strike to the arm and barely dodge a shot that would have taken his head clean off. But as soon as he did, another plowed into his hip, the armor only partially deflecting it. *This was a mistake*, Noah thought. These were Paragons. How stupid was he to think that he and Erik could ever—

Suddenly, he heard a low cry coming from behind the Xalans.

The SDI had charged up the hill nearly as soon as the first missile struck. The Xalans had been distracted enough to let them reach higher ground. Noah breathed a sigh of relief and locked the pain away and swatted a confused Xalan as the SDI armor smashed into the Paragons.

Above him, an SDI interceptor screamed as it plunged to the earth, fire venting from every port, one of its wings missing. It slammed into the hillside and erupted in a fireball. Through the smoke, Noah could see Natalie dueling with the dark ship, ten times more agile than she'd ever been with Noah at the helm.

The prototype fighter twisted and turned to avoid the dark ship's ordnance, sending shots back in return that seemed to cripple whichever weapons system had just fired. Noah cringed as the white-and-gold fighter took a glancing blow from an autocannon, but the ship righted itself and continued flying, even as it started to smoke.

Back on the ground, Xalans and Sorans were slaughtering each other. Erik was still fighting but was bleeding freely from the gouges in his arm's plating. Noah picked up a rifle from a dead soldier nearby and emptied it into the backs of the Paragons who had turned to deal with the SDI racing up the hill. Noah tightened his grip on the hammer and spun it around with his free arm. The glowing head slammed into a Xalan charging at him with a long pike, and the force of impact was so great the creature was reduced to little more than a loose collection of bones, skin, and metal by the time he hit the outer wall of the compound, cracking the smooth stone.

Another SDI ship was sliding sideways in the air in a flat spin, smoke pouring from its engines. The ship careened into the forest further down the mountain, with only a few Sorans managing to spill out the sides before impact. Looking up, Noah saw that the dark ship was vomiting silvery smoke from cracks in its armor. The AI fighter still zoomed around the larger craft at lightning speed, pelting it from every angle. The dark ship was slowly losing elevation. It brushed a rocky cliff face clumsily and sent an avalanche of dislodged rocks cascading down the side. Natalie was damaged, but relentless. Finally, after one last hull breach, the disc ship dropped all the way to the forest floor a half mile away, and the entire area shook intensely. Lucas held his breath for an explosion that never came. The AI had done her job, as promised.

The battle on the ground was all but over. The SDI had suffered heavy losses but overwhelmed the Xalans thanks to him and Erik breaking the line.

An SDI commander pulled off his helmet and Noah saw a young man he didn't know with dirty-blond hair, brown eyes, and a pointed beard.

"Thanks for the assist," he said solemnly, eyeing his dead troops. Medics were attending to the wounded. There were maybe only a dozen Sorans left standing. "Who's flying that thing?" he asked, motioning to the pearl fighter streaking by above them.

"You don't want to know," Noah muttered. The ship set down at the base of the hill, and was soon joined by another craft. Noah recognized the transport Theta and Zeta had taken from the colony. It landed gracefully next to the fighter.

It was only then that Noah saw new figures approaching. Sakai, Kyra, and Malorious Auran were marching up the battle-scarred hill toward them with a small contingent of soldiers. Noah smiled, but winced as he remembered the blade still stuck in him and the fire gnawing at his ribs. But there wasn't time for hugs and kisses. He pulled the shard of metal out, teeth grinding as he did so, and flung it to the ground. Kyra and Sakai both looked worried when they saw the state of him.

"We need to get inside," Erik said, shooting sealant gel into his arm wounds. "The Corsair is in there." He motioned toward the towering complex. This wasn't like their colony; it appeared to be one enormous, interconnected structure rather than a spread-out encampment.

"Send a squad to the black ship," Noah said. "Pry it open and find the Earthborn. They should be inside."

The commander nodded and motioned toward the five escort soldiers, who started jogging north toward where smoke was rising from the forest.

"You should never have come," Noah said, turning to the two girls and the old man. "I'm sorry to have put you in danger."

"We can make our own choices, same as you," Kyra said smartly. Noah noticed she had a scattergun on her back, and as the wind blew her sleeve to the side, he saw a slender silver knife strapped to the inside of her forearm.

"They're my family too." Sakai nodded, gripping her pistol a little tighter.

"Keeper Auran," Noah said, dropping the issue. "What is this place? What can you tell us about it?"

Auran shook his head.

"This was erected after my tenure with the program, I'm sure of it. I'm afraid I can't tell you what this place is, other than I assume it is another facility like the one I helped build to raise the lot of you. Let us hope we can save more of your brothers and sisters from this damnable creature, if that is the case."

The central doors of the main entryway were already flung open, the metal warped and contorted by psionic force. Erik and Noah led the SDI in, weapons at the ready. Theta and Zeta had now scaled the hill and joined up with the girls in the back. It was strange to see Theta clutching an oversized Xalan energy rifle, presumably looted from a dead Paragon. She looked mortified, and Kyra was trying to comfort her. *None of them should be here,* Noah thought as he crept through the dark hallway. But he knew they would need every man, woman, or Xalan they had to confront the Corsair. Too many SDI had died outside. *This is a mistake,* Noah thought again, unable to shake the notion. He considered telling everyone to turn back, load up in the transport, and get out. He didn't know these other Earthborn, what were they to him? Why should he risk his life, and the lives of all those he cared about just to save them?

But then he turned the corner, and knew they had to press on.

The room before them was brightly colored and the walls were painted with cheery suns and green planets. The floor was littered with an assortment of toys ranging from simple holoballs like the one Noah used to have a child, to plush pillows in the shape of spaceships. There were tiny chairs next to the tiny tables playing muted holographic cartoons. On animal-themed placemats sat small, neatly cut sandwiches, half-eaten.

They're just children, Noah thought. Sakai let out a gasp behind him, and he turned around.

In a shadowy corner of the room, there were two bodies slumped against the wall. Two young women, probably not much older than he, lay bloodied with gaping wounds in their chests that made it look like half their organs had simultaneously exploded. Zeta peered at the ID badges they wore.

"Caretakers," she said. "Soran."

"Where are the children?" Kyra asked, turning away from the horror.

"I'm getting a reading further in," said the SDI commander. "A large cluster of life readouts."

"Come on, they're still inside," Noah said, leaving the playroom through a door on the opposite side of the room. He ducked under a banner that said "Happy Birth Day Jericho!" in rainbow-colored letters.

There were more dead lining the halls, limbs torn, heads missing, chests ruptured like the girls they'd just seen. Noah held his breath each time he saw a new body, sick from each, but relieved none were children. Scans revealed all were Soran. A more brightly lit room loomed up ahead through another pair of destroyed doors.

This was a larger chamber. It lacked much color at all, and there were certainly no toys to be found. Rather, the floor was filled with small pods that Noah recognized as a birthing tanks. Noah was the only one in the room who hadn't been born in such a device.

But the tanks were empty. All of them. Some were a bit dusty and appeared as if they hadn't been used in a while. But others were broken open, the glass shattered and the holographic readouts blinking with strongly worded warnings.

The SDI fanned out, guns at the ready. Sakai lowered her pistol and ran her fingers through one of the displays on the tank. Theta and Kyra joined her.

"LYON/VERIA: EXT. 21.19.10237," she said, frowning.

Kyra looked at the tank next to her.

"KADOMA/HERAKLION: EXT. 13.01.10237," she said.

"What?" Erik asked. "Why are they labeled like that?"

Noah looked over at Malorious Auran, who had lost all the color in his face. Noah's stomach started to churn, though he didn't understand why.

Noah looked through the empty tanks, seeing more and more of his friends' names. His heart stopped when he saw his own.

"NOAH/SAKAI: EXT. 3.38.10237," it read.

It was Auran who finally spoke.

"Extraction. My gods. They went ahead with it. I strictly forbade it! It had to be with consent! And you were not *ready*."

EXT. Extraction? And that was a date, all within the year. Noah saw Erik standing next to him, staring at a shattered tank that read: "ERIK/PENZA: EXT. 30.12.10237."

"What *is* this?" Erik said, backing up. The girls were now racing from tank to tank, hands over their mouths. Noah finally put it together.

"They're ours . . ." he said, turning to Auran and Erik. "They're our children."

Auran's silence was all the answer he needed. Erik's eyes widened.

"That's not possible," he said, turning frantically to Auran. "They said it wasn't possible."

Sakai had now reached the tank with her and Noah's name on it and let out a half scream, half sob. She frantically raced through the readout to find out more details, more answers, but to no avail.

There was a soft, wet cough from the center of the room. Every rifle flipped toward the direction of the sound.

Noah moved through the tanks and saw the blood before he saw the woman. She came into view, propped up against a central console. Her face was heavily lined, and she looked ancient. Through the blood Noah could see her ID, which read "DIR. TARLA." Auran gasped as he saw her. So did Theta.

"*You*," the young Xalan said with uncharacteristic venom. She turned to them, a claw pointed at the woman. "She helped imprison Lucas. She was there when we escaped. When they all tried to kill us!"

"Jahane," said Auran. "What is this madness? What have you done?"

She let out a short laugh, which caused blood to spurt out of her mouth. The tips of two white ribs were poking out through her tunic.

"I need medical attention," she said. "I need—"

"Start talking," Noah said sternly. She glowered at him.

"You said they weren't ready," she said, wheezing, turning to Auran. "Stoller thought otherwise. He commissioned the project nearly as soon as he forced you out."

"What project?" Sakai spat out. "Why did you do this? *How* did you do this?"

"You Earthborn started multiplying the moment your hormones told you to." Her moss-green eyes met Sakai's furious gaze. "We said you were sterilized like Keeper Auran wanted, but Chancellor Stoller wanted to accelerate the project once he took office. None of you were ever infertile. As such, we didn't create Colony Two, *you* did."

"But . . . we would have *known*," Sakai said, looking at the tank with her name on it. "How—"

"Ever catch the 'parasite,' my pretty young friend? Did any of your friends?"

Sakai's eyes widened. "That was . . ."

"We'd—" Jahane coughed, spraying blood onto the floor. "We'd come in at night and perform the extraction as soon as the bio-readouts were flagged. Ensured complete unconsciousness of everyone present. Minimal recovery time. No one ever even suspected."

"How many?" Noah asked. "How many are there?"

Jahane looked up at him; she was fading. Auran stood with his arms folded and wasn't bothering to help her. No one was. She continued, hoping more information would save her.

"Eighty-six, last count. Though that abomination came through and took them all. Like he was picking berries from the bush, and discarding the staff like they were rotten fruit."

Eighty-six. Eighty-six second-generation Earthborn. And at least one was his, from what he could see. He looked out across the room at all the other tanks they hadn't examined yet. His heart was racing.

There were tears in Sakai's eyes.

"Why did you have to take them from us? Why couldn't you let us have them?" she said, her voice cracking.

"Chancellor Stoller insisted on a new training program when he took office. He wanted the new Earthborn to grow up to be his pets. Wanted to run fresh experiments that Keeper Auran refused to consider with the first crop. There were actually over a hundred at one point, but some of the tests . . . didn't go well. Tricky, that biology of yours."

Erik raised his pistol at her.

"You had no right," he said icily.

Another bloody cough.

"We had *every* right. You are guests of this planet. You're lucky we let you breed *at all.*"

Erik moved closer to her, gun raised.

"And you," she said, locking eyes with him. "All those times, sneaking off the colony to bed those poor Soran girls from the dance clubs. Do you have idea how many died once you put a child in them with your carelessness? Mother and offspring both. Your poisoned *human* genes. I'd say no less than a half dozen of each perished from your lust."

Erik's face contorted with indescribable pain and rage. His finger rested lightly against the trigger.

"If the two species can't mate, frankly, I don't know why Stoller or any of them wanted *more* of you. If it were up to me I would have erased your entire subspecies for the good of Sor—"

A loud bang echoed throughout the room, and Jahane's head snapped back, spraying blood up the side of the console. Erik looked down at his own gun, stunned, then realized it hadn't fired.

Everyone turned to see Malorious Auran holding Sakai's pistol in a shaking hand, the barrel smoking.

"Wretched woman," he said. "If only I'd had the courage years ago."

He turned to all of them, lowering the pistol.

"I am sorry," he said, voice quaking. "I am so, so sorry. I should have stayed. I should have looked after you all."

Kyra put her hand on his shoulder, and Sakai gently took her pistol back.

Everyone's head turned when they suddenly heard a sharp cry bouncing off the metal walls of the room. An infant's cry.

They left Jahane's crumpled body and sprinted down the corridor. Only Keeper Auran stayed behind to unravel what other secrets the woman had buried in the colony's data tree. Noah couldn't read the names of the tanks as they raced by. *I'm a father,* he thought, as the cry pierced the air again. *I'm a father.* The emotion of it was so complex, it was impossible to categorize. Rage, fear, joy, all jumbled together. He couldn't look at Sakai or Kyra. He was scared of what he would see on their faces. Another high-pitched wail.

At the end of the dimly lit hall, they found the source of the commotion. A child was crawling around at the base of a large metal door, wailing. It couldn't have been more than eight months old, though Noah couldn't tell its gender. It had dark skin and green eyes. Sakai quickly holstered her pistol and scooped the child up in her arms.

"It's okay, it's okay," she said, rocking the baby, who immediately quieted down. Kyra gave a reassuring smile to the child who stared at her blankly, but reached out to grab her finger when she brought it near.

A loud groan came from the sides of the door as the mass of metal began to move sideways. Sakai turned her back to the opening, shielding the child, as everyone else raised their weapons.

The room was cavernous, baked in blue light. Children hung suspended in the air. They turned slowly, their eyes closed, their small chests rising and falling. Noah couldn't count them, but he could guess. Eighty-five.

And at the center of them all, there he was, charred arms raised at his sides, floating eight feet above a raised docking platform. The Black Corsair, the man who had once been Mars Maston, in the middle of the collection. His blue eyes burned brightly.

"At last," he said, his voice a multitude.

The SDI fanned out, all aiming their rifles at him.

"Don't! Don't shoot!" Sakai cried out. "You could hit the children!"

The SDI troops never had time to fire anyway. Almost as soon as Sakai finished speaking, the dozen-odd men contorted and screamed. Noah watched in horror as their limbs and heads were ripped off, and their chests were imploded or exploded by an unseen psionic force. The young blond SDI commander died after being torn messily in half, shrieking as it happened. Noah could hear his bones snap like branches breaking in a hurricane wind.

Noah tried to raise his gun, but his whole body suddenly spasmed and then froze. Both his rifle and his hammer clattered to the floor, and he saw Erik involuntarily drop his pistols. Neither of them could move, their arms locked rigidly at their sides. They began to float a few feet off the ground. Noah looked and saw Sakai also trapped, the rescued babe now floating out of her arms to join the others in the sky. Theta and Zeta were similarly stuck, hovering a foot or so off the floor.

"The Fourth Order has been punished," the Corsair Maston said as he motioned toward the dismembered bodies of the SDI troopers on the floor. "The allied Xalans will be questioned. The humans will serve the Archon's purpose."

He peered at Kyra, the only one not dead or frozen in place.

"Civilian Soran, expendable." He raised his arm toward her, Noah tried to cry out, but couldn't.

"Wait!" she called out, raising her own hand.

Her blue eyes were wide, racing side to side, and she was trembling. Noah had never seen her look so afraid. *You can't surrender,* he thought, straining against his imprisonment. *He's a monster, not a man.* And yet, the Corsair listened.

Then, her demeanor changed. A new emotion crept across her face like she'd slid on a mask. Noah had seen it before. He'd seen it when she looked at him that night aboard Stoller's ship.

It was . . . love.

"Mars," she called out, stepping out into the light. "It's over."

The ruined Maston peered at her suspiciously. She took another few steps forward and slowly let her scattergun tumble onto the ground.

Noah looked back and forth between Maston and Kyra. *What is she doing?*

Kyra reached the stairs, all living eyes in the room on her.

"You've served the Archon well," she said. "And he's kept his promise."

Maston's blackened features slowly shifted from anger to disbelief.

"*Corinthia* . . ." he exhaled. "It cannot be."

Noah hung in the air as chills ran down his spine. He thrashed against his invisible chains, but could only move his eyes. He knew what she was doing, what she was trying to do, but it was insane, and unfathomably dangerous. And yet, he felt himself drift a little lower.

Kyra ascended the steps, blond hair dancing on her shoulders, her bodysuit a brilliant white, unstained from the bloody battle outside. A teenage Corinthia Vale, if there ever was one. Erik and Sakai watched her with looks of static fear.

"It's over, Mars," she repeated, wearing a wide smile Noah could have sworn was genuine. Maston blinked wet, electric eyes and began to descend himself. "You've won," she continued.

And then, the Black Corsair, ravager of fleets, bane of Sora, and terror of all mankind . . . smiled. His feet touched the platform as Kyra reached the last step. All around him, the unconscious children were gently falling to the floor, and so were the live adults. Noah felt his feet touch the ground, though he still could not move. His rifle had bounced yards away, but his hammer was within his reach, if he could only bend down to reach it. He saw Erik eyeing his own pistol from his rigid position across the room.

Kyra strode toward Maston. Once she reached him, she raised her hand to his cheek, brushing the cracked, charred skin with her fingers.

Noah strained every muscle of his body trying to move. He could flex his fingers now, but that was all. He was trying to choke out words.

"N-no . . ." was all he could manage, his constricted throat emitting only a strangled whisper.

But then, Maston looked into her eyes. Her ocean-blue eyes.

"You aren't her," he said breathlessly.

"You aren't him," Kyra said with a look of utter pity. But even a moment's distraction was enough. With a flick of her wrist, the knife was out of her sleeve, into her hand, and the blade was driven into his throat just as he grabbed for the handle. Blood spurted out all over Kyra's white clothes as she stumbled backward away from the gasping Corsair.

When she turned to look at Noah, the fear had flooded back into her face. Noah was free the instant the blade went in and dipped to scoop up his hammer and race toward the pair of them. Kyra was still looking into his eyes as the staggering Corsair raised his blood-soaked arm.

The crack of her neck echoed throughout the room.

So did Noah's scream.

Her blue eyes went vacant, and she crumpled to the floor.

Four other cries were bouncing around the chamber. Sakai held both hands to her mouth, and Theta and Zeta made unearthly wailing noises as they scrambled toward Kyra's falling body.

Erik was still shouting as he raced at the Corsair. The disoriented creature veered toward him, one hand clawing at the knife in his throat, the other raised toward Noah's brother. Even with his long strides, Noah was still too far away to do anything.

A bright gold beam shot out of Erik's pistol and caught the Corsair right between his middle two fingers. He let out an deafening howl as his forearm was split all the way up to his elbow, and Erik continued to charge forward unimpeded, leveling another shot. But Noah reached him first.

He brought the hammer around in a diagonal arc and caught Maston in the collarbone just below where the knife was lodged. He heard a dozen bones shatter as the Corsair was smashed down into the circular loading platform. Noah stood over him and raised the hammer, this time bringing it down toward the Corsair's head. His blue eyes flickered, then, for a moment, turned brown and filled with endless sorrow just before they disappeared behind the darksteel. The entire room shook from the blow. Noah pounded again and again unless the upper half of the Corsair's body was nothing more than a stain on the warped metal. Noah dropped to his knees, dreading what he would see when he turned around.

There was his brother, holding Kyra, her head bent at a tragic angle, her blue eyes staring straight up, seeing nothing.

Auran had followed them. He ran to reach her and scanned her with something small and metal pulled from his robe. As he turned to Noah, the look on his face was pure agony.

"I'm sorry," the old man said. But Noah didn't hear him. There was a deafening ringing in his ears, and every inch of him was completely numb. Again Auran spoke, and this time the words pierced Noah through the heart.

"She's gone."

38

Lucas felt feverish the whole voyage, and his head ached each time waves broke against the hull of the ship. He kept to himself, crouched in a dark corner, his hood shielding his face from the few refugees who had made it onboard. Most were weeping and moaning in the dimly lit area. His mind had been jumbled ever since the Xalan ships had fallen out of the sky. He scratched his arm, and black flakes of skin peppered the floor. Peering inside his armor, he saw the darkness was starting to crawl onto his chest. His mind felt like cracked glass that would shatter completely at the slightest provocation.

It's too much, he thought.

The power, the responsibility, all of it.

He watched families huddled together in the hold, the rich and poor together, all in torn, wet rags. Most had lost all their possessions, but they had at least kept their lives. That was more than could be said for many others on the planet. He couldn't watch another world face extinction. It had to end here. He knew he had to find the Archon, but they the best way was through the Corsair, which was why he had to reach the colony. Well, that and to protect his family, and the young human men and women now being hunted because of Lucas's displays of immense power. Why would the Archon need to sack a planet by force when he could raise an army of human Shadows to make the Sorans all bend their knee, or simply exterminate each other with little loss of Xalan life? That had to be why Lucas had been kept alive. But he refused to become a puppet again. He thought of the Soran soldiers on the ships he'd turned against one another at the listening post. He'd killed many enemies and even a few friends, but not so many innocents as in those few, brief moments. Not like that. It ripped at his insides, even now.

But he thought of the looks Torwind, Wisher, and the others had given him as he tortured the pillaging Xalans. He could barely even remember doing it. His grip on reality was starting to slip. How long until he turned into what Maston was? How cruel could he become?

He wanted to be rid of the powers now. These "gifts." Before, he thought he needed them to help win the war, but now he feared if he didn't shed his corruptive abilities, he might assist in ending the Great War the *wrong* way. Which was what the Archon had always planned.

Lucas kept his head down and put his hands to his temples. In his limited tunnel of vision appeared two tiny bare feet, muddied and bloody. He raised his head.

A boy stood there, no older than seven. He wore an oversized coat that nearly reached his bare feet. A damp bandage clung to the side of his head. It was crimson at the ear.

"I knew it was you," the boy said, bending low to peek under Lucas's hood. "Nobody believes me."

"I'm not him," Lucas said automatically, meeting the boy's gaze with his iced eyes. The child's eyes were almost as blue as his. "Go back to your parents."

"You are so," the boy said, pouting. "You look different, but you are so."

Lucas glared at the child, and thought about mentally forcing him away. But before he could, the boy sat down and leaned against the wall next to him.

"Will you save us again?" the boy asked earnestly. "I wasn't born the last time, but I heard about it from my parents. They said you were a hero. But they said you died."

Lucas scoffed, and rubbed his eyes.

"Maybe I did die. Maybe all of this is just a dream."

Immediately the boy reached out and gave Lucas's good arm a hard pinch.

"Ow!" he exclaimed, rubbing the spot. "What was that for?"

"You aren't dead," the boy said matter-of-factly. "This isn't the Forest. My parents said it's a nice place. This isn't a nice place."

"It certainly isn't," Lucas agreed.

"Why aren't you with Miss Asha?" the boy asked, relentless.

"I'm trying to find her," Lucas said. "That's why I'm on this ship. And to find my sons."

"And to save us," the boy added.

"That too, hopefully," Lucas sighed.

Lucas scanned the other clusters of people onboard, trying to find any worried-looking parents so he could send the kid back to them.

"I hope the Forest is nice," the boy said. "I hope everyone there is happy."

The Blessed Forest. The Soran's mythical, eternal paradise of light and life. There was a time Lucas had believed in heaven, but those days were long past. He'd seen death now. It wasn't pretty or joyful. It was an abyss. Sometimes Lucas was scared he'd stared into it for too long. And once he returned from the brink, he was never the same. Never *could* be the same.

"They're happy," he said. It was the only thing to say, he supposed.

"They can see Mira again," the boy said, rubbing his eyes sleepily.

"Who can?" Lucas asked. "And who's Mira?"

"My parents," the boy said, eyes downcast. "My sister. They're all in the Forest now."

The boy yawned.

"Find Miss Asha and make the monsters go away. Kyneth and Zurana won't, so you have to. Like you did before."

Lucas stared out into the room. No one was looking for the boy.

"I'm not who I was before."

He looked down, but the boy was fast asleep on his arm. He pulled his cloak around so that it covered his bare feet. Every so often, he'd look down to make sure the child was still there. It was increasingly hard to tell what was real and what wasn't anymore. Who was to say that this boy wasn't some broken-off piece of his subconscious? But the mop of matted black hair never left his arm, and soon he drifted off as well, utter exhaustion having seeped into every inch of him.

The burning woods of Losara was no place for children. Lucas left the sleeping child wrapped in his cloak as he stole away to disembark when they reached the proper longitude. He found a row of all-terrain hoverskiffs in the top level of the cargo hold, which meant he could avoid a lengthy swim and sprint to the colony. Most of the deck crew were inside the ship, but those on the surface battling the wind simply stared as a man emerged from below deck and drove a skiff straight off the edge of the boat into the choppy sea. Just before plunging into the waves, Lucas gunned the craft so that it shot toward the shoreline, leaving a spray of white saltwater in its wake. Then a spray of sand and stone when it hit the beach, then a spray of leaves and ash as he burst into the forest, dodging trees, boulders, and flames. It seemed like nearly half the countryside was on fire, and there was no rain this far north. He kept trying his comm, but found nothing but static. Looking up, he now saw only a few Xalan ships retreating to a point on the horizon. Asha's battle was miraculously won, which hopefully meant she would have reached the colony by now. Lucas hoped he wasn't too late to stop what Maston had planned for the installation. No one else should have to be subjected to what he had endured during the sickening Shadow transformation. If he survived this war, he would burn every such facility to the ground, both Xala's Genetic Science Enclave and whatever Soran horror show Madric Stoller had dreamed up. Lucas didn't care if Stoller's son said his father's experiments failed. Even a program with only the slimmest chance to create more beasts like him and Maston, or Omicron and the Desecrator, was too great a threat. Lucas would be the last Shadow, one way or another.

Through the smoke, Lucas saw a mountain ahead. Nestled in the face was a white structure with sharp spires reaching toward the heavens.

I'm here, he thought, and accelerated through the last charred trees into the clearing.

Lucas had never been to Colony One, the place that had raised his sons while he was imprisoned on Earth. And he would likely never see the beautiful place it once was, except in the videos Noah had shown him. The complex was a ruin, all blackened stone, melted metal, and dismembered bodies.

But the living were there as well. At least three interceptors were on the ground, and SDI soldiers were racing around putting out fires and lining up the dead in neat rows. They all jolted upright when they saw him, and many pointed energy weapons at him. He leapt off the skiff, which slid to a halt in the air, and scanned the panicked faces of the soldiers. She had to be there.

"Lucas!" came the cry, and he could breathe again. Asha broke through a line of soldiers and ran to throw her arms around him. She was out of military finery and back into power armor, black with soot. Her sword was slung across her back, and somehow she'd reacquired her silver Magnum.

And there he was too. The relief on Alpha's face was clear, but he looked worried too as his eyes crawled over Lucas's blackened arm.

"Where are they?" Lucas asked, pulling back from her. "Where are the boys?"

Asha shook her head.

"We got a brief transmission from them a little while ago. It was mostly fuzz, but it was Malorious Auran, and all we could make out was that they were returning here."

"From where?" Lucas asked, but Asha shrugged.

"I couldn't reach him again."

"It appears the Corsair buried some sort of jamming system nearby," Alpha said, still eyeing Lucas's arm. "I am attempting to locate it."

"Where's your family?" Lucas asked. "And the Earthborn?"

He scanned the bodies, but many were covered and the others were older. "Where—"

Lucas was interrupted as a transport rounded the mountainside, streaking past the white tower on the black cliff. It was Soran, and he immediately recognized the small pearl-and-gold fighter flying next to it. Lucas half expected a dark, flat ship to be chasing them, but they were the only craft in the sky. He and Asha shared a smile.

SDI soldiers parted as the large ship set down on the charred practice field in the middle of the complex. The rear ramp lowered, and Lucas's eyes widened.

Two dozen or more teenagers walked out of the dark entryway, some limping, many injured. He recognized a few from the pictures Noah had shown him. The Earthborn.

But they weren't alone.

Any of them that could manage it were escorting children and infants. A tall, blond girl with a shell-shocked look held the hands of two toddlers who waddled down the ramp onto the dirt. A large, dark-skinned boy held a pair of snow-white babes in his arms, with a two-year-old in a sling across his back. They just kept coming, the young men and women, and the very young children with them. But where were his sons?

The Earthborn met the soldiers and medics rushed to attend to both them and the children. Nearly all of the little ones were crying, and the Earthborn all seemed too stunned to speak.

Towering over the humans were the lanky, pale forms of Theta and Zeta, both stonefaced but apparently unhurt. Alpha raced to embrace them, and the words they exchanged needed no translation.

Then, at the back of the group, he saw them.

Erik limped down the ramp, holding his hip with one hand, a large pistol in his other. The look on his face was unfiltered rage, and he didn't even seem to notice his parents in front of him. And then Lucas understood why.

Out came Noah, flanked by a tear-stained Sakai and the gaunt Malorious Auran. In Noah's arms was a fragile shape. White, spattered with red. Her golden hair blew in the hot wind, and her skin was pale. Kyra's eyes were closed, and Lucas knew from the pain on his son's face that she would never open them again.

That girl was the future, he thought, feeling a dull ache take root in his heart. *That girl was the best of all of us. Like Corinthia before her. How could this happen? How could this happen again?*

Noah reached his father, and Lucas gently put his hand on the girl's arm. Her flesh was ice.

A thought dawned on him. He had to try. No matter how impossible it seemed, he had to try.

Lucas focused like he never had before. Drawing on every bit of pain, shutting out the entire rest of the world. The only people in existence were him and this empty shell of a girl.

Live, he thought. *Live.*

But he felt no discomfort. No cold in his mind.

LIVE, he commanded.

She lay there in his son's arms, unstirring, the air thick with the wails of children. He saw nothing in her. Nothing in her but the abyss.

"Live . . ." he finally whispered out loud, choking back a sob, but he knew it was useless.

Even his power had limits. He was no god after all.

The ship was in chaos.

The SDI supercruiser *Kyneth's Hammer* had descended to form a new base of operations, the *Colossus* remaining in high orbit with the rest of the fleet rallied around it.

Noah had lost consciousness after coming onboard and was being treated for a litany of wounds including a sliced lung and a plasma-ruptured liver. A harried-looking Malorious Auran had locked himself in a room with his granddaughter's body, and wouldn't come out. They could hear weeping through the door, so they left him alone to contend with his grief. Sakai and a few of her siblings were overseeing the new Earthborn children they'd uncovered at Colony Two. Lucas and Asha were stunned to suddenly realize they were grandparents, many times over. But no one knew which children belonged to which Earthborn, and now wasn't the time for mass DNA testing.

Rather, it fell to Erik and Theta to relay all that had happened at Colonies One and Two. Neither he nor Theta wanted to explain how Kyra fell, but Lucas had seen what the Corsair was capable of and understood. Through her sacrifice and the courage of his sons, the Corsair was finally dead. It was a huge blow to the Archon, as was the recent reclamation assault on Sora. But they had new problems now.

The Archon's forces were solidifying half a world away. The remaining fleet was clustered over Rhylos, with millions of troops on the ground, flooding the entire continent. And there were still plenty of invading Xalans ravaging nearly every major city across the planet, with not enough SDI to intervene. They had won the last few battles, but it felt like they were still losing the war. The only bright spot was that the planet's capital, the sprawling megacity Elyria, had been relatively untouched so far. It was well defended by the SDI, but curiously, the Xalans showed little interest in the populous city after only a few airstrikes and attempted incursions during the invasion. As such, refugees from the entire continent were flooding into Elyria as a safe haven, and its population had nearly tripled overnight.

It wouldn't be possible to surprise the Archon again, and his fleet was still formidable, even after they had thrown nearly everything at him out in orbit. They'd lost over half their ships, and their ground forces were being pulled from conflict to conflict by the rampaging Xalans. The grisly scene Lucas had seen in Kun-lai was repeating itself all over the globe, according to the Stream and military intel.

Asha was back in command, conferencing with her generals and admirals, many of whom hadn't yet been briefed that Lucas was alive, including his old friends Kiati and Toruk.

"I will administer an increased dosage," Alpha said after the last briefing wrapped. "Perhaps it is still not too late."

"It is," Lucas sighed, looking at his blackened arm. "There's no going back now. I can feel it. And it's not just my skin. It's worming its way into my brain. You wouldn't believe the things I've seen. The things I've done."

"You are still in control," Alpha said as he readied the familiar-looking syringe. While that had been true of the last few hours, Lucas wasn't confident it would last. He felt himself growing more numb with each passing hour. As if his soul were slowly bleeding out of him from some unseen wound. Alpha was trying to remain composed as he injected Lucas with needle after needle, but Lucas could feel the fear pouring off him in waves. Was his friend scared *for* him, or scared *of* him?

Asha walked in the room, rubbing her eyes after assuredly another frustrating session with the military council. She looked exhausted and, for the first time since Lucas had returned from Earth, older.

She sat down across from Lucas and Alpha in the makeshift laboratory of the *Hammer*. Her hair was falling out of a messy bun, and her
fatigues hung loosely off her.

"It feels like the end," she said at last, staring at both of them.
Alpha had run out of injections to give Lucas, but he felt nothing, as
if the syringes had been completely empty. There was no stopping the
transformation now, they both knew that. But that's not what Asha
was talking about. She motioned to a cloud of ships that was being
broadcast over the few remaining Stream layers. It hovered over tall
red cliffs. The projected image was presented without commentary;
most news outlets on the surface had been destroyed or evacuated.

"They're massed over Rhylos in a formation we can't possibly hope
to assault. We can't take them by surprise again. At any second they
could launch a thousand antimatter city-erasers and we could barely
hope to stop a fraction of them."

"The Archon said he wouldn't do that," Lucas said, rubbing his
arm where the needle holes had healed already. "He doesn't want to
destroy Sora like he did Earth."

"Even so," Asha said. "Taking the planet without completely
destroying it is well within his reach. He already has half our biggest
military bases under his command. He's cleared out most of the major
cities in the southern hemisphere and is creeping north. God only
knows why Elyria still stands."

She was speaking like a leader. Like the Chancellor.

"We could reclaim Xala while it is left undefended," Alpha suggested.

Asha shook her head.

"They took every ship with them, yes, but no offense to your
homeworld, Xala is useless to everyone now. They've traded up for
Sora, like they always wanted."

"What of the colony planets?" Alpha pressed.

"Sure, we could run, Stoller was right about that," she said. "But to
what end? We'd lose nine tenths of the population in the attempt, and
the rest would be hunted down within what, a few years?"

"The Archon," Lucas said. "He's the key to all of it. Without his
leadership, the generals would be in disarray. There is no more Council.

Only him. I saw it; he's coordinating every move and maneuver personally. With him dead, we would have a chance."

"You keep telling us he can't be killed," Asha said.

"Everyone said the same about the Corsair, and yet here we are."

"I mean no offense to your brave sons," Alpha said, "but that was a miracle, and the Archon has no such weakness like that twisted version of Commander Maston. That unfortunate girl gave her life to end his, but he was a threat that pales before the danger and mystery of the Archon."

"I can resist him," Lucas said.

"Ah yes, this *Circle*," Alpha mused. Lucas had told them of his ghostly visions of Omicron and the Desecrator, though from the worried glances they'd exchanged, he was concerned they thought it was merely a part of his mental degradation. And maybe it was, for all he knew.

"If only those monsters were as helpful in life as they are in death," Alpha growled. "I wish—"

But he was cut off by a loud squeal from the Stream feed behind him. All three of them turned toward it.

The entire screen was now devoted to one image, the Archon himself. His mouthless face and star-filled eyes seemed to stare directly into Lucas. When he spoke, the voice was in his mind, all their minds. Asha and Alpha cringed when they heard it, but Lucas was used to it by now. It was almost . . . soothing. He quickly shook that thought out of his head.

"The time has come to step out from the shadows, where I have waited long enough," the Archon said. Lucas could make out the Xalan ships behind him stationed at Rhylos.

"This age of Sora is at an end," he continued. "A new one begins this day. Some of you desire a long, painful death, full of bloodshed and violence. Others are wiser, and will accept their fate with open arms. The decision is yours, and it matters not to me which path you choose. Both will reach the same destination.

"I speak not to you, Sora, but to your cherished hero, Lucas of Earth. The dead man who lives, but only just. I request his presence at my side, and I grow tired of scouring the surface and the stars for him. Lucas, you shall appear before me by day's end. I anticipate your reluctance, but I assure you, you will come."

Lucas looked at Asha and Alpha, both of whom shared the same stunned expression. The Archon continued.

"Behold, Elyria, perhaps the greatest city in this galaxy, by any measure."

The shot changed to one of the capital, surrounded by SDI ships, flooded with refugees. The buildings stretched into the sky while, just outside the city, the tower of the Grand Palace loomed over all.

"The untouched haven of this bloody war," the Archon said. "Perhaps you have mistaken me as foolish or merciful, but I say this to you: why target a metropolis full of sixty million souls, when in just a short while, over a hundred and fifty million fight to flood into the same space?"

Oh god, Lucas thought, and from the look on Asha's face, she understood too. Elyria was a trap. *That* was the reason it hadn't been touched. There was an enormous chunk of the fleet devoted to defending it, and civilians had been pouring in for nearly two days now.

"Over the course of the invasion, my aerial forces injected a series of antimatter bombs into the surface surrounding the city. There are two ways these devices will now detonate. First, if there is any sign of evacuation, either military or civilian. Second, if Lucas does not appear at my side when the sun sets on this continent of dust."

Even at a distance, they felt they could hear the cries of all those in Elyria rising up from the ground. Asha's comm was screeching with generals trying to get ahold of her, panicked voices all talking over each other.

"You should know I do not play these petty Soran and Xalan games of boasts and bluffs," the Archon said, his eyes narrowing.

There was a brief flash of light that made all of them wince. The sound that followed was a rush of rolling thunder, and a white sphere of pure energy expanded near the base of the Grand Palace on the outskirts of the city.

The palace had been his home once.

He'd been welcomed there by Talis Vale.

Charmed by her daughter, Corinthia.

Annoyed by Mars Maston.

Mentored by Malorious Auran.

Joked with Sol'tanni Silo.

He remembered the nights with Asha.

Little Noah and Kyra playing in the nursery.

Erik being born and christened the First Son of Sora.

And now, the Grand Palace fell in mammoth stone and metal shards, collapsing onto an atomized base, falling to the earth in a giant cloud of dust and ash. It was gone, erased from the skyline completely in a matter of seconds, along with the tens of thousands assuredly sheltered inside. The shockwave shattered a million panes of glass in the greater city itself, yet the blue flame of the explosion never reached its edge.

None of them had any words. Even the screaming in Elyria had gone silent. Only the Archon spoke, reappearing in place of the destruction.

"Day's end," he said again, and disappeared into darkness.

"I'm going," Lucas said as he issued orders to the SDI to ready a transport a few minutes later in the hangar of the *Hammer*. Alpha and Asha both shot glances at him like he had finally gone fully insane.

"It's the only way to get close to him. And maybe, somehow, I can kill him."

"Or maybe, somehow, he's going to turn you into the next Corsair," Asha shot back. "Have you seen yourself? You're a few square feet of skin away from being completely roasted. Your eyes are so blue it hurts to look at them."

"The more powerful I am, the more of a chance I stand against him."

"You know nothing about the Archon, truly," Alpha said, his tone equally worried. "Only the whispers of ghosts. That is not enough. We need more data. We need—"

"We need what?" Lucas shouted, rising to his feet. "He's going to detonate the entire city of Elyria unless I'm there in what, four hours? We know two things the Archon wants, the destruction of Sora and me. I'd rather give him one than the other."

"You may give him both in the process," Alpha said quietly.

Lucas walked to the window and watched the curved horizon of Sora burn.

"You know you can't stop me," he said, a fact bordering on a threat.

"This is wrong," Asha said, her green eyes alive with sadness and rage. "Barely anyone knew you were still alive. If the public sees you back from the dead, surrendering yourself to the Xalans, they will lose what little hope they have left."

"The need for hope has passed. It's time for action now. They will either understand when this is over, or they will be dead," Lucas said solemnly. No one could argue with that.

Lucas had seen the horrors of this kind of war before. On Earth it lasted mere weeks, but Sora would not see that kind of mercy. The Xalans would tear up the enormous planet and exterminate its citizens for years, decades even. But if he could at least stop a hundred and fifty million deaths in the next few hours, he would. And in his eyes, it gave him a chance to end it all. The Archon had to have a weakness, a flaw, something.

He doesn't, said a quiet voice in his mind. *Even resisting his power, you were still like a toy to him.*

Lucas thought back to the Archon's ship. He'd detonated an entire null core nearly on top of the creature, and on the Stream he didn't even appear injured.

What if they're right? the voice continued. *What if you're the next Corsair?*

"Then so be it!" Lucas roared out loud, shocking Asha and Alpha, and everyone else around.

"You are not well," Alpha cautioned. "You need—"

"I need nothing," Lucas snapped. He eyed the transport; it had no weapons, no cargo, just as requested.

Yes you do, said the voice. *You need them. Like you've always needed them.*

He'd never ask. Though he knew he would never have to.

"Let's go," Asha said. Alpha nodded, his golden eyes stern. It was never even a question. Lucas could make them stay. He knew that, if he really wanted to.

But he was tired of being alone.

Their journey would end as it began.

39

"*No!*" Noah shouted as he dragged his warhammer across the ground of the docking bay, the darksteel spike gouging the metal floor. He hoisted it up over his weakened shoulder, cringing, but he still pressed on toward the group standing around the transport. Beside him was his brother, far less imposing, but striding forward with fury that caused fully armored SDI soldiers to scamper out of his way.

"Not again," Erik called out. "You are *not* doing this again!"

Lucas, Asha, and Alpha all turned to look at them. Their father was disintegrating before their eyes, blackness starting to creep up his neck now, eclipsing the already dark veins lurking there. They'd heard the Archon's message, seen the devastation at Elyria, and knew what Lucas would do next. And they wouldn't be left behind. Not again. Not after what the Archon had done to Kyra through the vessel of the Corsair.

"*You* leave us behind to go get yourself blown up on Xala," Noah said, pointing at Lucas.

"And *you* dump us in the colony so you can try to get yourself killed across half a dozen planets," Erik said to Asha.

"Boys, I know you're upset after what happened to—" Asha began.

"You *don't* know," Noah shot back. "You got him back," he said, motioning to Lucas. "She's gone. She died to try and help end this wretched war, and we're not going to sit back doing nothing while you three march off to martyr yourselves the same way."

Asha and Alpha looked at each other while Lucas brooded behind them. After a pause, he spoke.

"Let them come," he said. "If they want to stare into the face of evil, they are welcome to it. If the Archon lives, all of our lives are forfeit regardless."

That didn't sound like Lucas at all, but Noah didn't care. Before Alpha or Asha could protest, they brushed past them and entered the loading dock of the transport. Noah met Lucas's bright eyes as he passed him. There was an understanding there, albeit tinged with madness. As Asha and Alpha turned to join them inside, Noah felt like part of a family for perhaps the very first time.

Noah swung the hammer through the air, seeing the blackened face of the Corsair with each phantom strike. His shoulder ached, his side burned, and the bandage was stained with red blood and yellow pus. The burned arm from his youth was now shaping up to be the least gory of his injuries, but he was beginning to not even feel pain.

He wrenched the hammer around and around, recalling the ancient tactics of the Yalos he'd been taught during Colony One training. Whipping the hammer's head downward, he stopped within an inch of the floor, lest he blow a hole straight into the engine room. He pictured the Corsair's body, smashed to a bloody pulp.

The ship they were in now was stripped completely bare, a husk of rust and metal with nothing in it but five doomed souls. *As it should be.* They soared past SDI ships and Xalan forces alike, no one stopping them, their broadcast signal letting them all know they were not to be touched. They were the Archon's now.

Noah swung the hammer around and nearly took the head off his brother, who had appeared in the room out of nowhere. Another two inches and Erik's face would have been spattered across the room, but Noah suspected he knew that. His brother wasn't stupid.

"Watch it," Noah said, all the same.

Erik eyed Noah as he continued to whirl the hammer around in pantomime combat, battling invisible enemies, sweat pouring down him, seeping into his bandages.

"I kissed her once," Erik offered suddenly. Noah stopped, and his eyes flared at his brother.

"Only once," he continued, his tone was solemn, not mocking. "It was one of the nights on the way back from Earth, when we were guarding her. We had talked for hours, about everything, anything. It seemed right."

Noah stood there with the hammer, his chest heaving.

"Why are you telling me this?"

Erik looked at him.

"Because that was the night she chose you," he said.

That threw Noah off guard.

"You knew? All this time?"

"She didn't say it then," he said. "But I felt it. It didn't change what she was to me, but I knew I'd never have her. I don't think *she* even understood yet, but I did."

"She never . . ." Noah began.

"Not then," Erik said. "Not for a while. But I know you found each other in the end. You need to work the mute button on the fighter comm better. Just because you can't hear me, that doesn't mean I can't hear you," he sneered.

He'd heard everything they'd said before the reclamation battle. That explained his silence. It explained a lot.

"A year ago, I would have fought you for her, or something stupid like that."

"What changed?"

"That girl was more than just something to fight over. She deserved to be protected. She deserved the love of billions, not just one or two of us. That's why Stoller was so afraid of her."

"I failed her," Noah said, his hammer sliding to the ground.

Erik nodded. "We all did. But she didn't fail us. She's the reason we're standing here. And who knows how many more have been saved after us, with that thing dead?"

Who was this man in front of him? It wasn't his brother, the hot-tempered, raging child he'd sparred with his entire life.

"I'm glad you found her, even for a little while," Erik continued. "It's a different sort of loss for me. I never had her at all. I don't know if that's worse or better."

"I can't say," Noah said, sitting back on a nearby bench, resting his forearms on his knees. "But I can't describe what it was like then. Nor can I say what it feels like now. There just aren't words."

"So you'll beat the hell out of the air until the feeling goes away?"

"Not air," Noah said. "And it won't go away."

"I know."

"Why did you come, Erik? Just vengeance? Or that glory you always wanted?"

Erik shrugged.

"Both, maybe. But things are different now. Before I left, I saw Sakai wrangling all those kids as the others tried to help her. I saw a pair of twins, a boy and a girl, no more than a year old. They had Asha's eyes. My eyes."

Noah had been numb to the idea that it was incredibly likely he was a father. Kyra's death had shaken him too deeply. He'd said a muted good-bye to Sakai, who seemed to still be in shock herself, and he gazed over the sea of children. No one knew who belonged to who, and Noah wondered if he'd ever know, now that he'd gotten on this ship.

"So you fight for them?" he asked.

"Revenge. Fame. Family. Take your pick," Erik said. "I'm no shining knight. But I knew I had to be here. Just like Lucas knew he had to go to Xala all those years ago. Did he do it because they killed his planet? Did he do it because Sora worshipped him? Did he do it for the two of us? Heroes aren't so black and white, I think."

"You're right," Noah said, gripping his hammer so tightly his knuckles threatened to burst through his skin. He was full of death and despair and hate and hollowness, each spreading through him like a rampaging disease. There was nothing but blackness in him.

There were few places to go on the small ship, and nowhere to get away from his own thoughts. The voyage was a short one, only three hours to Rhylos, but it felt like an eternity. Watching the devastation out his windows only reminded him of Kyra's death. Erik was handling it better than he was, and that unnerved him.

She loved you, not him, he thought. *That's twice the burden.*

But looking into his brother's eyes, he wasn't sure he could say that was true.

In a cramped corridor, he found Asha, having just left the CIC. She looked unsettled. Noah wondered what Lucas had done now.

"Everything alright?" he asked as she approached, and she slumped against the wall.

"He's trying," she said. "That's all he can do."

Noah stopped and stood next to her. It was hard to believe his mother was still technically High Chancellor, though she'd turned over control of the military to her cabal of advisors before she departed. Even now, they were likely formulating last-ditch preparations in case the five of them failed. This wasn't like when his parents went to Xala. They had no plan, only a goal. Kill the Archon. And one misstep could leave any or all of them dead, not to mention hundreds of millions at Elyria and billions elsewhere on the planet. The weight of it pressed hard on all of them, but Asha more than any. She'd been fighting this war on the front lines longer than any of them.

She sank down to the cold metal floor. Noah followed, his aching muscles and bones thanking him for the respite. He'd be sore from all his work with the warhammer tomorrow, provided he lived that long.

Asha stared into his eyes, and knew his thoughts.

"You know, I lost someone too," she said, brushing her hair back.

"I know," Noah said. "But at least you found him again in the end, even if he's a different version of himself."

"It is still him. It is still your father in there, somewhere. Struggling to break free. He'll find his way back, I'm sure of it."

Noah was less confident, though he hoped it was true.

"But I wasn't talking about Lucas," she continued, shaking her head.

"Who, then?"

Asha looked up at the light fixture, which shrunk her pupils to pins.

"God, I was only a little older than you then," she said. "It was back on Earth. After the war. Before I met Lucas."

"You always said everyone lost someone then."

She nodded.

"Some more than most," she said quietly.

"Who was he?" Noah pressed.

"His name was Christian," she said, stretching out the fingers on her left hand and looking at them wistfully. "He was everything to me, a lifetime ago."

"And he died."

"He was murdered," she said stiffly. "Saving me from some wretched thing that called itself a man."

Noah was silent. He hadn't heard about this chapter in his mother's life. All the stories they told about her were of epic victories in battle, or at the very least, hard-fought defeats. It was difficult to picture Asha needing "saving."

"Christian died sobbing. His killer lived. I still hate myself for that, even though he's long dead now."

"I'm sorry," Noah offered.

"Don't be," she said. "It was another life. And even though I loved him, his death made me strong. The hate fueled me. Turned me into something else. Allowed me to survive as the entire planet died."

"So I'm supposed to just use all this hate to propel me forward from here?"

Asha shook her head.

"No. Becoming stronger is one thing, but being consumed by rage is another. I would have died in the desert if not for the mercy of Alpha, and the level head of your father. I was a demon. That still breaks through sometimes, but you have to let the pain shape you without letting it define you."

Noah thought on that. He understood what she meant, but he kept seeing Kyra's frozen, lifeless eyes as she drifted down to the floor. It was hard to see anything but those eyes wherever he looked.

"You'll never forget her," Asha said. "And you shouldn't. But the pain, it can be forgotten. And the love, it can return. Though I'm sure neither seems likely right now."

Noah stared at the ground.

"If I found that man again, I'd kill him," she said. "And probably not quickly. But it wouldn't bring Christian back. That's something you already know, having killed that twisted version of Mars. It's not enough. It never will be. Healing isn't a switch, it's a journey. And a long, hard one at that."

He nodded slowly.

"You were born of the worst of old Earth," she said. "The son of a mass murderer, cannibal, and rapist. We tried to shield you from that fact, but I see now that you should wear it with pride. You are living proof that the greatest kind of evil can transform into something good again. Christian's death was evil, but it brought me to Lucas. It brought me to you. To this world. To a moment where maybe we can save an entire species. Kyra's death was evil, but it can bring you somewhere good if you let it. It may take years and years, as it did with me, but it will take you there all the same. Someday."

Noah blinked. He saw her eyes again. But not glassy and dead. Alive with life, full of love.

"All moments end, you simply have to live long enough to repeat them."

He ran his hand over his mouth.

"I'll be with you every step of the way, no matter what happens next."

He felt her there. He felt her warmth. Her smile.

"I just can't see myself without you."

"Noah?"

Asha looked at him, concerned.

"Someday," he said, turning to her.

"Someday," she repeated.

And then, it was time.

The five of them were gathered in the cramped CIC, watching the sun set over Rhylos. They'd made their deadline. Or at least they hoped they had. Their comms were now completely dead, no doubt jammed by the Xalan army that now called the desert continent home.

Even though there had been thousands of ships at the reclamation battle on both sides, the void of space still made their skirmish seem relatively small by comparison. Not so on the surface, where the Archon had gathered an enormous portion of his remaining forces, and the sight of it took their breath away.

The ships weren't just floating, they were circling. They formed a massive pillar in the sky, everything from destroyers to fighters, locked in a tight orbit around a central point, stretching from the surface miles into the orange sky. It was a funnel cloud of Xalan armor, black and sharp. A swarm in a holding pattern.

But it wasn't just the air. The ground moved, swaying with a million black bodies that carpeted the surface so the red sand underneath was barely visible. They stretched all the way to the horizon, set up in makeshift camps alongside vehicles, tanks, and hovercraft barely skimming the surface. It wasn't a million. Noah had seen a million people at the promenade of the now-destroyed Grand Palace. This was a hundred times that many.

At first Noah wondered why they didn't just lob every massive warhead they had at this obvious cluster, but even a cursory glance showed that no missile or bomb could ever hope to make it through this kind of defense with thousands of anti-air turrets scattered on the ground and shieldships integrated into the swirling fleet above. Going after the Archon directly was the only possible option, given the scope of the force before them. He felt as they had when they'd posed as prisoners at Solarion Station. But there was no next step. Everything was an unknown. And however menacing the young Commander Hayne had been, the Archon was another class of evil and power. One none of them had ever seen before. None except Lucas.

A dark ship broke off from the drifting funnel of the Xalan fleet and flew to meet them. Noah was unsurprised to find their ship disabled within seconds, drifting uselessly toward the much larger craft.

The clank of metal on metal suddenly jolted loose all the fear Noah had been keeping locked away regarding this entire endeavor.

What are we doing here? he asked himself. For revenge. For glory. For family. Everything his brother had set forth as reasons seemed so petty now in the face of certain death.

You'll see her again, he thought. But his faith had been shaken so many times over the past few months that he wasn't even sure he believed that anymore. Yet still he prayed. He hadn't stopped praying for most of the flight. It had kept him safe so far. *But not her,* said the voice.

They were inside the larger ship now and could see nothing in the hangar bay. A rustle of whispers and they decided they should probably move toward the exit bay, but before they could, they were deafened by the shearing of metal.

Noah watched in amazement and horror as the entire viewscreen and nose of the ship was pulled off of the transport by an unseen force. The rusted metal tore like paper, and once it was all shorn away, the entire front half of the CIC, including all the controls to the ship, was flung into the darkness in the corner of the hangar. All of them were untouched.

"*Forward*," came the voice, needles and knives in Noah's head.

The five of them walked cautiously into the darkness, where they found the creature they sought.

Noah had only seen the Archon during his brief video message to Sora, but in person he was far more imposing, even unarmored and unarmed. His skin shimmered like it was wet, and he was taller and lankier than most Xalans. His claws were long, thin razors, and he had no sharp Xalan teeth, as he had no mouth at all. There were no rings in his eyes, only a swirl of stars of every color, and no color. They said he wasn't Xalan at all, but he *had* to be on some level. For every difference from a typical Xalan, there were two similarities. The thing in front of him . . . didn't make sense. And that's what chilled him the most.

"You are accompanied by quite a vanguard," the Archon said, looking over the group of them. They were all armed to the teeth, each with hands hovering over their weapons of choice. Noah had his hammer and a rifle, Erik his pistols, Asha her Magnum and sword. Even Alpha had a scattergun. Only Lucas was unarmed. Perhaps it was certain death to bear arms against the Archon, but they had to try. Noah waited for a signal to attack, but Lucas simply stared at the Archon.

"They are my family," Lucas said.

"More humans." The Archon nodded. "And this new 'Chancellor' among them. They will join you by ascending to immortality soon enough. I see you are making great strides with your transformation."

The blackness had reached Lucas's jawline now. His blue eyes blazed angrily.

"And you," the Archon said, turning to Alpha. "You have caused me many problems these past years. Your whole clan had so much promise. It was a shame to execute them for treason."

Alpha glowered at him. "You claim they died at *your* hand?"

"There is nothing that has occurred in the history of Xala that was not at my hand," the Archon said.

It was clear Alpha didn't know quite what to make of that, but he seethed all the same.

"I suppose you mean to kill me," the Archon continued, sounding almost bored. "Go on, make your attempt."

Asha didn't need to be asked twice. She raised her Magnum, but she was the only one. Noah found himself frozen, unable to lift his rifle. Alpha and Erik struggled similarly to aim their own weapons. Asha's finger hovered over the Magnum's trigger, but she couldn't fire.

Noah hated this feeling. It was exactly how he was rendered helpless as the Corsair killed Kyra. He strained every muscle, but received nothing for his effort but pain. The psionic power of the Archon was too much to bear.

But then there was Lucas. Somehow, he'd found a way past the Archon's influence and dove at the creature. Noah saw the glint of a black blade that had been hidden in the armor plating of his forearm, and it raced toward the Archon's galactic eye faster than Noah could even process.

But it didn't reach its target. Noah blinked and the Archon was a foot to the left, grabbing Lucas by the neck and slamming him into the ground. The Archon stamped down on his arm which shattered the plating, the blade, and probably the bone, judging by how Lucas cried out.

"Futile, as ever," the Archon said, his voice echoing in all their minds. "I will grow tired of this quickly, so I will ensure we can avoid this sort of occurrence going forward."

He looked toward Asha's Magnum, which was still pointed where the Archon had been standing moments earlier, her finger millimeters from the trigger.

The Archon's eyes brightened momentarily as he mentally pulled the weapon from her grasp, and it floated in the air in front of all of them. Noah was still frozen, but his eyes followed the slowly drifting gun as it came to rest in the air in front of the Archon.

And then the gun came apart. It didn't break or shatter; it simply started to disassemble itself in midair. The barrel, grip, trigger, hammer, the ammunition chamber, and fifty other pieces Noah couldn't identify slowly detached themselves from one another and floated separately in the air. Asha's eyes widened. Noah knew she'd had that weapon since Earth, though she'd never shared the exact significance of it.

Suddenly every piece clattered to the ground except one, the barrel. It twisted in the air as the Archon observed it, and then suddenly bits and pieces of it started falling away from it. The metal barrel was being sliced like a vegetable, and incredibly thin rings of metal cascaded to the ground as it grew smaller and smaller until there were only two identical rings left. As they rotated, they were so thin, they could barely be seen when they turned sideways.

"It seems the millions at Elyria are not enough to stay your hands. Perhaps this will be."

The rings, no bigger than a coin and thinner than a razor, disappeared from sight. Then, they reappeared, floating in the air once more. But this time as the light caught them, they glistened red.

Noah felt a twinge of pain in his neck, just above the collar of his armor. He touched the spot, and when he pulled his fingers back, saw a small smear of red. He look over at his Erik, who also had his hand at a similar point next to his throat. When he took it away, Noah saw a small, thin red line on his brother's neck, but there was no blood spilling from it. He touched his own cut again, and this time, the wound was dry.

"What—" he began.

Lucas and Asha were looking frantically between the two of them.

"What did you do?" Lucas growled. It felt like a bee sting. Noah didn't understand.

"To ensure our next endeavor proceeds without incident, I have severed arteries in your sons' necks."

The two razor discs dropped to the floor and clinked lightly next to the other pieces of the Magnum scattered there.

"I don't—" Noah tried again. He felt almost no pain at all. And there was no more blood. How—

"They continue to live only because I now guide the blood through their detached veins with psionic force. Such a task requires precise, constant concentration."

Lucas's eyes narrowed.

"Another outburst like before and they will die in seconds if you cause me to shift my attention to defend myself," the Archon continued.

Noah clutched the wound instinctively, though he knew that his life was now literally in the hands of the creature before him. The blood still coursed on a proper path through a torn artery because the Archon *willed* it. This was a power this world, any world, had never known.

Noah was shaking. He couldn't help himself. Erik had gone pale as the moon, and kept touching the sliver of a cut, checking for fresh blood. There was none.

"What . . . do you . . . want," Lucas said slowly, every muscle tense, his chest heaving with rage.

"Your cooperation," the Archon said coolly. "And when I have it, your sons will be healed. I would not waste such prize human specimens on petty spite or vengeance. Your kind has proven too valuable."

"So valuable you killed our entire planet," Asha said.

"I was unaware of the potential of your subspecies," the Archon replied, turning his stone gaze toward her. "The Earth campaign was rife with unfortunate errors I do not mean to repeat."

"What *are* you, demon?" Alpha growled.

"Come," the Archon said, turning away and walking into the darkness of the ship, "and you will learn."

40

His cell inside the ship was pure light, a five-sided box of searing forcefields that even Lucas with all his power couldn't hope to get past. Only the floor was metal—pure darksteel that had to be at least six feet thick. Lucas supposed with enough time and effort he could break through it and tear the entire ship apart with his bare hands, hoping the Archon would die in the ensuing fiery crash. But there was Elyria to consider, and now his family.

Why did you let them come? he thought. *Of course they would become hostages.*

But he knew it could have been far worse if there were no one there with him. He felt like he was losing himself more and more with each passing minute. And who could bring him back from the brink if not his family? He often found his mind wandering and warping as of late, but one look at them snapped him back into reality. He needed them here, but hated that their lives were at risk.

They were all in danger anyway, he supposed. Nowhere was safe now. But still, Colony One or the *Colossus* wouldn't have left his sons seconds away from death.

They're strong boys, they'll endure, he told himself. But he was fearful all the same.

The others had all been separated and imprisoned elsewhere, the Archon promising their destination was close at hand. Lucas had no idea what to expect, but was preparing himself, trying to hold together the slipping pieces of his sanity.

"Fight it," came a voice in the darkness outside the searing yellow light of the cage. The hair stood up on the back of Lucas's neck. It was a voice he knew. "Trust me, you won't like what happens when it takes over."

Mars Maston walked through the incinerating wall of light like it wasn't even there. Maston, not the Corsair. The man in front of him was as tall and dashing as he ever was in life, skin tanned, eyes brown, hair curled and jet black. He was wearing the military dress blues he'd donned when Lucas first met him during the Earth Gala, all those years ago, full of stiff, straight lines and gleaming medals. His dark eyes flashed; his face betrayed a hint of a smile.

"Is this real?" Lucas said, head reeling. "Or am I completely lost now?"

Maston shrugged.

"The definition of 'real' is a bit perplexing here. It's a strange place, this Circle."

Another vision from the Circle then, like the Desecrator and Omicron before him. But this was no monster, it was the man.

"But you're you," Lucas said stupidly. "Like you were before. Weren't you only a clone? Didn't the Archon drive you insane?"

Maston nodded and slowly walked around the cramped space, staring up at the corners of the cube. He cast no shadow in the light of the cage.

"Things are much clearer on the other side. I suppose that thing that died wasn't really me, but it had all my memories. All *his* memories, however you want to say it. As I said, it's a bit confusing."

"Do you remember, though?" Lucas asked. Maston's face darkened and Lucas knew the answer before he spoke.

"It feels like a bad dream, but I know it happened. So many dead at my hand. You've only seen the aftermath of what the Archon forced me to do. Imagine living through it, unable to change course."

"I have," Lucas said, remembering the thousands he'd killed at the listening post.

Maston shook his head. "I know what you've done, but it still pales in comparison to the chaos I've wrought. And then, the girl. That . . . young Cora. A clone?"

"A clone, yes, but more than that," Lucas said soberly.

"That was the most tragic of all."

"For you, or her?"

Maston stared into the nothingness outside the cell, his gaze a thousand miles away.

"She almost brought me back. Just for a moment. But then the madness returned, and killed her. My death was a mercy after that."

Maston looked away.

"I'm not here about that. We need to talk."

"You want to be free of the Circle too, then," Lucas said, already knowing where this was going.

Maston nodded and folded his arms.

"And you know what has to happen," he said.

Lucas picked nervously at the black skin on his wrist.

"Believe me, our goals are the same, but how do you kill an immortal?"

Maston shook his head.

"Not immortal. Though that's what he'd have you believe."

"Do you know what he is, then?" Lucas asked.

"I know enough," Maston said, "to know he can be killed. The rest you'll discover soon."

"What am I supposed to do?" Lucas asked. "I'm talking to thin air, and about to become the next . . . you."

"You're different," Maston said coolly. "But you already know that. You're all they talk about here, you know."

Lucas looked around, and a jolt ran through him as he saw electric blue eyes blinking in the darkness around the lightcell. There were dozens.

"They're here?"

"We're always here," Maston said. "And most of us want the same thing. The Archon executed many 'disloyal' Shadows after the resistance took up arms. Only a few survived like your friend Tau."

"That's what Omicron and the Desecrator were saying, though it's hard to trust two monsters that tried to kill you."

"Trust me, then," Maston said sharply. "The Archon must die, and you're the only one who can kill him."

Lucas shook his head violently.

"How?" he said loudly, his arms lifting from his sides. "I did what the Desecrator said. I know my pain inside and out, enough to resist him. But it's not enough."

"Of course resistance isn't enough, it's only the first step," Maston shot back.

"What's the second, then?"

There were whispers in the shadows around them. Blue eyes blinked. Lucas swore he caught a flash of a pair of orange rings in the black.

"They think that the Circle can be bent before it's broken," Maston said. "With enough power. Your power."

"Bent?" Lucas asked, cocking his head. "What do you mean?"

"I mean bent," Maston said, and streaked his finger along the light-cell wall. It made a trail and a low hiss, with just a tiny wisp of smoke. Lucas's eyes widened. *Did he—*

"But more is required," Maston said, passing his hand through Lucas's arm. He felt a dull chill, but nothing more.

"There's no more power to find, no more pain to draw on," Lucas said.

More whispers. Maston glared at the eyes in the darkness.

"They laugh at me," he said. "But I know the way forward."

"What way?" Lucas asked.

"In my final moments, I did something I never thought I could."

He paused, and gazed at the floor.

"I let go."

Lucas was confused.

"Let go of what?"

"All of it," Maston said. "Cora, Tulwar, Talis, Vitalla, Rhylos, Makari, everything. All of it. *All* the pain."

Lucas remained silent.

"In that final second, I felt power like I never had before. I was myself again, or whoever Mars Maston used to be. I was transformed."

"But you died," Lucas said.

"But what if I hadn't? What if *you* don't?" Maston pressed. "What if the key to true power isn't simply hoarding pain, but *releasing* it?"

More whispers and Maston shot the unseen Shadows a sharp look.

"All I know is what I felt in that moment, and that I stand before you now a man, not a monster."

"Are you telling me it's a cure?" Lucas asked, incredulous.

"A cure, a weapon, both, neither. I can't say for sure. But these other fools have no better ideas, clinging to the notions the Archon himself implanted in them."

"What happens then, if I *bend* the Circle?" Lucas asked.

"Who can say?" Maston shrugged. "But it's a better alternative to simply letting the pain consume you and allowing the transformation to complete. You'll kill millions without even knowing it, and there may be no hope for you, nor anyone you love after that."

"But there was for you."

"I saw a glimmer of what was possible," Maston said. "But that shard of light was enough to convince me there's a way out of the darkness for all of us. Let the pain go, if you can. It may only be possible facing certain death, but I imagine that will happen often, given what's about to take place."

"Where is he taking us?" Lucas asked.

"To the truth," Maston said. "And that will change everything if you survive this war."

"I don't understand."

"You don't have to, yet. But remember what I said. That's why I came here. I don't know if I'm the friend you once had, but I feel like the man I was, that's all I can say. If you ever trusted him, trust me."

And with that, Mars Maston turned and walked through the wall of light, and the blue eyes slowly snapped shut all around the room. Lucas was alone again.

There wasn't much time to reflect on anything Maston had said. Soon enough, the ship lurched to a halt, and Lucas's stomach jumped as the ship rapidly descended. The craft touched down softly on the earth. One by one, the light walls flickered, then faded. There were no eyes in the darkness this time.

The opposite door opened with a labored groan, and Lucas walked off his prison platform toward a lit hallway. He followed the lights to an exit where he found everyone else waiting for him already.

Asha, Alpha, and his sons were there, standing in the red dust of Rhylos, hands clamped in metal bindings. Noah and Erik still had red slices on their necks, but there was only dry blood around the wounds. The Archon stood next to them, beckoning Lucas to exit the ship. When he did, the sight of his surroundings sent a chill surging through him.

He'd seen the massive cyclone of Xalan ships from afar, but now he realized they were *inside* the spiral, at the point on the surface they were all circling. Looking straight up, the slowly moving Xalan ships extended as far as Lucas could see, like some enormous school of fish. The fighters were minnows. Interceptors were sharks, motherships whales. And a few craft so massive they were like undiscovered leviathans, lurking deep in the depths of the ocean. The diameter of the fleet's orbit was about two miles, he gathered, with all of them clustered in the center.

On the ground it was another scene entirely. Countless armored Xalans stood at attention, all facing them in eerie silence. Around the Archon himself was a personal guard of a half dozen Shadows, thick with muscle and armor plating, eyes full of quiet rage. Lucas noticed that a few of them held the weapons they'd brought. One had Asha's sword, the other Noah's hammer, though with their size they looked like toys strapped to their hips. His family looked anxious, but intact. Lucas couldn't see any new injuries on any of them, other than the menacing cuts on his sons' necks, threatening to erupt at any moment. His own arm still ached from being crushed under the Archon's heel.

"Come," the Archon said finally, and turned away from him. Lucas walked up to the others.

"Are you alright?" he asked Asha, putting his hands into hers, which were bound by metal. He could rip the bindings off all of them, but what would that accomplish? There was no need to provoke the Archon further until he knew he could actually end him. But he was far from confident in his ability to do so, despite what Maston had said. *Let go of the pain? How?*

It wasn't just a switch he could flip, though the hurt within him dimmed a bit whenever he looked into Asha's eyes.

"I'm fine," she said weakly. "What's the plan?"

"To wait," Lucas said. Erik snorted, but said nothing.

"Come!" the Archon said, and suddenly the four who were bound in front of him were wrenched forward a few feet. Noah stumbled and dropped to his knees, but everyone else kept their footing. Lucas glared at the Archon, but everyone starting moving toward him. Lucas walked alongside the Archon, his family in tow behind him. He was suddenly uncomfortable that the Archon *didn't* have him chained, even more so when he noticed a cloud of camera bots swirling around the procession. *Is he broadcasting this?* Walking alongside the Archon unbound made it look like he was already his pet, his new Corsair. But he wasn't. Not yet. Not ever. *I'll die before I ever turn completely*, he thought. Though he carried a deep fear he might not be given a choice.

As they walked with the Archon leading the way and the honor guard of the Shadows behind, the other Xalans spread out before them and lowered themselves to their backward-bending knees as they passed. The gesture spread outward like a ripple, and soon every Xalan they could see was kneeling.

It was only then that Lucas glimpsed where they were walking. Sticking out of the lone and level sands was a rock formation, a jagged spire of red stone poking out at all angles in a malformed tent shape. It was probably two hundred feet high at its peak and looked like it could be a natural formation.

But as they grew closer, he could see some very unnatural things about it. A door had been carved at the base, and surrounding it were faded white symbols encircling the entrance. Lucas recognized the language.

"Ba'siri," Asha said from behind him. Lucas had learned the language in half an hour one day when he was bored at the Merenes base.

"It says, '*Leave thy sins in the sands, for you enter sacred ground*,'" Lucas said as they drew closer to the archway.

"It's a temple," Noah said. "An old one."

"What are we doing here?" Lucas asked the Archon.

"Communing with your gods, of course," the Archon replied with no hint of humor.

They soon reached the entrance and the Archon cast open the huge stone doors with a small wave of his hand. Alpha had stopped to try and look at the mural etched on the stone slabs, but a Shadow shoved him forward with a huge black claw.

The only lights inside were ancient candles. If the place ever had been a church, it was long abandoned. The prayer stones were covered in dust and many were overturned or split. A statue of Kyneth lay shattered on the ground, and Zurana's head was missing, though she was still upright and at least thirty feet tall. There were pages of paper books decaying on the ground, and the red walls were full of carvings that were either cracked or had been worn away completely.

In the center of it all was a large circle on the ground, placed right below the apex of the domed roof. Something had once been painted on the ceiling, but only glimpses of faces or limbs or stars or swords could be seen.

As they drew closer to the circle on the ground, however, they could see a staircase spiraling downward. The stone had all its edges worn away, but the Archon wasted no time descending. More candles were lit on the walls, and the Shadows nudged the lot of them toward the first stair. They had no choice but to follow, and Lucas noticed that all the Shadows were staying behind at the mouth of the staircase. *Well that's progress, at least,* Lucas thought. *Let the pain go,* he repeated to himself, but his mind was racing a million miles a minute, trying to understand where they were going, formulating escape plans, assassination attempts, anything and everything to get them out of this.

The stairs seemed to go on forever, but eventually they ended on the floor of a very large cave. There were no candles, and no camera bots had followed them down, Lucas realized.

And yet, there was light. The walls glowed with a strange luminescence. Some natural occurrence, perhaps. But there was something very unnatural about this place.

They found bones. Old ones, covered in dust and discolored to dull gray. Sorans, it seemed, dead thousands of years. There was writing on the walls here too, but it was all runes, not a language Lucas recognized. The frenzied scrawling made the symbols seem like they were drawn by madmen.

"I don't like this," Asha whispered to him through her teeth. "What are we doing here?"

"I don't know," Lucas whispered back, but his voice bounced all around the cave walls, even as he was trying to be quiet. There were no secrets here.

The Archon said nothing as he moved through the cave toward a wall that appeared to be nothing more than a giant slab of stone. A dead end.

"He's crazy," Erik said, not bothering to lower his voice.

Lucas decided enough was enough, and when the Archon stopped to gaze at the wall, he turned and ripped the bindings off Alpha, then Asha, then the boys, all in just a few seconds. Each rubbed their wrists, and the torn metal bouncing on the hard stone echoed all around the cavern. Lucas looked to his left and saw a sharp stalactite hanging from the ceiling. The stone was three feet long and dangerously sharp at the end. The Archon's back was still turned. Lucas was contemplating the danger to his sons and to Elyria if he leaped toward him with the jagged point in hand when suddenly the entire cave shook.

"Earthquake!" Alpha cried out, his translator accurately portraying the panic they all felt. They struggled to keep their footing, and Lucas watched his stalactite dagger shatter, along with all the others nearby.

Ahead he saw what was really happening. The Archon had raised his clawed hand, and the cave wall was sliding upward, shaking the entire cavern violently. Soon, there was a dozen or so feet of space underneath it.

"Come," the Archon said, as he strolled through the new opening. Reluctantly, they all followed. Lucas gaped at the wall as they passed under it, and on the other side they could see it wasn't a wall as much as it was a boulder. It had to weigh a hundred tons. *How can he be that powerful?* Lucas thought, and knew everyone else was thinking the same thing. After they were through, the stone slid down behind them. Even though it landed softly, it still shook the cave like a bomb had gone off.

Streams of glowing ore in the walls lit their way, and after a few twists and turns, they reached one more chamber, this one smaller.

The ore glowed brighter here, and seemed to snake through the walls toward a central point.

They all saw it at once.

It was metal. Or had been long ago. The shape in front of them appeared to have once been a sphere. It was lodged in the wall twenty or so yards above them. It couldn't have been much larger than two dozen feet in diameter.

The sphere had lost much of its symmetry as panels had been pried out of it. On the inside of the rusted and stone-like metal was machinery that looked long dead. Inside, as they drew closer, they could see something in the center.

Seats.

Two of them.

"A throne?" Asha asked breathlessly.

"It's a ship," Lucas said slowly. The light of the ore bathed all of them. It was so concentrated around the ship it looked like they were gazing into an eclipse.

Lucas moved toward it and tripped over a bone. Looking around, he saw many skeletons, some decaying into dust, but many still bleach white. There were remnants of prayer stones scattered around too, but crudely made and worn down to mere lumps of rock. What few symbols were still painted on the walls were completely unreadable.

"What is this place?" Alpha asked, his translator flickering in the dark.

"Fifty thousand years ago, the first Sorans called it the Tomb of the Gods," the Archon replied, his starry eyes glinting. "But it was buried, lost, forgotten in time."

Lucas looked at the two seats covered in chalky dust, lodged in the wall above.

"The truth . . ." he said mindlessly, but no one seemed to hear.

"Now it is time," the Archon said. "I will not suffer another failure. First, a demonstration."

He waved his claw and everyone but Erik was wrenched backward, away from the small ship in the wall. Lucas raced forward but found razors digging into his shoulder, and the Archon tearing him backward with unmatched physical force.

Erik turned toward them all just as an unseen nudge sent him stumbling another few feet. He looked at the floor around him. It was littered with skulls. His son's eyes widened in terror.

And then he was bathed in a golden light.

The cries of the four of them reverberated through the chamber.

Then the light was gone, shrinking to a pinpoint in the central console between the two seats.

Erik turned back toward them. Alive. Unhurt. Only stunned.

The torn-open panels of the ship displayed a few dim, flickering crimson lights, then went out. The ancient craft groaned almost angrily.

Everyone was released and ran toward Erik, who slowly backed away from the ship, shaken but intact. Lucas didn't even notice the blood streaming from his collarbone where the Archon's claws had sunk in.

"I normally execute the failures," the Archon said. "The bones of Sorans, humans, Oni, and all the rest lie before you. They all failed."

He turned toward Lucas.

"You will not."

Lucas didn't exactly understand what was happening, but he knew what was being asked of him. He had stopped breathing when he thought Erik had been cooked alive. All their hearts were still racing. He could feel it. They'd seen dozens, hundreds of battles between them all, but he'd never seen fear in their eyes like this.

He would do what was required.

Lucas kicked away a pair of skulls and strode forward toward the ship. The Archon's eyes lit up with delight.

The light found him.

Though it hadn't burned Erik, it was noticeably warming in the cool cave. He stared into the bright point of light coming from the ship ahead, unblinking, bathing in its brilliance. He could feel the light searching him, flooding through him. It was a bizarre sensation, and he felt momentarily delirious. He could hear voices calling out from behind him, but he remained transfixed, staring at the light.

And then they descended.

The Archon laughed in his mind as the figures floated toward him like angels. The others were silent now. The beings smiled as their feet touched the ground without a sound.

How?

More jagged laughter, but he barely heard it. He was staring at two humans. Or something close. A man and a woman, clad in pale flight suits that clung to their bodies like a second skin. Lucas turned to see if the others could see them, or if he had breached the edge of insanity at last. The looks in their eyes told him they were seeing exactly the same thing.

The two figures stood to his right and left, their smiles strangely reassuring. The ship behind them was now alive with light and color, even in its ravaged state. The Archon paced around the three of them like he was stalking prey.

Impossible, Lucas thought as he stretched out his hand. It passed through the shoulder of the man. *A hologram*. But more lifelike than he'd ever seen. A perfect recreation of a man, down to the shadows he cast from the glowing ore. The woman was the same. Their skin was bronze, the man had auburn hair with flint-gray eyes. The woman had cascading blond locks and her irises were pools of blue-green. Both were beautiful, almost impossibly so. It was hard to look away from either. Not that he wanted to.

"Speak, fools," the Archon said as he circled back around behind Lucas. The pair of them obeyed.

"Greetings, child," the woman said, her lips parting to show a warm, white smile.

"We are glad to meet you at last, even if only the memory of us remains," the man said, his voice calm and smooth like water.

"You must have questions, and we have answers," the woman said, clasping her hands together.

"It has been long enough now where you have become as we were, discovering your gifts, your ability to shape the world around you, and those within it."

They kept alternating.

"That is why we have revealed ourselves to you now, after all this time. To tell our story. Your story. You are smart enough now, strong enough, to find the others and tell this tale on our behalf. To unite the worlds, and learn from our tragedies."

"I don't—" Lucas began, but the pair talked over him. It was clear he was supposed to simply listen. It occurred to him for the first time they were speaking his native tongue, English.

"We are the Exos. The last of the Exos. We come from a galaxy so distant, the light of its birth is still not visible here. For hundreds of thousands of years, we lived in peace in the Garden. A chain of star systems full of lush planets filled with endless greenery. At first we threatened to destroy the beauty of nature as our technology grew and our cities expanded, but eventually we learned to live in harmony, ensuring the Garden's eternal existence. We created jungles out of desert worlds. Forests out of gas giants. The Garden grew. We had our troubles, like any civilization, but we were content. At peace. Fifty thousand years of genetic research had eliminated disease, extended our lives almost infinitely. Our bodies healed themselves constantly from the ravages of age, and we developed new and wonderful abilities to move matter and communicate with our minds. It seemed there would be no end to our era of scientific progress and discovery. We lived to solve the mysteries of the universe, and delighted in unlocking the unseen wonders of nature."

"Everything changed when the Az'ghal came. We knew we were not alone in the universe. We made contact with a few of the other races, shared our knowledge, lived in harmony. But the Az'ghal were something else. They would not bargain, they would not listen, they would not even speak. They lived only to destroy."

"They were a race that feasted on other worlds the way a beast devours prey. They stripped planets bare, purging their inhabitants to extinction, taking what they wanted and leaving nothing behind."

"We had weapons, and with them we fought. The war seemed winnable, until the day it was not. The Az'ghal were a savage, bloodthirsty race. Even if we had more advanced technology, they had been waging wars for a million years. They lacked even a shred of mercy, decency, or restraint. Their numbers seemed without end; their ships were so numerous they eclipsed the stars."

"Eventually they broke our lines, swarmed the Garden, and the forests burned. The war raged for centuries and we almost drove them off, but in the end we fell to their relentless assault and endless hordes. Billions were hunted down and extinguished. They tracked us through every planet, every star system, every tiny, hidden moon. There was no escape. There was nowhere to hide."

"And then, *The Answer*."

"The only answer."

"*The Answer* was a ship unlike any before it. We had developed cores with the ability to travel between nearby galaxies, a previously insurmountable distance, but *The Answer* was something else altogether."

"The device our brightest minds designed required every last shred of energy our planets could muster. They called it the 'infinity core.' The power it required was unmatched, and could only be housed in a specific shape, and work within a ship of a specific size. And so *The Answer* was born. A single ship, as we had no time nor resources to build others."

"The distance it could travel was nearly infinite, though it couldn't be directed, and its destination was at the mercy of chaos. The size of the craft only allowed two of us, so we were chosen. We were the best of the last of us, they said, the most likely to survive what was to come, the most able to do what needed to be done. We boarded *The Answer* and destroyed all our research, just as our last stronghold was being consumed by the Az'ghal. We fired the infinity core, never knowing if we would live again."

"We did."

"This is the galaxy in which we arrived, nearly two hundred thousand years ago. The core brought us here. Some would say by luck, others by divine providence. It was our new home. Our last hope. Far from the Az'ghal. Far from our burned worlds. The answer, the true answer, was to start over completely. To birth a new civilization free from our past burdens."

"It would have to be pure. A fresh start. We were a trillion years away from our old technology; our ship contained the infinity core and room for us alone. There was no way to alter the genes of our offspring, and so far away from danger, we knew our civilization would have all the time in the world to grow on its own. Our children were weak, their lifespans short as ours once were, but they would endure. Our first planet was this one, now called Sora. Our offspring grew and thrived and discovered the answers of the universe on their own, with only cursory guidance from us. A civilization cannot be constructed as many think; it must be grown organically. Our first few failures were evidence of that."

"When one colony took root, we moved on to the next world. And the next. And the next."

"We traveled the stars in search of planets that could sustain life, and would spend a thousand years at each, setting up colonies we hoped could survive, and thrive. There were hardships, struggles, but our children were strong. Some planets boasted primitive life forms already when we arrived, but our descendants were dominant. Our vision was being realized. Our people were saved."

"Over a hundred thousand years we spent bringing this galaxy to life. The years changed our story countless times, until the truth was merely a memory. We left it that way, and decided it was best not to interfere. Not until you were ready, as you are standing before us today. We may be nothing but dust now, but we live on through you. Through all of you."

"Our children gave us many names over the millennia. We were once L'yii and Njhalo, but in their new tongues they called us Kyneth and Zurana, Adam and Eve, Saato and Valli, and countless others. Sometimes we were ancestors, sometimes gods. Sometimes we were forgotten entirely."

"As our health finally faded, we returned to Sora, our greatest hope for the future. We rested here, until you found us, evolved into near perfect beings as we knew you would. Now it is time to find the others."

"This is our last gift to you, Exos."

427

The woman reached forward and touched Lucas's forehead with three fingers. His eyes went white and in his mind he saw the beauty of a spiral galaxy, their own, and glowing points of light scattered all around it. Numbers floated over each of them. Each string etched itself into his mind immediately.

"Find them," the man said. "Make our family whole. You are ready. Share with them all you know. Raise up a strong, united civilization. You are the Exos reborn. You will thrive free from the danger of the Az'ghal, who are trapped across the stars. Even if in time they uncover the power of our infinity core, they will never be able to find this place. The core cannot be guided or controlled, and the universe is too vast for pure chance to lead them here. You are safe, and together you will be greater than we ever were."

"Find them," the woman repeated, and then they were gone.

Lucas saw the galaxy in his mind, slowly spinning. He blinked and the image faded.

And then the Archon was before him.

"How safe do you feel, Exos?"

Lucas understood, and fresh fear seized him.

"You're Az'ghal," he said. The entire story was unbelievable, but now everything was coming together in his mind. Except for the impossible appearance of the creature before him.

"How . . ."

"In time," the Archon interrupted, "but I have not waited over ten thousand years to be delayed a minute more. Give them to me."

"Give . . . what?" he stammered. His head was reeling. He felt feverish and his heart hammered against his ribs. The gods were real.

"The coordinates. The locations of your damnable Exos brethren scattered throughout this wretched galaxy."

Extinction. That's what the Archon wanted. A roadmap to find all the other human, Exos colonies in the galaxy to finish the war his people started. He'd found seven worlds already, but this would give him how many? Lucas searched his mind.

A hundred and eight, he realized, and the enormity of the situation took his breath away. A hundred and eight worlds out there full of others just like him. Billions of souls, if not trillions, the Archon would destroy with his Xalan horde.

The Xalans. He leads him. He looks like them. How . . . ?

And just when everything made sense, nothing did. There were still so many questions. He looked at the ship, but though it was still lit, the Exos did not return.

"I will not ask again," the Archon growled. The entire chamber started to shake. Stones began to float up from the ground. The creature's anger was all-consuming.

Lucas's mind raced through the thousands of numbers that had been engraved in the canals of his cerebral cortex. He stared at them as if they were floating in the air in front of him. Each line a piece of a puzzle that would end with the total eradication of humanity.

The cave was still. The stones hit the ground.

"Then we will start with the stray," the Archon said coldly.

He simply looked at Noah, and a fountain of blood erupted from the small cut on his neck. His son fell to the ground. Choking. Dying.

Lucas charged the Archon, but immediately found the creature's crushing hand around his throat. He watched Noah claw at his neck as Asha and Alpha tried to stop the bleeding.

"He has seconds," the Archon said. "And the other will follow."

Lucas looked into the pair of cruel, galactic eyes before him. There was no trace of mercy, decency, or restraint. Only a vast and endless evil.

41

Noah was alone. It was dark, and he was floating. Space? No. His arms and legs pushed through liquid, and air escaped from his lungs in large pockets. Too large.

He was drowning.

The panic set in immediately, and he flailed and floundered. He was a strong swimmer, but it was hard to tell where the surface was. There didn't seem to be a shred of light anywhere. More air escaped his lungs as he choked back a scream, and he followed the bubbles upward this time. Strong strokes. As strong as he could manage.

He breached the surface of the water only to be slapped in the face by waves. Coughing, he expelled the remaining water from his chest, but his mouth was thick with the taste of iron. In the darkness he couldn't see, but he knew he was swimming in blood.

The sky was cloudless, but also starless. The only light was coming from a point in the distance, a flickering flame. Noah coughed again and turned toward it, his long limbs paddling through the choppy ocean of blood as he tried to ignore the taste.

The light grew closer, but his muscles burned and he was tempted to vomit as metal and salt drained into his stomach.

He couldn't remember what had happened moments before he'd appeared underwater. He only remembered blood.

The crimson waters fought him at every stroke, but still the light grew. *A fire*, he realized, and he drained every last bit of his strength to surge forward. The beach was a half mile away. Then a quarter. Then five hundred feet. Then his feet brushed against the soft sands near the shore.

He trudged up the beach toward the blazing fire, his clothes clinging to him. The sand seemed like it had once been white, but it was stained a pale red from the frothy blood. Before him, a silent, black jungle loomed. Here, there was only the fire.

And her.

She was weeping as he circled around the demonic-looking bonfire planted in a circle of stones on the sand. Dried blood was caked on her skin, and it colored her hair. All but a few blond wisps.

But her eyes were still blue.

"Kyra . . ." he said. He took a step toward her, and the fire roared, sending smoke and ash into his eyes. He winced and coughed, and took another step around the pit.

She was huddled with her arms clasped around her knees. Her eyes were full of tears. And terror.

"Noah," she said. "Why did you leave?"

"I didn't," he replied, his own eyes wet now. "You did, and I'm so, so sorry."

"We were happy here."

Had he been to this place before?

"I don't understand. But I'm here now. We can be together."

She shook her head violently.

"Not here. And not when you still have so much to do."

Noah looked up. There were now stars in the sky in a few select clusters.

"I need you," he said, turning back to her.

"I'm scared," she said, looking around nervously. "The nights are cold here."

"We'll stay by the fire."

"The fire is the coldest of all."

Noah looked up again. *Not stars, eyes.*

He felt something pull at him, like a hook through his navel. He lurched back, his hand just inches away from brushing Kyra's cheek. The fire flared and then he flew back, being dragged through the sand. Kyra watched with despair in her shimmering blue eyes.

"No!" he cried out as he was wrenched backward again. Back to the sea. Back to the blood.

Kyra was gone. The fire became a golden pillar of light that stretched all the way to the sky. He was pulled under the waves, into the blackness. Down deeper and deeper and the pressure cracked his bones and the blood filled his lungs. Until—

Noah grabbed his chest and sucked in all the air he could. He lurched upright and found himself in the dimly lit cave with those galactic eyes staring directly at him. His family was crowded around, and he immediately remembered what had happened. His hand raced to his neck, but though he found dry blood, there was no cut. No pain.

"He's back," Erik declared, his voice sharp but his face visibly relieved. His cut was gone as well.

"I was . . ." Noah stammered. "She was . . ."

"Calm down," Asha said, rubbing the sides of his arms, which were rife with bumps under his armor. Everything was blurred, and there were spots in his vision.

"He has lost a great deal of blood," Alpha said, scanning him with a device attached to his powersuit.

Noah sat up further and saw Lucas looking anxiously at him. His father was typing furiously on a scroll with the Archon looking on approvingly. Asha told him what Lucas was doing.

"The-the coordinates," Noah said. "He can't—"

So many lives at stake. All the untold billions out there, waiting to be contacted. Lucas couldn't sacrifice them to this monster for his sake.

But it's not just you. It's Erik and Asha and Alpha. It's Elyria and the rest of the world. Would he do anything else if he were in Lucas's skin? Noah stood up and nearly lost his balance. Erik caught him under the elbow.

"You can't . . ." Noah said. Lucas could only look at him. His father barely even looked human anymore. The black skin was creeping up the sides of his jaw now, and the dark veins were crisscrossing his entire face. Only a few patches of white skin remained. His eyes shone bluer than ever in the dim cave.

Asha turned and whispered in his ear, "The Archon can't use the coordinates if he's dead."

That was always the plan, wasn't it? Kill the Archon? But now the fate of many worlds were in their hands, not just one. And they seemed no closer to their goal.

Noah tried to push the vision of Kyra on the hellish island from his mind. *There are no hells,* he told himself. *The gods are human.* Well, Exos, at least. The story seemed impossible, but it had to be true given everything they knew about the humans scattered across the galaxy. They were all the descendants of refugees, a race trying to start over from the brink of a holocaust.

They said we would be safe, Noah thought. But looking at the sinister creature before him, they were clearly anything but.

"Explain it," said Alpha to the Archon. "Your presence here. Your control of Xala. None of it makes sense."

"The spawn wishes to speak with his god?" the Archon said, bemused. He glanced at Lucas who glared at him but continued to enter numbers at lightning speed. Noah wondered what the map Lucas saw in his mind looked like. Erik rubbed his neck where the cut had been only minutes earlier.

"I wish to know the full extent of your twisted power fantasy," Alpha growled.

"You are the very image of your father," the Archon said. "And also headstrong, but the most brilliant of them all."

"Do not speak of my clan," Alpha warned him.

"You presume to command me? Your entire race would not exist had I not willed it."

"The Sorans made the Xalans," Asha said, glancing nervously at Lucas who seemed now to be in a trance, staring at the glowing virtual page in front of him. More numbers. Too many numbers. Each sequence a new, doomed world.

"Did they now?" the Archon said.

"It's a fact. It's history," she said.

"And who do you believe *wrote* your history?" the Archon said.

"Explain yourself, creature," Alpha said again. "No more of these games."

"This is not a game. It is all it has ever been. A war."

The Archon looked at the broken ship in the wall.

"In every ecosystem there are predators and prey. It is true in your forests, your oceans, anywhere life exists. But the same is true of galaxies. Civilizations rule their little rocks, dominating lesser creatures and each other as if they are the largest, most dangerous beings in the universe."

He paused.

"They are not.

"The Az'ghal are as old as time. Forged in the fires of a thousand dying stars, and bred and born to kill all those who would deem themselves kings of floating rocks. We swept through hundreds of races, devouring their citizens and consuming everything their worlds had to offer to fuel our next conquest. We started our endless hunt within our own star system, then our own galaxy. Eventually we developed cores to travel within our local cluster. Everywhere, more life. Everywhere, more death.

"In time we grew more powerful than we ever dreamed, able to control matter itself with our minds. We evolved our psionic gifts naturally, over millions of years, and once they spread throughout our population, truly no one could stand before us. And none did. None but the Exos.

"To look at them, it was easy to scoff. They were numerous, yes, spread across their garden planets, living in so-called harmony. But they were weak. Fleshy creatures of brittle bones and soft skin. They surely could not stand before the invincible might of the Az'ghal.

"But too many victories had made us complacent. The war was fierce, and raged for ten times longer than any we had endured before. Though their bodies were fragile, their machines were fearsome, and worse yet, through their demonic technology they developed a synthetic way to implant psionic abilities in their own people. They did not have the purity of evolution behind them, but their chosen warriors could match our own. Further still, a few among them had the power to warp the very minds of our soldiers, infecting them with madness, or turning them on one another. They were a foe the likes of which we had never seen. The Exos were almost the end of us.

"But in the end, we were victorious. The Az'ghal do not know defeat. We do not even have a word for it in our tongue. It was bloody, but the flesh men fell, and we hunted them to absolute and utter extinction, long after the war itself had been won.

"Or so we thought.

"It was fifty years later we discovered their 'Answer,' their final escape plan to tear a hole in the universe, and live wherever it led. We excavated what we could from the wreckage of their facility. We saw a plan to not simply escape, but reproduce. To grow an entire new civilization of Exos on the other side of space and time, recovering their strength, re-establishing their empire.

"'Let them go,' some of our leaders said. 'They are worlds away, and only two in a small ship. What threat could they pose?'

"But the rest of us remembered the war. How many were lost and how it might have been us erased, instead of them. And the Exos were a young race. Extremely intelligent. It had taken them barely a few hundred thousand years to grow into a united civilization that almost defeated us. We, the Az'ghal, old as time and death itself. They could not be allowed to breed and thrive and return. They must be destroyed, along with whatever new world they hoped to build.

"It took another hundred years to draft plans for this 'infinity core' and another hundred after that to deduce a way to repeat the exact firing sequence of the original vessel. The Exos believed the core was impossible to control. That they could never be tracked. They were mistaken. The simply had not had enough time to realize the full potential of the device they had created. We ensured they died before they did. It humors me now to hear they thought they were safe. That their children were safe."

"But they only sent you," Erik interrupted.

"The ship we created was small, like theirs. It could house only a single pilot. There were thousands considered, but only I was chosen. I was a scientist, once, though they made me an admiral after the burning of the Gaal Spiral. I understood the technology, and was also prepared for a long hunt, if it came to that. I was our best, sent to chase after theirs.

"We calculated the coordinates and firing sequence correctly, but there was another compounding factor we did not, could not anticipate."

"The time shift," Alpha said slowly. Noah didn't understand.

"When you travel between stars utilizing a normal core," the Archon continued, "it takes months to make a journey that should take years. But the infinity core was different. The journey was over in an instant from my perspective, but when I arrived in this new galaxy, I found that time had fled away from me. Nearly two hundred thousand years had passed since the Exos first departed. When I left, my people were trying to develop prototypes of new infinity core ships. Larger ones that could hold more than one of us. Five, a hundred, an army, eventually. But for all I knew, they could have arrived the next day, in another hundred thousand years, or never. The time shift was impossible to account for. Soon enough, I realized I was truly alone.

"I tracked the Exos ship as I was meant to, but what I found was Sora, in the height of its supposed golden age. Another wretched planet full of Exos, hugely populous and on the verge of countless technological breakthroughs. The kind that put my people in so much danger. It was then I knew my mission was far more important than it had ever been before. The Exos themselves were dust when I found them, and though I tore apart their ship, accessing their files for further information was impossible. I would have to destroy this world alone.

"But soon I deduced it was not the only one. I discovered Thuul next. Its people were primitive, but still Exos. Then hundreds of years later, I found the next colony. And the next. I realized there could be countless fertilized planets, each in various stages of development. Some were empty, extinguished by war and disease. Some had surged ahead and achieved wonders. But none of the few planets I found were a larger threat than this *Sora*. So how does one soul kill a civilization?"

"The way a seed becomes a forest," Alpha said quietly. His gray skin had gone white, and he looked sick.

Sharp laughter.

"Indeed, but my first attempt was clumsier than that. The Sorans had birthed the first few truly intelligent AIs. Moving in shadow, I invaded facilities unseen, rewrote code. Programmed them to be far more clever than their masters anticipated.

"The metal minds were dangerous, but more ineffective than I imagined. And though I set their wrath in motion, I had no control over them. I watched them nearly take the planet, and I watched them fail. All that survived were dismantled, and the technology was outlawed, existing only in black markets and secret laboratories. Too sparse to be used again for an uprising.

"But the Sorans, they were on an eternal quest to create servants to spare them from their dreaded tasks of labor. When the robots did not suffice, they created their organic descendants. The first Xalans.

"These creatures were blank genetic slates. They had the spark of Soran life inside them, but they were docile, harmless. Their intelligence and independence was locked deep away inside them. I sought to unleash it."

"No," Alpha said, stopping him. "It was Zero. The first true Xalan. He shaped us. He put the light in our eyes."

"And who put the light in his?" the Archon scoffed. "Who wrote the genetic mutations into the DNA of the others? The lust for freedom. The capacity for violence. The physical changes. These things did not *evolve*. I engineered them."

What little color Alpha had left drained from his face.

"It was I who sowed the seeds of rebellion, but in the end, the creatures were still too weak. They were cast off to that wretched rock, Xala. But in the end, it was the best gift the Sorans could have given me. There I was free to shape the people to my will. Working through their own leaders, forever shrouded in darkness, never revealing my true intentions. I believed they would not fight and die for me, a stranger from across the stars. But they would for their families. For their pride.

"Over the years I invented the lie that the Xalans were a sovereign race, ravaged by Sora, their planet destroyed and their technology stolen. I cultivated their rage for centuries, whipping up the exploding population into a bloodlust. I whispered in their ear of other planets where Sorans lurked. Thuul, Makari, Earth, and all the rest. We raided those worlds before Sora even knew they existed, and waged a war that Sora never believed we could fight. I gave them technology light-years ahead of their own. I cultivated the best and brightest of them to develop and implement it. And I made sure to cull those who were perhaps *too* intelligent, and more disruptive than useful as a result."

He glanced at Alpha, who was seething.

"But still, it was not fast enough. The Xalans I evolved were war-like, but not yet Az'ghal. I borrowed a trick from the Exos, and started forcing more and more dangerous mutations. What few subjects sur-vived were darkened by the process, but knew unlimited power. First, only strength and speed, but recently the psionic gifts have come."

"The Shadows," Asha said.

"Shadows to his flame," came a whispered voice in the darkness. It was Lucas.

His typing had slowed, and he was listening like the rest of them. There was a dark look in his bright eyes.

"But I realized my task was endless," the Archon continued. "In ten thousand years of searching, I discovered only seven Exos worlds. I stole back to Sora, to this place, and uncovered hints of remaining data that pointed toward a larger, inaccessible cluster of information. One that could only be transported directly into a user's mind. The format implied the data was a map. I knew the Exos would not die and leave no words to their children as to where their brothers and sisters and cousins were all hiding throughout the galaxy.

"I dragged humans, Sorans, Oni, all of the others from every world into this chamber. I forced them into the light, but each was rejected, and I struck them down in turn. I knew the Exos were waiting. Wait-ing for someone with the gift. That was when they would trust their own children enough with the truth. They thought Sora would reach this apex first, which is why they rested here.

"I tried with the one you called the Corsair, the first to survive the Shadow transformation process. But the Exos rejected him all the same, likely due to his madness, or his cloned DNA."

"But not me," Lucas said. "You needed me."

"When you survived, the *human*, I believed I had my key at last. Your massive power only confirmed what I suspected, and by the time we arrived here, I knew victory was at hand. No more need to stalk through the stars, sniffing out the stench of Exos. Now I have a map. And these worlds will fall now more quickly than ever before. I grow old, at last, but now I will see this through. All of New Exos will burn. If my Az'ghal brethren ever arrive, they may not find me, but they will see the ashes of a hundred worlds. They will rejoice in my life's work, and I will live forever, immortalized in legend."

The room was silent as the Archon finished his lengthy, terrible tale. He was the architect of all of this. The doom of one race, and the enslavement of another.

Noah laughed. Everyone turned toward him like he was mad. Perhaps he was. All he could think of was Kyra, and how if she was here, she would likely try and talk the Archon into surrendering, and letting both sides live in peace. *And she probably could do it too.* Noah covered his mouth and blamed his momentary insanity on the blood loss.

"Is the data entered?" the Archon said, taking the scroll from Lucas and projecting a galactic map into the air. A hundred and eight points of green light greeted him.

"It is," Lucas said solemnly.

"If you are lying, it is the woman who dies."

"I'm not."

"Then it is time for your final gift."

Lucas moved quickly, but not faster than the Archon. As if from nowhere, a three-pronged needle appeared in the Archon's clawed hand. Lucas tried to lunge at him, but the Archon caught him by the chest, and the needles dug into his back. Everyone raced forward but were thrown back by a quick pulse of energy. The vials drained neon into Lucas's spine, just between his shoulder blades, and he sagged down to his knees. He fell to his hands, the crest of his head touching the ground.

He lurched, shook, then swung himself upright.

His face was calm.

His skin was charred.

His eyes were blue, and empty.

"Your savior, transformed," the Archon said. His laughter raked through their minds as Lucas stared blankly past all of them. A shadow of a man.

There was an icy chill in the air as they ascended back to the surface. They were lost now, Noah realized as he looked at the faces of Asha and Alpha. Their despair was tangible, and it weighed on all of them as they trudged back up the stone steps of the cathedral. Lucas was gone completely. He placed one foot in front of the other, just as they did, but his gaze was infinite. Perhaps he'd been a twisted man these past few months as the darkness consumed him, but he was still a man. But now? All Noah had to do was steal a glimpse of his eyes, and see that there was none of his father left. *The Corsair lives.* The thought sent shivers through him. His head was still reeling from the fountain of blood that had escaped his neck in the cavern below. It had dried on the front of his armor, and the silver had almost entirely turned crimson.

A ring of Shadows greeted them at the surface, leering at them with sharp teeth, their own confiscated weapons hanging off their plating. Noah eyed his hammer. *One swing*, he thought. One spike into the Archon's face and it could all be over. It was such a simple thought, but one far outside the bounds of possibility.

The group was herded back through the large sandstone doors and out into the red waste of Rhylos. Millions of Xalans greeted them with a chorus of growls and snarls.

"It is done," the Archon said suddenly in their minds, and the minds of the millions before them. Noah noticed the cluster of camerabots was back, streaming their every move to all of Sora, no doubt.

"Their hero is now my herald," the Archon continued, motioning to Lucas, who gazed over the raucous crowd with indifference.

"The conquest begins again, and Xala shall rise not just on this world, but on countless others as well!"

The Xalans didn't know the Archon's truth, revealed down in the pit below, but they cheered the idea of conquest all the same. It was all many of them had ever known. *Az'ghal in training*, Noah thought. But no less dangerous, as they'd shown.

"But first, a demonstration," the Archon said, turning toward their pitiful band. "A lesson to the people of this world that it is useless to resist their own extinction."

He shot a sharp look toward the nearby Xalans who slowly backed outward, forming a circle around them. Only their group and the Archon's Shadow guard remained. Lucas was looking up at the circling funnel of Xalan ships above, immune to what was happening around him.

Another nod from the Archon, and Noah felt a claw sink into his armor plating. He was dragged backward toward the edge of the ring. Erik and Alpha were being wrestled away as well, and soon it was just the Archon, Asha, and Lucas in the center of the red stone floor.

"What's happening?" Erik asked, looking to Alpha, who remained silent. Noah recognized the fear in his face. He didn't even seem to notice the Shadow's claws in his arms, sending trickles of black blood down his skin. He was watching the camerabots, which were all trained on the three figures on the sand.

"A demonstration . . ." he said quietly. "*An execution.*"

Fear seized Noah as well as he suddenly understood what was about to happen.

The Archon started to rise, unaided, into the air. Many Xalans instinctively dropped to their knees, reverent to such power, but their Shadow captors remained upright, their grips iron.

"Citizens of Sora," he said, star-filled eyes swirling. "A test. Your champion, against mine."

Asha looked at him, horrified. Lucas remained expressionless.

"Arm her," the Archon commanded toward a nearby Shadow. The creature took Asha's black sword from his belt and tossed it toward her. It landed with its blade digging into the red stone under the swirling sands.

"Your new High Chancellor, Asha the Earthborn. Adored hero of many worlds, the most fearsome warrior your people have produced in millennia. May she honor you here today."

He turned to the charred man standing across from her.

"And here, her former equal. Now a thousand times her better. Her Lucas. Now *my* Lucas."

Lucas turned at the sound of his name to stare absently at the Archon.

"He can't . . ." Noah began with no one to hear him over the howls of the Xalans.

Asha stared down at the sword sticking out of the ground, and back up at the Archon.

"I won't fight him," she said coldly. "Not for you."

The Archon's sharp laughter raked their minds.

"Of course not for me, Chancellor. For them."

He brought up a trio of floating holoscreens, which showed multiple aerial shots of Elyria. Its streets were filled with military and civilians alike, all staring at viewscreens that were in turn showing Asha watching them. As crowded as the plains of Rhylos were with Xalans, there were three times as many Sorans jammed into Elyria. All standing on top of enough antimatter to obliterate them in seconds.

"Have you forgotten? You are their mother now. And let us not overlook your actual children."

Noah felt his rib cage constrict, like some massive metal snake was wrapped around him, crushing him. He tried to cry out, but the air had already left his lungs. His eyes bulged and he saw Erik struggling in similar pain next to him. The Shadows let both of them drop to their knees, and their bodies twisted in agony. Alpha was making unintelligible sounds and thrashing wildly, trying to free himself to reach them.

And then, the pain was gone, and Noah panted with his nose nearly touching the sand. He looked up and saw the fear in Asha's eyes.

"Slowly," the Archon said to Lucas. "Give the appearance of a contest, at least."

The blank look on Lucas's face was suddenly replaced by something far worse. Fury. Without hesitation, he leapt toward the woman he once loved.

"Lucas, wait!" she cried in the split second before he reached her.

But Asha didn't have time to consider any more principled stands. She whipped her sword out of the ground and used the flat of the blade to deflect a thunderous punch from Lucas. The impact sent her cartwheeling across the desert floor, and the area was now buzzing with the sounds of the Xalans beating on their armor plating with their claws. The camerabots weaved around each other to catch every angle of the spectacle.

Asha leapt to her feet but Lucas was on her already. Noah had never seen anything move so fast. Not even the last Corsair. Asha took a forearm smash that visibly cracked the armor on her abdomen and sent her skidding across the ground. Somehow, she kept a grip on her sword and used the pommel to deflect a kick from the instantly appearing Lucas, who was immediately at her side again, no matter how far she was thrown. His eyes were molten, his movements precise and mechanical.

A lightning fast series of punches landed all over Asha and she was visibly bloodied by the end of the barrage. Lucas leveled a straight kick at her, but she found the strength to leap over the top of him, assisted by her barely functional power armor. She looped her sword around so the flat of the blade struck his back. It did nothing, naturally, but a quick flick of her thumb sent electricity surging through Lucas, and his back arched in momentary pain.

Noah's first instinct was to cheer, but he realized it wasn't some monster she was fighting. It was his father. *No, it isn't*, said a voice in his mind. *Not anymore.*

"Lucas, stop!" she cried again as he convulsed, keeping his feet.

Though the shock had stunned Lucas for a half second, it had no lingering effects, nor did her words. He whipped around and caught Asha in the jaw with a kick that sent her spiraling end over end before she crashed awkwardly to the desert floor. He followed up with a sharp kick to her ribs that lofted her into the air before he smashed her back down with two fists to her spine. She'd lost her sword now, and scrambled for it, wincing in pain, bleeding from a dozen places.

Her fingers found the handle and she whipped it around toward him. She slashed left and right as she backed away, but Lucas dodged each swing with ease. Finally, the razor's edge nearly caught his throat, but the blade appeared frozen. Shifting his position, Noah realized Lucas had actually caught the sword in between his thumb and forefinger.

No one is that fast, Noah thought. Even the Xalans were stunned, and momentarily ceased their clanging.

Asha wasted no time, however, flicking the pommel again. But Lucas released his grip before the electricity found him, and kicked Asha in the chest as she and the crackling sword flew away from him.

The fight was leaving her now. Noah could see it in her unfocused eyes. She scrambled backward as Lucas approached, walking at a leisurely pace this time. Asha tried to cry out, but couldn't find her voice amid bruised lungs and broken ribs. She held the sword aloft, but there was a whir of motion, and Lucas kicked the blade downward into the sand. It flew from her grip and bounced on the stone. When it came to a rest, the darksteel blade was bent to a painful angle.

Asha looked as battered as her weapon. She struggled to her feet, but was helped by Lucas, his hand locked around her throat. His grip bent the metal plating on her armor inward, and his eyes burned with rage. Only strangled gasps escaped from Asha's throat.

Noah couldn't hear what he was shouting, nor did he feel the claws of the Shadow digging through his armor and into his flesh as he thrashed violently against his grip. Lucas turned his head slowly toward the Archon, who nodded approvingly.

A single word escaped from Asha's collapsing throat, her green eyes brimming with blood and tears.

42

"Lucas!"

Lucas blinked.

Where was he? The last thing he remembered was a cave. Pain in his back. His head was swimming. He could hear primal shouts and screams around him, but everything was a bleary mess.

"Lucas."

His eyes started focus. The voice. It called to him through the darkness. What had he dreamt about? He was fighting bandits, cannibals, Xalans, Shadows, the Archon himself. But that wasn't real, was it?

"Lucas . . ."

The voice was growing fainter now. The light crept into his eyes and he saw a shape above him. *An angel,* he thought. But it was Asha, in all her radiance. Those heartstopping light green eyes. That knowing smile, the one she showed only to him.

But no. There was no smile. And her beautiful eyes were marred with black-and-brown bruises, her tearducts filled with blood.

He looked down and saw his own arm was raised, and his hand was a vice around her neck. The green irises disappeared as her eyes rolled back into her head.

"No!" he cried out, all of his senses returning in full at once. He dropped her immediately, and she collapsed to the ground in a heap, gasping for air. There was blood on the sand. So much blood.

"Finish her," came the cold voice in his mind. He bent down to help Asha, and turned to find the Archon hovering behind him. One look at him, and the Archon knew Lucas had returned to fill his body once more.

"Impossible . . ."

The Archon extended his clawed hand.

But before he could rip either of them apart, something screamed in the distant horizon. Ships. A sky full of ships.

The SDI and resistance fleets had formed a giant floating spear. They sped toward the tornado of Xalan vessels above them, and all Xalan eyes turned toward the fleet. But on the cliffs in the distance, Lucas saw the shimmer of silver-and-pearl SDI ground armor taking up positions around the Xalan encampment.

"They come at last," the Archon said, the last-ditch attack clearly not a surprise. "Annihilate them," he said to the millions around him. Ships started breaking off the vortex formation to meet the Sorans and Xalans in the open sky. This was it then, the last hope. Lucas counted the ships in an instant. It was nearly everything they had.

He also calculated that it wasn't enough. Sora had lost too much in the reclamation assault, and were dramatically outnumbered. They'd lost the element of surprise as well. This was desperation, pure and simple. Lucas eyed the lead ship, a Guardian dreadnought. Kiati was undoubtedly inside. He spotted Tau's hulking destroyer and Toruk's long-winged bomber. They were all there. Every last one. And they were about to be reduced to ash.

"You did it," came a weak voice from the ground. "I knew you could come back." Asha smiled through chipped teeth. Lucas felt like he was about to collapse. Had he really done this to her?

"*My god*," he said, cradling her as gently as he could manage in his charred arms. He could taste the ash on his lips. "I'm so sorry. I didn't—"

"It's up to you now," she interrupted, looking up at the two fleets about to collide. The Xalans were taking up defensive positions all around them, guarding against the aggressors on the cliffs.

Looking at Asha's broken form, Lucas had never felt more pain than he did at that moment. His chest heaved with sorrow and anger, he was shaking uncontrollably.

"Use it," she said, brushing his cheek with bloodstained fingers. Flecks of ash fell off his skin like snowflakes.

He saw himself in her eyes. His face burnt to cinders. His eyes shards of blue ice. But as he focused, they grew lighter. And lighter. Asha's pupils shrank from their brilliance.

Lucas didn't need to utter a word this time. He simply stood up, and the world exploded.

Something shot through the Xalan troops like a wave, and all around them, gray and black creatures clutched their heads like something was trying to claw its way out of their skulls. They fell out of formation, and many began writhing on the ground.

Above, enemy Xalan ships began weaving oddly in the sky. A few crashed into one another, and some simply fell straight down. The break in formation was enough for the SDI to unleash an enormous barrage of ordnance against the much larger force, and the Xalan front line evaporated in a string of explosions.

On the ground, Lucas watched as his sons wrenched their weapons away from the crippled Shadows who were also clutching their heads. Noah drove the spike of his hammer through the chest of his captor, and Erik split the head of his Shadow with a bright gold laser. Even Alpha found a way to slit the throat of his guard with his mechanical claw.

It all had taken place in just a few seconds. The Archon looked around at his crumbling army with wide eyes, the stars shrunken into pinpoints.

"No!" the Az'ghal cried out, and in an instant, he was on Lucas.

Lucas didn't feel the needles of the claws until they pierced his heart. The last thing he saw was Asha's face, eyes closed, half buried in bloody sand.

He woke in the crater.

It was empty, all shifting sand mixed with the scattered metal bones of long-dead buildings. Portland. Where it all started.

Sometimes he wondered if he had died that day. If when he'd put his rifle in his mouth, he'd pulled the trigger, instead of seeing the flickering lights of Alpha's ship buried in the sand. Maybe all of this was a dream. Maybe all of this had been hell the entire time.

But no, that would be too easy.

He could see his breath in the night air. He walked along the sand, his ashen feet leaving black footprints in his wake.

Is this it then? Is this what death feels like?

Was he a part of the Circle now? Trapped on some plane of the Archon's consciousness? A lonely prison for the powerful. Then where were the others?

But in the distance, three familiar shades danced through the shifting shadows. Their wispy white robes fluttered in a breeze he couldn't feel. He walked toward them.

"Please," he said, almost sobbing. "I need help."

The three turned toward him. Cora, Natalie, Sonya. Their faces beautiful, this time. Sorrowful, not stern.

"Forgive me," he said. "Forgive me for all I've done."

"That is not for us to give," said Corinthia.

"I want to let it go," Lucas said. "All the pain. I don't want it anymore."

"We cannot free you of it," Natalie said.

"Tell me how," Lucas pleaded.

"You know," said Sonya. She smiled a sad smile, and drifted close to kiss him on the cheek. The touch of her lips was ice.

Lucas turned and found another shade. This one shrouded in darkness and twisting shadow.

"Forgive me," he asked Asha. "For all the pain I've caused."

Blood trickled from her eyes, nose, and mouth.

"I am not your answer, either," she said, shaking her head.

"You brought me back. You can free me," he said, shaking.

"Only one person can do that."

She kissed him as well. Only her lips burned.

And then she was gone, and Lucas was alone.

He turned, and found him. Found them.

It was him, clad in a stiff shirt and tie, a typical workday before the war. His jaw was lined with a five o'clock shadow. There was vodka on his breath.

But then next to him, another vision. This one a gaunt survivor with hollow cheeks and a swollen stomach. He wore camouflage pants and held a dusty assault rifle with a name etched into the stock.

And next to him, a regal-looking man in a high-collared suit with piercing eyes and well-combed hair. How he'd been presented to the Soran public when he'd first arrived.

Then next to that one, a stern-faced soldier, clad in blood-spattered armor, the kind he'd worn on the suicide mission to Xala. In his arms he held his famed rifle, its casing cracked and core smoking.

In the center of them all, the dark one. The one he didn't want to look at. Blue eyes blazed in the dim light of the crater.

"You know," they said together. "Who you must forgive."

All of the men before him, all the versions of himself had done terrible, awful things at one time or another. They'd turned their back on friends and family, risking their lives or getting them killed. These versions of him had murdered dozens, hundreds, even thousands to survive. Lucas had carried the oppressive, unyielding weight of that for a long time.

Too long.

He searched inside himself and found the nest of pain in his heart that had spread to every inch of him.

"Forgive yourself," the figures said in unison. "And be free of it."

He found the vile ball of hate and pain and guilt inside him, and felt it dissolve into nothing. The black tendrils retracted from his insides. They released his heart, his mind. They had no more power over him.

Lucas was free.

"Now you understand," said Mars Maston, standing in front of him, the other figures gone. He was flanked by Omicron, the Desecrator, and at least a dozen other pairs of blue eyes in the darkness.

"I would not have guessed it possible," Omicron mused.

"The Archon must die," the Desecrator said sharply.

"And he shall," Maston said.

"I *don't* understand," Lucas protested. "What have I done?" He looked around the crater. It was still barren, but he could see the sun rising now over the lip of the looming wall across from him.

"You've bent the Circle," Maston said.

"What does that mean?" Lucas asked.

"Open your eyes, and learn," Omicron said.

Lucas did.

Maston and the Shadows stood before him, though the crater was gone and replaced with the Rhylosi red waste. The Xalans had recovered and were now engaged in a heated ground and aerial battle with countless SDI troops. The floating holoscreens that once showed Elyria now were blank white squares of static, and every so often one was pierced by a passing plasma round. The Archon was hovering above the fray, mentally shouting orders Lucas could hear in his own mind. Lucas watched him thrust his claw upward and psionically shear a passing SDI fighter in half.

Turning around, Lucas saw Alpha helping Asha to her feet, Noah and Erik defending them from the Xalan horde. Half of Noah's armor had been torn off, and the exposed skin of his arm and shoulder was almost entirely covered in blood. Alpha's hand was pressed to a horrible-looking plasma burn on his abdomen. Erik's face was a mess, and it looked like he might have lost an eye. But all were upright and fighting. Asha looked worse than any of them, but she caught his glance and smiled weakly as she leaned on Alpha for support.

Lucas looked down at his hands. The ash flakes that coated his skin were peeling off and floating up toward the sky. Underneath was soft, pale flesh. Smooth and unblemished. He felt his face, and found more ash rising from his skin.

"A cure . . ." he said breathlessly.

"A weapon," Maston replied, still standing in front of him with the others.

"I don't understand," Lucas said, looking across the group of Shadows in front of him. "Are you . . ."

"The Circle is bent," the Desecrator rumbled. "Let us break it."

There was a wall of about five hundred Xalans between them and the Archon, but the Shadows tore through the blockade of metal and flesh like paper. Father and son, Omicron and the Desecrator, were a blur of claws and teeth, shredding Xalan armor and tearing any creature limb from limb that got in their way. The other unnamed Shadows, at one time executed by the Archon, fanned outward and ripped into the Xalan army. Lucas watched as two took down one of the Archon's muscled Shadow personal guards, and soon the warrior was nothing more than a torso.

Lucas walked calmly through the chaos, unable to tear his eyes away from his newfound pink skin. No shots hit him, and every Xalan that drew close was ripped back and mangled by a summoned Shadow. Lucas followed behind Omicron, the Desecrator, and Maston, who were cleaving a path toward the Archon up ahead. Maston was without claws, but held a knife nearly as long as his forearm, and it served the same purpose. He hacked and slashed his way through Xalans left and right, though no drops of black blood ever touched his pristine uniform. Lucas swore he heard him laughing.

The Xalans thinned out and the path to the Archon himself was clear. He turned to Lucas and the advancing Shadows.

"It cannot be," he said, fear in his voice.

His tone changed to a snarl.

"You will die here today with the rest of your wretched Exos!"

Lucas walked toward him as Shadows tore Xalans out of his way.

"Only one race faces extinction in this galaxy," he said coldly. "The Az'ghal."

The Desecrator launched himself into the air on his long, furious insect wings. His jaws caught the Archon's shoulder and he tore at the meat, sending dark blood spraying into the air. The Archon had no mouth, but Lucas heard him scream all the same. The pair tumbled down to the ground, where Omicron leapt on the Archon and plunged a black claw into his gut with a fearsome war cry. Mars Maston was last to arrive, his enormous knife diving down into the Az'ghal's chest. The Archon's featureless face contorted in agony, and the immortal took his final breath.

"Lucas!" came a shout from behind him. He turned.

It was Asha, being helped by Alpha and Noah with Erik close by. All wore stunned looks.

He turned back toward the Archon. There was nothing but a corpse on the ground, surrounded by silver-black blood, its galactic eyes now completely dark. Maston and the others were gone. Looking around, Lucas saw no more Shadows. Only the bodies of the Xalans they'd butchered.

"What happened?" Noah asked, clutching his injured arm. "How did you do that?"

"The Shadows . . ." Lucas stammered, "Didn't you see?"

Everyone looked at each other blankly.

"You tore them all apart," Erik said, his face a mask of blood. "Didn't you?"

"No, I—" Lucas turned around again. Mars Maston was right in front of him, completely undisheveled. Even his knife was spotless.

"Was the Circle even real?" Lucas asked him, suddenly confused.

Maston smiled, and then vanished.

The Archon's black, dead eyes watched the tatters of his fleet flee overhead, now lost without direction, pursued mercilessly by the SDI. On the ground, Xalans stepped on his corpse as they sprinted across the sands, but those who would not surrender would find no quarter on Sora.

Lucas looked toward his family and caught Asha as she staggered over to him.

"It's over," she said. He held her until the first Soran ships touched down around them.

Epilogue

Peace is more difficult than war, Alpha mused as he rubbed his temples, sitting at the far end of a long, elaborately carved tulwood table inlaid with holographic projectors. Through the dancing maps and documents made of light, the other participants at the summit could be seen. Men and Xalans alike sat together at one table. *That much is progress, at least*, he thought.

The war was over, at last. Though not without cost.

It was unknown precisely how many had died in the Archon's invasion of Sora, but the toll was in the billions for both races. That included the nearly two hundred million whose ashes rested in the great interlocking craters of Elyria, the city vaporized by the Archon in the moments before his death. For all they'd done to stop him, they couldn't save Sora's greatest metropolis, nor all those who had taken shelter there. It weighed heavily on Alpha, and he often thought if he'd stayed behind, perhaps he could have disabled the explosives in time. *There is no point dwelling on what might have been*, he constantly told himself, but the thought was still hard to shake. He was alive, his friends and family were as well, and that would have to be enough.

The destruction of Elyria was why they were now gathered in a new space station constructed to house representatives of both races, to try and come together and learn how to live in peace.

There was no more High Chancellor of Sora, nor a new Ruling Council of Xalans. There was only the Forum, a collection of hundreds of Xalans and Sorans, with a few Oni members as well. And, as their population grew, Earth's humans would come to be represented. Getting so many to agree on anything was difficult, if not often impossible, but it was a preferred alternative to giving individuals the power to control entire planets, as far too many had abused their station recently between Talis Vale, Madric Stoller, and the Archon's puppets on the Council. Progress was slow this way, but healing had begun.

"Can you update us on the status of the Makari settlements?" a slim, dark woman asked Toruk. She was a representative from one of the larger Soran continents, but Alpha couldn't recall the name.

"We have finished dividing the regrown northern forests," Toruk answered, clad in his finest bone armor for the formal occasion. Alpha thought he looked rather out of place in the room, but he supposed he wasn't one to talk. He flittered his six metal fingers across the tabletop.

"There have been a few shouting matches, but nothing insurmountable," the Oni chieftain continued. He grew more eloquent by the day.

"Some Oni have begun teaching the Xalans how to hunt and fish in the forests," Zeta added helpfully. Alpha's mate had spent most of the year since the war's end helping with the integration of Makari. Her remark drew a few snorts from some of the Xalans present, but Alpha silenced them with a sharp look.

"And what of Earth?" Maeren Stoller asked. Madric Stoller had retired from public life, escaping criminal charges in the process, but his daughter remained a military fixture. She had no desire to rule, however, and seemed far more grounded than her father.

"The new colony there has been established," Alpha answered. "The climate has normalized in enough areas to make habitation viable again. Readings indicate the rest of the planet will heal in time, though it will take many decades yet. Keeper Auran should be arriving there shortly to supervise the young ones."

"Xala is progressing as well," General Tau chimed in, his voice two octaves lower than anyone else in the room. With his strength, the Shadow could have easily tried to seize power for himself in the wake of the war, but he remained committed to cooperation, and to putting his days of killing behind him. Alpha had been working on a cure to try to reverse what had been done to him and the few remaining Shadows that hadn't turned outlaw and fled to the stars.

Alpha nodded.

"The limited reproduction of the Archon's terraformers has proven fruitful in select areas. The technology is at least one gift the monster left us."

Xala was still a cesspool, and largely abandoned now as its people fled to the other planets in the quadrant, but Alpha was determined to revive it. He might not live to see it thrive, but perhaps his children would. Or his grandchildren after them. He'd recently returned from a visit to his former homeworld, and found his breath taken away at the sight of a small grove of stunted trees growing in the courtyard of the shuttered Genetic Science Enclave. It was perhaps a pathetic cluster of botany, but it was the most green he'd seen in one place on Xala his entire life.

"I know no one wants to bring this up," said Grand Admiral Kiati, her fiery hair pulled into high ponytail, her hands folded across her chestplate. "But we need to talk about Lucas. Are we sure he's ready for this new mission? After all this time, we still don't really understand what happened in Rhylos."

"He is ready," Alpha said firmly. "They both are."

"But you've seen the footage," a sharp-featured man said, some ambassador from the Broken Shore. "You've seen what he did."

Alpha had, in addition to watching it unfold live. The archived video was chilling. In it, Lucas walked through the army of Xalans as they all were sliced to pieces around him as if by invisible blades. The camerabots' feed was cut before the death of the Archon himself, so that remained a mystery to most. But not Alpha; he'd seen the creature fall.

"The man was afflicted with powers no mortal being should ever know," he said. "That is behind him now."

Alpha didn't know how to rationalize Lucas's story about the Circle of Shadows, including Omicron, the Desecrator, and Mars Maston appearing to dismantle the Archon and his army. He wasn't sure Lucas knew what to make of it either, and some doors were better left closed.

"But you have been monitoring him?" An older, wrinkled Xalan with violet rings in her eyes spoke up from across the table. "He has stabilized? He is fully cured?"

"The data shows nothing out of the ordinary," Alpha reassured his audience. *That is not strictly true,* he thought, but even he didn't understand certain fluctuations in Lucas's biological readouts. But for all intents and purposes, his friend was himself again. *There is still blue in his eyes,* Alpha thought, thinking of the bright, microscopic flecks drifting in pools of gray. But again, there was no need to raise alarm, not given the task Lucas had been assigned now, in any case. It was too important, and no one was better suited.

"We are coming to the end of our session," Alpha said, eyeing a holographic time readout. "Damage assessment updates will be on the docket first thing tomorrow morning. I am postponing settlement transport conflicts until the following day."

That brought a loud chorus of annoyed groans from the room, and Alpha simply shook his head and waved his claws. The holographic table shut down and slowly the makeshift government stopped griping and moved toward the exits.

Alpha felt a claw on his shoulder, and turned to find Zeta smiling with her soft blue eyes.

"You are doing your best with them," she said. "It is all that can be expected of you."

"This damnable string of crises will never end," he said, sighing.

"It is a welcome substitute for war," Zeta said. "No one dies from arguing over trade disputes or settlement integration procedures."

"Not yet, anyway," Alpha said. "In any case, hopefully matters will normalize by the time our daughter has grown."

"Or perhaps our son," Zeta said, placing a claw softly on her protruding abdomen. Alpha put his lone organic hand on top of hers.

"Yes," he said warmly. "Indeed."

"Have you heard from Theta?" Zeta said, her tone tinged with worry.

"A week ago," Alpha said, surveying the darkened room and Sora slowly spinning outside. "She says they will return to Earth soon, though she failed to mention where she was presently. Naturally, she has blocked her tracking signal. I have taught her too well."

"She is just experiencing life, I suppose," Zeta said. "We should at least allow her that, after all she has endured."

"I would prefer her to experience life in the company of someone less foolhardy," Alpha grumbled. But he looked at Zeta, round with child, bathed in the glow of Sora, and couldn't be anything other than content.

—

"Can you still hear me?" Theta asked. Even in the middle of the club floor with deep bass pumping all around him, her voice was still deafening in Erik's ear.

"I said yes," he said, clutching the ear painfully. "I told you, I'll signal you when I'm at the door."

Erik muted her to avoid any further damage to his eardrum and kept pushing his way through the lively crowd. His face was lightmasked; a holographic image covered his features thanks to a small piece of metal clipped to his hairline. It would have been conspicuous if nearly everyone else in the club wasn't wearing something similar due to the theme of the night. "Glowface," they called it, and it was supposed to be delightful when you were buzzing on a cocktail of alcohol and Paradise.

But Erik was stone sober.

He shoved his way through writhing bodies until a flailing pair of girls blocked his way. Their dancing was occasionally rhythmic, but disjointed enough that the influence of narcotics was obvious. One with neon pink hair, wearing little more than silk bandages and lightbands, caught him by the shoulder and started gyrating in his direction. She peered into his brightly lit face, her nose an inch from his own.

"Heyyy," she said slowly, peering into his eyes. "Aren't you—"

"Busy," he said, placing his hands on her shoulders and herding her in the direction of her equally scantily clad friend.

Finally, Erik reached the edge of the dance floor and ducked behind the main stage, where performers were waving their hands through the air, playing various virtual instruments that produced the music of the evening. Elyria was no more, but its nightlife scene had moved across the border to nearby King's Falls, a waterside metropolis guarding the largest river on the continent. It had taken him a long time to find this specific club, but he wasn't interested in the party downstairs.

"I'm here," he whispered into the air, shoving a door open. The hallway was brightly lit compared to the dance floor, and it momentarily burned his eyes. His right one was still light sensitive a year later; he'd had to get it regrown after it had been gouged by a rogue Xalan claw in Rhylos. It was a more painful process than his fingers had been, and the socket still itched terribly.

"There's a problem," he said, eyeing a rather large pair of men standing next to a rather large pair of metal doors at the end of the hall. "There wasn't supposed to be anyone down here."

"It must be an unscheduled change," she said. "Perhaps he is paranoid."

Or just smart, Erik thought.

"You sure the cameras are looped?"

"They are . . . now," she said. And that was good enough for him.

Erik adopted a drunken stagger and stumbled toward the towering security guards. The man on the right held his hand up even as he was still twenty feet away.

"You can't be in here," he said through the grating of a metal helmet. "I'm going to have to ask you to exit the way you entered."

"I saw her come thisssway," Erik slurred, looking around confused. "She wasss coming home wit' me." A fake hiccup followed.

The other guard approached now and the two took him by either arm.

"Come on, lighthead," one said. "I'm sure you'll find another one out there."

"Your armor is so *smooth,*" Erik said, falsely delirious, widening his eyes and running his palm across the plated forearm of the taller guard, sliding it toward the pistol attached to his ribcage.

"Don't—Hey!" the guard exclaimed as he realized what was happening.

Erik had grown four inches the past year. He was taller. Stronger. Faster. And this was far from his first fight since the war ended.

In a split second, the pistol was out, and the first guard crumbled after a stun round pierced his helmet. At close range, the protective metal did nothing. The other guard drew his weapon, but Erik slammed the butt of the pistol into his wrist, which caused him to lose his grip. He reached for the much larger rifle on his back, but Erik shot him in the leg, making his armor seize up and lock tight. The guard cried out as he stumbled to the left against the wall, and Erik blasted the side of his head with another blue flash of light.

"No one saw that, right?" he asked the air. No alarms were sounding at least.

"No one except for me," Theta said. The metal doors opened, and there she was.

The white Xalan had also grown, nearly reaching seven feet now. *The cameras had better be looped*, Erik thought, *since you don't get more suspicious than a snow-white Xalan wandering your back hallways.* He trusted her word that security was down, and there were no more guards coming out of the woodwork to apprehend them. She had a full view of every hallway on a scroll in front of her, and nothing was amiss despite Erik's colorful entrance. He joined Theta in the lift. She had rigged the controls with an electronic crack, and soon they were rocketing up to the restricted penthouse floor. She'd entered through the fifth subbasement, where the security junctions were housed. It was a bit less obvious than moving through the dance floor. Erik had confirmed with enough of the patrons that he was indeed there. Supposedly he'd thrown a massive party in the suite barely twelve hours ago.

Retirement suited Madric Stoller.

The door opened, and four armored guards in the hallway turned to see the First Son of Sora and a pure white Xalan standing in the lift. Before one even uttered a syllable into their comm, Theta opened her claw and out sprang four small silver discs that whizzed magnetically to the breastplates of each of the guards. In half a second, their armor was completely locked down from a fizzling electric pulse, and the discs had drilled micro-holes through the plating to deliver quick puffs of naxgas inside the suits. All fell together in unison.

"I designed those myself," she said proudly as she casually strode through the contorted bodies. "They will not wake for hours, and will have to manually pry themselves out of their armor." Her translator made a noise that might have been a giggle.

Be that as it may, Erik didn't want to take more than a few minutes.

A larger disc with a lockcrack inside opened the final set of doors, and they strode into a dark, lavish penthouse suite that had a gorgeous view of what used to be Elyria, but was now cluster of craters formed out of the ashes of the dead.

Theta found the data core almost instantly, a small but elaborate piece of machinery.

"I shouldn't have brought you," Erik said, looking around the empty suite cautiously.

"This is why I am here," Theta said firmly. "His financial security measures cannot be compromised remotely."

She knelt in front of the core and began furiously typing into the holographic controls. She bypassed the login instantly, and began to dive deep into the annals of the core.

Erik walked around the common area of the suite, almost tripping over empty bottles of enormously expensive vaporwine. On every flat surface lay at least a handful of vials used to ingest any number of illegal substances, and there wasn't a piece of furniture that wasn't stained with some kind of liquid. Erik stared at the craters through the thirty-foot windows. They were lit by excavation crews, still digging for charred bones a year later. And they were still finding plenty, the Stream said.

"Where am I diverting the funds, again?" Theta asked, her face lit up by the glow of the core.

"Dump everything into the Reconstruction and Restoration Fund," Erik said. "Make it from a few thousand sources, though, and impossible to revert."

"Everything?" Theta said, gold-ringed eyes wide.

Erik grinned.

"Well, maybe carve out a bit for us too."

Theta nodded.

"Will a hundred thousand marks suffice?"

Erik cocked his head.

"Let's make it an even hundred million. That still leaves a few trillion or so for charity."

Theta tapped a few more keys, and Madric Stoller's accounts, legal and illegal, evaporated in microseconds. *Sorry about your inheritance, Finn*, Erik thought. *But I have a family to support.*

He'd go back to Earth soon, he thought. He just had to take care of this first. The money would do wonders for the new colony, his children. All the children. That much he could give them, at least, though he knew it would be some time before he could truly become a father. *If ever*, he thought. *They're better off with Noah.*

"You're running," Noah had told him when he left. "The war is over."

It wasn't. Not for Erik. One more guilty party had to pay. After everything Madric Stoller had done, Erik knew it was up to him to be the hand of fate, rebalancing the scale.

He started walking up the curved glass staircase in the foyer.

"*Erik*," Theta hissed through her translator. "*Don't. The funds are disbursed. We can depart without issue.*"

"You can," Erik said, looking down at her. "I can't."

He tried to ignore the sadness in her golden eyes.

Entering the suite's bedchamber, he gingerly stepped over a naked girl on the floor, lying next to a drying clump of vomit. She was breathing, but unconscious.

The second girl was nearly enveloped in the folds of Stoller himself. He lay on the bed like some fleshy, cancerous tumor. Mercifully, a robe the size of a tent covered most of him. He'd practically doubled in girth since his last public appearance, gorging himself on every pleasure imaginable, if the disaster of the hotel penthouse was any indication. He snored through his thick mustache, and his gold-rimmed glasses were askew on his face. The girl had tan skin with thick black hair, and Noah counted more than a handful of bruises across her face and chest. A distinctive sunburst tattoo on her collar indicated she wasn't a mere partygoer, but had at one point been the property of a Solarion trafficking gang.

Noah drew the heavy pistol from under his long-tail coat. It was practically a relic, rusted and worn, but it still worked. Tannon's father had carried it to war and back, as had he. Now it would avenge him, along with all the crimes that had been carried out against Lucas, Asha, Alpha, the Earthborn. And her. Especially her.

She didn't love you, a voice said in his head. *Not like she loved him.*

It doesn't matter, he told himself, and cocked the gun. Pale red lights came alive on either side of the metal.

"It's time," Erik said out loud. Stoller stirred, and then woke, blinking sleepily through heavy lids. His eyes widened, seeing Erik standing over him, pistol raised. He adjusted his glasses instinctively.

"Erik?" he said, alarmed. "How did—? Guards!"

No one came. No one would. Even the girl nestled in his armpit didn't stir as he bolted upright.

"What do you want?" Stoller asked, realizing what had likely befallen his security detail.

"Justice," Erik said through gritted teeth. The gun was heavy, and it drifted a foot from Stoller's bloated face.

"This is a misunderstanding," Stoller said, instantly on the verge of tears. "Is this about the girl? The clone?"

That earned him a sharp rap with the butt of the pistol, which broke the bridge of his stubbed nose and snapped his glasses in half.

"She had a name," Erik said as Stoller wailed, clutching his bloodied nose.

"Please, son!" he cried. "The war has ended!"

"So they keep telling me."

"This is a time for peace, forgiveness!"

Erik glanced at the bruised sex slave next to Stoller, who was still motionless. It didn't look like the events of the evening had been very peaceful.

"I am not your son," he said coldly.

"You are not," Madric Stoller said, his tone darkening after seeing the look in Erik's eyes. "I would *never* allow a son of mine to carry on with a wretched, soulless, cloned whore!"

"She had a name," Erik said flatly.

462

The flash of the barrel lit up the room, but the sound still didn't rouse the unconscious figures sleeping in shadow.

Theta greeted him with a grim look as he came back down the stairs. But he caught a gleam of triumph in her eyes.

"Is it done?" she asked, her question answered by the flecks of blood on his clothing. He nodded.

"Where to now?" he asked, wiping off his face with a discarded shirt hanging off the back of a chair.

"Anywhere," Theta said breathlessly, turning pale pink in the darkness. "Earth?" she suggested.

"Earth can wait," Erik said, looking out into the night sky over the Elyrian craters. "Zaela says SolSec is trying to take back the station. And I hear the Fourth Order has reformed in the north of Rhylos."

"Old enemies," Theta said.

"New battles," Erik said, arms folded, staring at the stars. "And someone needs to fight them."

—

Bali was beautiful.

The island chain was one of the first to reappear as the oceans slowly filled in after months of targeted torrential downpours on Earth. The terraformers were slowly reshaping the planet, and they'd been assured that the water level would rise no further in this area once called "Indonesia" before the planet's destruction.

The new colony had been planted on the top of a burned city, now leveled and cleared away. The palm trees were small, but growing quickly thanks to genetic enhancement, and soon the jungles of the island would be lush again. Someday, perhaps the same could be said of the rest of the planet.

Noah had healed as well, after spilling a worrying amount of blood in Rhylos before the SDI crushed the last of the Archon's forces. Noah's arm had been torn up with shrapnel, but all of it had since been removed and his marred skin regrown. By twist of fate, the injury was also on his burned side, the injury he'd carried with him since his initial escape from Earth as an infant. But now all those scars were finally gone, the area smooth. The new skin still felt stranger than the deformity. He'd borne that mark a long time.

Noah walked through what had been developed as a town square in their little micro village. Though there were only a few more than thirty of the original Earthborn, there were now nearly three times that many human children there as well, rescued from Colony Two, with a few more born in the year since. Gone were their Soran caretakers, as they were all considered adults now. Here they grew their own food, completed their own chores, and did so using only minimal amounts of machinery. It was a more primal sort of life than they'd been used to, but Noah was relieved to be picking fruit instead of crushing heads with his hammer. The weapon hung over the mantle of his small wooden house, and he hoped he'd never wield it again.

Not to say there was no conflict. There was still an arena in town where the Earthborn would spar for fun or to settle disputes. With Erik gone, no one had broken any bones to date. Noah had been challenged a few times, but remained resistant to the idea for a long while. Finally, a few weeks ago he allowed Wuhan to pull him into the ring for old time's sake. An hour later, both were bruised, exhausted, and laughing painfully through aching ribs.

Two children sprinted by, skipping over the cobblestone with little regard for pedestrian traffic. Erik's twins, Noah knew, just by the backs of their heads. In fact, six of the children here were Erik's, from four different Earthborn girls.

No wonder he fled, Noah said, but perhaps that wasn't fair. Few had endured as much as Erik, and he would allow his brother some time to sail the stars if that's what would help heal him.

This was all Noah needed.

"Daddy!" came a voice behind him. Little Kyoto was nearly three now, named after a city from his mother's home country. In his hand was that of the unsteady year-and-a-half-old Halden, named for a city in Norway, where Noah had been born amid ash and flame. They were his only two, and they were enough. Kyoto was dark-haired like his mother, but as tall as Noah had been at that age. Conversely,

Halden was blond but tiny. Both were worryingly interested in the practice weapons around the arena, however, and Noah had caught them attacking rocks with sword-like twigs on more than one occasion, giggling wildly to themselves.

"They found you," said Sakai, drawing up behind them. Her once-voluminous hair had been cut short, and her tan skin had darkened further in the sun.

"They did," he said, smiling.

It had been a long journey for the pair of them to find common ground again, but with two shared children in their lives, they were trying to settle back into an old rhythm. But Noah knew she still hurt, and she had to know that he did as well. Kyra didn't consume his mind anymore, but still, rarely a day passed where he didn't think of her at least once. If he escaped dwelling on her during the day, she'd almost always appear in his dreams.

He was letting go, slowly. But he wasn't sure what would ever truly heal that wound.

"Are you still headed to the mountain?" Sakai asked, eyeing the path ahead.

"I'll be quick," Noah said.

"I want to come!" Kyoto said. Halden just giggled.

"When you're older," Noah said. "It's very windy with lots of sharp rocks."

"I'm not afraid," Kyoto said matter-of-factly. Halden mimicked his brother's sternness by crossing his arms.

"I know," Noah said.

"I'm gonna be a Guardian someday," the boy said.

"Or a very talented silvercoat," Sakai interjected.

"No, a Guardian!" Kyoto pouted. "Like gramma Asha."

"You can be anything," Noah said, putting his hand on his tiny shoulder. Sakai rolled her eyes, and led them away. She turned back and a quick smile escaped her lips.

The mountain was not all that dangerous, in truth. It lacked the steep slope of the rock that had held the White Spire back on Sora, and was more just a rather large hill. Still, it was where Noah went to think. And pray.

But there are no gods, he constantly told himself. Even so, he routinely sat down on a makeshift prayer stone and spoke to them all the same. Perhaps it was tradition, or perhaps he didn't mind praying to dead ancestors instead of actual gods. Sometimes he imagined he could speak to Tannon again. Or Celton. Or her. Sometimes he swore they spoke back.

When he arrived this time, he was surprised to find his stone already occupied. Malorious Auran sat on the smooth rock, his legs not folded in prayer, but hanging over the edge, his hands on his knees. He looked winded.

"I apologize," he said, "for defacing your stone, but even a small mountain is enormous for a man of my years."

Noah strode forward and embraced him heartily, the old man of skin and bones wrapped in Noah's towering, muscled form.

"No worries," he said, pulling back. "When did you arrive?"

"A short while ago. Young Quezon informed me you were heading to this location, so I figured I would meet you rather than chase you all over town."

Auran sat down and glanced at his travel pack, which sat on the other side of the stone. It was rough and brown and the top was open to the air. Noah suddenly hoped Auran had brought lunch, but the man made no moves toward it.

"Will you be staying?" Noah asked.

"For a spell," Auran said. "I hope you do not mind."

"Of course not," Noah said, grateful to have someone to help organize their little band of humans. Earth was not theirs alone, of course; a whole planet devoted to little more than a hundred would be wasteful. In other habitable parts of the planet, Soran and Xalan colonies were already springing up. Some were even mixed communities. But for now, because of their sparse numbers, the humans were kept isolated. Dangerous genetic incompatibility made a human/Soran settlement unwise at this point.

"Why were you looking for me specifically?" Noah said, catching Auran looking toward his sack again.

"I cannot see an old friend?" Auran said, laughing. "But in truth I need to discuss something. Someone."

Noah knew.

"Kyra."

"I am sure you still feel her absence strongly, as do I."

Noah could only nod.

"Some may think me something of a monster, creating a clone in that way. An echo of the young Corinthia."

"It's just genetic refinement," Noah said. "She was her own person."

"That she was," Auran agreed. "But the work I did on them both, it seems even I didn't understand the full extent of it."

"What do you mean?" Noah asked.

"I spent years refining those genes, each strand of DNA. I weeded out every possible defect, every abnormality. Both children were as genetically flawless as any Sora had ever known. That resulted in unmatched beauty, effortless charm, and a brilliant mind. Born leaders, both of them."

Noah needed no convincing of that.

"But . . . that was not all they were capable of, it seems," Auran said. "And Kyra will influence the entire course of mankind, even in death."

Auran was starting to sound delirious.

"Keeper, what are you saying?"

Auran stood up from the stone and walked over to the sack on the ground. From it, he pulled a sleeping infant. Little more than a newborn. He cradled it in his arms and brought it over to Noah.

His insides froze, then melted all at once.

"This can't be—"

"After Kyra died," he said, putting a papery hand behind the infant's head. "I scanned her body and was stunned to learn she was with child. I immediately preserved the temperature in her core, and raced to extract the embryo onboard the SDI vessel where we were stationed. I told no one, and built a makeshift tank for a child I assumed would die shortly, no doubt born of human and Soran union," he said, eyeing Noah knowingly. "She did not."

"What are you saying?" Noah said, barely able to speak.

"In perfecting Soran DNA to create Kyra, it seems I inadvertently solved the riddle of our two species' incompatible biology, even before I knew of your existence. Whatever in evolution had driven us apart over a hundred thousand years or more, I had somehow mended. The child lived, and all my data said her mother would have as well, had she not met with a cruel end first."

Kyra's child. His child. He couldn't—

"I wanted to be sure of her continued survival, which is why I have withheld the little one from you until now. But I can assure you, she will grow to be strong and healthy. The first of a new people, both Soran *and* human."

Noah was speechless. The child had woken, and blinked big, beautiful blue eyes at him. Wisps of white-blond hair rested on her forehead.

"She is the first, but will not be the last. I have isolated the rogue mutation causing incompatibility between subspecies. I can develop a cure. I can unite all humans and Sorans and Oni and whomever else we find out there in the stars. We can be one people, one race. We can be Exos," he said, eyes twinkling. Only a few knew that secret, and it seemed Auran was among them.

"The only tragedy is that even new life cannot defeat death," he continued. "But I hope you take some solace in your daughter, and will raise her to remember her mother fondly. From what I have seen of both you and Sakai, I know she will be loved."

The child smiled. Noah felt tears streaming down his face.

"She will," he said, his voice wavering.

Auran smiled, and handed Noah his daughter. He stood up from the stone as Noah dropped to a knee, barely able to support himself as he was shaking from the revelation.

"What shall you name her?" Auran said. "Another Earth city?"

Noah looked into the endless blue eyes below him.

"Elyria," he said, his voice breaking. "Her name is Elyria."

—

Lucas dreamed of planets burning.

He could hear the billions screaming. Smell the smoke rising out of forests, see cities crumbling into ash and ruin.

He was powerless to stop it, only a witness to the extinction. Night after night. And always there the figure was, floating in space above the blazing worlds. The galactic eyes, the jagged voice. The Archon.

"The Az'ghal will return. You know the destruction I have wrought; imagine when the army arrives.

"They will come in a million years. In ten thousand. In a hundred. They will come tomorrow.

"They will exterminate New Exos. They will tear through this galaxy like a raging storm. Nothing will remain. Your children. Their children. Every descendant of every line. Extinguished.

"Live with that knowledge, if you can. May your every waking moment be filled with dread for the horror that is to come."

Lucas woke in a panic, as he always did. And Asha bolted up to soothe him, as she always did.

"Someday it'll stop," she said, propping herself upright in the sheets.

Lucas slowly caught his breath and wiped his brow.

"I don't think so," he said.

"Then make sure your days are filled with only pleasant things," she said, her lips parting into a smile. She kissed him and flung the sheet away from her, revealing bronze skin on the white linen, and the Archon's warning fled from his mind. He lost himself in her. She brought him back at Rhylos. She brought him back now as well, every day. He was cured, Alpha said, but still he never quite felt like himself. The strength and speed were gone. His mind was his own, except for the dreams. No more Circle, if it ever existed at all. No more madness, if that was the explanation instead. But still, he'd been touched by both the darkness of the Archon and the light of the Exos, and he could feel both raging inside him. Only she could quell the storm. When he looked into her eyes, and she gave him that smile, he was Lucas again. The best version of himself.

And that's who he needed to be today.

He suddenly glanced at the time readout.

"Shit, we're late!" he said, bolting out of bed. Asha was in less of a hurry, and lazily stretched out in the tangled sheets in a way that made Lucas want to climb back in with her for another hour. But they couldn't. Even she realized that eventually and slid out of bed and sauntered over to the outfit that had been laid out for her. A sleek jade dress that made her eyes shine more brightly than ever. For Lucas, it was a tailored suit blending Soran and Earth garments. He felt naked without a weapon, but it was obvious that would send the wrong message.

"Thirty minutes to arrival," the captain said over the ship's intercom. The blue-green of the space-time tunnel still drifted outside their room's viewscreen. They were arriving in a luxury liner, not a warship, though Lucas wondered if that would always be the case.

The map had stayed with him. The swirling galaxy was forever etched in his mind, even after he transformed back from Shadow to human. All the numbers, all the coordinates. Every Exos settlement across the galaxy. And so the search began.

There were only disappointments in the beginning.

The first world had been devastated by the impact of a comet, and whatever civilization once lived there was obliterated fifty thousand years ago.

The second contained only husks of stone castles and ivory palaces, filled with the bones of the dead who had been wiped out by a worldwide plague in ages past.

The third was nothing but craters and radiation. The Xalans hadn't attacked them. Instead, they'd wiped themselves out through internal wars, and nothing remained but death and insects.

But the fourth was Nahiva.

It was nearly as big as Earth, not untouched by war, famine, or disease, but not destroyed by them either. Lucas had felt tears in his eyes when the scouting information from long-range scans showed the first pictures of the blue-and-green world. The images were magnified and sprawling cities came into view. Spiderwebs of life, criss-crossing the surface of the planet. Gray and solemn in the day, alive with light at night. *They survived. They thrived.*

Lucas soon realized Nahiva was what Earth almost became, had it endured just a little longer. Its people, the Hota, a new name to add alongside Soran, human, and Oni, were proud of their recent push into space. They'd set up bases on both of their moons, and it had been a global event when their latest long-range craft had touched down on their neighboring, dusty planet for the first time. Lucas watched the world cheer as their spacewalker made a footprint in the black sands.

They still had vehicles with wheels. They had only started dabbling in genetic modification, preventing birth defects and choosing eye color. They were a long way from null cores, but they were a bright people. Lucas loved the Hota even before he met them. And now he would get the chance.

It took some time for Soran linguists to decipher the many tongues of the planet, but once they did, the broadcasts began.

"We are here."

"We are like you."

"We want to meet you."

"We have knowledge to share."

"We come in peace."

The initial panic on Nahiva turned into celebration in the weeks and months that followed first contact. Arrangements were made. Ambassadors were chosen. It was nearly unanimous who Sora wanted to send as the two lead emissaries.

"You ready for this?" Lucas asked Asha as he zipped her into her dress.

"Are you?" she replied, turning toward him.

"We've done this before," he said. "Kind of."

"This is different," she said.

Lucas stared out the viewscreen. He would smile and nod and talk about space travel and other planets full of humans and all their cultural differences. But eventually they would have to know. They would all have to know.

Finding the others, all the others, wasn't just about peaceful harmony, the way the Exos intended. They had to sow the seeds to raise an army a hundred planets strong.

"They will come in a million years. In ten thousand. In a hundred. They will come tomorrow," the Archon's voice rang in his head.

When they did come, could ten planets hold back the Az'ghal? Could a hundred? Whatever the case, they had to be united. They had to share all their knowledge, bring every civilization out of the dark ages. If Toruk could go from tribal chieftain to starship captain in ten years, anything was possible. The Hota seemed more than willing to learn. They would be a good first step, but Lucas feared the second, and the third, and all the ones after that. Who knew what sort of worlds they would find out there? And always, the Az'ghal loomed.

Still, Lucas had to be satisfied with what had been won. His body and mind were his again. His family was safe, and growing. Earth was healing, Sora was rebuilding, Xala was a free nation. There was a whole galaxy to explore. So many lost civilizations to find and connect. Nahiva was just the beginning. For the first time in perhaps his entire life, Lucas finally had hope. For his family, for his people. It was the dawn of the most important age of human history, and he was on its blinding edge.

The ship finally slowed to a crawl, the haze giving way to stars again, now rearranged in unfamiliar patterns. They moved through the ship as it drew closer to the planet, past all the other dignitaries, scientists, and affable public figures who would meet with the Hota in the coming days, weeks, and years. Lucas squeezed Asha's hand as they made their way to the landing bay. He wished his children and Alpha were there, but they had their own concerns. At least he had her. She was more than enough. Asha had once been the face of the Great War. Now she would be the face of this new peace.

"They've assembled in the docking area below," said a Soran aide holding a scroll filled with crawling data streams. "And it's all being broadcast back to Sora."

"God, I hate cameras," Lucas said, eyeing the tiny swirling robots around them.

"No pressure," Asha said with a smile. She turned to glance out the window of the bay and put her hand to her mouth.

"My god," she said breathlessly. "It's like we're coming home again."

Lucas saw what she meant. Nahiva's skyscrapers were stone and metal and glass. Not the towering platinum monstrosities of the hugely advanced Sora, but closer in scale to the cities of Earth. Cars drove on actual paved roads like tiny insects below. Jets that couldn't leave orbit zoomed past them as they descended. It was all incredibly surreal. The architecture was unique, the vehicles were stylized strangely, and the continents were different shapes, but it felt like Earth all the same. A civilization on the verge of greatness.

A swell of movement on the ground was visible as they got lower, and Lucas realized it was people, gathered by the millions to watch the spaceship descend. To watch the aliens come. Lucas remembered the hovering Xalan craft over New York. *Never again*, he thought, remembering the violence that followed. *We come in peace.*

The metal landing pads of the ship made contact with concrete, and the doors opened slowly. The light of a foreign sun found them, and the roar of the crowd was deafening. Nobles in long robes smiled kindly at them, waiting patiently for them to emerge. The Hota. More humans. More family.

Lucas looked at Asha one more time, and the two stepped forward into the future.